YOU GIVE WITCH A BAD NAME

A WICKED WITCHES OF THE MIDWEST SHORT BOOKS 11-15

AMANDA M. LEE

WINCHESTERSHAW PUBLICATIONS

Copyright © 2017 by Amanda M. Lee

All rights reserved.

No part of this book may be reproduced in any form or by any electronic or mechanical means, including information storage and retrieval systems, without written permission from the author, except for the use of brief quotations in a book review.

❦ Created with Vellum

FOUR-LEAF CLOVER

A WICKED WITCHES OF THE MIDWEST SHORT

ONE

"I love this time of year."

My cousin Bay, her blond hair wild because of the storm raging outside, fixed me with a bright smile as she scuffed her feet against the doormat upon entering Hypnotic. I made a face, convinced she had to be messing with me, and turned my attention back to cleaning the shelves in my magic shop. "You're joking, right?"

Bay shook her head and stripped out of her coat, hanging it on the chair at the edge of the sitting area before rubbing her hands together to warm them. "I was being serious."

"You're soaking wet."

"Yes, but I love a good storm. Of course, walking in a big storm is another story. What are you doing?" Bay lazily stretched out on the couch, propping her feet on the table and flashing a smile. She looked to be in a good mood, which I found baffling because it was dark and dreary outside. The occasional flashes of lightning didn't help lighten my unease. I don't consider myself a worrier by nature – no, really – but I've never been nearly as fond of storms as Bay.

"I'm straightening the shelves for the big pre-Halloween sale this weekend," I replied, taking a moment to admire the diamond ring glittering on my left ring finger. It was a recent addition – I'd been engaged for exactly two weeks – and I couldn't stop staring at the stone whenever I got the chance. "I expect we'll do a lot of business because there's a big tour coming from the west side of the state. It's more than fifty women."

Bay arched an eyebrow, surprised. "I knew it was big, but that's a lot of Halloween enthusiasts hitting Hemlock Cove all at once. I guess I didn't realize exactly how big the group was going to be when the tourist committee dropped off its ads this week."

Hemlock Cove, formerly known as Walkerville, is the only home I've ever known. Years ago, when the manufacturing base died off and the town was struggling, the council representatives opted to rebrand in an effort to tempt tourists. Walkerville became Hemlock Cove, a kitschy draw for paranormal fans. It boasts a festival every other weekend and gossip around every corner.

Essentially Hemlock Cove is a normal town where the business owners pretend to be witches, warlocks and the like so visitors will be entertained by the odd atmosphere and hopefully tell their friends about us. The truly weird thing is that I'm really a witch. No, you heard that right. My name is Clove Winchester and I'm a witch, although I'm not nearly as wicked as the rest of my family.

So, while Hemlock Cove's rebranding constitutes acting for a lot of people, it involves a bit of juggling for my family. We're real witches pretending to be normal humans pretending to be fake witches. Did you get that? It's totally confusing. I know. Wait, what were we talking about again? Oh, yeah. The group of tourists.

"They're due to arrive soon. My understanding is all of the inns in the area are completely booked," I said.

Bay pursed her lips. "Halloween isn't even here yet. It's going to be a madhouse when it does arrive. The influx of tourists around Halloween and Thanksgiving grows every year."

"It's a madhouse no matter what. I happen to love a madhouse, mind you, because it means more money for the shop, but it also means more work."

"Not for me." Bay ran Hemlock Cove's weekly newspaper. It was basically two pages of news and three pages of ads and fluff material, but she enjoyed her work. "Still, I feel for you."

"How much?"

Bay cocked an eyebrow. "Is that a trick question?"

"No."

"See, I'm sensing a trick question." Bay shifted on the sofa. "If you want me to do something, you need to ask ... and in your sweet voice."

"Will you do it if I ask nicely?"

"Maybe. Probably. Most likely."

That wasn't the answer I was looking for. "Will you or won't you?"

Bay wasn't an idiot. There was no way she would agree to a favor before she heard what it entailed. She has a cynical quality. Quite frankly, everyone in my family boasts that quality except for me. I find cynicism a waste of time.

"What do you want me to do, Clove?" Bay asked, her voice firm. "I'm not agreeing to anything without an explanation ... and probably some cookies."

I narrowed my dark eyes and stared her down. I learned how to bully people with the best of them – my great-aunt is a master when it comes to making rational people do irrational things – but Bay was used to dealing with far worse, so she merely shot me a bored look before turning her attention to her fingernails.

"There are cookies on a plate on the counter," I offered.

"I know. I saw them. Why do you think I mentioned cookies?"

I scowled, annoyed. "Most cousins would volunteer to help out of the goodness of their hearts."

"I'm not most cousins," Bay pointed out. "If you want a good cousin, ask Thistle."

Thistle is the third corner of our cousin triangle, and she's even more difficult to deal with than Bay. There was no way she would help without a significant bribe. Bay tends to waffle depending on her mood.

"Thistle isn't here," I pointed out. "She's picking up lunch." Something occurred to me. "A lunch you're eating and we paid for. If you want your food, you'll have to help."

Bay snorted, the sound making my stomach twist. "Do you know how many restaurants are in this town?"

I pointed toward the window, the lightning flashing at an opportune time and reminding Bay how nasty it was outside. "Do you want to brave that if you don't have to?"

Bay shrugged. "I still haven't heard what the favor is. The more you avoid answering, the more I believe it's something awful and it will be worth getting wet to avoid."

I let loose a heavy sigh and scorched my cousin with a dark look. "Why do always have to be so difficult?"

"Why do you always have to be so manipulative?"

Manipulative? Bay and Thistle trot that word out all of the time. I'm never manipulative. Er, well, mostly. Okay, I'm manipulative some of the time. I can't help it, though. You either have to be manipulative or bossy to survive in my family. Being manipulative is so much easier. And I trend toward general laziness when given the option.

I opened my mouth to answer, something acerbic on the tip of my tongue, but my response was cut short when the front door blew open and Thistle stomped inside. She had a box gripped tightly in her hands and her hair – which was a vivid orange this month to commemorate Halloween – stood on end as water dripped from the tips.

"Good morning, sunshine," Bay called out, amused.

I shot Bay a dirty look as I moved to Thistle's side and removed the box of food from her chilled hands. Thankfully everything was safely ensconced in plastic containers inside so our diner offerings weren't ruined.

"How is it out there?" I asked.

Thistle shot me a look that could've made paint peel and ripped off her drenched coat. "Did you seriously just ask me that?" she barked.

"Someone is in a lovely mood," Bay said, holding out her hands and wiggling her fingers. "Gimme. I'm starving."

"You have to agree to do me a favor before I give you food," I shot back.

Bay tilted her head to the side, annoyed. "Seriously? Are we back to the blackmail?"

"I don't consider it blackmail," I answered. "I consider it ... aggressive negotiation."

"The only thing that's going to be aggressive is me if you don't give me my lunch," Bay warned. "I'm not joking. I'll make you eat dirt. It's raining, so it will actually be mud, and that's so much grosser because there will be worms ... and slugs ... and whatever hangs out in mud."

"You'll get wet if you try."

"I don't care."

I chewed my bottom lip as I regarded her. She didn't look worried I would keep her meal from her greedy little hands. "Fine." I blew out a sigh and handed her the box. "You're a terrible cousin. I hope you know that."

"What did I miss?" Thistle asked, kicking off her shoes. She left them next to the heat vent to dry before braving the elements a second time later in the afternoon. "Why are you guys fighting?"

"We're not fighting," Bay replied. "Clove is merely trying to manipulate me. I refuse to fall victim to her antics."

Thistle rolled her eyes, her annoyance obvious. "You're only messing with her because you're bored. Landon has been out of town for days because he caught a case out in Kingsley, and you're going through withdrawal or something. Admit it."

Bay averted her gaze. "That is not even remotely true. I am a strong and independent woman. I don't need a man to complete me."

Bay's boyfriend, Landon Michaels, is an FBI agent. His office is in Traverse City, but he does his best to brave the forty-five-minute trek as often as possible so Bay isn't forced to sleep alone. I think it's kind of cute. Thistle calls it co-dependent. Because I live with my boyfriend and Thistle is making plans to do the same, I'm not sure we have a lot of room to talk.

"You keep telling people that," Thistle snarked, causing me to cuff the back of her head and make a face. I wasn't thrilled with Bay, but that didn't mean I wanted her feelings hurt.

"I want Bay to do a favor for me, but she won't agree unless I tell her what it is in advance," I explained. "I'm pretty sure that goes against the cousin code."

Thistle snorted, amused. "What cousin code? The only code I'm aware of is the one in which it's every witch for herself when our mothers and Aunt Tillie get going. I don't remember any other cousin code."

"Oh, it exists. I've read it. I believe the biggest portion of it says that you have to give your help freely and without sarcasm when a cousin is in need."

"Yeah, well, I would never agree to that," Thistle said, taking her food container from Bay and locking gazes with me. "If you won't tell her what you want, that must mean it's annoying and ridiculous."

"That's what I said," Bay interjected, grinning.

"You didn't say that," I argued.

"I thought it."

"That's not the same thing." I rolled my neck to loosen the stress building in my shoulders and leaned forward so I could collect my lunch. I didn't get a chance, though, because the bell over the front door jangled, signifying someone entered the store. With the weather unbelievably scary outside, I figured it had to be one of our boyfriends.

I glanced over my shoulder and jerked upright when I saw the tall and lean woman standing inside the door. Her long black hair was perfectly in place despite the wind, her ankle-length skirt showing no signs of dampness, and her makeup wasn't so much as smeared. If I wasn't already a witch and knew that bedhead and bad hair days are inevitable for everyone, I would think she was somehow magical.

"I ... can I help you?"

Bay and Thistle shifted their attention to the woman, seemingly as surprised as me to be interrupted. Thistle plastered a welcoming smile on her face while Bay merely leaned back on the couch and appeared pleasant instead of surly.

"I was just walking past the store and thought I would stop in." The woman's voice was strangely melodic as her odd gray eyes washed over me. "I love shops like this. It's so ... cute."

Bay pressed her lips together to keep from laughing as she exchanged an amused glance with Thistle. Because I was standing, I was fairly certain I would be the one helping our new guest as my lunch cooled on the coffee table.

"We think it's cute, too," I said, trying to keep my eyes from traveling to the woman's sandals. How can she walk around in the rain and cold pelting the town without socks? Seriously, that makes no sense. "Do you need something specific?"

"Actually, I'm here to offer you something specific." The woman pulled back the caped hood she wore, revealing a full wrist of metallic bangle bracelets, and extended her hand. "I am Madam Rosa."

"Madam Rosa?" I cocked an eyebrow as I shook her hand. "Is that an official name or … something else?"

"It is my work name," Madam Rosa replied. "I am psychic. In fact, I'm the most powerful conduit north of the Mason-Dixon line."

Huh. I couldn't help but wonder if that was an important distinction. "Well, um, you came to the right place," I offered. "Hemlock Cove loves psychics."

"And witches and warlocks," Bay added helpfully.

"And little old ladies in strange leggings causing mischief and blaming it on everyone else," Thistle interjected, popping an onion ring into her mouth. Apparently she'd lost interest in putting on a good show for our lone customer. I guess I couldn't blame her.

Instead of being offended, Madam Rosa merely smiled. "You're funny. You're also lucky you found a man who could double as a saint on Sunday to put up with you."

Thistle furrowed her brow, confused by the conversational turn. "Excuse me?"

"The man you love," Madam Rosa prodded. "He has the patience of a saint. He needs it to deal with you."

Bay snorted, amused. "She pegged you."

"Oh, shut up," Thistle grumbled.

"And you. You also have the perfect man, don't you?" Madam Rosa turned her attention to Bay. "He's not nearly as patient, but he loves with his whole heart. That's the thing you need most, because you crave reassurance and strength of character when dealing with your man."

Bay's mouth dropped open. "I … um … ."

"She's psychic," Thistle reminded her. "She pegged you."

"Shut your hole," Bay muttered, smacking the back of Thistle's head and focusing on Madam Rosa. "Have you been talking to others about us? Have you been trying to get information so you can come in and apply for a job?"

"I don't need to talk to others," Madam Rosa replied. "I can see into your minds. That's my gift. As for the job, I thought I could offer my services for a few weeks. I never stay in one place very long, but I like the vibe here very much."

"If you can see into my mind, what am I thinking right now?" Thistle challenged.

Madam Rosa didn't hesitate. "You're thinking that you want me to meet another member of your family – an elderly woman, I believe – because you think she would have a great time messing with me."

Thistle wrinkled her nose, dumbfounded. After a few moments of silence she leaned back in her seat and glanced at Bay. "She's good. I was wondering what Aunt Tillie would make of her."

"You were also wondering if you could sucker your cousin into bringing you cookies," Madam Rosa added, jerking her thumb in my direction. "She's already standing and you're feeling entitled."

I didn't want to laugh, but the surprised look on Thistle's face caught me off guard. "That's fairly impressive," I said after a beat. "You're very entertaining. Unfortunately, we do our own cards and readings. We don't have an opening."

"Oh, that's too bad." Madam Rosa said the words but she didn't put a lot of weight behind them. "Perhaps I will see if I can get my own booth at the festival this weekend. I have good timing. I didn't even know you were having a festival until I saw the preparations underway when I was walking around town this morning."

"We always have a festival," Bay supplied. "I'm sure you could get a tent. I think there's still an opening or two. Try talking to Mrs. Little down at the porcelain unicorn store. It's the one undergoing construction, but she's always in there making sure the work is done correctly. She would know."

"I thank you for your time," Madam Rosa's expression was serene as she turned to go. She stilled before her hand hit the doorknob. "I have something I want to leave with you." She dug in her purse and extracted a large coin, pressing it into my hand and giving it a good squeeze before taking a step back. "For ... luck."

I wasn't sure what to make of the gesture so I merely stared at the coin for a moment, flipping it over. "This looks old."

"Oh, it is."

"Then you should keep it," I said, holding out my hand. "It's yours. You don't need to give me anything. You don't even know me."

"Oh, I know you," Madam Rosa said, grinning. "You just don't know it yet."

I wanted to say something as she walked through the door, but my mind was blank. As soon as she was gone, I shifted to find Bay and Thistle laughing, their shoulders shaking as they swiped at their eyes.

"She's very good," Thistle said. "I hope she gets a tent, because she could be very entertaining this weekend."

I balked. "You didn't believe her?"

"She was unbelievably vague," Thistle replied. "I mean ... she knew I had a boyfriend but didn't go into specifics because she could risk being wrong. She was vague on Bay's stuff, too."

"But in some ways she wasn't vague," I pressed.

"I think you're seeing something you don't want to see," Bay offered. "What's the deal with the coin? What's on it?"

"It looks like one of those old costume coins," I replied, staring at the item in my hand. "It's metal, but I think it's iron rather than gold or silver."

"Since she's looking for work, I'm guessing you're right," Thistle said, turning her attention back to her lunch.

"Still, the symbol is interesting," I added.

"What is it?"

"A four-leaf clover."

"Well, she did wish you luck," Bay mused. "Now, sit down and eat your lunch. I believe you had a favor you wanted to ask me, and I haven't decided how I'm going to answer yet."

"I only wanted you to help me clean the store so I don't have to do it alone," I said. "Thistle is leaving early to help Marcus at the stable, and I don't want to do all of the work alone."

"Yeah, I don't want to do that."

"I told you," Thistle said, giggling. "You should've figured out a different way to phrase it or something. If you're going to manipulate her you need to do it when she's distracted and not bored because she's pining for her boyfriend."

"You take that back!" Bay slapped Thistle's arm. "I'm not pining for anyone."

"You've been sleeping in his shirt," Thistle said dryly. "I saw you in it this morning. You're pining like a crazy woman."

"You're dead to me," Bay said.

I tuned out the rest of their conversation – it was just more of the same, after all – and focused on the coin. There was something familiar about it, although I was sure I'd never seen one like it before in my life. It looked harmless, yet I couldn't put my finger on why it bothered me. There was something odd about Madam Rosa, too. Now I just had to figure out what.

TWO

"There was a robbery at the bank!"

Bay had been gone only thirty minutes before she lunged back through the front door and nearly knocked me off the stepladder I was on to dust the shelves.

"What do you mean?" Thistle asked, confused. She wiped her hands on a towel as she wandered out of the storage room where she'd been bagging herbs. "The bank was robbed?"

"Well, technically someone attempted to rob it," Bay clarified. "Some dude wearing a hoodie went in and handed the teller a note, said he had a gun, and demanded money. It happened, like, twenty minutes ago."

Thistle's eyebrow winged up. "Did he get any money?"

"No. Shana Stevenson was behind the counter. She smacked him in the face with that candy jar she keeps there, and then he took off."

Thistle snorted. "That will teach him. Still, that's kind of creepy. Did he ever show a gun?"

"No, and I'm going to guess that means he didn't really have one." Bay rubbed her hands together to ward off the chill. "Still, it's weird, right? Who comes to Hemlock Cove to rob the bank?"

"An idiot." Thistle shook her head and turned back to the storage room.

I focused on Bay a moment, conflicted. "Do you think this person will try to rob other businesses?" I had no idea why my mind went there, but I couldn't help myself. Bay and Thistle call me a "kvetch" because they think I'm whiny. I think "practical," and occasionally "brilliant," are much better terms.

"I don't know, but I wouldn't worry about it," Bay said, her blue eyes clouding briefly, as if reading my mind. "You and Thistle don't keep a lot of cash on hand. I doubt this guy really had a gun."

"What if he does have a gun, though?"

Bay shrugged. "It's hardly the first time you've had a gun held on you. Aunt Tillie had her shotgun out so she could clean it just last week and she pointed it at us when we wouldn't stop making those jokes about taking her hunting and leaving her on a farm to live out the rest of her days."

"I told you that was a mean joke," I said. "She didn't like it. She was sad and covering."

"She wasn't sad," Bay scoffed. "She was plotting her revenge. Why do you think your socks smelled like sauerkraut Thursday?"

Something clicked in my head. "I thought it was just me!"

"It was all of us," Bay shouted, shaking her head. "She's a mean woman."

"She's still our aunt."

"That doesn't mean she's not mean." Bay reached for the door handle. "I have to go back and close down the newspaper office, and then I'm heading home. I'm afraid if I wait too much longer I'll need an ark to get there."

"Good luck." I offered a half-hearted wave. "I'm going to finish up here and head home myself. Now that I know there's a robber out there, I'm kind of … agitated."

Bay's smile was mischievous. "That's because you're a kvetch."

"I am not!"

"Oh, you totally are," Thistle called from the storage room. "Thankfully for us, we're used to it."

TWO HOURS later I let myself into the Dandridge, the restored lighthouse where I lived with my fiancé Sam Cornell, and let out a sigh as I kicked off my damp shoes. It had been a strange afternoon – there was no getting around that – and the only thing I wanted to do was curl up in front of the fire with a cup of tea.

Sam met me in the living room, a curious look on his face as he looked me up and down. "You don't look happy. Let me guess, did Thistle do something to annoy you?"

Sam's smile was cute and flirty, but I was hardly in the mood to encourage that kind of interaction – at least until I was in warm pajamas with no hint of a chill invading my bones. "Thistle always does something to annoy me," I replied, reaching for the button on my jeans and glancing around. The walk from the parking lot to the Dandridge had been a long one and my clothing was so wet it dripped. I didn't want to create a mess – which I would have to clean up – and sent Sam a pleading look. "I don't suppose you could run upstairs and get me warm pajamas?"

Sam took pity on me, running his hand over my damp hair and pressing a quick kiss to my forehead. "Absolutely. I'm sorry you had such a miserable day."

"The day itself wasn't bad," I clarified. "It was simply ... different."

Sam arched an eyebrow, but otherwise remained silent. By the time he returned with dry pajamas I was already stripped down. Five minutes later he had me tucked under a blanket in front of the fire and was running a comb through my snarled hair.

"I hope you don't catch a cold from being out in the rain so long," Sam offered, his eyes serious as they looked me over. "Now isn't the time for you to get sick. It's going to be a busy week around here, especially with so much work to do on the tanker."

"I thought all of that was taken care of." Sam bought a tanker ship to use as a haunted attraction several months before. We'd been working overtime to get it ready to open for the holiday season. It wasn't finished, but we planned to open the top deck this year and then work steadily throughout the spring and summer to get the area below deck ready for next Halloween. "What more do we have to do?"

"Just small things," Sam replied, slinging an arm over my shoulder and tugging me closer so I could share his warmth. "We can't put the actual decorations out until the day we open because of the weather. Can you imagine if we left all of that stuff out there today? We'd have to start from scratch."

"It is bad," I agreed, tracing my fingers over the palm of his hand as I got comfortable. "I didn't realize it was supposed to be this rough out."

"It's supposed to get worse before it gets better. I'm worried we could lose power tonight."

I wasn't thrilled about the possibility. I love living in the Dandridge – it's beautiful, quaint and homey, after all – but the isolation frays my nerves at times. "What happens if we lose power?"

Sam smirked. "Well, I was thinking we could spend the day in bed. I mean … it might be dangerous to maneuver those stairs without any ambient light."

I rolled my eyes. "You suggest we spend the day in bed when it's sunny and humid out."

"You could get dehydrated if you're not careful."

I barked out a laugh, amused. "You're cute. I can't take the day off from work, though. We have that big tourist group coming in. I'm sure they'll visit the store. I'm more worried about not being able to shower and clean up more than anything else."

"I guess if that's a real concern then we could run out to the guesthouse," Sam suggested, referring to the small house I previously shared with Thistle and Bay. It was located on the Winchester family property, only a few minutes' walk from The Overlook, the inn my mother and aunts operate. "I'm sure they would let you shower there."

"The guesthouse isn't on the generator," I pointed out. "We'd have to go to the inn to shower. I'm sure my mother wouldn't care, though."

Even though he tried to hide it, I didn't miss the way Sam cringed.

"What?" I prodded.

"It's just … I would rather smell like a dirty armpit than risk Aunt Tillie sneaking up on me when I'm in the shower."

The visual was so absurd I could do nothing but chuckle. "Why would she want to see you in the shower?"

"Why does she do anything?"

That was a good point. Still … . "If she was going to sneak up on anyone it would be Landon."

Sam shifted, knitting his eyebrows. "Are you saying Landon is hotter than me?"

"Of course not. I'm saying Landon has a shorter fuse and Aunt Tillie absolutely loves messing with him. She turns it into a game."

"Ah, well, that makes sense." Sam relaxed, if only marginally. "As long as you don't think Landon is hotter than me, I'm fine."

"You're definitely hotter than Landon."

"Thank you."

"That long hair and smoldering intensity most women find attractive is barely a blip on my radar."

Sam's smile slipped. "For some reason, that doesn't make me feel better. It makes me feel worse."

"Oh, let it go." I blew out a sigh. These rare moments of sitting together, alone, with nothing to do but talk were always some of my favorites. We'd been extremely busy for weeks. It was nice to have a moment of quiet. "Tell me about your day."

"I worked on the tanker most of the day and did a little yard cleanup before the rain started," Sam replied, rubbing the back of my neck. "It was a pretty boring day for me. What about you?"

"Mostly we just cleaned and straightened the store. Thistle put together a bunch of baskets with herbs to use as free samplers. We figured it couldn't hurt and might draw people in to buy more items."

"That sounds like a good idea."

"We also had a weird lady come into the shop. Her name was Madam Rosa and she declared herself the best psychic this side of the Mason-Dixon Line."

Sam snorted, amused. "That's a bold statement to make in the presence of the wacky Winchester witches."

"She was nice and had some interesting insights," I said. "She was weird, though. She gave me a coin. I pulled it from my pajama pants pocket – I'd removed it from my jeans while waiting for Sam to bring pajamas – and held it out so he could take it. "She said something about luck, and then we suggested she see if she could get a tent for this weekend's festival."

"That sounds like a good idea," Sam said, his expression thoughtful as he stared at the coin. "If she's as good at reading people as you say, she'll probably clean up with the crowd coming in this week."

"You think she's a fake?"

Sam shrugged, noncommittal. "I didn't meet her. I'm not sure I can answer that. I guess I would say that most of the people who claim to be psychic are frauds, but that's just my gut answer."

"You're cynical, just like Bay and Thistle."

"I don't mind the comparison to Bay, but likening me to Thistle is so insulting," Sam teased, poking my side. "This coin is neat. It looks old."

"Yeah, I'm sure it's iron instead of silver or gold, but I kind of like it."

"It has a four-leaf clover on it." Sam smiled.

"It's for luck."

"You've certainly been my four-leaf clover," Sam said, kissing my cheek. "You've been lucky for me … and then some."

"Oh, that's kind of sweet."

"That's the way I roll." Sam handed the coin back to me and watched as I pocketed it. "It's kind of weird that woman was out in the storm today, huh?"

"Yeah, we definitely weren't expecting customers. We thought it would be a set-up day. Only a crazy person would go out in today's weather if they didn't have to." Something niggled at the back of my brain and I realized I hadn't told Sam the biggest tidbit I had to share. "Oh, and someone tried to rob the bank!"

Sam's eyebrows nearly flew off his forehead as he shifted his attention to me. "Are you serious?"

"That's what Bay said," I replied. "She stopped by for lunch and then left after. She came back about thirty minutes later and said someone tried to rob the bank, He wore a hoodie, but didn't show a gun."

"Did he say he had a gun?"

I nodded. "Shana Stevenson smacked him with that candy dish she has behind her little wall and he took off."

"Did they call the police?"

Now it was my turn to shrug. "I have no idea. I assume so."

"Well, I hope we don't have a desperate guy with a gun running around," Sam mused. "If he can't get money from the bank, he might try to rob stores. I don't want you to come into contact with this guy."

I widened my eyes, surprised. "That's what I said! Bay and Thistle pooh-poohed me."

"Bay and Thistle are mean when they want to be," Sam said, smiling as he slipped his arm around my waist and tugged me closer. "I get you. I understand the way your mind works. Mine works the same way."

My chest warmed at his earnest expression. There was something so delightful about the way he made me feel – as if I was the only woman in the world – I couldn't help but love him even more. "I guess we're the perfect match, huh?"

Sam tapped the stone on my engagement ring. "Forever, right?"

"And ever ... and ever ... and ever." I dissolved into giggles as Sam tickled me, enjoying the fact that I was home, warm and safe. I couldn't ask for much more.

I DIDN'T REALIZE I'd dozed off until I felt Sam's shoulder jerk beneath my head. It took me a few minutes to get my bearings, and when I did, an unmistakable banging sound assailed my ears. It was loud, yet it sounded as if it came from far away, which was confusing.

"What is that?"

"I'm not sure," Sam said, sliding out from beneath me and moving toward the window that faced the lake. It was dark outside, and when I joined him I couldn't see anything at first. Then, when lightning split the sky, I saw it. The tanker was rocking against the dock construction site.

"Son of a ... !"

I shifted my eyes to Sam, concerned. "What should we do?"

"I have to check on it," Sam replied. "I'm not sure there's anything we can do, but ... if the ropes have come undone ... I need to reattach them. It's probably a lost cause, but ... ."

I made up my mind on the spot. "I'll come with you."

"There's no sense in that," Sam argued. "If I can't do it alone, you won't be much help. I would rather know you're safe here. I won't be gone long."

I opened my mouth to argue, but it was too late. Sam smacked a firm kiss against my lips before striding out the door. I watched the empty space for a moment, my mind blank. Then I realized he didn't take a coat and my courage caught up to my hammering heart.

I scampered outside in the darkness, taking a moment to stare at the lake. I didn't see Sam until lightning flashed again. He was moving, and he was moving fast. Instead of thinking through my actions, I broke into a run and followed him.

"Sam!"

Between the waves crashing against the tanker and dock and the thunder rumbling, he didn't even glance over his shoulder. I knew he hadn't heard me, yet I continued my pursuit.

"Sam!"

Still nothing.

I increased my pace, my short legs pumping as fast as I could make them move. I hadn't bothered putting on shoes – which was a mistake – and my socks were soaked mere seconds after stepping outside. By the time I hit the dock area I'd lost sight of Sam. I tried calling for him again, but he didn't materialize.

For one moment – illuminated by a vicious flash of lightning – I wondered if I'd already lost him. Maybe he fell into the lake. Maybe he was drowning and I had no idea where to look. Maybe he was crushed between the tanker and the dock.

A hint of movement caught my attention out of the corner of my eye and I bolted in that direction. Instead of finding Sam, though, I found one of the ropes meant to secure the tanker fluttering in the wind. I grabbed it without thinking. I had every intention of tying it to the dock stanchion and moving on. The tanker reared at that moment, though, and I was caught off guard. I didn't let go, and was yanked forward.

I hit the water before I had a chance to register what was happening. I managed to surface, gasping for breath, but it was so dark I had trouble orienting myself.

"Sam!"

I was desperate, and because I'm pessimistic at times, I couldn't help but wonder if he'd even realize I followed him until it was too late. I clawed at the edge of the dock with each wave that hoisted me, but the wood was so slippery I couldn't gain a grip to pull myself up.

I wearily kicked my legs even as the water rocked over my head time and again. I coughed, trying to evict the frigid water from my lungs. I didn't have enough time before another wave crashed over me, though.

I brushed my hand against my thigh, making contact with the coin. It didn't feel lucky at all.

I geared up for one final attempt to pull myself out of the water, and this time when I reached up I felt something warm snag my wrist.

"Sam?"

I sputtered as he braced his feet against the stanchion and dragged me from the lake, pulling my small body on top of his. He pushed my soaked hair away from my face and gazed into my eyes, his pallor white.

"Are you okay?"

"I ... ." I broke off into another coughing fit.

"Why did you follow me?" Sam's voice cracked as he hugged me, his dark hair plastered to his forehead. "I didn't even see you until the last second. You could've died."

"I was trying to help." I managed to get the words out, but it was difficult because my body shook uncontrollably from the freezing water and the shock.

"Good job." Sam struggled to his feet and then swept me up in his arms, being careful to give the edge of the dock a wide berth as we headed toward the pathway that led back to the Dandridge. "Do you have any idea how lucky you are?"

Lucky? The word echoed in my head even as I plastered myself against him and tried to absorb his warmth. Was I lucky? "I'm sorry."

"Don't be sorry," Sam chided. "I'm getting you back to the Dandridge right now. It's okay. We're okay. It's … everything is okay."

"What about the tanker?"

"There's nothing we can do right now," he replied. "Two of the lines are holding. We just need to hope they can withstand the storm. We can't fix this, so we have to protect ourselves. That's the most important thing. Maybe we'll get lucky and everything will be all right."

"And if we're not lucky?"

Sam answered without hesitation. "I have you. I already consider myself the luckiest man in the world. We can't control the uncontrollable. All we can do is wait."

THREE

Sam dropped me at the shop the next morning. He made a big show of kissing me on the cheek when he walked me to the door – offering Thistle a small wave before looking both ways and crossing the street to return to his vehicle. He seemed distracted, and even though he checked the tanker as soon as the sun came up and everything was okay, I couldn't shake the feeling something haunted him.

"What's up with that?" Thistle asked, her gaze following Sam as he trudged toward his truck. "He doesn't usually walk you to the door when he drops you off. Speaking of that, he usually doesn't drop you off. Did something happen to your car?"

"I think he's a little clingy," I admitted, dropping my purse behind the counter and grabbing a doughnut from the plate on the counter. It was fresh and smelled almost heavenly. "Did our mothers make fresh doughnuts today? I can't believe I missed that."

"Yes, doughnut day is surely the best day of the month." Thistle's words were teasing, her eyes contemplative. "Why is he clingy? I thought everything was wonderful since you guys got engaged. The only thing you're missing is a pet unicorn to complete the magical picture when you're walking around these days."

I knew she was making fun of me, but I couldn't muster the energy to care. "Ha, ha."

Thistle sobered. "Seriously. What's wrong? Why is he clingy all of a sudden?"

"Something might've happened last night," I hedged, averting my gaze. Sometimes I think my family members can see right into my soul. That's not one of our witchy gifts, but it could very well be one of those intangible talents only people who swim in the same gene pool can identify.

"Something might've happened?" Thistle isn't the type of person to beat around the witch hazel bush. "What might've happened?"

"Well ... there was an incident last night."

Thistle scorched me with a dark look. "That thing you do to avoid discussions you don't want to have – where you drag things out to such lengths you believe people will become bored and distracted and stop pressing you on the issue – you know that never works on me. Why do you keep doing it?"

"I didn't know I was doing it." That was a total lie. I knew I was doing it. I also realize it rarely works. That doesn't mean it never works. It's always worth a shot.

"You're such a bad liar," Thistle muttered, shaking her head. "I'm serious, though. What happened last night to make Sam clingy?"

I told her. There was no sense lying. When I was done, I expected sympathy. What I got was open disdain.

"Are you an idiot?" Thistle exploded. "You would have to be to go out to that tanker in the middle of the night with a storm raging! That's on top of the fact that you didn't wear shoes and you tried to tie a huge tanker to the dock by yourself. Did you eat a stupid pill for lunch yesterday and tell no one about it?"

I heaved a sigh and ran my tongue over my teeth as I decided how to answer. The go-to reaction in the Winchester household is snark. I like to buck the rules and offer reactions that aren't expected. Why? It irritates my family. Everyone gets to the same place eventually. We simply take different roads.

"You're really hurting my feelings," I sniffed. "I could've died last night and you're attacking me. How is that fair?"

Thistle extended a warning finger, annoyed. "Don't do that. You know I hate it when you do that."

That's exactly why I did it, of course. "You don't have to worry. Sam already yelled at me for being such an idiot."

"Oh, well, I like him even better now. Did he use that word?"

"I believe he called me brave and thanked me for trying to help and then said next time I should pick an activity that isn't so terrifying," I replied. "He claims he almost had a heart attack."

Thistle made a face that was so exaggerated it bordered on comical. "He is such a wuss. Why didn't he really let you have it?"

"Probably because I was shaking and cold. I was ... afraid. He put me in a hot bath and made me stay there until my lips weren't blue any longer."

Thistle had the grace to look abashed. "Oh, well, I guess he did okay."

"You're all heart." I pinched her shoulder to shake her out of her doldrums. "It's weird, though. Right before he pulled me out of the lake there was a moment when I didn't think I would surface again if I went under one more time. I had that coin in my pocket and I brushed my hand against it and ... there he was."

Thistle tilted her head to the side. "You're not actually telling me that you think the coin saved you?"

"Madam Rosa said it would bring me luck."

"I think luck would've been not falling into the lake."

"Or it could've been Sam showing up at the exact right moment," I pressed. "Also, this morning I wanted pancakes for breakfast. Sam said we were out of eggs and I rubbed the coin while I was trying to decide what I wanted and he suddenly found eggs. It was like magic."

"Or he just cleared the cobwebs from his eyes and saw what was right in front of him the entire time," Thistle countered. "Do you know how many times I've looked in the refrigerator and said we were out of something only to have Bay check one minute later and find the thing we were out of?"

"No. Do you?"

"Like … five or something."

I didn't bother smothering my giggle. "Surely that's magical and mysterious."

"You know what I mean," Thistle prodded. "I sincerely doubt Madam Rosa gifted you with a magic coin that allows you to conjure breakfast food from thin air."

I blew out a sigh, resigned. "I know you're right. It's just … weird. I distinctly remember wondering if Sam would blame himself for not noticing me approach the boat if I died, and then I felt the coin. The next thing I knew he was pulling me out of the water and carrying me to the lighthouse."

Instead of being snarky, which was her normal attitude, Thistle opted to be earnest. "We're all lucky he found you. Don't do that again, by the way. If you die then Aunt Tillie is going to have to find a new kvetch and that won't end well for Bay."

I rolled my eyes, annoyed. "You'd miss me if I died."

"Probably," Thistle conceded, her smile impish. "Bay doesn't let me bully her as much as you do."

"You're a terrible cousin."

"I can live with that," Thistle said, turning back to the store. "Let's finish what needs to be done. I expect to be busy today."

And just like that, my death-defying night adventure was shelved and the reality of the day embraced. That's how it works in a tourist town. You have to take the business wherever you can get it, even if you had a bad night or an off morning. I had no choice but to focus, so that's what I did, pushing the coin out of my mind and fixating on the work. It had a calming effect on me, which was exactly what I needed.

TWO HOURS later the store was clean, stocked and smelled of clove. Thistle was in charge of filling the diffuser, and I knew she was in a conciliatory mood – well, at least for her – because she picked the clove-scented oil. That's my favorite (for obvious reasons), so the fact that she picked it meant she really was glad I survived. What? I'm not making something out of nothing.

"I think we're ready," Thistle announced, dusting her hands on her skirt and glancing around. "It looks good."

"Thank you."

Thistle narrowed her eyes. "Thank you? I toiled in here for hours, too."

"I must've missed that," I teased, smirking as I sat on the chair at the edge of the rug and sighed. "It does look good, though. Do we know when the tour group is supposed to arrive?"

"I'm not sure." Thistle sat on the couch and rested her feet on the coffee table. "I tried calling the inn about an hour ago, but I got my mother on the phone and she wouldn't stop talking about pumpkin cookies and ... well ... you know how that goes."

I did indeed. Of all of us, Thistle was the most unlike her mother. Sure, she had Twila's sense of drama and creative streak, but she was much meaner than her mother. Twila lived her life in the clouds. Thistle preferred mucking around in the dirt. I wasn't sure which was worse. Okay, who am I kidding? Being mean is so much worse.

"Maybe I should call," I suggested. "I might have better luck."

"Hey, there you go. You can rub your lucky coin while you're doing it."

I rolled my eyes and proceeded to ignore her as I retrieved my phone. I pulled the coin out as I did, flashing it to Thistle before hitting the appropriate contact button. Belinda, the woman who works as an assistant at the inn, answered on the second ring.

"Hello."

"Who did you get?" Thistle sneered.

"Hi, Belinda." I sang out the name as if I was reciting a lyrical poem, causing Thistle to make a disgusted face. Belinda really was the best option. "It's Clove."

"Hi, Clove." Belinda sounded friendly but distracted.

"I'm sorry to bother you," I said. "I'm just wondering if you know when that tour group is supposed to arrive."

"They're already here," Belinda replied. "They arrived about twenty minutes ago. We got twelve of them and they're ... lovely."

"I'm not sure what that means."

"I think I'll let you meet them yourself and make up your own mind," Belinda said. "They're all getting settled in their rooms right now, and let's just say ... um ... they seem extremely enamored of the inn, town ... and especially Aunt Tillie."

"Oh, well, that's terrifying."

"What's terrifying?" Thistle looked bored as she stared at the ceiling and picked at the fabric on the couch.

"The new guests have arrived, and they love Aunt Tillie," I answered.

"Oh, that's definitely terrifying."

"Did you need anything else?" Belinda asked. She clearly had other things on her mind.

"I guess that's it. Do you think the guests will come to town today or will they spend the entire afternoon getting settled?"

"Oh, they're staying at the inn. They keep following Aunt Tillie around with cameras. They're not going anywhere that doesn't involve Aunt Tillie ... and we all know how she feels about visiting town."

We do indeed. "She only makes the trip if she can irritate someone, and Mrs. Little's store is still being repaired so she doesn't have time to worry about Aunt Tillie. It would be a wasted trip."

"Precisely."

Thistle pursed her lips as I disconnected and cast me a dubious look. "So ... are we getting business today or not?"

"Not unless Aunt Tillie decides to visit."

"I'd rather go broke."

She wasn't alone. I opened my mouth to add my agreement to the comment when the sound of someone screaming outside drew my attention. Thistle jumped to her feet and beat me to the door even though I was closer and standing. She yanked it open, ignoring the jangle of the bell, and bolted outside.

I followed for lack of anything better to do, even though I wasn't keen on seeing anything horrifying. If I could help, I would. As long as it wasn't dangerous, that is. I would let Thistle handle the dangerous end.

The only person on the street was a redheaded woman I didn't recognize. She gripped the lapels of her coat, tugging them tight as she screamed a second time.

Thistle hurried to the woman, her eyes darting in eight different directions as she tried to ascertain the problem. "What's wrong?"

"I was robbed."

Thistle arched an eyebrow, confused. "I'm sorry ... you were robbed?"

The woman nodded, her lower lip trembling, and then she sank to her knees on the chilly concrete. "He took everything!"

TWENTY MINUTES later Chief Terry handed the woman – her name was Nancy Jarvis – over to one of his officers so she would have an escort to the inn she was staying at, and he found Thistle and me inside the store. He looked weary, but not particularly worried.

"Did you get anything more out of her?" Thistle asked, handing him a mug of coffee before he answered. We were all ridiculously fond of Chief Terry, and even though he was closest with Bay he served as a father figure to all of us throughout the years.

"Yeah, she says that a guy in a hoodie approached her and insinuated he had a gun in his pocket," Chief Terry replied, nodding in thanks to Thistle as he sipped the coffee. "She says he had the hoodie tied so tight she couldn't see his features – except that he was white with dark eyes – and that she was so afraid she let him walk off with her purse and Christmas purchases."

Her Christmas purchases? "Who buys Christmas gifts before Halloween?"

"Someone visiting a witch town who has a Goth daughter, apparently," Chief Terry replied. "I asked the same question. She's visiting Hemlock Cove with her sister. She thought her daughter would love a lot of the things we have to offer. She thought she would stock up early."

"Oh, well, that makes sense," I murmured, rolling my neck. "That's awful, though. Who steals someone's Christmas money?"

"An asshat," Thistle replied without hesitation. "Did anyone else see this guy?"

"That's what I was going to ask you." Chief Terry's gaze bounced between Thistle and me. "You guys were closest. Did you see anything?"

I shook my head. "No. We were focused on each other. We didn't look out the window. We didn't notice anything until we heard the scream."

"Is this the same guy who tried to rob the bank yesterday?" Thistle asked.

"Your guess is as good as mine, but I seriously doubt we have two idiots wandering around in hoodies pretending to have guns," Chief Terry answered.

"How do you know he's pretending?" I asked.

"Because if you have a gun, you show it. That makes people acquiesce much more quickly. It also keeps you from getting banged in the head with a glass candy bowl."

I didn't want to laugh – it was a serious situation, after all – but I couldn't help but delight in his wry expression. "You have a point. Still … should we be on the lookout for this guy?"

"I think everyone should be on the lookout for this guy," Chief Terry replied. "He's clearly desperate for money. Desperate people are dangerous people. It doesn't matter whether they have a weapon or not."

"Well, we'll keep our eyes open and our senses keen," I said. "Good luck finding him."

"Thanks," Chief Terry said, draining the rest of his coffee. "I have a feeling I'm going to need it once all of these tourists hit town. I'll see you girls later for dinner. I'm going to do my rounds and see if I can find out anything about this guy."

"See you soon."

FOUR

"How are you feeling?"

Sam barely bothered acknowledging my cousins before joining me on the library couch at The Overlook later that night. I went straight to the inn with Thistle because Sam was busy on the tanker. He appeared happy to see me – which I enjoyed because it made Thistle roll her eyes. What? I have to get my kicks where I can. Irritating Thistle is one of my favorite things. I don't often get to do it, because she's evil enough to be faster than me when it comes to aggravating people.

"I'm fine," I said, grabbing his hand as he tried to press it to my forehead. "I'm not sick. You don't have to worry."

Sam wasn't convinced. "Are you sure? Maybe we should stop at the market on our way home and pick up some orange juice and soup, you know, just to be on the safe side."

"Oh, good grief," Thistle snarled, annoyed. She flopped on the chair across the way and leaned her head back to stare at the ceiling. "Do you have to be such a woman?"

"I am a woman," I reminded her.

"I was talking to Sam." Even though her words were clipped, Thistle's eyes twinkled as she locked gazes with him. She clearly wanted someone to argue with, and Sam made an intriguing target.

"I don't care what you say," Sam shot back. "You weren't there. You didn't see what happened."

Thistle sobered. "Listen, I know you're upset, and I don't blame you. I was just ... ." She trailed off, unsure.

"Just what?" Sam prodded.

"Being her," I filled in, patting his hand. "She can't help herself. She got the biggest dose of Aunt Tillie in her genetic makeup when we were born, so she really can't stop herself from being a terrible person."

Thistle narrowed her eyes to dangerous slits. "That's the meanest thing you've ever said to me."

"What's the meanest thing she's ever said to you?" Bay asked, strolling into the room. She looked tired, shadows under her eyes, but she forced a bright smile.

"What's wrong with you?" Thistle asked, immediately picking up on Bay's ragged appearance.

"Nothing is wrong with me," Bay shot back. "Why do you think something is wrong with me?"

"Because you look like hell."

Bay blew a raspberry in Thistle's direction before focusing on me. "I heard you had a scary incident last night. I'm glad everything turned out okay."

"I'm fine," I offered. "You don't look fine, though."

Bay scowled. "Are you saying I look like hell? If so, I'll put my foot in your butt and bury your face in the flowerbed outside. Aunt Tillie swears up and down Bigfoot pooped in the flower urn on the porch. Do you want to find out if that's true with your face?"

I rolled my eyes. You can always tell when Bay is about to slip over the edge, because she lashes out in unexpected ways. "You haven't been sleeping, have you?" I prodded.

"I've been sleeping."

"No. You miss Landon. Admit it."

"You're crazy," Bay muttered, crossing her arms over her chest. "And to think I came in here because I was worried about you."

"You came in here because you want to avoid our mothers and Aunt Tillie," Thistle countered, contorting her body so her legs hung over the side of the chair and her head rested on the armrest. "That's the reason we're all in here. You're not fooling anybody."

Bay scorched Thistle with a look that would've shriveled a normal human. Thistle, though, is pretty far from normal, so she didn't so much as blanch.

"I think we should focus on Bay's feelings," I interjected, hoping to head off a fight. "Clearly she's lonely."

"I am not lonely," Bay barked. "I am perfectly capable of entertaining myself. I did it for years before Landon showed up."

"Yes, but now that Landon is your love muffin you pine for him when he's away," Thistle teased. "It's so cute I want to puke. No, wait. It's so cute I want to punch you in the face and then puke."

"You're not helping," I warned, extending a finger in Thistle's direction. "Why do you always have to be such a pain?"

"I think it's a gift."

"I think you just like attention, whether it's negative or positive. Aunt Tillie is the same way."

The verbal jab landed exactly where I wanted it to ... Thistle's emotional glass jaw.

"You take that back," Thistle hissed, her lips twisting. "I am nothing like that crazy woman."

As if sensing things were about to get out of hand – a regular occurrence in this house, and most of the time it's not out of malice but boredom – Sam opted to change the course of the conversation. "Did anything happen at work today?"

"Other than a woman getting robbed on the street and losing her Christmas shopping money, no," Thistle answered. "Oh, Clove tripped over the rug and landed on the couch, which was so funny I wish I had taped it. She also called for our lunch order, and because she was the forty-fifth customer of the day at the deli we won free sandwiches for a month."

Sam arched an eyebrow, surprised. "You tripped and fell?"

"See, and I thought the most interesting part of that conversation was when I won sandwiches for a month," I said.

"I thought the most interesting part was the woman who got robbed," Bay countered. "I mean … she lost all of her Christmas money. You've got to hope the jerk who robbed her has a big dose of karma coming his way."

"That would be nice," I agreed, bobbing my head. "I wish there was something we could do for her."

"We could find the robber and kick him in his naughty bits," Thistle suggested.

"You only want to kick someone," Bay argued. "How will that help anyone?"

"It might make the victim feel better."

"If she got to kick him in his naughty bits it might make her feel better," Bay argued. "You doing it is just potentially amusing and mean."

"Can we stop talking about kicking people in their naughty bits?" Sam asked, shifting uncomfortably on the couch. "Go back to the part where you tripped. Are you okay? You've had a rough twenty-four hours."

"I'm fine," I replied, amused. "I tripped over the edge of the rug and fell face first into the couch. It was lucky really. It didn't hurt at all."

"Yes, 'lucky,'" Thistle mimicked, making a face. "That's all she keeps talking about. Luck. She's convinced that coin Madam Rosa gave her yesterday is magical and she's benefitting from its powers."

"That's not what I said," I protested, my cheeks warming.

"That's exactly what you said," Thistle shot back.

"How have you been lucky?" Sam challenged. "You tripped over a rug and almost drowned in the lake last night."

"Yes, but I brushed against the coin right before you saved me. I was convinced I was going under for the last time, but then I felt the coin and you appeared out of nowhere … as if you were my knight in shining armor." I was going for cute because I was desperate to keep Sam from focusing on the negative. If I have one complaint about him

– which I don't, for the record – it's that he tends to tread water on the pessimistic side of the pool.

"Oh, well, that's adorable." Sam tweaked my nose. "You've still had a run of bad luck. That coin can hardly be lucky, given that."

"It's all how you look at it," I argued. "I believe I touched the coin and you found me. I believe I touched the coin and that's why I landed on the couch instead of the hard floor. I believe I touched the coin before ordering lunch and now we have free sandwiches for a month. That's on top of the fact that I touched the coin before calling the inn and got Belinda. She almost never answers the phone. To me, those are all lucky things."

Bay was understandably dubious. "And you think the coin is making these lucky things happen for you?"

I nodded, refusing to back down. "I do."

"Well, I guess it's possible."

Bay's capitulation took me by surprise. "You do?"

"Of course I do. We've seen magically imbued objects before. Usually they're cursed with bad mojo, but I don't see why it wouldn't be possible for someone to put a luck spell on a coin."

"Especially someone looking for a job," Thistle added. "Have we considered that Madam Rosa gave Clove the luck charm because she realized Clove was the easiest mark?"

"Hey!" Even when I'm not at the center of a conversation Thistle manages to get obnoxious digs in.

Thistle's smile was serene. "That wasn't meant as an insult. You took it wrong."

"How else am I supposed to take it?"

"Like an adult who doesn't get her feelings hurt over nothing," Thistle replied. "I wasn't trying to upset you. I was merely making an observation."

I didn't believe that for a second, but I decided to let it slide. "I believe the coin is lucky. I think Madam Rosa gave it to me because I'm the nicest of the three of us. She saw that after talking with us for only a few minutes. I think there's a lesson in there."

"Yes," Thistle agreed. "You're incredibly gullible."

"No, it's a lesson about karma," I argued. "I'm a good person, so I got the lucky coin. Good things keep happening to me because of that. On the flip side, the robber is a bad person, and he stole a woman's Christmas shopping money. He has bad karma and he will rue the day he set foot in Hemlock Cove."

Bay and Thistle snorted in unison.

"He'll rue the day?" Thistle shook her head. "Sometimes I think you get your theatrical side from my mother. We should switch mothers."

I love Aunt Twila, don't get me wrong, but I internally shuddered. She's a handful and loopy on a good day. I can take only so much. "I'm good, thanks."

"I don't blame you," Thistle said. "I … ." She trailed off as she narrowed her eyes and stared toward the library door. I followed her gaze and frowned when I saw Aunt Tillie scurry through – a floppy hat perched on her head – and slide between the chairs Bay and Thistle shared.

"What are you doing, old lady?" Thistle asked, changing course. "Are you undercover? Are you Nancy Drew-ing it?"

"I don't think she would be Nancy Drew," Bay countered before Aunt Tillie could answer. "She's more like that lady from *Murder She Wrote* – if Jessica Fletcher was evil and enjoyed cursing her great-nieces for no good reason."

Aunt Tillie fixed Bay with a petulant look. "I always have a good reason … and Jessica Fletcher has nothing on me. I'm an excellent investigator. I could do it for a living if I wanted to. I don't, though. Do you want to know why?"

"Because your big, floppy hat would get in the way?" Thistle asked, wrinkling her nose as she got a better look at the hat. "Is that a plastic flower pinned close to the brim there?"

"It's for natural camouflage," Aunt Tillie replied. "If you pick too much of one color you stand out – even if it's a muted color. I include small accents that allow me to fit in with the décor. And, by the way, smart mouth, I'm not an investigator because I believe everyone should be able to keep secrets from 'The Man.' I never want to be 'The Man,' because I don't pry into other people's business."

I couldn't help but giggle at the assertion. Aunt Tillie never met a secret she didn't want to drag out of someone. "I like your hat. I think it's very sensible to want to fit in with the décor. Are you wearing it because the guests are so enamored with you? Belinda said they were following you everywhere."

"They think I'm a celebrity," Aunt Tillie hissed, her eyes darting toward the door. "They think I'm like that Kim Kardashian or something. It's freaking me out."

"Oh, that's freaking all of us out," Thistle intoned, smirking.

"See, I think you're much more *Real Housewives of Beverly Hills* than *Keeping Up With the Kardashians*," Bay mused. "You're an attention whore, so you could be a Kardashian, but you would be all over a slap fight at a fancy restaurant."

"Good point," Thistle said, grinning.

"Do you think this is funny?" Aunt Tillie challenged, annoyed. "I'm being stalked!"

"I think it has funny elements," Thistle replied. "Quick, Clove, give her your lucky coin and the magic will protect her from becoming a Kardashian. While I'm not keen on helping her, I can't live in close proximity to a Kardashian."

"Join the club," Sam said, smirking.

I balked. "I'm not giving her my coin. She'll use it for evil and ruin the magic."

"What coin?" Aunt Tillie asked, turning her attention to me for the first time. "You look tired, little kvetch. You should get more sleep. I expect this one to look depressed and angsty because she misses 'The Man,' but your man is sitting right next to you."

"I'm just tired. And as for the coin, well, it's a long story."

Thistle launched into the tale, her amusement growing as she picked her way through the tale. When she was done, Aunt Tillie's eyes gleamed as she shifted her eyes to me.

"Let me see this coin," Aunt Tillie ordered.

"No way."

"Let me see it."

"No. It's mine."

Aunt Tillie heaved a sigh as she shuffled closer. She'd seemingly given up on hiding from her stalkers. "Let me see it. I'm not going to steal it."

I wasn't so sure. Aunt Tillie had a tendency to "liberate" things she wanted. She usually waited until we weren't looking to appropriate what she desired but she wasn't exactly known for being shy. "I ... ."

"Let me see it!" Aunt Tillie barked, her annoyance taking control.

"Sheesh. All right." I dug in my pocket and reluctantly handed her the coin, watching as she studied it.

"What do you think?" Bay asked a few moments later. "Is it magical?"

"I'm not sure what it is," Aunt Tillie replied, sticking the coin in her mouth so she could bite it. "Iron."

"We kind of already figured that out," Thistle offered. "No one is going to give a gold or silver coin to a random stranger."

"I'm not familiar with all of these markings," Aunt Tillie said, ignoring Thistle's snark.

"That's a four-leaf clover," I supplied.

"Thank you, Clove. I never would've figured that out on my own," Aunt Tillie deadpanned.

I crossed my arms over my chest. "I was trying to help."

"And you did a marvelous job, honey," Sam said, running his hand down the back of my head as his eyes remained on Aunt Tillie. "Do you think that coin is magical?"

"I think this coin is interesting," Aunt Tillie answered after a beat. "It doesn't feel completely magical – I'm not sensing a curse or anything – but it doesn't feel normal either."

"So you basically have nothing for us," Thistle summed up.

Aunt Tillie burned holes into Thistle's forehead as she handed the coin back to me. "Oh, I've got something for you. Do you want to know what it is?"

Thistle almost always steps over a boundary before recognizing it for what it is. This was no exception. "Not particularly."

"Well, I'm going to tell you anyway," Aunt Tillie said, straightening her shoulders. "You're on my list. You're not just on it, mouth. You've got the first two slots all to yourself."

"Oh, why?" Thistle whined. "Shouldn't you be focused on your fan club?"

As if on cue, a middle-aged woman dressed all in black clapped her hands as she appeared in the doorframe. "I found her," she sang out.

"Holy rabid rats, Batman," Aunt Tillie hissed, skirting around the edge of Bay's chair. "They're relentless."

"Run, old lady," Thistle suggested. "They're coming for you!"

Aunt Tillie scurried toward the door, but she stilled long enough to cast a baleful look over her shoulder. "I'll be coming for you later, mouth. Mark my words."

Thistle looked resigned as she watched her go. "Well, that was fun. Do you think my punishment will be tolerable or bacon-scented?"

"I think you're in for worse than a smell," I answered.

"What about you? Are you going to be punished with me?"

I shook my head as I held up the coin. "Nope."

Thistle snorted. "I guess we'll have to wait and see," she said, pushing herself to a standing position.

"I guess so," I agreed.

"So, we're going with the Winchester normal?" Bay asked.

Thistle and I nodded in unison.

"It's every witch for herself," I said. "I hope Aunt Tillie takes pity on your poor, wretched souls."

FIVE

Sam was more relaxed the next morning, a good night's sleep brushing away the last of his worry. He found my insistence that the coin brought me luck humorous, but unlike my cousins, he never insulted me when he didn't agree with one of my beliefs.

He remained at the Dandridge to work while I headed into town. It was a sunny fall day, a nice change from the rain that plagued us the past week. I couldn't help but enjoy my walk from the parking lot to the store.

Thistle was already working when I entered, the smile she reserved for customers in place as she helped a woman choose candles. Even though my cousin has the patience of a petulant child in a candy store, she's a marvel when it comes to helping people peruse our little assortment of odd offerings.

"I just don't know," the woman said, tapping her bottom lip. "There are so many to choose from."

"Take your time," Thistle suggested. "There's no reason to hurry. Give them all a good sniff again." She turned her attention to me. "You're late."

"Like two minutes," I protested, annoyed.

Thistle snorted. "Late is late."

"You sound like Aunt Tillie."

At mention of my great-aunt's name, the woman brightened and shifted. "You know Tillie Winchester?"

Uh-oh. I immediately knew where this conversation was going and was happy to leave Thistle to handle the situation. I averted my gaze and walked behind the counter, shedding my coat. "I'll make coffee since you haven't gotten around to it yet."

I could feel Thistle's eyes scorching holes into the back of my head, but opted to ignore her. "How does a little café mocha sound?"

"Just great," Thistle gritted out before returning her full attention to the customer. "Tillie Winchester is our great-aunt."

"Oh, you're so lucky," the customer enthused, clutching a skull candle closer to her chest. "What was it like growing up with her? Did you live in the same house? That's the rumor. I'll bet she was a terrific role model."

I didn't mean to snicker out loud, but I couldn't help myself. "Sure. If your idea of a role model is a woman who makes you sneak into the cemetery to steal flowers because the dead people won't miss them anyway."

The woman ignored my derisive tone. "People say she uses real magic." Her voice was barely a whisper. She seemed almost awed to be in the presence of Winchester greatness.

"Look, Dolores … ." Thistle started with an edge in her tone, but quickly recovered. "Your name is Dolores, right? I think that's what you told me when you came in."

The woman nodded. "That's right."

"The thing is … um … everyone in town is magical," Thistle lied, adopting a hokey tone she pulled out only when telling little white lies and tall tales for the customers. "It's true that Aunt Tillie's gift is stronger than most, but she's hardly a special case."

I found Thistle's response interesting. She was trying to deflect attention from Aunt Tillie, which seemed completely unlike her. Aunt Tillie was annoyed by her fan club, so normally Thistle would encourage the fan club to increase its efforts just so she could sit back and watch the show. This was a strange development.

"That's not what Mrs. Little said," Dolores argued.

I stilled, my shoulders tightening, and shifted my eyes to the woman. She seemed sincere, almost as if she was mired in a bout of celebrity worship rather than visiting a tourist town with fake witches and wizards. "Mrs. Little?"

"She's head of the tourist committee," Dolores explained. "She's the one we spoke with on the phone. We were very clear that we wanted real witches and not fake ones. She swore up and down that Hemlock Cove has real witches."

Crud. Margaret Little was Aunt Tillie's sworn enemy. No joke. If Aunt Tillie were a superhero, Mrs. Little would be the villain she has to fight to save the world from evil death rays and the like. She's the Lex Luthor to Aunt Tillie's Superman, the Joker to Aunt Tillie's Batman, the falling ratings to Aunt Tillie's Kardashian.

"Hemlock Cove is full of real witches," Thistle said, wetting her lips. "Did Mrs. Little point you in Aunt Tillie's direction for a specific reason?"

"She said that Tillie Winchester is the most powerful witch in the land and she never conducts demonstrations unless people show her the appropriate worship," Dolores replied. "I want to make sure that I show the appropriate worship for a witch befitting Tillie's stature. I already missed out on staying at The Overlook because it was booked solid by the time I called, so I want to make sure I handle the rest in the correct manner."

"Uh-huh." Thistle glanced at me, her expression unreadable. "And did Mrs. Little provide the appropriate way to worship Aunt Tillie?"

"Well, it's a secret, but since you're family you probably know." Dolores winked for emphasis, but the gesture came off as creepy rather than charming.

"Yes, we know all about worshipping Aunt Tillie," Thistle intoned. "Tell me exactly what Mrs. Little said … and don't leave anything out. It's an important ritual and I would hate for you to miss a step."

"Okay. That sounds reasonable. How much time do you have?"

I internally groaned as I pressed my eyes shut. This wasn't good.

Aunt Tillie would blow a gasket when she found out what Mrs. Little was up to.

I VOLUNTEERED to pick up lunch shortly before noon. I thought Thistle would put up a fight, but she'd grown to enjoy her role as an Aunt Tillie expert. Instead of using her powers for good, which is what I would've done, she opted to play both sides against the middle. That essentially means she turned the visitors against Mrs. Little while also encouraging them to do things that would drive Aunt Tillie crazy. I couldn't help but be relieved I no longer lived on the family property, because it was going to be all out war by the time Thistle was done.

I hummed to myself as I shuffled down the sidewalk, scuffing the bottom of my boots as I walked and enjoying the way the falling leaves crinkled as I stepped on them. The diner was only a few blocks away, and I was so lost in thought I didn't realize I was about to run into someone until it was almost too late.

I turned swiftly, my fingers brushing the coin in my pocket as I struggled not to tip over the curb. As if by magic I regained my footing – something of a miracle, because I'm known as a klutz – and landed squarely on both feet. I recognized the person I almost hit from the previous day. It was the woman who had been robbed. I was almost positive her name was Nancy Jarvis.

"I'm so sorry," I offered, horrified. "I didn't even see you. Are you okay?"

The woman's eyes were sad and vacant as she lifted them to my face. "I'm fine." There was absolutely no life to her demeanor.

"I recognize you," I said, my voice soft. "You probably don't remember me, but I'm one of the people who found you on the sidewalk right after you were robbed."

"I remember you," Nancy said, forcing a tight-lipped smile. "You were very kind."

"I wish I could've done more." I chewed my bottom lip, uncertain.

"Chief Terry said all of your Christmas gifts were stolen ... along with your money."

"Yes." Nancy nodded. "I'm sure it didn't seem like a lot of money to other people, but that five-hundred bucks was very important to me."

"I'm sure it was." My heart went out to her. She looked lost. "I can't help you out with the money, but I could offer you kind of a trade. If you're interested, that is."

Nancy lifted an eyebrow, suspicious. "What kind of trade? I'm a mother and I don't do anything kinky."

"Not that," I said hurriedly. "And ... eww. Do I look like the kind of person who does kinky stuff?"

Nancy shrugged. "It takes all kinds. I didn't think a guy in a hoodie would rob me yesterday, and look how that turned out."

"You have a point," I conceded. "It's just ... I know that you were shopping for your daughter and that she likes gothic things. I own the store down that way. Hypnotic. It's a magic shop, but we have a lot of different items for sale."

"Yes, I saw it when I was shopping yesterday." Nancy followed my finger with her eyes. "I was going to go in before ... well, I guess that doesn't really matter now. I have no Christmas gifts and no money."

"That's just it. I can help you with the Christmas gifts."

"How?"

"I own that shop with my cousin and it's supposed to be absolutely slammed this week because of a tour group," I replied. "I figured if you worked a few shifts for us you could pick out some items for your daughter for Christmas and still have plenty of time to enjoy the festivities while you're visiting Hemlock Cove. We have cool home-made candles and tarot cards. We have unique mortars and pestles, and hand-painted Ouija boards. It's full of things teenagers would love."

Nancy widened her eyes, her expression thoughtful as she glanced at the store. "You would do that?"

"I don't see why not. You need Christmas gifts and we need help. It's a nice trade-off."

Instead of smiling, as I expected, Nancy's eyes filled with tears. "I don't know what to say."

"Oh, please don't cry." My stomach twisted. "It was just a suggestion. I'm not trying to force you into doing anything you're not comfortable with."

"I'm not crying because I'm sad," Nancy supplied. "I'm crying because that's the nicest offer I've had in days. I would love to take you up on it."

"Oh, well, great," I said, recovering. "How about you come to the store tomorrow – let's say about nine in the morning – and we'll get started."

"I can't tell you how grateful I am for this." Nancy grabbed my hand and gripped it tightly. "You're a wonderful woman. You have a blinding flash of karma coming your way for this. I'm sure of it."

I smiled as I watched her leave, amused. I know it's wrong to pat yourself on the shoulder, but I couldn't help but feel good about brightening Nancy Jarvis' day. The emotion lasted only until I turned and found Chief Terry standing on the sidewalk behind me. He wasn't alone. Landon Michaels, Bay's boyfriend, stood next to him.

I found myself feeling defensive without understanding why. "What are you looking at?"

Chief Terry snorted as he shook his head, amused. "You."

"I ... why?"

"Because we heard the tail end of that conversation," Landon replied, his long dark hair brushing his shoulders as his eyes flashed with warmth. "You're a very good person."

I tilted my head, considering the words. "I try to be. I couldn't offer her much, but I did my best."

"I think what you offered her is plenty," Chief Terry said, resting his hand on my shoulder. "You always were the sweetest member of your little trio. Er, well, other than when you went through that stretch of time where you constantly claimed your eyes leaked so you could manipulate me."

Landon barked out a laugh, delighted. "Oh, I'll bet she was cute when she was using her witchy powers of persuasion on you."

Chief Terry made a disgusted face. "Picture her as an eight-year-old. She was even smaller then, and she could muster tears out of thin air. It was beyond frustrating."

"I didn't fake those tears," I said. "I was really that sensitive."

"Who do you think you're snowing?" Chief Terry asked, tapping my nose. "I'm on to your shenanigans."

I shrugged. "You were on to them even then, but you still let me cry."

"You seemed to enjoy it," Chief Terry said. "You were a good girl, for the most part. And I can chalk up almost all of your bad behavior to Tillie's influence. I don't blame you."

"That was our intention." I beamed when Chief Terry scowled and then focused on Landon. "Does Bay know you're here? She's been a little sad the past few days."

Landon's smile slipped. "What's wrong with her? Is she sick? I just got into town. I haven't seen her yet."

"She's not sick. She's just ... a girl."

"I have no idea what that means." Landon tugged a hand through his hair. "She's been a girl since I met her."

"She's missed you, that's all." I didn't bother hiding my smirk. "She's lonely when you're not around, especially ever since I moved out and Thistle is ... well ... Thistle."

"Yes, Thistle is a true joy," Landon muttered, shifting his eyes to the newspaper building. Bay's car was parked in front, and he looked almost relieved to see it. "My boss sent me to help with The Hoodie Bandit, so I'll be in town for a few days."

I couldn't help but be dubious. "The Hoodie Bandit? Seriously? The FBI sent an agent because a dude in a hoodie robbed a woman?"

"That's what I said," Chief Terry muttered dryly. "We all know Captain Fussypants here begged his boss to let him visit. He can't seem to stay away from his blonde."

"You say that like it's a bad thing," Landon replied. "I happen to love my blonde. I'm an independent person, though. I don't need her constant companionship to function."

I snorted, amused. "That's almost exactly what Bay said. Then she proceeded to pout for what felt like days."

Landon sighed. "I'll go see her right now. We're okay for a few minutes, right?"

Terry shrugged. "I don't know. I think this hoodie bandit is clearly gearing up for a terrorist attack on Hemlock Cove. I think I need your constant attention. I'm not sure I can spare you."

Landon's knit his eyebrows, frustrated. "You only saying that to torture me."

"I'm only saying that because I'm mildly curious what you'll do," Chief Terry admitted. "I'm fairly certain nothing will keep you from that newspaper building – or the editor inside – but I've always had a scientific mind and I enjoy conducting experiments."

Landon heaved an exaggerated sigh. "Do you want me to beg?"

Chief Terry tilted his head to the side, considering. "Yes."

Landon worked his jaw, his eyes flashing. He had a choice, and I couldn't help but wonder which way he would go. Finally Landon gripped his hands together and forced a smile. "Do you mind if I stop at the newspaper and question the editor about any information she may have gleaned on our robber?"

Chief Terry barked out a laugh. "That was pretty slick the way you phrased that. Go ahead. If she's upset, I want you to make her feel better ... just not in a gross way."

"No promises," Landon shot back as he moved toward the building.

I watched him go, amused at the spring in his step. After a few seconds I turned my eyes back to Chief Terry and found him watching me. "What?"

He shook his head. "Nothing. You're a good girl. You're genuinely happy for Bay even though the situation has nothing to do with you. I like that about you. I always have."

I blushed at the compliment. "I ... thank you."

"Oh, you're still cute," Chief Terry said, grinning. "Even when your eyes leak."

I ignored the teasing and forced my mind to important matters. "Any leads on The Hoodie Bandit?"

"None so far. We have the Feds here now, though. Surely a crack agent like Landon Michaels can solve the case in no time flat."

"You're enjoying this far too much," I chided him. "I think it's cute."

"Oh, I think it's cute," Chief Terry said. "That doesn't mean I don't like making fun of him. He makes it very easy."

He did indeed.

SIX

"You did what?" Thistle made a face as she crossed her legs at the ankles and glared at me.

"I offered to let Nancy Jarvis work for us in exchange for items from the shop." I'd been proud of myself for going out of my way to help a person in need … right up until the moment Thistle made me feel like an idiot. She does that often, just for the record. Bay says I should stand up to her more often, but Bay makes me feel like an idiot on a regular basis, too, so I'm not sure I should trust her.

"But … why?"

"Because she was upset and I felt bad for her."

"But we don't even know her."

"Last time I checked, I didn't need to know someone to have empathy for them," I pointed out. "She's sad and afraid. If I can make her feel better, I'm going to do it. Besides, what does it matter? It's a few candles and an Ouija board or something. It's not as if it will break us."

"I didn't say it would break us." Thistle's eyes flashed. "I just … ." She broke off and held up her hands in defeat. I almost didn't recognize the gesture because Thistle is the type of person who never admits defeat. "You know what? You're right. We could use the help, and it's a nice gesture. I don't have a problem with it."

I narrowed my eyes, suspicious. "Are you just saying that so you can turn it around on me later and make a big deal about it?"

"No. I'm saying it because it's true."

"It will mean good karma for us." I'm an optimist at heart.

"And the Goddess knows I need good karma after the crap I pulled with those women earlier," Thistle mused. "I wonder if Aunt Tillie has found out why those women are worshipping her."

That was a pretty good question. "Are you going to tell her about Mrs. Little?"

Thistle answered without hesitation. "Yes."

"Are you going to wait until those women drive Aunt Tillie around the bend and she's threatening curses against people other than you?"

"Yes."

"Are you enjoying this more than good karma rules allow?"

"Oh, yeah." Thistle's smile was lazy. "I can't seem to stop myself from enjoying this. It's like the perfect storm. Aunt Tillie is going to lose her mind and I'm going to swoop in at the exact right moment and tell her that Mrs. Little is responsible. She'll be so furious she won't be able to remember my part in all of this. It will be glorious."

I had my doubts, but I didn't bother admitting them to Thistle. It's rare that she's in a good mood, and I wanted to take advantage of the situation as much as possible. "So ... you're okay with Nancy working for us for a few days, right?"

"I am," Thistle confirmed. "Perhaps this is your lucky coin coming into play again. Maybe she'll help us out of a bind when we're busy, and we'll help her make Christmas special for a teenager who probably doesn't deserve anything more than a lump of coal in her stocking."

"You don't know that," I protested. "For all we know Nancy's daughter could be an absolute delight."

"She's a teenager."

"So?"

"Think back to when we were teenagers."

Crudsticks. I hate it when she has a point. "Fine. She's probably a devil in disguise – if she even bothers to put on a disguise – but that doesn't mean her mother doesn't love her."

"Of course not," Thistle scoffed. "Our mothers loved us, and we certainly didn't deserve it."

"I always deserved it."

"And that's why everyone thinks you're a kvetch."

"No one but you thinks I'm a kvetch," I snapped, my patience wearing thin.

"That's not true. Everyone thinks you're a kvetch." Aunt Tillie appeared at the edge of the couch, almost as if teleporting to the location via magic – which is impossible, in case anyone is keeping score – and fixed me with a pointed look. "Why are you denying being a kvetch, by the way? That's your thing. You should own it."

I jolted at her sudden appearance, glancing over my shoulder to stare at the door. "How did you get in here?"

"I walked in through the front door."

"But ... the chimes over the door didn't jangle," I pointed out. "Shouldn't they have jangled?"

Aunt Tillie held her hands palms up. "You're asking the wrong person. I'm not an expert on wind chimes."

"I guess we finally found something you can't do professionally," Thistle teased, her lips twitching. "Wind chime testing is out."

"This one is a kvetch," Aunt Tillie said, gesturing toward me. "You're something worse, mouth. Now get off your lazy behind and lock the front door. I'm undercover. I can't risk anyone stumbling across my location."

Thistle didn't make a move toward the door, instead furrowing her brow as she regarded Aunt Tillie. Our great-aunt has interesting taste in clothing, to put it mildly. She was dressed in muted colors today – black cargo pants and a matching T-shirt – and instead of standing out she faded into the background. That wasn't like her at all.

"Are you hiding from your fan club?" I asked.

"I don't have a fan club," Aunt Tillie replied. "I have stalkers. There's a difference."

"I'm not sure the majority of Hollywood starlets would agree with you there, but for the sake of argument, how do you figure you're being stalked?"

"Every time I turn around someone annoying is standing behind me," Aunt Tillie answered. "They sneak up on me. No, that's not the right word. They creep. Yeah, that's better. They creep up behind me. They follow me down hallways and into my greenhouse. Do you know someone walked into my greenhouse without knocking?"

"They should be drawn and quartered," Thistle drawled.

"How am I supposed to work in my ... special field ... when people are following me? It's undignified, I tell you."

Aunt Tillie's "special field" is actually a side pot business ... accompanied by her illegal wine business ... and she's been making noise about building a still. She magically warded her field so people don't accidentally stumble across it, but that doesn't mean someone following her wouldn't get an eyeful if she wasn't careful.

"It's just about harvest time, isn't it?" I asked, my mind busy.

"Yes, you little stoner," Aunt Tillie shot back. "Don't even think of trying to go in there to harvest without me."

"I'm not an idiot."

Aunt Tillie arched a challenging eyebrow.

"I wasn't thinking about it," I protested, my voice hopping. "Why do you always assume the worst?"

"Because you share genes with me and I know what I would do in your place," Aunt Tillie shot back.

"She has a point," Thistle said. "You don't have to worry about us harvesting without you, though. We remember the great Marijuana Meltdown of 2007. We couldn't stop rhyming for days."

"That's what you get for being snoopy little monsters." Aunt Tillie was blasé. "Now, not that I'm not happy to shoot the breeze with you – I'm not, but I'll pretend I am so you don't think I'm rude – I actually have a reason for being here."

"I'm terrified to ask, but here it comes," Thistle intoned. "What do you want?"

"Well, I'm glad you asked." Aunt Tillie's smile told me the exact opposite was true. "For the good of everyone – but especially for the sake of my mental health – I need that coin. I'm in need of a bit of luck, and I understand you have an endless supply of it."

I narrowed my eyes and instinctively turned so the pocket housing the coin was further away from her. "No way."

Aunt Tillie wasn't about to be dissuaded. "Give it to me." She extended her hand and shook it in front of my face."

"I said no." I slapped her hand away, wrinkling my nose and adopting my best stern expression. "I didn't bring it with me. I left it at the Dandridge this morning."

Aunt Tillie rolled her eyes so hard she almost toppled over into Thistle's lap. "You're such a bad liar. How did I raise such a bad liar?"

Thistle snorted. "You didn't raise us. You just took us with you when you were doing something illegal because the cops were less likely to arrest you if you had three innocent faces to trot out. The fact that one of those faces could manufacture tears with minimal effort was merely a bonus."

"Especially because Chief Terry refused to do something that would've upset Bay," I added.

"Don't kid yourself. Terry would've gone out of his way to protect all of you." Aunt Tillie rolled her neck until it cracked. "Bay is definitely his favorite, but he loves both of you, too."

"I know. I saw him on the sidewalk today and he told me he was proud of me."

"That's because he's a good man and he knows how to make people feel better," Aunt Tillie said. "Except me. He's never cared about making me feel better."

"That's probably because you've been a thorn in his butt so many times he's lost count," Thistle said sagely. "By the way, not to turn this to a topic that will agitate you, but have you figured out why all of these women are following you around?"

Part of me was happy that Thistle couldn't leave things alone and pointed the conversation away from my new good luck charm. For some irrational reason, I couldn't help picturing myself as Gollum in the *Lord of the Rings* movies and felt a desperate need to protect my precious when Aunt Tillie demanded I hand it over. Where in Hecate's pocket did that come from?

"I have no idea, and I can't force myself to talk to one of these women long enough to find out," Aunt Tillie replied. "Do you know?"

"I have no idea."

To the untrained observer, Thistle looked as if she was telling the truth. She was an accomplished liar when she put in only moderate effort. The way Aunt Tillie narrowed her eyes told me that she didn't believe my smug cousin, though.

"What do you know?" Aunt Tillie lowered her voice to a dangerous level. "I can tell you know something. Don't bother denying it."

"I don't know anything!" Thistle's voice took on a screechy tone. "Why are you always so suspicious? Can't you simply believe me because I'm your niece and you love me?"

"Did you just meet me?"

"Yeah, I knew that was taking it a step too far," Thistle grumbled. "I have no idea why the women are following you other than one of them heard some rumor that you're the most powerful witch in the land and they're prepared to worship you because of it."

Aunt Tillie pursed her lips. I could practically see her mind working. "Well, whoever started that rumor is a genius. That doesn't mean I like it. I wonder who told them that."

"I asked, but they all named different women in their group," Thistle offered. This time I was completely impressed with her lying ability. "It sounds like one of them heard a rumor and spread it as fact to the rest of them."

"Well, it is a fact." Aunt Tillie crossed her arms over her chest. "I can't blame them for worshipping me. I'm quite extraordinary."

"You should be studied," Thistle agreed, causing me to bite my lip to keep from laughing.

"I don't want to encourage them, though," Aunt Tillie said. "Do you have any idea how annoying it is to have people following you around all of the time? I'm all-powerful and brilliant. That doesn't mean I want people bugging me."

"Duly noted," Thistle said, catching my eye as she smirked. "So, back to the important issues. Why do you think Clove's coin will be able to help you?"

I scorched her with a look. I couldn't believe she had the audacity to turn the conversation back to my coin when I had much juicier dirt on her. "Oh, no," I said. "I think we should focus on the fiend who told those women that Aunt Tillie was the most powerful witch in the Midwest. That's potentially dangerous, and the person spreading that rumor should be taken in hand. So should anyone – any witch even – who has information on who this megalomaniac is and keeps it to herself."

Thistle made a face that would've been comical under different circumstances. Oh, who am I kidding? It was comical now. Somehow I managed to keep from laughing out loud.

"I'm more interested in the coin for the time being," Aunt Tillie said. "Now ... gimme."

"No." I rolled out of my chair and away from Aunt Tillie, annoyed. "It's mine. Madam Rosa gave it to me. You can't have it."

"You're being ridiculous," Aunt Tillie sputtered. "In this family we share. That's the number one rule in the Winchester household. Now ... share." She shook her hand in front of my face.

"I thought the number one rule in our family was not to get caught," Thistle mused. "You always added the caveat that if we did get caught to make sure we didn't take anyone else down with us ... especially you ... so we should always have alibis at the ready in case 'The Man' stopped by for a chat."

Aunt Tillie rolled her eyes. "That's a rule, too. It's not the number one rule, though. That thing I said about sharing is."

"Since when?" I challenged. "You always told us as teenagers that sharing was for ninnies."

"I only told you that when you got into my wine ... and pot ... and herbs ... and anything else that was mine," Aunt Tillie argued.

"So basically you're saying that I'm supposed to share with you, but you're not supposed to reciprocate, right?" I challenged.

"Exactly." Aunt Tillie moved her hand again. "Gimme."

"No. It's mine."

"Hold up." Thistle climbed to her feet and stepped between us, her eyes flashing. "What if I said I have a compromise that will make everyone happy?"

"I would say you've been harvesting my field without permission," Aunt Tillie answered, not missing a beat.

Thistle ignored the snarky response. "What if we all worked together as a group to test the coin to see if it works?"

Aunt Tillie's eyebrows arched up. "What do you have in mind?"

Thistle's demented smile was enough to make my stomach twist when her gaze landed on me. "I have a lot of ideas. I think we should try as many of them as possible."

That didn't sound good for my physical or mental well-being. "But …."

"That is a great idea," Aunt Tillie said, cutting me off. "Where should we start?"

Thistle pointed toward the ladder. "I was thinking we might try a few physical tests, and then maybe we can buy some lottery tickets."

"You're totally my favorite great-niece today," Aunt Tillie enthused. "Let's do it."

SEVEN

"Ow! That hurt!"

I ruefully rubbed my bottom as I turned a hateful glare in the direction of Thistle and Aunt Tillie. I was on the floor, a pillow under my rear end, and my cousin and great-aunt appeared to be amused by my recent show of luck. I, on the other hand, was starting to grate under the pressure.

"That didn't hurt," Thistle scoffed, annoyed. "You landed on a huge pillow."

She was right. It didn't hurt. I landed hard enough that it should've hurt, though. My mind reacted before my body, and I couldn't stop myself from complaining. Our luck challenges lasted most of the afternoon, Thistle waiting on the customers as Aunt Tillie thought of a wild array of experiments. Every time my newfound luck came out to play they were awed and amused. I felt bolder as the hours ticked by, but I also had a niggling source of worry. What happened if I came to rely on the coin and it failed?

Still, it had been an illuminating afternoon.

We won five hundred bucks on a scratch-off lottery ticket – which Aunt Tillie put in her pocket when no one was looking.

We played poker, and I won eight hands in a row. We played for

Hershey's Kisses, but I noticed Aunt Tillie scooped all of my winnings into her purse when I was distracted grabbing more candles from the storage room.

We took to racing outside. I beat Thistle four times in a row before demanding we stop. Hey, I don't want to sweat if it's not for a good cause. Thistle has longer legs and always beat me in footraces when we were younger, so she should've won.

Aunt Tillie hid a quarter in the stable. I found it within four minutes. Thistle's boyfriend Marcus owned the stable. He merely shook his head as he watched us cavort. He appeared intrigued, but happy to let us meander about on our own.

Aunt Tillie suggested a horse race, but I put the kibosh on that. Ever since Bay was thrown from a horse in the spring I'd been leery of getting on one.

The most recent test involved placing a pillow in the middle of the room and then climbing on a ladder. Thistle then kicked the ladder out from under me, and each time I landed on the pillow instead of the hardwood floor surrounding it. I was nervous the first two times, but got used to the fall after that. Thistle relished her power in that scenario ... right up until she realized I wasn't getting hurt.

"I think the coin is really magical," Thistle announced, crossing her arms over her chest. "I mean ... that's freaking amazing."

"It really is," Aunt Tillie said, shuffling closer to me. "You're a very lucky person, Clove." I felt her hand in my pocket and jerked away, ignoring the innocent look she pasted on her face.

"You are terrible. I'm not giving you my coin." I stomped behind the counter and grabbed my phone. I'd had my fill of experiments for the day. "In fact, I'm kind of done. I'm going home."

"You can't go home," Aunt Tillie argued. "I haven't stolen the coin from you yet. That's not fair."

I rolled my eyes. "Do you ever listen to yourself?"

"Every chance I get."

I did my best to tune her out as I glanced at the phone screen, my heart rolling when I realized I'd missed a text during my most recent fall. "Hey, guys!"

"You hold her down, Thistle," Aunt Tillie ordered. "I'll get the coin."

"I'm not helping you," Thistle shot back. "Making you more powerful is a terrible idea. That's how evil dictatorships start."

"You're on my list."

"Guys!" I yelled as I moved toward the door, paying them little heed. "Bay texted two minutes ago. She said someone was trying to break into the newspaper building and she asked us to call the police."

Thistle stilled. "That is the lamest lie I've ever heard."

"It's not a lie!"

"Why wouldn't she call the police herself?"

"Because she didn't want the intruder to hear her," I snapped. I held up the phone for proof. "Bay's in trouble!"

My family may be persnickety and full of annoying people who get joy out of messing with others, but the one thing every Winchester puts above all else is family loyalty. If Bay was really in trouble, we had to get to her.

"I'll call Chief Terry," Thistle said, grabbing her phone. "Odds are we'll beat him there, though."

"Odds are I'm going to beat someone," Aunt Tillie announced. "That hoodie-wearing psycho had better watch out, because I'm in a mood."

She said that as if it was a new thing. The woman is always in a mood.

IT TOOK us less than three minutes to run to the newspaper building. Despite her age, Aunt Tillie is surprisingly spry. She didn't put up a whisper of complaint as we rushed in that direction. For a woman who does nothing but grouse, it was quite the accomplishment.

"Clove, you take the back door," Thistle ordered, keeping her voice low. "I'll take Aunt Tillie through the front door with me."

I balked. "Are you joking?"

"No."

"You want me to go alone?" Here's the thing: I am not a coward.

I'm completely brave and willing to sacrifice my life for a family member and all that other crap I'm supposed to say and think when someone I love is in danger. I don't want to die if there's no reason, though. If I'm going to lose my life, the sacrifice had better be worth it.

"You won't be alone," Thistle argued. "The back door is hidden by that storage room, if you remember correctly. It's far more likely that Aunt Tillie and I will see the robber than you will."

"Then why don't I go with you and offer backup?"

"Because we need to cover both doors in case The Hoodie Bandit rabbits. We really need to come up with a better name for him, too. The Hoodie Bandit makes him sound like a slacker looking for pot instead of a robber threatening the lives of Hemlock Cove's finest."

I made a face. "Is that really what we should be worrying about right now?"

"How about The Hooded Marauder?" Aunt Tillie suggested.

"That's much better." Thistle nodded and then made small shooing motions with her hands. "Go to the back door."

"I ... don't want to."

"Then go through the front with Aunt Tillie and face the danger," Thistle challenged. "We can't put Aunt Tillie at the back door."

"Mostly because I don't want to walk that far," Aunt Tillie interjected.

Thistle ignored her. "Clove, those are your only two options."

I tilted my head to the side as I considered what to do. The fact that Bay could be in danger finally propelled me to a decision. "I'll go in through the back."

"Good girl."

I left Thistle and Aunt Tillie and trudged toward the back of the building, casting the occasional glance over my shoulder. By the time I rounded the corner that led to the back door my heart was hammering and my palms were sweaty. I rubbed my hands over my jeans to alleviate some of the moisture before reaching for the handle.

At that exact moment the door flew open and a hooded figure bolted out. He seemed as surprised to see me as I did him. I had a split second to register my surprise and soak up as many details as possible before the man grabbed my shoulders and tossed me off the narrow steps.

"Get out of the way," he growled.

He tossed me with enough force that I should've flown over the railing and possibly broken my neck on an awkward landing – no, I'm not being dramatic. Instead, the pocket of my jeans caught on the jagged edge of the metal railing and I merely glanced to the side as he bolted to freedom.

The unmistakable sound of pounding feet assailed my ears, and when I shifted my attention to the open doorway I found Thistle staring in the direction of the departing figure, her chest heaving.

"Why didn't you stop him?" she barked.

I rolled my eyes. "I'm fine. Thank you so much for asking."

Thistle made an exaggerated face. "And the kvetch strikes again."

I can't tell you how tired I am of hearing that word.

I SAT ON the edge of Bay's desk as she recounted her tale. She'd barely gotten into it before Landon burst through the door, his eyes furious as he scanned the room.

"Bay?"

"I'm okay," Bay offered, standing so he could see that she was unmarked and free of blood stains. "I'm sorry I texted you the way I did, but I wasn't sure what else to do."

"Oh, I see how it is," Thistle complained. "You texted him before you texted us. We were your second choice."

"Of course you were," Bay said. "He has a gun."

"And I'm strong and manly," Landon muttered, tugging Bay close for a hug. He ran his hand down the back of her head and whispered something in her ear. I had no idea what it was, but there was something tender about his expression. He loves Bay in an all-encompassing way. She doesn't always see it, but I do. They're unbelievably sweet when they want to be. They also fight when one of them decides to be stubborn, but sometimes I think they do that simply because they enjoy the way the other looks when they're angry. It gets their blood pumping.

"Okay, tell me what happened," Landon prodded when he pulled his head back.

"It was weird," Bay replied. "I was in here working on my computer, just emailing some articles to the page designer. I locked the office door when I came in because I didn't want to deal with tourists. I was determined to get out of work early because you showed up earlier to surprise me."

"That sounds like a good plan," Landon murmured.

"Anyway, I was at my desk when I swear I heard someone outside the front door," Bay said. "I parked behind the building, and most people recognize my car, so anyone local should've known that I was here. I went to the front door because I thought that maybe Brian showed up and forgot his key, but when I looked through the peephole I saw a guy in a hoodie."

"Did he look up at you?" Landon asked. "Did he have a gun?"

"I didn't see a weapon. All I saw was white skin around his dark eyes."

"I saw the eyes, too," I offered. "He pushed me out of the way on the back porch, and I was up close and personal with him. I can't put my finger on it, but there was something familiar about those eyes."

"Do you think he's a local?" Landon asked.

I nodded. "I think I recognize him. I just … I need to think. I'm sure if I have a little time when I'm not so traumatized that it will come to me."

Thistle rolled her eyes. "Traumatized? You saw him for like two seconds. How were you traumatized?"

"It seemed longer to me," I sniffed.

Landon ignored my interaction with Thistle and focused on Bay. "How did he get in the office?"

"He jimmied the lock," Bay replied. "I was in the lobby and saw him working the handle. I knew it was only a matter of time until it gave. It's old."

"Well, it's getting replaced before we leave here today," Landon said. "What did you do?"

"I texted you. You didn't get back to me right away and I didn't want to risk calling because I didn't want him to hear my voice. I thought there was a chance he didn't know I was inside and I could get away with hiding in a closet."

"That was smart." Landon let his hands roam over Bay's shoulders. "How long did it take him to get in?"

"About three minutes. I used my phone to message Clove, but she didn't get back to me right away either. Then I stuffed my phone in my bra and hid in the closet."

"You put your phone in your bra?" Despite the serious nature of the situation, Landon couldn't help but smile. "What a lucky phone."

Aunt Tillie cuffed the back of his head and scowled. "Only you could turn something like this into a reason to act perverted."

"Oh, don't sell yourself short," Landon teased. "I'll bet you could do it, too, if you set your mind to it."

Aunt Tillie was agitated, but I didn't miss the way her lips twitched. "You're a funny guy."

"I'm here all week." Landon shifted his contemplative eyes to Bay. "Did he know you were in the closet?" I couldn't be sure, but he almost looked as if he didn't want to know the answer.

"I don't think so, but I can't be sure," Bay replied. "I was inside trying to control my breathing when I heard Aunt Tillie yell about taking down The Hooded Marauder. The next thing I knew, I heard pounding footsteps and Thistle yelling for me."

"The Hooded Marauder? Do I even want to know?"

"It's like The Riddler, only weirder," I offered.

"That explains everything," Landon deadpanned. "Well, at least you're okay." He rested his brow against Bay's for a moment before sobering. "I'm going to have the uniforms check for prints on the handle. Did he touch anything else?"

Bay shrugged. "I honestly didn't see."

"I didn't either," Thistle said.

"He put his hands on me," I supplied, pointing toward my arm. "Right here."

"Oh, here we go," Thistle complained. "We're never going to hear the end of this. It's going to be like the time she claimed she saved the town from blowing up because she thought she smelled a gas leak."

"I did smell gas!"

"It was on your pants," Thistle argued.

I crossed my arms over my chest and ignored her challenging glare. "What are you going to do, Landon? I mean, if this guy keeps getting bolder, that can't be good for any of us. I didn't see a weapon, but that doesn't mean he can't get one."

"I'm not afraid of any weapon," Aunt Tillie sneered. "He probably has a tiny one in his pants, and that's the reason he feels the need to manhandle women."

"Thank you so much for that visual," I said dryly.

"You're welcome."

"I'm not sure what I'm going to do right now," Landon admitted. "We're checking for fingerprints, and I'm hoping once Clove has a chance to process what she saw that she'll figure out the missing piece of the puzzle.

"All I can say with any certainty is that I'm replacing that lock and fawning all over my woman for the rest of the night," he said. "That's my plan until further notice."

Bay arched a confrontational eyebrow. "Your woman?"

Landon refused to back down. "Yup."

"I'm going to punish you for that later."

For the first time since finding out she was okay, Landon flashed a genuine smile. "That's the best thing I've heard all day."

EIGHT

Nancy arrived at the store five minutes early the next day. She seemed nervous but eager, and I immediately set her to work stocking shelves. The new gaggle of tourists seemed keen about grabbing as many herbs as possible, so that meant we were low in the front of the store. Thankfully, Thistle bagged extra in anticipation of the large group, so we had plenty ready to go in the back.

"Did you hear what happened at the newspaper office yesterday?" Nancy asked, sitting on the floor, her legs crossed, and reading some of the herb labels. Thistle made them up on her computer and they were nicer than anything I'd seen on comparable products at other area stores. They had an antique feel to them.

I nodded my head, momentarily fingering the coin before turning my attention to the voodoo dolls display. "I was there."

"You were?" Nancy widened her eyes. "Why were you there?"

"Because my cousin is the editor. She texted when the guy tried to get in the building," I explained. "Her boyfriend is an FBI agent, but he was out following a lead with Chief Terry. They couldn't get to her in time, so we went instead."

"Who is we?"

"Thistle and me ... and my Aunt Tillie."

"Aunt Tillie?" Nancy looked conflicted, as if she wanted to ask a question but was afraid she would offend me.

"You can ask," I said, offering a kind smile. "Everyone is curious about her. They can't seem to help themselves."

Nancy smiled, sheepish. "Is she as scary as everyone makes her out to be? I've heard everyone talking for the past two days, and she seems to be the only person everyone believes to be the real deal."

That was definitely an interesting development. We're all the real deal, although Aunt Tillie definitely is stronger than the rest of us ... sometimes combined. "I don't know if 'scary' is the right word," I hedged. "She has a good heart."

"And?"

"And evil fingers," I added, smiling when Thistle walked through the front door. She carried a tray with multiple gourmet coffees perched on it, and she looked less than thrilled to be working so early in the day. "Good morning, sunshine."

"Don't make me kick you in the face," Thistle warned, resting the tray on the counter before greeting Nancy with a head bob. "I'm glad you're here, and I'm sorry about what happened to your Christmas money."

Nancy seemed shy in the face of Thistle's entrance. "That's okay," she said after a beat. "Thank you for allowing me to work so I can earn some Christmas gifts for my daughter."

"Don't worry about it. We have everything a teenager could possibly love." Sometimes Thistle is a pain in the butt – okay, she's almost always a pain in multiple body parts – but she has a good heart. I could tell she would go out of her way to make Nancy feel welcome. "Speaking of that, has Chief Terry been in contact about the guy who robbed you? Now that he scared the crap out of Bay, I expect Landon to go on a rampage until he's found."

"Chief Terry said he would be in touch," Nancy answered. "He's been very nice, but I don't expect to get my money back. I think that would be asking for too much ... and I'm about the unluckiest person in the world."

Thistle and I exchanged a quick look at the mention of "luck," and then turned our attention back to Nancy.

"I think everything will work out," Thistle said. "I'm a big proponent of karma."

"And this Landon … this FBI agent … you think he'll find out who did this?" Nancy looked hopeful despite her obvious resignation.

"I do," Thistle confirmed. "He's worked up over someone breaking into the newspaper office. He's sticking close to Bay."

"How will he work if he's sticking close to his girlfriend?" Nancy asked.

Thistle jerked her thumb in the direction of the door as Landon pulled it open and ushered Bay in. "Because he's shifting babysitting duties to us." Thistle's smile was evil, as if she enjoyed Bay's outrage as our blonde cousin openly glared at her boyfriend.

"You can't tell me what to do," Bay barked, annoyed.

"I'm not telling you what to do." Landon was clearly in no mood to argue, but he wasn't about to let Bay run roughshod over his concerns. "I'm asking you to work from the store today. I think we'll have this guy by the end of the day, and then you can do whatever your heart desires."

Bay made a face. "Landon, this guy would have to be an idiot to try to get into the newspaper office again. You changed the lock yourself."

"And I'm an FBI agent, not a handyman," Landon shot back. "Why do you think Chief Terry is checking over my work right now?"

"Honestly? I thought you just wanted him to clap you on the back and say, 'Good job, son. You're manly and strong and handy with a hammer.'"

Despite the serious nature of the situation, Landon couldn't stop himself from smirking. "Very cute. I'll show you how handy I am later."

"Oh, puke," Thistle complained, shaking her head. "How can you guys go from fighting one second and staring at each other with heart-shaped eyes the next?"

"It's a gift," Landon replied, resting his hand on Bay's shoulder. "Chief Terry believes that we have a good lead with the loggers up at

Dead Man's Hill. They're new to the area, and witnesses say all of them have been wearing hoodies. It's a good place to start."

"That doesn't mean I need to work here," Bay pointed out. "I'll be safe at the office. I promise."

"I would prefer you be safe here," Landon said. "Look at it this way: At the office you don't have Thistle and Clove to amuse you. Clove thinks she has a magic coin, for crying out loud. That has to be entertaining."

"Thanks," I said dryly, sticking out my tongue.

Landon ignored the snarky display. "And don't forget Thistle," he prodded. "She's playing a very dangerous game with Aunt Tillie and Mrs. Little. She's playing both sides against the middle, and we both know that's going to blow up in her face and she'll end up cursed."

Bay's expression softened. "That could be fun."

"It will be great fun if you're caught in the crossfire and smell like bacon for the next few days," Landon said, tugging a strand of Bay's hair behind her ear. "I'll feel better if you stay here. You'll be entertained if you stay here. Isn't that the best of both worlds?"

Bay heaved a sigh, resigned. "Will you call me when you know more?"

"I will."

"Okay." Bay held up her hands in defeat. "You owe me a massage later. I expect my emotional distress to be overpowering by the end of the day."

Landon's lips twitched as he leaned forward and gave her a kiss. "I will gladly let you punish me to your heart's content." He sobered as he turned his attention to Thistle and me. "Watch my sweetie."

"We'll do our best," I said.

"Watch yourselves, too," Landon added. "We have no idea how dangerous he is."

I nodded in understanding. "We'll stick together like glue."

"Normally that promise would fill me with dread, but I'm strangely happy for it today." Landon tapped the end of Bay's nose. "I love you. Be good."

A whimsical sigh escaped Nancy as she watched Landon go, a far-off expression on her face. "He's ... dreamy."

"He's okay," Thistle said. "He's bossy."

"So are you," I pointed out.

"He has his moments," Bay said, turning to the stocking action. "So who wants to entertain me?"

Thistle made a groaning sound. "This is going to bite."

"YOU GUYS ARE COUSINS, not sisters, right?"

We took a break for lunch, settling on the couch and chairs in the center of the store. After a few hours of listening to us mess with one another, Nancy was feeling a lot more relaxed.

"We're cousins, but we were raised in the same house together," I answered. "Most people assume we're sisters, even though we look nothing alike."

"We look like our mothers," Thistle supplied. "They're sisters, but they don't look alike."

"I'm surprised you admit that," Bay teased, closing her laptop and placing it on the coffee table before reaching for her container of take-out. "You usually hate it when people think you look like your mother."

"Look who's talking," Thistle shot back. "You hate looking like your mother."

"No, I hate being compared to my mother," Bay clarified. "She's a bossy control freak."

"Everyone in our family is a bossy control freak," I pointed out. "Except for me, of course. I'm delightful."

Thistle made an exaggerated face that caused me to giggle. "Yes, you're the most delightful kvetch in all the land," she drawled.

I narrowed my eyes. "I hope you know that orange hair color makes you look like a demented clown."

"Don't ever say that," Thistle warned. "You know how I feel about clowns."

"We all feel the same way about clowns," Bay said, involuntarily shuddering as she shifted her eyes to the front window. "Chief Terry and Landon should be out at Dead Man's Hill by now. Do you really think they'll find the culprit?"

I'd been thinking about that myself, something that had been niggling the back of my brain all afternoon. "I kind of have a theory about that."

Bay shifted her eyes to me. "And?"

"Well, I'm afraid you're going to think I'm crazy."

"We already think you're crazy," Thistle said. "Another bout of crazy won't make it worse."

"I'm not so sure, but I'll tell you anyway," I said. "I swear there was something familiar about those eyes when I saw the guy running out of the newspaper office. I just can't put my finger on it. I've never seen the guys out at Dead Man's Hill, so how could I recognize the eyes if it's one of them?"

Bay shrugged. "Maybe you didn't recognize him. Maybe you only thought you did."

"I considered that," I conceded. "That doesn't feel right, though. I don't think I know who it is well, but I do think I've seen him before."

"Okay, if that's true that would mean The Hooded Marauder is someone local, not an individual just passing through town," Thistle noted.

Bay snorted. "I can't believe you're using that moniker now. That's just so ... Aunt Tillie."

"I think it's better than The Hoodie Bandit," Thistle shot back. "That's not nearly as ominous as this situation clearly demands."

"And we're all about being ominous," Bay teased. "I didn't see his face. I hid in the closet like a coward. I kind of wish I'd been braver so I could know what you were talking about."

"I thought there was something familiar about him when he approached me, too," Nancy said. "I don't know the locals, so that can't be it."

I pursed my lips, intrigued. "Maybe we should retrace your footsteps," I suggested. "You haven't been around very long, so we can see where your memories and mine overlap."

"That's not a bad suggestion," Bay offered. "How long have you been in town, Nancy?"

"This is my third day. I'll be here for another two."

"What inn are you staying at?"

"The Dragonfly."

Bay stilled, flicking her eyes to me. "Well, that's kind of coincidental."

"Why?" Nancy asked, shifting on her chair. "Is there something wrong with The Dragonfly?"

"No," I answered hurriedly. "Our fathers own it."

"Oh. Jack, Warren and Teddy are your fathers?" Nancy appeared contemplative, but not overly surprised. "Now that you mention it, that makes sense. I saw you girls in photographs on the wall out there. I never really considered it until now."

"We're in photographs?" Thistle arched an eyebrow. "Those must be new. I don't remember seeing them last time we were there."

"That's because we're terrible at visiting," Bay said. "Think about the guests, Nancy. When you look at any of them, do you think they could be the robber?"

Nancy shook her head. "It's almost all women staying out there right now. Your fathers are very popular."

"I'll bet," Thistle snickered. "What about the help? I know our fathers do most of the work on their own, but I believe they have regular cooks and maids."

"I've seen the cooks, and I don't think it's them," Nancy replied. "They're caught up in their own little world."

"Where have you been?" I asked.

"Well, I've visited the bakery, the stables, most of the stores along Main Street. And I've eaten in the diner at least three times."

"We know it's not Marcus," Bay mused, tapping her bottom lip. "I doubt very much it's Mrs. Gunderson from the bakery. I wouldn't put it past Mrs. Little because she's evil, but she has her hands full with the unicorn shop being rebuilt after the fire and that whole gaslighting Aunt Tillie thing that she seems obsessed about."

"What about people you've seen around town?" Thistle pressed.

"This place is thick with tourists right now. Maybe you saw a tourist who happened to come into the store?"

"I've seen mostly women since I arrived," Nancy said. "That big group arrived after I did, but they're all middle-aged women."

"And they're all obsessed with Aunt Tillie and don't care about robbing people," Bay said. "Who else?"

"There's a family I saw at the stable," Nancy offered. "It's a father and two teenaged sons, along with a wife and a daughter. I guess it could be one of them."

"I'll ask Marcus and see what he thinks," Thistle said. "Anyone else?"

"Other than the robbery, the most notable thing that happened to me was a woman dressed like a fortune teller in the diner. She told me things would get better relatively soon. She was nice, but obviously a fraud."

"Madam Rosa," I muttered, shaking my head. I wasn't convinced she was a fraud, but that was an argument for another time. "We must be missing something."

"I think we need to focus less on who and more on how to trap them," Thistle suggested. "I have an idea about that, if anyone is interested."

Bay narrowed her eyes as my stomach clenched. Thistle having an idea was akin to throwing gas on a pile of leaves and then acting surprised when they ignited into a conflagration when a match was added to the mix.

"What's your idea?" Bay asked after a beat.

"We need to direct The Hooded Marauder to a place we can control, right?"

"We need to stop calling him that because it bugs me," Bay replied.

Thistle ignored her. "Why don't we have a few loud conversations on the street about the money Aunt Tillie will be coming into when her harvest is cleared?"

Wait … what? "You can't be serious." I realized where Thistle was going with the suggestion before she expounded on it. "You want to use Aunt Tillie's pot field for bait?"

"Why not?" Thistle asked, shrugging. "We can control the location and it's isolated, so no innocent people will stumble across it. Aunt Tillie wants to get away from her fan club, so I'm guessing she'll agree. She hates 'The Man,' but she loves catching and punishing evildoers. What could possibly go wrong?"

That was a loaded question if ever I heard one. "Do you really want me to answer that?"

Thistle ignored me and focused on Bay. "You know it's a good idea."

Bay's expression told me she agreed, which meant I was the lone voice of reason. "It's a terrible idea," I barked. "This will blow up in our faces."

Bay and Thistle locked gazes, both pretending I wasn't in the room.

"If we do this, we'll need Aunt Tillie's help," Bay warned. "We can't do it without her."

"I'm aware of that," Thistle said. "I still think it's our best option."

Bay capitulated almost immediately. "Okay. Let's do it."

"'Okay? Let's do it?'" I sounded shrill, but I was beyond caring. "This is going to be a nightmare. You realize that, right?"

Bay and Thistle ignored me as they started planning. I shouldn't have been surprised. They always ignore me when they don't want to admit I'm smarter than they are.

"When this goes wrong – and we all know it will – I want you to do a little dance when you tell everyone I was right and you were wrong," I declared. "I'll want presents, too."

Thistle reached for her phone. "I'll call Aunt Tillie and get her down here. She's bound to have some good ideas."

And there's a sentence I never thought I would hear slip past Thistle's pouty lips. Where did my luck go?

NINE

"I just want to repeat that this is a terrible idea."

Fall in Michigan means the daylight grows shorter, so it's practically dark by six most nights. Tonight was no exception, so the second dinner ended I slipped outside with Bay, Thistle and Aunt Tillie.

Landon and Chief Terry missed the meal because they were at the police station questioning the loggers. They remained convinced they were on the right path. I disagreed. We waited until our mothers were distracted with dessert – an absolutely divine-looking carrot cake – and then slipped out the back door. We had no idea where Aunt Tillie disappeared to until she popped up on the back patio, decked out in camouflage and wearing a black combat helmet.

"Of course you think it's a bad idea," Aunt Tillie said. She crouched behind a bush as she stared at the field. Because it was magically cloaked, only we could see it. That didn't mean an outsider couldn't catch a glimpse of Aunt Tillie if she was working in the field … and wanted to draw them in. It simply meant Aunt Tillie could control who saw what and when. She liked having that power.

"Do you want to know your biggest problem?" Aunt Tillie asked, turning to me.

I shook my head. "Not even remotely."

"I'm going to tell you." Aunt Tillie blew past my shake of the head with a pointed stare. "Your problem is that you're too scared of life. You need to learn to enjoy things a little more, go on an adventure from time to time."

"Is that what this is?" I challenged. "Is this an adventure?"

"Of course it's an adventure. We're hiding in the bushes to catch The Hooded Marauder. How is that not an adventure?"

She had a point, but still … . "I don't think putting ourselves at risk is the same thing as an adventure," I pointed out. "An adventure is looking for buried treasure … or a pirate ship on a rainy day."

"Okay, that's the plot of *The Goonies*," Bay said. "They also got chased by robbers and almost fell into a pit because they played the wrong notes on a bone piano. They almost died. And they believed that was an awesome adventure."

"I didn't consider that," I hedged, annoyed. "I … this is still a bad idea. What if he shows and is armed? We made a big show of making sure everyone knew there was going to be someone with money out here tonight. What if this guy decides he can't make another mistake and really brings a gun?"

"I've got that covered," Aunt Tillie replied, digging in the large bag she insisted on bringing from the inn and pulling out an ancient shotgun. I widened my eyes, dumbfounded. "If The Hooded Marauder shows his ugly face, I'll blow it off."

Bay slapped Aunt Tillie's hand and grabbed the shotgun, shaking her head as she stared at the weapon. "What were you thinking?"

"We're trying to catch a bad person," Aunt Tillie replied. "I thought we needed a way to protect ourselves."

"You said we weren't in danger," I reminded her. "If we're not in danger, why do we need a gun?"

Aunt Tillie shrugged. "Sometimes it's simply fun to shoot at people."

"Hide that gun," Thistle ordered Bay, shaking her head. "What is wrong with you? We can't shoot someone."

"If they come out here trespassing with the intent to steal, we most certainly can shoot them," Aunt Tillie argued. "That's my right, according to the Constitution."

"You have the right to bear arms, not shoot some hapless person wandering around in the woods at night," Bay countered. "There's a big difference ... you ninny."

Aunt Tillie extended a craggy finger. "You're on my list, Bay."

"Give her the gun." Thistle took the shotgun from Bay and handed it back to Aunt Tillie. "Make sure we're not in your path if you shoot that thing," she instructed.

"Wait a second," I protested. "You can't purposely arm her and tell her to do whatever she wants."

"I can do whatever I want," Thistle said. "And as long as she doesn't kill someone, I don't care what she does. That worn out old gun probably can't fire more than 20 yards, and the shells are filled with birdshot. Unless she's standing next to someone, the best she can do is make them feel like they're in a hail storm."

"What a completely responsible attitude," I deadpanned, shaking my head as I stared at the field. "Run me through this again. How are we going to draw a robber if he can't see anything?"

"That's where Aunt Tillie comes in," Thistle replied. "She's going to go out and pretend to be working in the field."

"I brought baggies and everything." Aunt Tillie held up a box of Glad sandwich bags for emphasis. "I figure I can do two things at once. I'll really harvest my haul and I'll catch an evildoer at the same time. That sounds like a productive night."

This entire thing was so surreal I was having trouble wrapping my mind around it. "Who in their right mind would go after Aunt Tillie? If it is someone we know – and I think we're all agreed that it has to be – they're going to know better than to attack her in the middle of the night on our property."

"In theory, yes," Bay agreed. "The thing is, whoever is doing this is clearly desperate. Why would you break into the newspaper office? I mean ... it's not as if we keep cash on the premises. That leads me to believe The Hoodie Bandit ... ."

"The Hooded Marauder," Aunt Tillie corrected.

Bay rolled her eyes. "The Hooded Marauder. Fine. That leads me to believe The Hooded Marauder is willing to steal items he thinks he can fence."

"Fence?" I couldn't stifle my laughter. "You've been spending too much time with Landon. Who uses that word?"

"She didn't get that from Landon," Aunt Tillie said. "She got it from *Orange is the New Black*. We've been binge-watching it while Landon is out of town. I'm considering becoming a lesbian. It looks fun."

I pressed my eyes shut and pretended I didn't hear the last part of that statement.

"Oh, you really do miss him when he's gone," Thistle teased, pinching Bay's cheek. "It's a little sad that you have to spend time with your great-aunt or you'd have nothing else to do."

Bay scowled. "That's not why. Have you ever considered I simply like her company?"

"Yeah," Aunt Tillie snapped. "I'm good company. I should have my own talk show, in fact. I could be the next Oprah."

"Yes, you could do it professionally," Thistle deadpanned.

"You bet your bottom I could," Aunt Tillie said, gripping the gun. "Are we ready to put this plan into motion? I think if we wait too long we'll scare off The Hooded Marauder and all of this will be for naught."

I rolled my eyes, resigned and irritated at the same time. "Naught? Oh, geez. I can't believe how dramatic this entire thing is getting."

"That's how we know it's going to be a good night. Let's move, girls. It's time."

TWENTY MINUTES of watching Aunt Tillie work in her field by the light of the moon was enough to give me a headache. I rested on the ground, the cold seeping into my bones, and cast the occasional look in Thistle and Bay's directions. They seemed much more at ease.

"I think ... ."

Bay slapped her hand over my mouth, causing me to widen my eyes and consider biting her fingers before she inclined her chin to the east. I let my eyes slide in that direction, my heart pounding when I caught sight of a shadowy figure picking its way through the underbrush.

The leaves had started falling about a week before, so the figure made crunching sounds as it moved in Aunt Tillie's direction. For her part – and I had to give her credit for appearing oblivious to what was happening behind her – Aunt Tillie went on about her task. She'd hidden the shotgun in the plants to her right so she could get to it easily, but if I didn't know her better I'd have thought she was unaware of the approaching danger.

"What do we do?" I asked, my whisper barely audible as I pushed back Bay's hand. "Do we attack?"

"Not yet," Bay replied. "We need him to get closer."

"What if he gets his hands on her?"

"Then he'll be sorry he ever met us," Thistle replied. "If he touches her, she'll rip his nuts off and feed them to her pet skunks."

Bay made a face. "What pet skunks?"

"You know what I mean."

I had no idea what she meant. "What are you even talking about?"

Bay shook her head and turned back to the field. The second the shadow crossed the line, she stood and moved to her left. She gave the figure a wide berth, clinging to the tree line so she could get behind the visitor.

Thistle followed suit, moving in silent strides as she kept her gaze trained on the field. I had a choice: I could either remain hiding behind the bushes like a coward or go with my cousins and engage in what was sure to be an outrageous fight. They would tell stories about it for weeks. I knew it. In the end, that's what tipped me over the edge. I didn't want to be omitted from the stories.

I moved forward on unsteady feet, my hands shaking as I shoved them into my pockets. It was only then that I remembered the coin, my thumb brushing against the uneven ridge of the metal. I had luck on my side, I reminded myself. We could do this.

My courage bolstered, I increased my pace and scampered closer to Thistle. We were almost at a point where we would be able to cut off the hooded figure – and he was clearly wearing a hoodie; it was distinct in the moonlight. That's when Bay made an error and accidentally stepped away from the tree line, her foot landing on a branch and causing the weathered wood to snap.

The sound echoed throughout the night, causing the stranger to lift his head and stare in our direction. I met the gaze first. He clearly looked right at me, making my blood run cold. Then he moved to race back in the direction from which he came.

"Get down!" Aunt Tillie roared, gripping the shotgun and swinging it in a big arc as she leveled it in the stranger's direction. "Cover your heads!"

I realized what she was going to do when it was too late to react and too late to stop her. I covered my head and dropped to the ground, making sure to press my shoulders as close to the cold earth as possible. Thistle and Bay did the same moments before Aunt Tillie pulled the trigger and a deafening roar filled the air.

Aunt Tillie didn't just fire once. She racked and fired three times, each echo seemingly lasting longer than the previous. Then the night descended into silence for a few seconds until absolute chaos erupted.

"Oh, my gawd! I've been shot!"

"**WHERE IS HE?**" I lifted my head and scanned the field, looking for hints of movement even as I kept one eye on Aunt Tillie and her gun.

"Did he drop?" Thistle asked, rolling to her feet and struggling to a standing position. She distractedly brushed debris from her clothes as she narrowed her eyes. "Did he keep running into the woods?"

"We'll never catch him if he did," Bay said, her expression rueful. "I'm sorry. I didn't see that branch until it was too late. If we'd held off for even another thirty seconds we would've had him."

"Who says we don't have him?" Aunt Tillie challenged, resting the butt of the gun against her hip and extending her hand. "He went down right there."

"Where?" I couldn't see anyone besides us in the field.

"There," Aunt Tillie repeated. "He's right there. He fell on the ground."

"That's because you shot me, you bitch!"

I heard the screech. I exchanged a quick look with Thistle before following her in the direction of the voice. We moved slowly, being careful that we didn't accidentally give the fallen robber a chance to recover and grab one of us to use as a shield.

By the time we found the man, I was a nervous wreck. All of my fear fled the moment I realized the person on the ground was rolling around and holding his knee, groaning as if he was giving birth instead of dealing with a few birdshot pellets.

"And who do we have here?" Thistle asked, dropping to her knees and reaching for the hoodie strings. "Don't even consider biting or hitting me. Aunt Tillie has a gun and she's not afraid to use it."

"I figured that out myself," the man gritted out.

Thistle jerked down the hood and frowned as she leaned away from the figure. There was something markedly familiar about the features, but I didn't recognize the man sitting on the ground nursing his knee. He had brown hair, buzzed close to the scalp. The dark eyes – more gray than brown – were contorted in pain as he made small whining noises. He sounded truly pathetic.

"Huh." Bay rubbed the back of her neck. "Does anyone recognize him?"

"I don't," Aunt Tillie said, moving closer. "I was kind of hoping it was Margaret Little. Is that wrong of me?"

"Yes," I answered, not missing a beat. I rubbed the coin in my pocket and something occurred to me. It was a ludicrous idea, of course, but ... there it was. "Guys, I don't think you're going to believe me, but ... that's Madam Rosa."

Thistle made a dubious face as she looked the man up and down. After a moment of quiet contemplation, she sucked in a breath. "Holy crap! You're right!"

"Wait, Madam Rosa is really a dude?" Bay was dumbfounded. "How is that possible?"

"It's called cross-dressing," Aunt Tillie supplied. "I saw a show on it when I was watching the Oxygen network the other day."

"Oh, well that explains everything," Thistle deadpanned, annoyed.

"Why do you dress like a woman and offer your services as a fortune teller?" I asked. "More importantly, why do you dress in a hoodie and rob people?"

Madam Rosa … er, whoever he was … opened his mouth to answer, but the sound was drowned out by heavy footsteps approaching from the opposite direction. I glanced over my shoulder and my heart lodging in my throat.

"Someone is coming," I hissed.

"And you're all in big trouble now," Madam Rosa howled. "Here comes my payback!"

TEN

Aunt Tillie moved swiftly, pointing the gun at the trees. Two figures exploded through the foliage, pulling up short when they saw the gun and frightened faces leveled at them.

"What's going on?" Chief Terry barked.

"Put that down," Landon ordered, pointing a finger at Aunt Tillie. "If you shoot me, I swear I'll come back and haunt you until the end of your days."

Aunt Tillie rolled her eyes, but lowered the gun. "We thought you were with The Hooded Marauder. Chill out. I wasn't going to shoot you."

"Who is The Hooded Marauder?" Chief Terry asked, giving Aunt Tillie a wide berth as he circled closer to us.

"That's what Aunt Tillie named The Hoodie Bandit," Bay supplied, her eyes busy as they bounced between Landon and Chief Terry. "I … um … we caught him, by the way. So … yay!"

Landon shot her a dirty look. "You're in so much trouble."

"Hey, this isn't my fault." Bay was instantly on the defensive. "You said the robber was out at Dead Man's Hill. We thought we were safe."

"Who do you think you're fooling?" Landon challenged. "You're all dressed in black and this one has a gun." He took hold of the stock of the shotgun and gently pulled it from Aunt Tillie's hands. "Did you shoot someone?"

Aunt Tillie nodded, solemn. "I shot The Hooded Marauder. We're all good now."

"You shot someone?" Chief Terry was beside himself as he pushed past me and focused on the figure cowering on the ground. "Who is this?"

"That's Madam Rosa," I supplied. "Apparently she's really a man."

"Oh, Criminy," Landon muttered, slapping his hand to his forehead. "Every time I think this family can't get any weirder you prove me wrong."

"It's not as if we're dressing up like women," Aunt Tillie pointed out. "Wait … that might've come out wrong."

Landon ignored her and knelt next to Madam Rosa. "Where are you hurt?"

"They shot me! I want them arrested," Madam Rosa barked.

Landon didn't appear bothered by the tone. "You're trespassing. They were within their rights to shoot you … not that I'm condoning it." Landon sent Aunt Tillie a weighted gaze. "You're in trouble, too."

"Oh, yes. I'm quaking in my combat boots," Aunt Tillie intoned, rolling her eyes. "Focus on the bad guy. Find out what he did with the stolen money. That's your job, right?"

Landon scowled. "I'm going to have a raging headache before the night is over. I just know it."

"I'll make you feel better," Bay offered, a winning smile on her face. "I promise you'll feel better once this all sinks in and we're sitting in front of the fire with hot chocolate."

"You bet you're going to make me feel better," Landon muttered, shaking his head. "So, Madam Rosa, is it? What's your real name?"

"My name was given to me by the gods," Madam Rosa gritted out, the veins in his neck straining as he gripped his knee. "This really burns. Is it supposed to burn like this?"

Aunt Tillie shrugged. "It's birdshot. It's not supposed to feel like puppies licking you. You're a bad man. You deserve bad things."

"What is your name?" Landon repeated. "I'll find out eventually. I

AMANDA M. LEE

have a feeling that once we run your prints we'll find a record as long as Aunt Tillie's tongue when she lies."

"You're on my list," Aunt Tillie warned.

"I was born Ron Gibson. I changed my name five years ago when I found my true calling."

"As a female fortune teller?" Landon pressed. "How did you fall into that line of work?"

"Is this really necessary?" Gibson's face contorted. "I'm in serious pain."

"We'll get to that in a few minutes," Chief Terry said. "You're clearly in no danger of dying."

"It doesn't feel that way."

"That's probably the karma seeping into your soul," I suggested. "Only a truly terrible person would pretend to be psychic and rob people."

"Stuff it," Gibson snapped. "It's a legitimate job. You should know. You do the same thing."

"She doesn't do remotely the same thing," Landon shot back. "She runs a store with her cousin. They sell handmade items and other tokens. They do the occasional reading, but they hardly wander up to random people on the street and steal from them."

"Whatever." Gibson's agitation was profound. "What do you want me to say? I think you've mistaken me for someone else. I was out walking in the woods when I saw that little old lady working and thought I'd offer my help. I thought she was lost."

"And you just happened to wear the same hoodie that the person who tried to rob the bank wore?" Landon challenged. "Clove saw you when you ran out the back of the newspaper offices. That building wasn't empty. What were your plans when you got inside? Were you willing to hurt someone to get what you wanted?"

Gibson swallowed hard when he realized how deathly serious Landon was. "I … that wasn't me."

As far as denial goes, it was the weakest I'd heard in quite some time. "It was you," I argued. "I knew there was something familiar about your eyes. The fact that I knew you as a woman threw me off.

I'm guessing that was deliberate. I didn't realize Madam Rosa and The Hooded Marauder were the same until I saw your entire face."

"We're going to find where you're staying and you'd better hope we can recover that money you stole from Nancy Jarvis," Landon said. "Then we're going to have a really long talk about going after my girlfriend."

"I didn't go after your girlfriend," Gibson protested. "I didn't realize anyone was in the building."

"And here I thought you said you were innocent," Thistle mused.

"It doesn't matter. We've got him dead to rights." Landon cuffed Gibson and then tugged him to a standing position. "Let's get him back to the inn so we can load him in the cruiser. I want to be done with him."

"This really hurts," Gibson whimpered, limping in exaggerated fashion. "I think my leg is falling off. I'm not making it up."

Landon shifted his eyes to Aunt Tillie, suspicious. "What was in that gun?"

"Just birdshot." Aunt Tillie said the words and offered her most innocent expression, but something lurked behind her eyes. Landon must've seen it, too, because he immediately started shaking his head.

"What else?" he pressed.

"Well, I might've cursed it so it burned a little extra something special," Aunt Tillie hedged. "You know, some lemon rind and hemlock essence."

"Isn't hemlock poison?" Landon asked, turning to Bay as panic swept through him.

"Not in these doses," Aunt Tillie answered. "It's all good. He won't die. He'll just wish he'd died."

"Well, I'm still going to swing by the hospital and let them look him over," Landon said, moving away from the field. He hadn't so much as looked at the pot plants, which made me realize he hadn't seen them. The cloaking spell was still working. "You ladies are lucky this ended so well. You could've been hurt."

"You're only angry because we caught the bad guy and you're left with nothing to do but act as a chauffeur," Aunt Tillie yelled to his back.

When Landon swiveled, his grin was impish. "You may have a point. Good job, everyone. You caught the bandit and saved the day."

Aunt Tillie preened under the compliment. "Thank you."

"You're still in trouble," Landon added. "I'd start running now."

Aunt Tillie snorted. "I could say the same thing about you. You have no idea what kind of curses I can link with birdshot. Trust me. You don't want to find out."

I WAS late to breakfast the next morning. Sam was already seated when I arrived. I offered a lame apology to the guests while steadfastly ignoring my mother's pointed glare.

"Sorry I'm late. I had an errand to run."

"That's okay," Sam said, pulling out my chair so I could sit. "I almost cried because I missed you so much, but I somehow pulled through the terrible ordeal and remained functional."

I rolled my eyes and dropped a kiss on his cheek. "It took me longer than I expected to return Nancy's money to her. Thank you for that, by the way, Landon. She was so thankful she started crying. You even found her Christmas gifts. With the stuff she earned from us, her daughter is going to have a marvelous holiday."

Landon shrugged, noncommittal. "Just doing my job. Once Gibson started talking we could hardly shut him up. We found a lot of items from various communities. We'll see that all of the stolen items make it back to their owners over the next few weeks."

"That's good."

"So Nancy was excited?" Bay asked. "I'm happy for her. I was worried she was going to have a rotten holiday after what happened, but she seems fairly strong. Now she can go back to enjoying her vacation."

"She's so relieved it's almost cute," I admitted. "I … um … gave her the coin, too." I had no idea why I admitted it. I planned to take the secret to my grave – or at least hold onto it for a few days so I could work the situation to my advantage and mess with my cousins.

"You did what?" Aunt Tillie practically exploded at the head of the table. "Are you crazy? That man ... er woman ... er man ... might've been crazy and evil, but that coin was a gift. How could you possibly give it away?"

"Because I don't need it." I saw no reason to lie. "I'm already lucky. I have a great man." I squeezed Sam's hand under the table. "I have a great family."

"Other than Aunt Tillie," Thistle interjected.

"Oh, well, that goes without saying," I teased.

Aunt Tillie glowered in my direction. "You're on my list."

I ignored her. "I don't know what it's like to really struggle," I supplied. "We've always had it good ... even when we've had it rough. We've never gone hungry or worried about getting Christmas gifts. If you guys were afraid that you couldn't give us what we needed when we were kids, you never showed it.

"Nancy is a single mom struggling to do her best. It seems as though she can never catch a break," I continued. "That coin can do nothing for me but serve as a source of entertainment ... and I'm sick of letting you guys kick me off ladders."

Sam's eyebrows shot up his forehead. "Kick you off ladders? When did that happen?"

I didn't reply, instead focusing on Aunt Tillie. "That coin can mean the difference between a life of poverty and maybe something better for Nancy and her daughter. That's why I gave it to her."

"That's assuming the coin is really lucky," Landon pointed out. "How do you know that the coin wasn't a fraud like Gibson? By the way, we ran his record. He's been arrested twenty-five times in four different states. He runs the same grift every time.

"He comes to a small town and pretends to be psychic," he continued. "In some cases he cons people to pay for readings. In others he robs them outright. He's been doing it for a long time."

"You got him to confess?" I couldn't help but be impressed. "How did you manage that?"

"It was pretty simple," Landon replied. "He was in a lot of pain and we refused to take him to the hospital until he told us everything. We couldn't shut him up after that."

"Well, I don't have a lot of sympathy for robbers, but I'm not sure that sounds appropriate," Winnie sniffed. "Isn't that against the rules?"

Landon shrugged. "Do you care?"

"I don't," Aunt Tillie replied. "Did the doctor get all the birdshot out?"

"She did," Landon confirmed. "She commented that someone had great aim."

"I wasn't aiming at anything," Aunt Tillie countered. "I just didn't want to hit the girls."

Landon stilled. "Was that a possibility?"

"Of course not."

Landon didn't look as if he believed her for a second, but he let it slide. "You ladies got lucky."

"We were smart and trapped a robber," Aunt Tillie corrected. "We deserve a reward ... especially since Clove gave away our good luck charm."

"It wasn't our charm," I pointed out. "It was my charm. I gave it to a person who needed it."

"Still, we could've used it for a few days before you got rid of it," Thistle pointed out. "We could've bought more lottery tickets."

"Or a still," Aunt Tillie added.

"Or you could just be thankful for what you have," I shot back. "You might not believe it, but you're lucky, too. You already have a certain level of magic. You don't need more."

"Speaking of magic," one of the women at the table said. She was a middle-aged woman with gray hair, and her eyes sparkled when she focused on Aunt Tillie. "We were kind of hoping you would show us how to cast a few spells today."

Aunt Tillie's face turned from mischievous to wan. "I'm sick. I was almost killed last night. I can't possibly muster the energy."

The woman's smile slipped. "You were in a great mood a few minutes ago."

"You imagined that."

Sam smirked as he shot a look in my direction, clearly enjoying himself. That's when I remembered one other piece of unfinished business. Instead of waiting for the right moment, I opted to drop the bomb in the middle of breakfast so I could enjoy watching its shockwaves play out.

"Speaking of imagining things, I heard a rumor while I was in town," I said, reaching for the syrup. "Apparently Mrs. Little is telling all of the tour groups you're the only real witch in town and that you can help people become powerful if they spend time with you."

The look on Aunt Tillie's face was murderous. "What?"

"You suck," Thistle muttered, shaking her head. "You're ruining my game."

I ignored her. "I also heard that Thistle knew all along, and she told people it was true." That wasn't entirely true, but it wasn't a complete lie either."

"You!" Aunt Tillie's voice was evil as she shifted her gaze to Thistle. "Oh, mouth, you have no idea the retribution coming your way."

"She's making it up," Thistle protested. "That's not true. Would I turn on you? You're my family."

That was a stupid question to ask, considering the situation.

"I'd start running now," Aunt Tillie warned. "Your punishment will be absolute."

"I vote for the bacon curse," Landon announced. "Because Bay was bad and didn't tell me what was going on last night, I think that should be her punishment."

Bay shot him a dirty look and pinched his side. "No. I don't enjoy smelling like bacon."

Landon pressed a finger to her lips. "Shh. I'm talking to Aunt Tillie."

"Oh, bacon is too good for this betrayal," Aunt Tillie said, pressing the palms of her hands to the table as she stood. "I have something better in mind."

"Just remember that I wasn't involved," I said. "This is all on Thistle."

"Don't worry, little kvetch. I know who to blame." Aunt Tillie strode toward the door. "Thistle is going to be sorry she ever met me. I swear it!"

Something told me Thistle already felt that way, but I decided to focus on my breakfast instead of the mayhem in the other room. "So, what is everyone doing today?"

And another normal day in the Winchester household was underway.

THISTLE WHILE YOU WORK

A WICKED WITCHES OF THE MIDWEST SHORT

ONE

"I'm confused. If we're supposed to do what the police say because we have to follow the rules but we're also supposed to make sure 'The Man' doesn't win, what happens when the 'The Man' tells us to do something?"

I arched an eyebrow as I glanced at Annie. She stood next to the antique shelf in the library, a book in her hand, and stared out the window at the blowing leaves. Nine years old and full of energy on most days, today she seemed more contemplative than anything else. She's been dealing with a lot – including the fact that she can see and talk to ghosts – so I've been going out of my way to spend time with her whenever possible.

People say I'm hard to deal with – and they're right – but for some reason I feel a maternal pull whenever I look at Annie. It's a sobering thought, because before she came on the scene I wasn't sure I ever wanted kids. She makes me doubt my earlier assertion … er, well, at least some of the time.

"I'm not sure what you're asking," I admitted, sliding a bookmark in the leather-bound book on my lap and turning my full attention to Annie. It was a cold and windy fall day – Halloween was only weeks away – and I was more than happy to be on babysitting duty instead of braving the elements to go work in the magic store I own with my cousin Clove.

"I'm saying that 'The Man' is out to get us, but he's also the boss of us, Thistle." Annie's expression was somber. "What is it that Aunt Tillie says? There's a flaw in the logic."

She's young, but she's got the mind of a girl twice her age.

"How am I supposed to know?" I asked, hoping I didn't sound cross. "I'm not as worried about 'The Man' as you and Aunt Tillie seem to be."

"Yes, but you're a witch."

"I am a witch. That doesn't mean I care about 'The Man.'"

"You're also my babysitter," Annie pressed. "My mom always says that I'm supposed to ask an adult if I'm confused, and you're the only adult around."

Yup. That's me. My name is Thistle Winchester and I'm a witch, storeowner, babysitter and apparently a fountain of useless information for young girls with endless amounts of curiosity. That's if Annie Martin is to be believed, that is. She's been living at the inn my mother and aunts run for months – ever since I found her on the street one day, dazed and confused from a car accident – and she's as much a member of the family as the individuals I share genes and bloodlines with.

"I'm starting to regret agreeing to babysit," I teased, poking her side and grabbing her around the waist so I could wrestle her to the couch. "You're asking some really annoying questions."

"Is that because you can't answer them?"

I frowned. "You spend too much time with Aunt Tillie. You know that, right?"

Annie immediately started shaking her head. She adored Aunt Tillie. She loved everything about my cantankerous great-aunt, including her penchant for finding trouble and a mouth that refuses to quit even after the batteries have died. "Aunt Tillie is the bee's knees."

I stilled, surprised. "I'm sorry ... what?"

"She's the bee's knees," Annie repeated. "She told me that, so I know it's true."

In the grand scheme of things, being the "bee's knees" was probably the most harmless tidbit Aunt Tillie had bestowed upon Annie since she joined our cozy family unit. The young girl was like a sponge, soaking up everything the women in my family said. Before joining us, she spent time on the run with her mother. It was a sad and lonely life. Now that she had people fighting to spend time with her she ate it up. She couldn't get enough of everyone, and loved the fact that we all doted on her. She'd particularly taken a shine to Aunt Tillie. Sadly, my great-aunt can officially lay claim to the Worst Babysitter Ever title. She seems to derive great joy from filling Annie's head with her version of The World According to Aunt Tillie. It's turned into a problem once or twice ... or ten times.

"Well, Aunt Tillie is more like Satan's knees, but that's hardly a cause for concern today," I said, smiling as Annie rested her head against my shoulder. "Are you looking forward to Christmas? It's only a few months away."

Annie nodded. "I just hope Santa can find me here."

"I promise that he'll find you. He knows everything, right? He won't forget where you live."

"What if I don't live here when it's Christmas time?" Annie's voice was so low I almost didn't hear her.

I opened my mouth to ask where else she would live, but her mother, Belinda Martin, picked that moment to swoop through the front door and distract me. Bundled up, Belinda stomped her wet boots on the front rug as she removed her coat and hung it on the rack in the corner. It was only then that she noticed we were in the library and plastered a bright smile on her face as she shuffled into the room.

"I didn't realize you were in here," Belinda said. "I thought maybe you would be in the kitchen filling your face full of the cookies I saw Winnie baking when I left a few hours ago."

"You said I couldn't have any," Annie reminded her mother.

"I said you couldn't go overboard," Belinda clarified. "One or two cookies won't hurt you."

"Now she tells me," Annie grumbled, crossing her arms over her chest and causing me to smirk.

"How was your errand?" I asked, focusing my full attention on Belinda. In truth, I only got involved in her plight because I felt responsible for Annie. Finding her on the street, dehydrated and injured, jolted me. I was obsessed with helping her, and that meant helping Belinda as well. After her time in the hospital, though, I'd grown quite close to Belinda, too. She was a good person with a wonderful heart.

"It went well," Belinda said, averting her gaze as she rubbed her hands together to warm them. "In fact, it went exceedingly well. It … was everything I hoped it would be."

That was an odd reaction … especially because I thought she was running to the grocery store. "What's going on?" I asked, leaning forward. I couldn't help but be intrigued.

"Um, why do you think anything is going on?" Belinda is a terrible liar, and her lack of talent in that department was on full display.

I pushed Annie to a standing position with my hands on her waist. "You should go get those cookies before you forget," I prodded.

Annie's eyes were suspicious as her gaze bounced between her mother and me. "But … ."

"Your mom might change her mind," I warned. Belinda would do nothing of the sort, but I wanted to talk to her alone in case Annie's presence was holding her back. You had to be careful about what you said in front of the young girl because she repeated almost everything … and often at the worst possible time.

"Okay, but I know you just want to talk when I'm not around to listen," Annie said.

I snorted. "How do you know that?"

"I'm not stupid."

"You're definitely not stupid." I playfully swatted her arm as she scurried out of the room, waiting until I was sure she was far enough away that she couldn't eavesdrop before continuing. "What's going on, Belinda?"

Belinda heaved a weary sigh. "How do you know something is going on? Is that one of your witchy gifts?"

Belinda was aware of the family secret – the truth came out rather recently – but she didn't seem bothered by our magical abilities. That didn't mean she was entirely comfortable with them. She did seem happy to have us around when it came to Annie's burgeoning ability, though. My cousin Bay has the same gift, and she's been a miracle worker when it came to helping Annie navigate the uncertainty that goes along with talking to spirits that only a handful of people can see.

"I can tell by the way you're acting." I hoped I sounded kind rather than accusatory. I can never tell when I've crossed a line until it's in my rearview mirror, and my go-to reaction is often snark. For some reason, that rubs people the wrong way. I have no idea why.

"And how am I acting?"

"Nervous."

Belinda rubbed her forehead and cast a quick look into the hallway before shutting the door and sitting on the chair across from the couch. Whatever she was keeping to herself was big ... and for some reason it filled my stomach with dread. What did Annie say about not being here for Christmas again? Could Belinda's big secret be that she's leaving? I know she's been looking for a house, but ... it's too soon. Oh, crap! This is going to suck. I just know it.

"It's just ... I've been on a waiting list to take a class," Belinda admitted, her expression rueful. "I know this might sound stupid to you because you've been running your own business since shortly after you graduated from high school, but I've been giving it a lot of thought, and I want to start my own cleaning business."

I didn't bother hiding my surprise. "That doesn't sound stupid at all," I argued. "In truth, given the fact that Hemlock Cove caters so heavily to tourists, it's probably a great idea. I know everyone is always looking for help when it comes to cleaning their shops. There are a bunch of inns in the area, too, and they often need deep cleaning before a big event."

"That's exactly what I thought," Belinda enthused. "I thought I could do a steady business and arrange my hours so that I work while Annie is in school. It will be an issue in the summer, but that's months away and ... well ... I figured I would work that out later.

"I mean, I can always take her along on some shifts as long as the customers allow it," she continued. "I might be able to find a responsible and reasonable babysitter, too."

"Or you could leave her with us," I suggested. "We'll watch her for free and enjoy it. Everyone here loves her. We love you, too. Why are you so worried about bringing this up? Why are you hiding it?"

Belinda shrugged, holding her hands palms up. "Because I already have a job and you guys have been so kind to me that I don't know how to put into words how grateful I am. I feel somehow ... disloyal ... for even considering this."

"You can't live your life based on what you think my family needs," I pointed out. "You have to do what you think is best for yourself and Annie. What's your plan?"

"Well, they're holding a special class for small-business owners in Traverse City next week," Belinda explained. "It's at the college and it's geared toward women. I was on a waiting list and got a call that I'd been accepted into the class after someone else dropped out."

"That's great."

"But ... how do I tell your mother and aunts that I'm considering leaving?" Belinda looked shredded at the prospect. "I love this place. I love all of you. What would've happened to me if you hadn't been kind of enough to take us in? What would've happened to Annie if you didn't watch her while I was in the hospital? I would've died in that car if you didn't go out of your way to find me."

"That doesn't mean you're beholden to us forever," I told her. "You don't owe us anything. You're part of the family. I'm guessing you're going to want to stay here while you work out the details in this – and everyone wants you to stay here, so don't worry about that – and then you'll decide how to progress once you've got a few months of work under your belt."

"Yes, but how can I afford to stay here? I won't have the money for that."

I tilted my head to the side, confused. "I'm not sure I understand," I hedged. "Why would you have to pay to stay here?"

"Because this is an inn," Belinda replied. "I work here. Part of my wages go toward the room you gave us on the third floor. You girls also help with babysitting ... and feed us ... and have made it so Annie has the run of the house and never gets bored."

"Why would that change?"

"Because I won't be able to work here." Belinda showed signs of frustration. "If I can't work here, how am I going to afford the room?"

Things clicked into place, but I couldn't help but wonder how long she'd twisted herself into knots over this scenario. "They can't rent that room out anyway," I reminded her. "It's on the third floor. They'll be fine with you starting your own business and staying here until you've saved up enough money for a down payment on a house."

"But ... will they really?" Belinda's expressions warred between hope and misery. "What if they kick me out?"

I leaned forward, sympathetic, and gripped her hand. "I understand why you're worked up about this, but I think you're making yourself sick for no good reason. Has my mother done something to make you think she would kick you out for any reason? Have my aunts?

"Heck, Aunt Tillie doesn't like anyone, but she'll be devastated when you finally do move away because she adores Annie," I continued. "You're twisting yourself in knots over nothing. Trust me."

"But ... how am I supposed to tell them?"

"Tell them the truth," I answered. "They'll be happy for you. They'll think this is a great idea. They'll help you the best way they know how. That's what they do. In truth, they're probably going to help you so much that you'll get annoyed with all of the help, no matter how well-meaning they all are."

"I think they're wonderful," Belinda gushed. "You're so lucky to have them in your life."

"Yes, well, imagine being a teenager with them and then repeat that statement," I teased, sobering as I returned to the topic at hand. "I promise everything will be okay. You can stay here as long as you want. Once you tell them what's going on they'll help no matter what."

Belinda laughed sheepishly and pressed the heel of her hand against her forehead. "Do you think that will include watching Annie while I'm out of town for a few days? I don't want to take her to Traverse City with me because she'll be bored."

"I think we can all take shifts with Annie and make it work," I said. "I can take her to the store with me some afternoons. Aunt Tillie is annoyed that it's cold, and she's always looking for a partner in crime.

"The woman is a mean old bat when she wants to be, but she's also loyal," I continued. "She'll never let anything happen to Annie. You know that."

"I do know that." Belinda sucked in a deep breath as she gripped her knees. "I probably should tell them now, huh? The longer I wait, the harder it's going to be."

"I'll go with you," I offered. "I think you'll be surprised at how easy this is actually going to be."

"I hope you're right."

I mustered an evil smile. "Haven't you realized it yet? I'm always right."

Belinda snorted. "You sounded like Aunt Tillie just then."

My smile slipped. "That's the meanest thing you've ever said to me."

Now it was Belinda's turn to beam. "I guess I really am part of the family, huh?"

"Most definitely."

TWO

"What a crock of crap!"

I arched an eyebrow and glanced over my shoulder as my cousin Clove showed Annie how to weigh herbs before bagging them. Belinda had left town for her conference the day before, which meant we were on Annie duty. In typical fashion, my Aunt Winnie stepped in and made up a chart so Annie was covered every moment of her day. Winnie is nothing if not organized. The problem with that approach is that nothing ever happens in a normal fashion when it comes to the Winchester witches, so the odds of sticking to the schedule were slim. It was still the first full day, though, which meant Annie headed to our magic shop, Hypnotic, as soon as she finished school for the afternoon. To keep her busy, Clove suggested giving her a few tasks. I thought it was a great idea. Annie, apparently, had other thoughts.

"Who taught you to say that?" Clove asked, leaning back as she widened her eyes. She sat cross-legged on the floor, her hand resting on her knee. The light caused the large stone in her engagement ring to glimmer, constantly catching my attention. I think she planned it that way. No, I'm not making it up. She's annoying like that, and she'd been able to talk about nothing but her wedding plans since her boyfriend, Sam Cornell, popped the question several weeks ago.

"Say what?" Annie asked, her tone reflecting annoyance.

Clove has infinite patience sometimes – this being one of them – and she refused to engage the child in a snark competition. "That crock of crap stuff?"

"Who do you think?" I asked, snorting.

Clove ignored me and remained focused on Annie. "Who?"

"Aunt Tillie says it all of the time," Annie said, adopting a tone of petulance. "I heard her say it last night when Landon stole the last cookie off the tray."

Clove pursed her lips as she stared down the girl, clearly conflicted. "I don't think you're supposed to say that. Your mother wouldn't like it."

"My mother says worse things," Annie challenged. "She accidentally stubbed her toe when she was packing the other night and she said the S-word."

"Well, that was an excited utterance, not a deliberate choice," Clove pointed out. "That can be forgiven."

Annie screwed her face up into an adorable expression. It was her "thinking" face, which made me internally laugh because she was clearly thinking of causing mayhem. "What's an excited udder?"

"That's something that only farmers should know about," I replied, smirking.

"Don't listen to her," Clove chided, wagging a finger when Annie glanced in my direction. Our young charge clearly thought I could get her out of working with Clove, and she was eager to test her boundaries. "An excited utterance is something you say when you're surprised or hurt. Like when you say 'oh, my' when someone surprises you."

"Or when you say the S-word when you stub your toe?" Annie asked.

"Yes, but you should never say the S-word if you can help it."

"What about the F-word?"

Clove's dark eyebrows flew up her forehead. "You should definitely never say the F-word."

"Landon said it to Bay last night," Annie complained.

I tilted my head to the side as I racked my brain. "I didn't hear Landon say the F-word to Bay. That's not generally his style."

"He said he wanted to fornicate."

I pressed my lips together to keep from laughing as I stared down Annie. "I know he didn't say that. He'd never use that expression." He would use a hundred different euphemisms for the same thing, but that wasn't a word that would easily roll off his tongue. "Where did you hear that word?"

"He said it," Annie protested.

In addition to being my cousin Bay's boyfriend, Landon Michaels was an FBI agent. There was no way he used the F-word – either version of it – in front of Annie. He could be a pain when he wanted to be, but he was careful about what he said in front of Annie. "He did not," I shot back, shaking my head. "Don't lie."

"Well, he wanted to say it," Annie argued, crossing her arms over her chest. "That's what Aunt Tillie said."

"Ah. Now we're getting somewhere." I crouched down so I was at the same level as Annie's face and fixed her with a pointed look. "What did Aunt Tillie say?"

"She said that Landon and Bay were going to fornicate. I thought that had something to do with a fork at first – you know, because he's always stuffing food in his mouth with his fork – but Aunt Tillie said I was wrong to think that."

"Aunt Tillie was wrong to say that," Clove countered. "That's not what fornicate means."

"And Aunt Tillie would never use that word in front of you," I added. "I'm guessing you were listening when you shouldn't have been. Is that what happened?"

Annie opened her mouth to argue and then snapped it shut.

"Answer me," I prodded.

"I plead the fifth," Annie announced. If I didn't know better, I'd think she got her stubbornness from our family. That was impossible, so I had to bite the inside of my cheek to keep from laughing.

"Don't bring up the F-word again," I instructed, straightening. "Fornicate is not a bad word."

"Then why did Aunt Tillie whisper it to Twila?"

"Because … ." I turned to Clove for help.

For her part, Clove adopted an innocent look. "Yeah, Thistle. Why did Aunt Tillie whisper it?"

"You're such a kvetch," I muttered, shaking my head. Thankfully for me, the bell over the door jangled, drawing my attention to the front door. My shoulders stiffened when I caught sight of the woman standing there. She seemed disheveled and out of place, her long gray hair swept away from her craggy face. "Can I help you?" I asked uncertainly.

"I'm looking for some orange juice. Can you point me toward the proper aisle?"

I exchanged a quick look with Clove and then instinctively put myself between the woman and Annie. I try to refrain from being judgmental – no, really – but there was something off about the woman. I could see it on first glance. Her long hair, once black, was shot through with a dustball gray, and she wore a dirty jacket. It wasn't that the woman's clothing was worn and tattered as much as it was filthy. She wore no makeup and had a wild look in her eyes.

"This isn't a grocery store," I replied evenly. "If you need a market, there's one about two blocks that way." I pointed for emphasis. "I'm sure they have some orange juice. In fact … um … if you need some money or help, I can go with you and buy the orange juice. How does that sound?"

Instead of reacting with gratitude, the woman narrowed her eyes and scorched me with a defiant glare. "I don't need you to buy me orange juice. I'm merely looking to buy orange juice. Is that suddenly a crime?"

Her reaction seemed rather extreme given the circumstances, but I decided to let it slide. "We don't have orange juice here. I'm sorry. We have tea if you want to brew your own at home, but that's all we have."

"But … I need orange juice." The woman was a conundrum. One second she seemed completely aware of her surroundings and coherent. The next she seemed lost and confused. I couldn't help but wonder if she'd accidentally walked away from a group home or something.

"Where do you live?" I asked, changing course.

"How is that any of your business?"

"I'm merely asking because you look lost," I answered, refusing to back down. "Do you need help? I'm willing to help if you need it. I just … I don't know what you need."

"I need orange juice," the woman repeated.

"We don't have orange juice."

"Then you're absolutely no good to me." The woman took me by surprise as she turned on her heel and stalked out the door. I padded to the window so I could watch her, scratching my cheek as she shuffled in the direction of the market.

"Where is she going?" Clove asked.

"Toward the market. At least it looks that way."

"What do you think we should do?" Clove asked, worried. "I don't think we should leave her to wander around by herself."

"Definitely not," I agreed, rummaging in my pocket for my phone. "I'll call Chief Terry. My first instinct was that she wandered away from a home or something. He might know. Even if he doesn't, he's better equipped to deal with her than we are."

"That's a good idea," Clove said, smiling as she turned back to Annie. "Are you ready to go back to weighing herbs?"

"No. It's a crock of crap."

Clove's smile tipped upside down. "I'm going to have a talk with Aunt Tillie about the amount of time she spends with you."

"Is that because you're a kvetch?" Annie appeared earnest when she asked the question, and I couldn't help but smile.

AN HOUR later Annie wasn't happy, but she helped Clove with the herbs without complaint while I stood behind the counter and double-checked the order sheet for the week. I'd almost forgotten about the strange woman until Margaret Little, Hemlock Cove's answer to the question "who is the evilest woman in town," strode through the front door of the shop.

"Hello, Thistle." Mrs. Little's tone was clipped. "How are you doing today?"

She was either high or assumed I'd somehow forgotten she was a terrible person who often went out of her way to make Aunt Tillie's life miserable. I often went out of my way to do the same, so you'd think we'd have a lot in common. You'd be wrong. No one likes Mrs. Little. It's one of those universal truths you can't shake.

"I'm wonderful, Mrs. Little." I adopted a grating tone that I knew would set her teeth on edge. "It's an absolutely marvelous day, isn't it?"

Clove raised her eyebrows as she rolled to her feet. It was as if she sensed trouble and wanted to head it off. "You keep doing what you're doing," she instructed Annie, her voice low. "I'll be right back."

Annie's eyes were wide as she glanced between Mrs. Little and me. "Are they about to do the F-word?"

Clove's made a shocked face. "No! Stop saying things like that."

Annie shrugged, seemingly unbothered by Clove's tone. "They look like they're going to fight."

"Oh, that F-word." Clove heaved a relieved sigh. "Yes, I think it's fair to say they're going to do that."

"At least I won't be bored," Annie said brightly.

Clove shook her head as she moved to join us, her eyes wary as they scanned Mrs. Little's face. We hadn't seen much of the woman lately – mostly because she was busy rebuilding her shop after it was firebombed a few weeks ago – and I hadn't missed her. Not even a little.

"I'm glad that you're having a marvelous day," Mrs. Little said, her demeanor stiff. "I have no intention of doing the F-word with you, though, so if that's your intention … ." She left the sentence hanging, essentially shifting the onus of the conversation to me. That was definitely on purpose.

"What do you want?" I asked, refusing to maintain my earlier sunny demeanor. It was too much effort and she wasn't worth it. "Whatever you think Aunt Tillie has done … well … I'm pretty sure you're misguided. She's been busy at the inn lately."

"Believe it or not, I'm not here about Tillie."

I didn't believe it for a second. "Uh-huh. And why are you here again?"

"Just because you say she's busy, that doesn't mean I believe Tillie is innocent of anything," Mrs. Little added. "She's the devil in tacky clothing."

"I'm pretty sure Aunt Tillie would consider that a compliment."

Mrs. Little rolled her eyes so hard I worried she might fall over. "Anyway, I'm here about an important issue. As you might recall, about two years ago I approached the city council with an idea to start a DDA."

"What's a DDA?" Clove asked, curious.

"A Downtown Development Authority," I replied. "They basically take money from business owners so they can plant flowers on every street corner."

"That is not what a DDA does," Mrs. Little argued.

"We already put flowers on our corner," Clove pointed out. "Why should we have to pay more when we already do it ourselves?"

"I just said that is not what a DDA does," Mrs. Little barked, her eyes flashing. "Do you listen?"

"Hey, you came in our store," I pointed out. "There's no reason to be a pain. We didn't ask for your company."

"And yet I'm here to make your life easier." Mrs. Little adopted a singsong voice that made me want to punch her rather than capitulate. I always want to punch her, though, so that wasn't much of a change.

"If I remember correctly, the town council agreed that a DDA wasn't necessary," I reminded her. "They said it was just a way to collect money when everyone was already doing their part to keep the town cute and up to code."

"That very well may have been true at the time, but I think a DDA is a good idea," Mrs. Little sniffed. "It would allow us to set some ... uniform ... rules for the area businesses."

My witchy senses tingled. "What kind of rules?"

"Well, for example, have you seen the mummy Ginny Gunderson has outside of her shop? It's covered in dirt and filth. It's very unattractive."

"That's a zombie," I snapped. "That's not dirt. That's blood."

"That makes it even worse," Mrs. Little said. "That's not the appropriate decoration for a tourist town. It's offensive."

"I'm pretty sure you're the offensive one," I shot back. "Either way, I don't care about the zombie. I'm betting this is just a way for you to put yourself in charge of something. Do DDA's have leaders?"

"That's hardly important," Mrs. Little said, averting her eyes. "Of course someone would have to run the program. I need every business in town to agree to it and sign my petition, and then we can get it past the town council."

Even if I liked the woman – which I don't, for the record – I wouldn't agree to this harebrained idea. "Um, no." I shook my head. "We're not signing that. We don't need or want a DDA."

Mrs. Little made a petulant face and glanced at Clove. "You think it's a good idea, right?"

"I think that you're up to something and I'm too tired to deal with it," Clove replied. "In fact, I think I'm done for the day. I think we should shut down a half hour early and go to the inn for dinner. They're making French onion soup."

I perked up at the news. "Seriously? That sounds great. Just let me grab Annie and we'll put the herbs away. Then we can make a run for the bluff."

"Did you forget I'm here?" Mrs. Little challenged. "I asked you a question."

"And I think we answered," I said, turning my attention to the floor where Annie sat a few moments earlier. It was empty. "Oh, geez. You scared her away. Great job."

"I did nothing of the sort," Mrs. Little protested. "She probably ran because you're terrible babysitters."

"Oh, whatever." I scanned the room and frowned when I couldn't find Annie. "Where did she go?"

"She's probably in the bathroom," Clove said, striding in that direction. "Just give me a second."

I watched her move, frowning when she quickly returned and shook her head. "She's not there."

My heart dropped at the news. "Then where is she?"

Clove held her hands up, helpless. "I don't know. She's just … gone."

THREE

"Annie?"

She didn't answer. She wasn't there to answer. No, I couldn't accept that. I stormed toward the hallway at the back of the store, the one that led to the back door (which we never used). It was empty, but the door was propped open. My temper got the better of me as I strode toward it.

"You're in a lot of trouble, Annie," I barked. "You can't just wander off like that without telling anyone."

I kicked the door so hard that it bounced back, making a metal clanging as it slammed into the brick façade. I scanned the alleyway behind the shop – it ran the entire length of the block – and frowned when I didn't immediately catch sight of Annie.

"This is not funny," I growled, moving toward the Dumpster behind the store and tilting my head to either side to see if she was hiding behind the oversized trash receptacle, perhaps playing a game. She wasn't there. "I'm not messing around, Annie. Come out right now. This isn't funny."

"Calm down." Clove appeared at my side and rested a hand on my forearm. "She's probably just messing around. There's no reason to panic."

"That's easy for you to say," I shot back. "She's not your responsibility."

Clove narrowed her chocolate eyes, annoyance evident. "She's everyone's responsibility because we all love her. But there's no reason to panic. This is Hemlock Cove, not Detroit. Even if she is playing a game, it's not as if it will take us long to find her."

She had a point. Still … . "Why would she do this?" I felt annoyed, helpless and worried all at the same time. "She knows it would drive us crazy."

"I think that's your answer," Clove replied. "She spends a lot of time with Aunt Tillie. In Aunt Tillie's world this is probably funny."

I tilted my head to the side, catching a glimpse of my holiday-colored hair reflected in the window across the way – it was orange, in anticipation of Halloween – and shook my head. "Aunt Tillie wouldn't find this funny. She's more for declaring war so you know it's coming rather than hiding in an effort to terrify people. She wouldn't have encouraged Annie to run away like this."

"I'm not saying she encouraged Annie to do anything," Clove clarified. "I'm saying that Annie sees Aunt Tillie getting away with whatever she feels like doing and wants to emulate her. Aunt Tillie would never tell her to run, but Annie is a child. She can't see how her actions hurt others until it's too late."

I rolled my neck until it cracked. Clove's words made sense. Still, I couldn't help but be agitated. "We need to find her."

"Then let's find her," Clove said. "I'll take this side of the alley and you take that side. We should find her pretty quickly."

"Make sure you check everywhere," I called out as she moved to the east. "She's small. She could hide behind something and we wouldn't even know it."

Clove's eyes twinkled as she glanced over her shoulder. "You seem to forget how small I was at that age. I know exactly where to look."

I could only hope she was right.

"**ANYTHING?**"

Twenty minutes later I'd been up and down the alleyway three times and hadn't found a single hint pointing toward Annie's whereabouts. Clove looked conflicted when she caught my gaze.

"I looked twice," Clove said, her voice small. "She's not there."

"She's not here either." My stomach twisted as I worked to control my snowballing panic. "I don't understand this. Where did she go?"

"I don't know." Clove is generally the opposite of calm under duress, but she was much calmer than me given the current circumstances. "I don't think we can risk looking for her alone any longer. We're wasting time."

"What do you mean?"

Clove held her hands palms up and shrugged. "We need help. We need to get Chief Terry involved so he can get his men out searching. Every second we wait now … well … it's a second Annie could be getting farther away."

I read between the lines of what she wasn't saying. "You think someone took her." I felt sick to my stomach and pressed the palm of my hand there in an effort to dislodge the discomfort. "You think she's been kidnapped."

"I didn't say that," Clove insisted, grabbing my wrist. "I think she wandered outside as part of a game. I also think it's possible someone stumbled across her. Maybe they took her someplace because they thought she was lost."

Or maybe they took her for another reason entirely. I made my decision on the spot. "You're right. We need Chief Terry. This is bigger than us now."

"Then let's get him."

I cast one more hopeful glance over my shoulder, hoping I'd somehow missed a secret hidey-hole and that Annie was watching us, a mischievous grin on her face, and everything would be okay. She didn't appear.

I fell into step next to Clove, my emotions muted and numb as I attempted to hold it together. "Yeah. Let's get Chief Terry. He'll know what to do."

"**WHAT DO YOU MEAN?**" Chief Terry Davenport sat behind his desk, a plate of doughnuts I recognized from the inn resting next to his computer. He seemed puzzled when Clove and I entered. Even after we told him why we were there he couldn't seem to get a grip on what we were saying.

"She's gone," Clove explained. "One second she was sitting on the floor of the store and the next she disappeared."

"But … how is that even possible?"

"We're not sure," Clove replied. "Mrs. Little came in and distracted us with that stupid idea to start a D&D club."

"DDA," I automatically corrected. "I would totally join a D&D club with Mrs. Little because it would be hilarious. We could film it for a reality show." It was meant to be a joke but my voice was so flat that it came out robotic.

"What's the difference?" Clove asked.

"One is a card game in which you battle with other players and one is a way for Mrs. Little to get control over the town's businesses," Chief Terry answered, his expression thoughtful as he rubbed his chin. "Are you sure Annie isn't hiding in the store?"

"We looked everywhere. She's not in the store. The back door was open. We searched the entire alley – several times – and she's gone. I … lost her." It was hard for me to grit out the words, and when I did, I wanted to dissolve into tears. That wouldn't help Annie, though, so I struggled to remain strong in the face of Chief Terry's sympathetic eyes. For some reason the pity there almost undid me.

"She can't have wandered far," Chief Terry said, getting to his feet. "I'm going to put a call out over the radio and have my officers converge on the town to search for her. I'll go back to the store with you girls and have a look myself. Then, if we still don't find her, we'll go business to business. It's a small town, Thistle. I'm sure she's okay."

I wanted to believe him. I was desperate to believe him. "Hemlock Cove may be small, but the woods surrounding it are thick," I pointed out. "What if she thought she was being funny and went into the woods and got lost?"

"She hasn't been gone for thirty minutes yet," Chief Terry pointed out. "That's hardly time to get lost."

He believed the words. I could tell. That didn't make me feel better. "We need to find her."

Chief Terry looked stricken when my voice cracked. "Honey, we'll find her." He rested a hand on my shoulder. "You girls took off plenty of times when you were that age. I always found you."

"We never took off this way," Clove sputtered, offended.

"You did it more times than I can count," Chief Terry shot back. "Bay took off at summer camp, for crying out loud. She was in the woods all by herself for hours. Kids take off all of the time. I swear we'll find her."

"Then let's do it," I said, gathering my nerve. "I don't like this. I want to find her right now."

"And that's exactly what we're going to do."

"**WHAT DO** WE HAVE?"

Landon Michaels, in addition to being Bay's boyfriend, is an FBI agent. When I saw him striding toward us as we regrouped in front of the police station three hours later, I didn't take it as a good sign.

"You called in the FBI?" I felt defeated when I locked gazes with Chief Terry.

"I called in Landon," Chief Terry replied. "We need as much help as we can get."

"It's a good thing." Bay, who joined the search not long after we started, hopped to her feet and threw her arms around Landon's neck as he approached.

He returned the embrace, running his hand down the back of her head as he briefly swayed. He was all business when he released her. "I'm taking it you still haven't found her."

"We've looked everywhere," Chief Terry said. "We've been through every store. We've searched every alley. We've walked around the woods on the edge of town. We can't find her."

"She's gone." Clove sounded mournful as she leaned her head

against the police station's brick wall. "I don't understand how we lost her. She was right there."

Landon's expression was sympathetic as he squeezed Clove's shoulder. "We'll find her."

"What if we don't?" I asked hollowly. "What if we never find her? What if she's wandering around the woods and ... ?"

"Don't go there," Landon warned, taking me by surprise when he grabbed my shoulders and gave them a moderate shake to get my attention. "If you give up now then we've already lost. Is that what you want?"

"No."

"Then don't." Landon licked his lips before turning to Chief Terry. "We need dogs."

Clove was horrified. "Cadaver dogs?"

Landon shook his head. "No. The state police have search dogs. We need them to follow Annie's scent."

"I already placed a call," Chief Terry informed him. "They should be here in twenty minutes."

"Which means we need an article of Annie's clothing to give them," Landon said, his gaze pointed when it landed on Clove. "Can you be responsible for that?"

Clove nodded. "Her coat's in Hypnotic."

That's when realization truly set in for me. "She didn't take her coat. It's cold out. I ... she's probably freezing."

"We'll find her," Landon said, gripping my elbow as he focused on Bay. "Sweetie, I need you to track down Marcus to see if he can get people out on his horses in the woods. He'll be able to cover more ground."

My heart rolled at mention of Marcus' name. I'd forgotten all about my boyfriend. "I didn't tell him. I should've told him right away, but ... I knew he would worry." Annie absolutely loves Marcus and the feeling is mutual. At first I didn't tell Marcus because I didn't want to panic him. Once it became more serious, I got distracted. He'd be angry I didn't tell him. "Maybe I should do it."

Landon shook his head, firm. "Thistle, I need you to stick close to me. You were the last one to see her, so your presence is important."

I narrowed my eyes. I had trouble believing that was true. "You're only saying that because you think I'm going to fall apart."

"Oh, golly, you're smarter than you look." Landon flicked me between the eyes. I knew he did it to fire me up, so I opted against picking a fight that would distract everyone from the important goal of finding Annie.

"I'll go with Marcus to search," Bay said. "I know the area as well as anyone."

"You be careful," Landon intoned, pulling Bay in for a quick hug. "Last time you got on a horse you fell and scared the life out of me."

"That's because a poltergeist was out to get me." Bay didn't bother faking a smile as she pressed a kiss to Landon's cheek. "I'll text if we find something."

"You make sure you're off that horse before dark," Landon instructed. "It gets dark early these days."

"And cold," I muttered. "So cold."

"We'll find Annie," Landon said, grabbing my arm so I had no choice but to swivel and face him. "We'll start hitting residential neighborhoods next. There's a good chance she wandered down a side street and someone invited her inside because it is so cold."

That was a possibility, and yet … . "If you found a child on the street, what would you do?"

"I would help," Landon replied, confused. "That's what you would do, too. That's what you did with Annie in the first place."

"Yes. I found her on the street. I brought her inside and got her something to drink and eat. Then I immediately called Chief Terry because I needed help. Isn't that the normal thing to do? Don't you call law enforcement when you find a missing child?"

"I … ." Landon broke off, unsure. "Maybe whoever it is lost track of time. Maybe Annie saw other kids playing on the street and went inside of a house and the parents don't even know she's there yet."

"But … how?"

"She could be playing with friends in a basement or bedroom,"

Landon answered. "There are a thousand different scenarios. Not all of them are bad."

"Not all of them are good either," I pointed out.

"No, they're not," Landon agreed, resigned. "If you focus on the bad, though, it's almost as if you're creating a self-fulfilling prophecy. Is that what you want to do?"

"Of course not. It's just ... she's so small. She was my responsibility and she's gone."

"Accidents happen," Landon said. "You can't blame yourself. We also can't waste time sitting around here. We need to get moving. We all have jobs to do. Can you do yours? Annie needs you to do it, but I can't waste time if you're not up to the challenge."

There was something about his voice that irked me. But I knew what he was trying to do. He would antagonize me until I focused. That was best for everyone, so it's exactly what he was attempting to accomplish.

"I'm up to the challenge," I said, squaring my shoulders. "I want to find her as much as anyone."

"I know you do," Landon said, gripping my shoulder. "That's exactly what we're going to do. Everyone knows his or her job, right? Then let's find Annie. She's out there waiting for us and we can't let her down."

FOUR

It was dark when we regrouped in front of the police station hours later. My legs ached from walking, my voice strained from yelling and my heart hurt from worry.

"Still nothing?" Bay rubbed her rear end as she moved to join us. She'd clearly spent a lot of time on a horse this afternoon. She wasn't used to riding, so she'd be sore for days. She didn't mount one second of complaint, though.

"No." Landon tugged Bay to him, taking a moment to bury his face in her golden hair. He looked exhausted, grim even, and I could tell that Annie's disappearance weighed heavily on him. He was in law enforcement, of course. He knew the terrible things that happened to children when they went missing.

Marcus, his expression hard to read, stared at me from the other side of Bay. I hadn't seen him since this morning when he rolled out of bed to start his day. He was usually unflappable, soothing in an unobtrusive way, but I couldn't help but notice the distance he maintained between us. That couldn't be good. He clearly blamed me for losing Annie. I agreed with the sentiment, so to have someone reinforce it almost made me feel better. Almost.

"I don't know what else we can do," Chief Terry said. "The state police dogs picked up her scent in the alley and followed it to the town line. Then they lost her in the underbrush. I ... don't know what to think."

"How is that possible?" Clove asked, rubbing the back of her neck. She was pale and drawn. I had no idea what she'd been doing over the past few hours, but she looked as if a light breeze could knock her over. "If she was on foot then they should've been able to find her."

"Not if someone took her," I said bitterly.

"They still should've been able to follow her," Clove persisted. "Even if they carried her, right? I mean ... they should've been able to find her."

"We don't know what happened," Landon said, his gaze dark as he rubbed Bay's back. He seemed to need to keep his hands busy. "Someone could've picked her up or ... the dogs could've lost her scent because it's wet out there. It's been raining a lot over the past few days."

"So what do we do now?" I asked. "Do you issue an Amber Alert? Do you bring in the National Guard?"

Chief Terry's gaze was sympathetic. "Honey, we can't issue an Amber Alert because we have no idea if she was kidnapped or walked away. Amber Alerts are for when we have a suspect and need the community to be on the lookout."

"Then call in the National Guard." I pushed forward stubbornly. "They can cover more ground."

"This isn't a natural disaster," Chief Terry argued. "We're doing the best that we can. We'll bring in helicopters tomorrow. They have infrared scanners. They might be able to detect her body heat.

"That will be difficult in this area because we have so much wildlife, but that's our best shot right now," he continued.

"That's it?" My temper ratcheted up a notch. "Are you honestly telling me that you're done for the night? You're just going to leave her out there?"

"What do you suggest I do, Thistle?" Chief Terry shot back. He was generally calm in the face of disaster, but weariness weighed heavily on his strong shoulders. "We can't keep looking in the dark. We'll lose more people. Someone could get hurt."

"Well, I'm not giving up." I crossed my arms over my chest. "I'll get a flashlight and look myself. If you think I'm giving up you're crazy."

"Of course you're not giving up," Landon said. "None of us are giving up. I just … what do you suggest we do?"

"We keep looking."

"And how are we supposed to find her when we can't see a foot in front of our faces?" Landon challenged. "We could step within five feet of her and not even know it."

"If she hears us she'll come."

"And what if she can't hear us?" Landon asked. "What if she's unconscious? What if she's hurt? We'll be walking around in circles and exhausting ourselves. We need to eat … and sleep … and regroup for tomorrow."

"I'm not leaving her!" I burst into tears, my control finally slipping. The sight was enough to jar Marcus into action. He moved to me and tugged me into his arms. I fought the effort. I didn't want to be consoled. "Don't! This is my fault. I did this."

"You didn't do this," Marcus murmured into my hair, smoothing it with his hand as he rocked back and forth. "It was an accident."

"Don't try making me feel better," I warned. "She was my responsibility. I promised Belinda I would watch her. She was right there! I know you blame me. I saw it on your face when you walked up with Bay. You should blame me. I … lost her."

The tears were so heavy they clogged my throat, and my shoulders shook as Marcus tightened his grip.

"I don't blame you, Thistle," Marcus said, his voice surprisingly strong. "You couldn't have seen this happening. Annie clearly chose to walk out the back door on her own. You were distracted.

"We can't be sure what happened to her after she took off – and that very well may have been out of her hands – but she made the initial decision herself," he continued. "I'm not angry because you lost her. I'm angry because you didn't call me sooner."

"Oh." That made sense. I would be angry if I were in his position, too. "I didn't want to worry you at first. I didn't want to frighten you. I thought we would find her right away and then … well … we didn't. I got distracted. I … ."

"You panicked," Marcus finished. "I know. I'm not angry any longer. There's no sense in being angry. It won't help anyone … especially Annie."

"We can't give up," I gritted, out, turning my pleading eyes to Landon. "There has to be something we can do."

Landon looked helpless as he held up his hands, the lines on his face making him appear ten years older. "I don't know what to do, Thistle. We've looked everywhere. The dogs lost the scent. What do you think we can do to fix this?"

"I … ."

"We need to cast a spell," Bay volunteered, taking me by surprise.

"A spell?" Clove shifted her eyes to Bay. "What kind of spell?"

"Not that I want to encourage the spell talk, but can you do something to find her?" Chief Terry asked hopefully.

A spell. Why hadn't I thought of that? Clearly my brain wasn't working. "We can perform the locator spell," I said, wiping my runny nose with my coat sleeve. "We can do it because the ball of light will appear in the darkness. It will lead us."

"Exactly," Bay said, bobbing her head. "We're witches. We might as well use our magic. We should've done it hours ago. I don't know why I didn't think of it."

"None of us thought of it," Clove said. "It's a good idea. Our biggest problem is that we're kind of bad at them. We need … help."

As if on cue, Aunt Tillie appeared out of the darkness on the sidewalk. She looked furious, her hands clenched at her sides. The combat helmet she wore had a light attached to it. She was clearly loaded for bear.

"Why do you think I'm here?" Aunt Tillie barked, drawing everyone's attention in her direction.

"You're here to help us," I said, relieved. Aunt Tillie was here. She was mean and terrible when she wanted to be, but she was also competent and loyal. She wouldn't let Annie go without a fight. She would find her ... and punish the Hecate out of whoever took her. "You're going to find her."

"Of course I'm going to find her," Aunt Tillie sniffed, annoyed. "You should've called me the second this happened. What were you thinking?"

"That she couldn't have gone far," I answered honestly.

"Yes, well, next time, don't think." Aunt Tillie smacked her index finger between my eyebrows. "You've made this much harder than it has to be."

"Then fix it," I demanded, gritting out the words. "Fix it and I'll declare you the Wickedest Witch of the Midwest and bow down to you for the rest of my life."

"Oh, geez." Aunt Tillie rolled her eyes. "Let's not get melodramatic, shall we? I'm going to find her ... and you're all going to call me a hero ... and you're all going to be on my list ... but there's no room for blame."

"Just find her. I don't care how."

Aunt Tillie's expression bordered on sympathetic, which was almost enough to send me on another crying jag.

"I'll find her, Mouth," Aunt Tillie said. "Don't fall apart on me now. I'm going to need you to do it."

AUNT TILLIE KEPT her wits about her when she cast the spell, using Bay's magic to help bolster it since she was the steadiest. I tried to lend a hand but was so uneasy Aunt Tillie ordered me to take a step back.

By the time the locator spell was fully functional I was an emotional mess. Marcus gripped my hand as we followed the swirling ball of light into the forest. He was steady as we trudged through the darkness, but I couldn't stop my hands from shaking.

"She must be freezing," I murmured. "She's probably so cold."

"She'll be okay," Marcus said, squeezing my hand. "Thistle, you need to snap out of this. I don't like the way you're acting. This isn't your fault and you cannot go on acting as if it is."

"If it's not my fault, whose fault is it?"

"There's not someone at fault every time something goes wrong," Marcus pointed out. "I love you, baby, but you've got a defeatist attitude right now and it's not going to help Annie. You need to pull it together."

"I'm not sure I can. My head is like a nest of bumblebees. I hear all of this humming and my heart hurts from the stinging. We need to find her. I just … this is too much."

"It's not too much," Aunt Tillie said, keeping one eye on the locator spell's spinning sphere as she fell into step beside me. "The Goddess never gives us more than we can handle."

"Isn't that the mantra of most religions?" Chief Terry asked. He was doing his best not to watch the ball of light … and failing miserably. He was well aware of our witchy ways, but often opted to ignore them because he wasn't sure how to wrap his head around it.

"Witchcraft is not a religion," Aunt Tillie countered. "It's a way of life."

"Good to know," Chief Terry intoned. "I don't suppose that ball of light can tell you if we're close, can it? We're pretty far into the forest right now. Why would she go this deep?"

Aunt Tillie shrugged, noncommittal. "Perhaps she got turned around. Perhaps someone else forced her to go this deep. The spell will find her. Give it time."

"It has to find her," I said. "I just … we cannot lose her."

Aunt Tillie's gaze was sharp when it landed on me. "We're not going to lose her. The child is smart and tough. For all we know she accidentally followed a ghost without realizing what she was doing and got lost.

"Annie isn't a normal child. She'll survive because she's meant to survive," she continued. "She's destined for greatness, that one. This isn't the end of anything. It's merely a … crack in the cauldron."

"I wish I had your faith."

"You're too busy beating yourself up to have any faith," Aunt Tillie shot back. "You need to keep flogging yourself because that's the only thing keeping you standing right now. I don't agree with it, but I get it.

You need to get over it as soon as possible, though. When we find Annie, she'll need you."

"How do you know that?"

"Because, loath as I am to admit it, you're her favorite," Aunt Tillie replied. "You found her on the road that day. She bonded with you. She's bound to be frightened and upset when we get her back. That means she'll want you."

The words warmed me. "Marcus is technically her favorite."

"She adores Marcus, but she loves you best," Aunt Tillie said. "I am, however, a close second."

I snorted, the sound taking me by surprise. That was such an Aunt Tillie thing to say. "Do you think we're close?"

"I definitely think we're close," Aunt Tillie said. "Let go of the guilt, Thistle. You'll do more harm than good with it if you're not careful."

"That's easy for you to say. You didn't lose her."

"No, but I lost you when you were younger." Aunt Tillie narrowed her eyes as she stared into the darkness, slowing her pace as the colored sphere shifted to the left. "You don't see me crying in my Cheerios because you spent eight hours lost in the woods, do you?"

I tilted my head to the side, conflicted. "That never happened."

"Yes, it did."

"No, it didn't. I would remember being traumatized because I was lost in the woods."

"You don't remember because I told you it was a game and then bribed you not to tell your mother how frightened you were when we found you," Aunt Tillie said, the muscle in her jaw tensing as she held up her hand to still everyone. "You took the bribe and milked the situation for three days. I … something is here."

I discarded Aunt Tillie's story, filing it away to bring up another time, and swiveled wildly. "Where? Annie? Are you here?"

The unmistakable sound of pounding footsteps assailed my ears and I jerked to the right when I heard a tree branch snap. Landon lifted his flashlight at the noise, extending an arm to shove Bay behind him should we find ourselves under attack from an unseen force.

Instead of an enemy, though, a small figure stumbled into our circle of searchers. It was Annie. Her hair was disheveled, her face filthy, and she looked to have any number of scrapes on her arms. She was ghostly pale and barely standing.

"Oh, Annie!" I raced to her, grabbing her close. Her skin was like ice, but I didn't care. "I thought we lost you. You're okay now. We have you. Everything is going to be perfectly okay."

And just like that, the pit of dread in my stomach broke apart. The guilt remained, but it wasn't nearly as sharp as before. Annie was here and she was safe. That's all that mattered.

FIVE

"Annie, are you okay? Are you hurt?"

I ran my hands over her slim shoulders, cringing at the cold emanating from her body. She didn't answer, and when I focused on her blank face all of the worry I'd managed to shove out of my soul returned with enough force to smack me across the face. She looked like an empty shell, nothing close to the gregarious child I lost hours before.

"What's wrong with her?" Clove asked, kneeling. "Has something happened to her?"

"Let me see." Marcus gently nudged me to the side so he could crouch low and attempt to meet Annie's gaze. She stared into nothing, registered nothing. "Sweetie, can you talk to me? Can you look at me?" His voice was so gentle it almost hurt to listen to him.

Landon shifted his flashlight and frowned when the beam landed on her feet. "Holy crap, she's barefoot! We need to warm her up right now."

My heart sank. "Does she have hypothermia?"

"We need to get her back to the inn," Chief Terry instructed, shifting out of his coat and wrapping it around Annie's shoulders. "We need to carry her."

"Then do it," Aunt Tillie barked. "Get her off the ground right now."

Marcus did as instructed, wrapping his arms around Annie's shaking body and cradling her to his chest. "She's trembling." He pressed a kiss to her hair. "It's okay, sweetheart. We'll get you back to the inn right now. It'll be okay."

"Marcus, wait." Aunt Tillie's face was serious as she shuffled forward and wrapped her hands around Annie's bare feet. She cringed at the icy digits but otherwise remained focused as she whispered something I couldn't quite make out and then blew on Annie's feet.

Out of curiosity, I extended my hand and found the cold dissipating as Annie instinctively flexed her toes. It wasn't much, but it was the first sign of life she'd managed since she barreled through the bushes.

"Let's go," Marcus said. "We need to get her in a warm bath and feed her. There's no reason to stay here."

"You go," Aunt Tillie instructed, remaining rooted to her spot. "Take Annie back and let Winnie, Marnie and Twila fuss over her. They'll know what to do. Call them when you're on the way and tell them what to expect."

"What about you?" I asked, casting a worried look over my shoulder. "What are you going to do?"

"I want to take a look around," Aunt Tillie replied mildly. She flashed a smile that didn't make it all the way to her eyes. Something else was lurking there, and she made shooing motions with her hand. "I'll be right behind you."

"Why are you staying out here?" Landon asked.

"I don't know. I sense ... something." Aunt Tillie turned her attention in the direction from which Annie ran. "I don't think we're alone."

"Then I'm staying with you," Landon said.

"I don't need a babysitter."

"That's good," Landon shot back. "You couldn't afford my services. I'm going with you. Don't bother arguing. If you think I'm leaving you to wander around the woods alone, you're crazy."

Even though it was dark, I didn't miss Aunt Tillie's exaggerated eye roll.

"Fine," she heaved out. "I'm in charge, though."

Landon's expression was blasé. "We'll both be in charge."

"I want to be more in charge."

"How about I go with you and we'll vote?" Bay suggested.

Aunt Tillie immediately started shaking her head. "You'll vote with him."

"You don't know that."

If I weren't so agitated by Annie's silence and Marcus' disgusted sighs I would've tossed my opinion into the Winchester argument pile, but I had no time to deal with their crap. "I don't care who is staying or going. We're going! This is about Annie, not your never-ending power struggle."

Landon didn't rise to the bait. "I'm staying with Aunt Tillie."

"So am I," Bay added.

"Fine," I said. "We'll meet you back at the inn. Don't stay out here too long. Everyone will worry if you do."

"There's no need to worry," Aunt Tillie offered. "I'm the wickedest witch of the Midwest, after all. Nothing bad will happen."

"I'm going to hold you to that."

"WE'VE GOT A BATH READY UPSTAIRS."

Winnie met us at the front door and extended her arms to take Annie from Marcus. He seemed reluctant to relinquish her, but arguing with Winnie is akin to driving a golf cart into a semi-truck and expecting to come out the winner, so Marcus acquiesced.

"Come into the dining room," Marnie ordered. "Winnie has Annie under control. We kept dinner warm for you. We'll make sure Annie eats as soon as she's done with her bath."

"She hasn't spoken since we found her," I said, rubbing my hands together as I trudged toward the table. "She hasn't said one word. She doesn't make eye contact."

"She's probably in shock," Marnie suggested, resting her hand on my shoulder. "I'm sure she'll be okay as soon as she warms up."

"Of course she will." My mother bustled in my direction, her flame-red hair glinting under the chandelier. "She just needs a few minutes to adjust. It's no different from that time Aunt Tillie lost you in the woods. You weren't chatty when we found you either."

My eyebrows winged up. "She mentioned that when we were out searching. I don't remember being lost in the woods."

"Oh, well, you probably blocked it out," Mom said. She didn't appear bothered in the least that she was casting my entire childhood into a lava vent and sitting back to watch it burn. "You were very upset."

I glanced at Marcus, frustrated. "Can you believe this?"

Marcus slipped his arm around my shoulders and led me to the table. "You obviously survived. There's no reason to get worked up about it."

"That's easy for you to say," I grumbled. "I just found out I was lost in the woods, and I don't remember it."

"It's for the best." Mom patted my shoulder. "We have meatloaf and potatoes. We made it special after we heard what happened. They're Annie's favorite. We also have French onion soup and bread bowls."

"Load me up," Marcus said, smiling. "I'm starving. I didn't realize how hungry I was until you mentioned meatloaf."

"How about you?" Mom turned to me.

I shook my head. "I'm not hungry."

"Oh, you're hungry," Mom argued. "Your stomach hasn't stopped growling since you walked through the door."

That couldn't be right, could it? As if on cue, my stomach picked that moment to rumble. It was only then that I realized was famished. Hours of worry and self-doubt had worked together to hollow me out. "I guess I could eat," I hedged.

"You'll definitely eat," Mom said, knitting her eyebrows. "Where is Aunt Tillie?"

"And Bay and Landon?" Marnie asked, scanning the empty foyer. "Were they in a different vehicle?"

"They stayed behind," I replied. "Aunt Tillie was acting weird."

"Aunt Tillie always acts weird," Clove noted. "I didn't think she was acting particularly odd given the circumstances."

"She insisted on hanging out in the woods," I argued.

"And Bay and Landon are with her," Clove said. "It will be fine. Don't get worked up."

"I'm not worked up!"

Marcus squeezed my knee under the table and shook his head. "You seem a little worked up. You need to calm down."

"Have a little wine." Marnie pushed a glass in front of me. "It's from Aunt Tillie's stash, though, so drink it slowly if you don't want to dance around the room with a lampshade on your head."

"That never happens," I grumbled, although I accepted and sipped the wine. I immediately felt warmer. "There's no reason to wear a lampshade."

"No, this family just gets naked," Marcus teased, poking my side. If he was still angry about the fact that I didn't call him right away after Annie disappeared, he didn't show it. He wasn't one to hold a grudge, but I sensed a serious conversation in my future.

"I have no intention of getting naked," I said, leaning back in the chair and lifting my eyes to the ceiling. "How long do you think they'll be up there?"

"At least thirty minutes," Marnie replied. "Annie needs to soak in the hot water."

"Aunt Tillie did something," I supplied. "She whispered something I couldn't hear and blew on Annie's toes. It warmed her up some right away. I've never seen her do that before."

"She did it to you after you were lost," Mom offered.

I rolled my eyes. "Someone needs to fill me in on this missing day of my life. How did I get lost? How did it happen? Why did it take you so long to find me?"

"You wandered away because you were angry with Aunt Tillie and she let you go because … well, she said it was payback but I'm not certain that's true … and you decided to teach everyone a lesson and walked off on your own," Mom answered. "She realized about eight hours later that you hadn't come back. She found you on her own."

"Eight hours later?" I was dumbfounded. "I was lost for eight hours before anyone noticed?"

"Bay noticed," Marnie replied. "She told us you were gone, but we thought she was just talking to hear herself talk. She was a chatty thing sometimes, and you had no choice but to tune her out."

I shook my head and glanced at Marcus. "We're lucky to be alive. All of us. Apparently we had almost nonexistent parental supervision."

Marcus chuckled. "We'll do better with our kids."

He said the words with an ease I didn't feel. "How can you possibly talk about kids when I lost one today?"

Marcus' eyes were steady as they locked with mine. "You cannot blame yourself for this. It was an accident. It could've happened to anyone."

"Of course it could," Mom said. "I once took you to the circus and grabbed another kid's hand. I thought she was you. It took me a good twenty minutes to realize my mistake. By then she'd had some cotton candy and you'd worked yourself into a royal snit by the ticket booth. Was that my fault?"

My mouth dropped open. "Seriously?"

"What? I bought you some cotton candy, too."

"Oh, well, that makes it perfectly okay," I muttered, anger pooling in my stomach. "You bought me cotton candy. It doesn't matter that you walked off and left me. Cotton candy makes everything A-okay."

Mom rolled her eyes. "Stop being so dramatic. You got two cotton candies because you wouldn't stop complaining. Your sugar buzz took two days to wear off. You're still alive."

I pressed the heel of my hand to my forehead and shifted my eyes to Marcus. "We can't ever have kids!"

Marcus chuckled. "We'll figure it out. I'm glad you're feeling a little better. The color is coming back to your cheeks."

"I won't feel like myself until Annie starts talking again."

"She will." Marcus leaned over and pressed a kiss to my forehead. "It'll be okay."

I rested my head on his shoulder for a moment, basking in his warmth. I jerked when I heard the front door open, swiveling to find Aunt Tillie, Bay and Landon walking through the door. They appeared to be arguing – which wasn't out of the ordinary – but I wasn't sure I was in the mood for a big blowup. I'm always in the mood for a big blowup, so that made me realize I was even more out of sorts than I initially understood.

"I did not purposely try to kill you," Aunt Tillie announced, sweeping into the room and heading for her normal spot at the head of the table. Her combat helmet was still in place and she seemed oblivious to its presence as she sat. "You're making a big deal out of nothing."

"You almost ran me down," Landon shot back. "You actually aimed my own vehicle at me and almost ran me down!"

"I didn't see you standing there," Aunt Tillie hedged. "I forgot to turn the lights on. It was dark. It was an oversight really."

Landon narrowed his eyes to dangerous slits. "You didn't have permission to drive my truck in the first place. You stole my keys from my pocket when I wasn't looking."

"That's an ugly lie," Aunt Tillie countered. "You dropped your keys, and I merely picked them up."

"I didn't drop my keys."

"You did so."

"I did not."

"You did so."

"I did not."

"Oh, shut up," I ordered, slapping the table for emphasis and earning dirty looks from both parties. "Is now really the time for an argument?"

"They're only doing it to keep warm," Bay explained, sitting in her usual spot. "It got cold out there fast. They're not really angry with each other."

"But she did try to kill me with my own truck," Landon muttered, sliding into the chair on Bay's right. "You can at least admit that."

"She missed you by a good five feet." Bay looked weary as she patted his knee. "You're okay."

"See," Aunt Tillie said, beaming.

"Don't push your luck," Bay warned, extending a finger. "I can take only so much."

"Whatever." Aunt Tillie shook her head and turned toward me. "Where is Annie?"

"Winnie took her upstairs for a bath the moment we hit the front door," I replied. "She should be down soon. I wanted to go with her, but Winnie just kind of took over."

"That's what she does," Aunt Tillie said. "Annie will feel better after a bath. Then we'll get some food in her and bundle her up in front of the fire. She'll be back to her old self before we know it."

"That sounds fabulous." I said the words even though part of me didn't believe Aunt Tillie was right. "Did you see anything in the woods?"

I didn't miss the quick glance Aunt Tillie shot in Landon and Bay's direction.

"No," Landon answered after a beat. "There was nothing out there."

"I'm not an idiot," I pressed. "I saw that look. You found something."

"We don't know if we found something," Bay clarified. "It's too ... weird ... to wrap our heads around."

That didn't sound good. "What did you find?"

"We'll talk about it later," Aunt Tillie said, turning her attention toward the stairs when she heard Winnie's voice. "It's nothing that needs to be brought up in front of Annie."

I turned to Bay, unconvinced. "Are you sure?"

"We'll talk about it later," Bay said, keeping her voice low. "It was weird. I'm honestly not sure what we found. For now, though, you need to let it go. Annie is our priority right now, and we need to focus on her."

I wanted to focus on Annie, so it wasn't difficult to push myself to a standing position and shuffle toward the hallway. "I won't forget this. You're going to tell me what's going on later."

"We'll tell you," Landon said, "but we can only focus on one thing at a time. Right now, that's Annie."

I was reluctant to let it go, but Annie needed me ... and I had every intention of being there for her every step of the way.

SIX

I went straight to Annie when I saw her round the corner in her fuzzy pajamas. Marcus beat me to her, though, scooping her into his arms and carrying her to the table so he could settle her on his lap. Winnie looked as if she was going to argue against the coddling for a moment, but I planted my hands on my hips, practically daring her to say something. Finally, she merely shook her head and moved to the end of the table.

"Is everyone hungry?" Winnie asked, feigning brightness.

Annie didn't respond. Marcus pushed her damp hair out of her face as he forced a smile. "Annie and I would like a huge plate of food. Isn't that right?"

Annie remained mute and stared blankly into space, causing my heart to roll. I risked a glance at Bay and saw her conflicted eyes resting on the girl. Landon absentmindedly rubbed the back of Bay's neck. He looked equally concerned.

"Well, I for one am dying for a good meal," I said, hoping I sounded chipper rather than deranged. It's a hard line for me to toe and I don't always recognize how creepy my expressions come across until it's too late. As if reading my mind, Bay shook her head and offered me a rueful look, so I took the smile down a notch. "How about some hot chocolate, Annie? That's your favorite."

"Oh, that's a good idea." Winnie, who had been fluttering her hands at the edge of the table, hurried into the kitchen while Marcus accepted the plate Twila slid in his direction. He kept one arm wrapped around Annie as he cut the meatloaf. He looked lost, and I felt helpless because there was nothing I could do to make the situation better.

"Do you want some mashed potatoes?" I asked hopefully. "You love mashed potatoes and gravy. You like to make a fort. I'm sure Marcus will make a fort for you."

"Of course I will." Marcus bobbed his head. "I love a good mashed potato fort as much as the next person."

"Okay, you need to knock that off," Aunt Tillie said. She'd been so zealous when digging into her dinner she'd managed to get mashed potatoes on her cheek. She either didn't notice or didn't care. I had a feeling it was a mixture of the two. "You'll freak her out if you keep doing that."

"Doing what?" I protested, annoyed. "I'm not doing anything."

"You're being a kvetch," Aunt Tillie shot back. "That's this one's job." She jerked a thumb in Clove's direction, earning a scowl for her efforts, but kept her eyes focused on me. "Be calm. Don't push her."

Aunt Tillie is stubborn. Sometimes it's her best trait, and sometimes it's her worst, depending on how the day is going. I can be just as bad, though, and now I refused to back down. "She needs to eat."

"And she will," Aunt Tillie said, extending a finger to cut me off when I opened my mouth to argue again. "Trust me."

I didn't have many options, so I merely rolled my neck until it cracked and fixed her with a challenging stare. "Wow me."

"I will." Aunt Tillie licked her lips and gripped her fork. "Annie, pick up your fork and eat your mashed potatoes."

"Oh, good grief," I muttered, annoyed. "That won't work."

Aunt Tillie ignored me. "Annie, pick up your fork and eat your mashed potatoes." Her voice was firmer this time.

Annie remained silent and staring for a full beat, and then, to my utter surprise, she lifted the fork from the side of her plate and dipped it into the mashed potatoes. She took a heaping forkful to her mouth and methodically began to eat. She didn't engage with anyone at the table as she did it, but she picked a rhythm and stuck to it.

I exhaled heavily, relieved. "I ... how did you do that?"

Aunt Tillie shrugged. "I'm magic."

"At least you didn't try to run her over with a truck," Landon grumbled.

"Oh, suck it up," Aunt Tillie sneered, her eyes flashing. "You're still alive and you have your love monkey to cuddle with tonight. You'll be fine."

Landon rolled his eyes, but the corners of his lips tipped up as he glanced at Bay. "Are you my love money?"

"I thought you were my love monkey," Bay teased, some of the weariness fleeing from her vivid blue eyes.

Landon gently rubbed his knuckles down the side of her face. "I'll be your love monkey if you eat your dinner quickly. I'm tired and want to head back to the guesthouse so we can get some sleep."

Sleep? How could they sleep when Annie hadn't spoken one word since we found her? "What about ... ?"

Landon offered a firm headshake as warning. "That can all wait until morning. She needs a good night's sleep."

"But ... ."

"Landon is right," Bay said. "She won't answer any questions tonight. Forcing her will only traumatize her."

"Oh, well, that's the smartest thing you've said all day," Aunt Tillie drawled. "I almost thought your hormones had taken over your brain the way you were falling all over Landon in the woods. But you seem to have regained your senses."

"How was I falling all over Landon?"

"You know what you were doing," Aunt Tillie replied. "All of that 'Landon, hold my hand. Landon, don't go too far. Landon, you're so hot.' It all drove me nuts."

Bay made a face. "I don't sound like that! And I never said 'Landon, you're so hot.' Stop making things up."

"You should've said that," Landon teased. "It doesn't matter, though. We can't push Annie to talk when she's not ready. We'll see how things are in the morning and go from there."

"She probably shouldn't stay alone in her room," I mused, running her hand down the back of Annie's head. "Maybe we should put her in a room with Marcus and me. We can sleep on either side of her and make her feel safe."

"That sounds like a good idea," Winnie said. "We have one open room, and it has a queen-sized bed. I can set you up in there."

"Sounds good," I said, smiling at Annie as I smoothed her hair. "You ate all of the mashed potatoes. Good job. You need to eat the corn now. You can have cake or pie if you want, too."

Annie didn't respond, instead using her fork to spear several corn kernels and slipping them into her mouth. She remained unresponsive, but I was happy to see the color returning to her cheeks.

"It's going to be okay, Annie," Marcus murmured into her hair. "We'll take care of you. We'll keep you safe."

I nodded as I attempted to anchor the emotion. "I won't fail you again. I promise."

"**ALL SNUG,** MY LITTLE BEDBUG?"

I had no idea why I said it – other than my mother used to say it to me when I was a kid – but I was so anxious as I tucked Annie into bed between Marcus and me an hour later that I was willing to fill the silence with anything. It didn't matter how ridiculous it sounded.

Marcus flashed a smile as he got comfortable. "This is kind of nice, huh?"

I arched an eyebrow and flitted a dubious look in Annie's direction. Her face was stony and she didn't appear to notice. "Not really."

"I don't mean the part where Annie got lost," Marcus said. "I mean this part. You and me sharing a bed with a little girl. Er, wait, that came out totally wrong and creepy."

I couldn't help but smile. He was adorable when flustered. "I think

I know what you mean," I said. "It's kind of like we have our own little family."

"Exactly." Marcus looked relieved. "We have a fire going, the bed is warm, and Annie is safe. It's a good night."

Annie's eyes were pressed shut. The only sign that she was still awake revolved around the way she clutched at the comforter.

"It's okay, Annie," I whispered, attempting to straighten her fingers in an effort to relax her. "Marcus and I are going to stay right here with you all night. I promise everything is going to be okay."

Annie made a small sighing sound as she shifted and put her head on Marcus' shoulder. I couldn't help but smile as he traced small patterns on the back of her hand.

"It'll be okay," Marcus repeated. "I'll be here when you wake up. You won't be alone at all tonight. I promise."

Almost as if she needed to hear the words before dropping off, Annie sighed again before her body went limp. Marcus recognized the moment she dropped off, and grinned at me over her head.

"See. This is nice."

I extended my hand over Annie's body and linked fingers with Marcus, creating a protective wall over Annie's small body. "We need her to tell us what happened. We have to know. We can't just ignore it and let her crawl inside of herself."

"We'll talk to her. We're simply waiting until tomorrow morning. There's no sense getting worked up."

"But ... ."

"Thistle, there's nothing we can do right now." Marcus' voice was firm. "We're both exhausted. It's been a long and trying day. Can we table it until morning? I'm begging you."

I wanted to push him further – mostly because my mind was so busy and I was doubtful I would ever manage to turn it off long enough to slip into sleep – but I couldn't argue with the sentiment. "I'm sorry."

Marcus squeezed my hand. "Don't be sorry. You're tired, baby. You need sleep. I need sleep. Annie is already out. Let's join her. Morning will be here soon enough. We can deal with our bigger issues then."

I pressed my lips together and nodded. "Okay."

"Thank you." Marcus lifted our joined hands and kissed my knuckles. "I love you. Go to sleep."

"I love you, too."

And, despite my assertion only moments before, I drifted off within seconds of closing my eyes. Apparently my body and mind didn't agree about the sleep thing. I couldn't help but be happy that my body won.

I DRIFTED IN A DARK DREAM, fear licking the corners of my mind as I jerked my head in a variety of different directions. I couldn't see anything. It was too dark. I could hear, though, and the sounds whipped around me as my terror almost overwhelmed my already fragile brain. Blowing leaves, whispers – oh, the whispers – and the sound of footsteps in the forest caused me to bolt to a sitting position, heaving out uncontrollable gasps as I focused on my surroundings.

I was still in the bed with Marcus and Annie. She tossed and turned fitfully, and Marcus rubbed his hand over her cheek to soothe her. "It's okay," he murmured. "It's just a dream."

Was it? A dream, I mean. Was it something she made up in her head or was it a memory? And what about me? Did I merely dream what I thought happened to her or did I somehow slip into her head and get a glimpse of a child's terror? In some respects, that made sense. I'd felt fear before, but nothing compared to the dream. Was it Annie's fear I felt?

"Are you okay?" Marcus asked, his eyes drifting over my features. "You look pale."

"I ... had a nightmare."

Marcus furrowed his brow, concerned. "You don't usually have bad dreams. It must be everything that happened today catching up to you."

I wanted to believe the assertion but I couldn't. "Sure."

I shifted my eyes to the door when it opened, gawking at Bay and Landon as they hovered in the doorway. Bay was dressed in fuzzy sleep pants and a hoodie and a Landon's hair was tousled from sleep. I met Bay's serious gaze over the muted light – Marcus left the lamp on low so Annie wouldn't wake in darkness – and I could see worry etched on Bay's face.

"What's going on?" I asked, keeping my voice low.

"I ... don't know." Bay shuffled into the room, her eyes fixed on Annie.

"She had a dream," Landon volunteered, sliding a worried look in Bay's direction. "She woke up gasping and couldn't catch her breath."

Marcus flicked his eyes to me. "So did Thistle. What did you dream?"

"I ... don't know." That wasn't a lie. I had no idea what I saw in the dream. I couldn't put a name to it other than fear.

"I think it was something from Annie's memory," Bay offered, moving closer to the bed. She sat at the end of the mattress, forcing Marcus to move his feet as she rested her hand on top of Annie's leg. "It was dark. I was in the woods but I couldn't see anything. I could hear the trees in the wind, though. I could hear footsteps. There was ... whispering."

"You heard the whispering?" The question was out of my mouth before I realized what I was saying. "It sounded like a woman, right?"

Bay widened her eyes and nodded. "You heard it, too?"

"How is that possible?" Landon asked, creeping closer. "How could you all share the same dream?"

"We've theorized before that Annie has a little witch in her blood," Bay mused. "She can see ghosts. That's not a human characteristic. That's a witch trait. Maybe she inadvertently called to us when she was frightened."

"Why couldn't she do that when she was lost in the woods?" Marcus asked, stroking the back of Annie's head to offer comfort. She'd ceased whimpering and relaxed into a normal sleeping pattern again. "If she could reach you on that level, why not earlier?"

"Probably because we're at our most unguarded in sleep," I answered, rubbing my forehead to ward off a building headache. "We're cognizant of our actions and thoughts when we're awake.

Someone can't just wander into our heads because we would actively work to keep them out."

"But it's different when you're asleep?" Landon asked. "Is that like subliminal messages? I mean, say I whisper that you want to smell like bacon for an hour while you're sleeping. Will you wake up and roll in bacon?"

I couldn't help but laugh. Landon's face was so earnest – and Bay's so annoyed – that it broke the heavy spell in the room.

"That'll never work," Bay answered. "However, if I whisper that you're going to want to give me an hour-long massage when we wake up, that will probably work."

Landon smirked. "Good to know."

"So you're basically saying that you have no idea what this means," Marcus prodded. "Do you think it was real or a nightmare?"

Bay shrugged. "We won't know until we question Annie in the morning."

"Which is four hours away," Landon noted. "We should get back to the guesthouse and at least try to get some sleep."

"Why did you come here?" I asked, genuinely curious. "You knew she was safe. I wouldn't let anything happen to her. Not twice, at least."

"I wanted to see her," Bay said through a wan smile. "I can't explain it."

"I get it." I blew out a sigh. "Landon is right. Morning will come early. We won't be able to deal with this until then."

"So we'll get some sleep and deal with it over breakfast," Landon said, grabbing Bay's hand and tugging her to him. "It will be easier to wrap our heads around when there's bacon."

Bay made an exaggerated face and shook her head. "You have a one-track mind."

"And believe it or not, you're that track," Landon said. "We'll see you guys in the morning. Try to get some sleep."

SEVEN

"Good morning."

I woke to find Marcus smiling at me from the other side of the bed, Annie's head resting on his shoulder. He looked adorable, his long hair tousled and his morning beard giving him a devilish quality.

"Morning."

I shifted so I could run my hand down the back of Annie's hair, and then linked my fingers with Marcus' so we could have a moment together before the tempest blew through.

"What are you thinking?" Marcus asked. "Did you have another dream?"

"Not that I recall." That was the truth. "I think I need to go back to where we found her and search the area."

"I don't think that's a good idea, but I'm happy to go with you."

I offered him a rueful smile. "You don't think it's a good idea, but you're happy to go with me? How does that work?"

Marcus shrugged. "I think you'll be chasing your tail out there, but I know you're not ready to give it up. I want to go with you to make sure you're safe."

It was a sweet sentiment, but that was the last thing I wanted. "I need to know if someone took her. I need to look around when we can actually see the terrain. Bay and Landon said they saw something weird, but didn't say what it was. I need to see it for myself."

Marcus' response was simple. "Then I'll go with you."

I shifted my eyes to Marcus' shirt and focused on Annie's fingers and the way they were curled into the fabric. She clung to him in sleep, so I knew she would need him when consciousness claimed her. "I think you're going to be otherwise engaged."

Marcus moved his eyes to the spot where I stared and patted Annie's hand until she loosened her grip. "I don't want you out there alone, Thistle. I love you. That's just ... not going to happen. There are plenty of people here who can watch Annie."

"She'll want you."

"Yes, but I want you." Marcus' tone was firm. He wasn't giving me a lot of wiggle room. "If someone is out there and that person did grab Annie ... well, I won't risk you. It's simply not going to happen."

I pursed my lips as I dragged my hand through my Halloween orange hair. He made a good argument, but I didn't need a babysitter. I decided to appeal to his sense of chivalry. "I'd feel better knowing you were watching her."

"And I would feel better if we watched her together," Marcus shot back. "That's clearly not going to happen, so we'll have to negotiate. I am not going to sit back and let you wander around the woods alone."

He was serious. There was no doubt about that. "Okay, well, I want you with Annie because I know you'll keep her safe. She won't be tempted to wander if you're here."

"Don't kid yourself. She's not going to wander today no matter what. I'll bet she doesn't leave the house."

"That's not what I want." I played with the ends of Annie's hair as I furrowed my brow. "I don't want her traumatized."

"I know that, but it's going to take a few days for her to get back to normal."

"I don't want her looking over her shoulder as if there is something out there stalking her," I argued. "Bay and I had the same nightmare. It was tied to Annie and her memories. I will find out what happened and make sure there's no threat to her in this town."

"Well, great," Marcus growled, his eyes flashing. "I'll babysit the kid while you put your life on the line. That shouldn't be hard for me to deal with at all."

I fought the urge to roll my eyes. There was no need for him to be so dramatic. "I'm not trying to bully you ... ."

Marcus cut me off. "That's exactly what you're trying to do."

I pretended I didn't hear him. "I have to go out there, and you have to stay here with Annie so she feels safe." I held up a hand to cut him off before he could mount further argument. "I don't plan on going into the woods alone."

Marcus was understandably suspicious. "You're not?"

"Nope. I'm taking Bay and Clove with me."

Marcus made a face that was so adorable I would've kissed it into submission if we were alone. Annie's presence didn't allow that, so all I could do was smile.

"Bay and Clove will get you into trouble," Marcus argued.

"I'm not looking to stay out of trouble," I reminded him. "I'm looking to make sure that other trouble, worse trouble, isn't lurking out there. Bay, Clove and I can handle anything when we're together."

Marcus didn't look convinced. "Thistle, I don't like this. I'd prefer leaving Bay and Clove here with Annie while I go with you. I have a cooler head."

"Than who?"

Marcus was unruffled and answered right away. "Any of you. Your entire family is prone to theatrical fits."

"Only my mother is prone to theatrical fits," I countered. "Everyone else is quite normal."

Marcus cocked a challenging eyebrow. "Aunt Tillie is normal?"

"I ... ." He had a point. "She's normal-ish," I said after a beat. "Bay, Clove and I will be perfectly safe in the woods. Why can't you trust us?"

"Because I love you and am looking forward to the day when we move in together," Marcus replied. "That's coming sooner than you realize. It's right around the corner, in fact. I'm not losing you before it happens."

It's hard to be angry with a man when he's so stinking cute and earnest. "You're not going to lose me."

"I know." Marcus bobbed his head. "That's why you're taking Landon and Aunt Tillie, too."

I opened my mouth to argue but didn't get a chance. Marcus firmly shook his head to make me aware of exactly how serious he was.

"That's the only way I'll agree to this," Marcus said. "I want Landon and Aunt Tillie there, too."

"But ... why?"

"Because Landon is an FBI agent and he often has a cool head when it comes to this stuff," Marcus replied. "As for Aunt Tillie, well, if you do run into someone out there she'll go for first blood. She loves Annie more than just about anyone. She'll curse first and ask questions later."

He had a point. Still .... "What if I don't agree to your terms?"

"Then I'll steal Landon's handcuffs and attach you to me. Good luck getting anything done if that happens."

I blew out a sigh, my bangs fluttering, resigned. "You drive a hard bargain."

"Do we have a deal?"

Marcus waited as I chewed my bottom lip. Finally I bobbed my head. "We have a deal."

"Good. The handcuffs thing sounds good in theory, but it would be nothing but a nightmare after an hour or so."

I chuckled. I couldn't help myself. "I love you."

Marcus squeezed my hand. "I love you, too. We'll figure it out. We got Annie back. That's the most important thing."

I wanted to agree with him, but something niggled the back of my brain. "We got Annie back, which is important, but now we need to focus on keeping her safe. I think something is out there."

"Then I trust you and the rest of your crew to find out what it is and put an end to it."

"Oh yeah. You can count on that."

"GOOD MORNING, SUNSHINE."

By the time we made it to the dining room table – Annie's hair standing on end as she refused to change out of her pajamas – Marcus and I had come to an agreement. even though he wasn't keen on separating for the day.

Annie was an entirely different story. From the moment she opened her eyes she wouldn't stop clinging to Marcus. He couldn't even sit in his own chair. She insisted on being on his lap and he was forced to feed her breakfast and forgo nourishment of his own because she kept burying her face in his shoulder when anyone else tried to speak to her.

Winnie, who was carrying the bacon platter, frowned when she saw Annie's reaction. "Sweetheart?"

"She's having a tough time getting going this morning," Marcus said, flashing an apologetic smile as he rubbed her back. "She's ... still tired, I guess."

"Yes, that must be it." Winnie didn't look convinced, but knew better than to push the issue. "I'm sure a good breakfast will help."

"Of course it will," Landon enthused, moving through the swinging door that separated the dining room and kitchen with Bay on his heels. "I smell bacon. There's nothing in the world that's not better with bacon."

Despite herself – Annie couldn't refrain from glancing over Marcus' shoulder and staring at Landon. Her eyes widened when Landon grabbed a handful of bacon strips and moved them to his plate, but otherwise she remained silent.

"Do you want some?" Landon asked, snapping a strip in half and crunching into it. "It's like a magical elixir. It will fix whatever is bothering you."

I considered warning Landon about pushing her, but there was something about the way Annie watched him that made me realize Landon knew what he was doing. He was with the FBI, so I figured he was trained to deal with all sorts of witnesses – including traumatized children. He seemed to have a relaxed air about him, all the while exuding confidence, and Annie couldn't take her eyes off of him.

"Do you want eggs?" Winnie asked, her eyes narrowed as her gaze bounced between Landon and Annie. She seemed to sense that he was the magical powerhouse this morning, too, and she was eager to make things easier.

"I would love eggs. Thank you." Landon beamed, making a show of swatting Bay's hand when she attempted to snag some of his bacon. "That's not for you. There's an entire platter right there. You can grab your own."

Bay made a petulant face. "I thought you loved me."

"I do."

"You love me but you won't share bacon with me?" Bay apparently understood the game Landon was attempting to play. I had a feeling it had something to do with acting as normal as possible. I could only watch, fascinated, as Annie stared in their direction.

"I would die for you, Bay," Landon replied simply. "Bacon is sacred, though. It's magical. You need to get your own bacon."

"That's so hurtful." Bay sniffed and shook her head. "I can't believe you prefer bacon to me."

"I didn't say I preferred bacon to you." Landon squeezed Bay's knee under the table. I recognized the action for what it was: reassurance that they were doing the right thing. I had to bite the inside of my cheek to keep from laughing. "I merely said that you need to get your own bacon."

It was a goofy conversation, but it was also flirty, mundane and familiar. It was something Annie saw at least three times a week. She seemed happy to witness it now.

"I think I'm going to make a bacon cake at some point and not invite you to have a slice of it. How does that sound?" Bay challenged.

Landon pursed his lips. "That's kind of a mean thing to say."

"You started it."

Landon held out a slice of bacon, taunting Bay with it as he made his fingers dance. Bay tried to snag the bacon slice, but Landon was too quick. "What are you going to give me for this bacon?"

"A kiss."

Landon smirked. "That's a nice start. I get kisses every single day, though. I want something else."

"Like what?"

"Like ... tell me something important," Landon suggested. "Tell me what you saw in your dream last night."

That's when things clicked into place for me. Landon and Bay were trying to cajole answers out of Annie. To do it, they talked about their part of the story first. They were doing it in front of her so she could listen and be up to speed on the investigation, but they were also doing it without talking down to her and treating her as a child. I had to admire the effort.

"I was in the woods," Bay replied. "It was dark and all I could hear was the rustling of the leaves and someone whispering. I knew I was being chased ... that someone was following me ... but I couldn't seem to find my way out of the darkness."

Annie leaned forward, putting a little bit of distance between Marcus and herself. "You got lost in the woods?"

They were the first words she'd uttered since we found her. She did a bit of crying – and a whole lot of clinging – but she hadn't spoken. Until now. I sucked in a breath as I watched her, letting Landon continue his questioning in his easygoing manner.

"I did," Bay confirmed, acting as if Annie speaking wasn't some sort of miracle. "I couldn't find my way, and I knew someone was following me. It was creepy."

"But it was a dream, right?" Annie's gaze was intense.

Bay shrugged. "It felt very real. It almost felt as if I was someone else, though."

"Maybe you were me." Annie's words were barely a whisper. "I had that dream, too."

"You did?" Bay feigned surprise. "Did you see who was whispering in your dream? You have younger eyes and probably got a better look at the person. It was too dark for me."

"I … ." Annie licked her lips, absently accepting the slice of bacon Landon slid in her direction. "There's a woman out there. She lives in the trees."

I tilted my head to the side, confused. "A woman lives in the trees?"

"She's afraid of people. But she's lonely. She doesn't like being alone." Annie's eyes brimmed with tears and Marcus pressed a kiss to her forehead. "She gave me a doll, but I dropped it when I was trying to find you."

"We saw the doll," Landon said carefully. "We found it I the woods last night."

Was that all they found? I didn't ask the question out loud.

"I don't want to see the doll again," Annie warned. "I don't like it. I don't like the tree woman either."

"You're very brave telling us this," Marcus prodded. "Did the woman take you from the store?"

Annie shook her head. "I walked out the back door because I was bored. I thought I would hide so you could find me, except … except someone was there and she made me go with her. I tried to call out for you, but she put her hand over my mouth."

Annie balled her fist up and pressed it to the corner of her mouth.

"I knew I was in trouble, and it was all my fault," she continued, tears coursing down her cheeks. "I shouldn't have snuck away. It was my fault."

"It wasn't your fault," I argued, grabbing her chin so she had no choice but to focus on me. "I swear it wasn't. I should've been watching you. You saved yourself, though. You were a big hero. We're so proud of you."

"But … she's still out there," Annie protested. "She kept saying she wanted me to live with her and that she'd been looking for me for a long time. I waited until she wasn't looking and ran. She chased me through the trees, but I ran forever. Then I heard you guys and … I just ran some more."

"You did well," Landon said, pointing toward the hand with bacon. "Eat that to build up your strength."

Annie did as she was told, mustering a small smile when Landon gave her another piece of bacon. "What about Bay? Are you going to give her some of your bacon?"

"Bay can always have some of my bacon," Landon answered. "You can, too. Only the two of you, though."

"I don't think anyone would risk touching your bacon," I pointed out.

"I'm just making sure I stated it for the record," Landon said, flashing a smile for Annie's benefit. "I have one more question: Did the woman take you to a house? Did she have a place where she was living?"

"It wasn't really a house," Annie answered. "It was kind of like a playhouse more than anything. It was in the middle of the woods. You would almost miss it if you weren't looking right at it."

"How close was it to where we found you?"

Annie shrugged. "I felt like I was running forever, but I don't know which way. I ... got lost and I could hear her behind me. She was following me."

"It's okay." Landon rested his hand on Annie's head and smiled. "We're going to find the woman. We're going to make sure everything is okay."

Annie widened her eyes, fear finding a foothold. "I don't want to go back!"

"You don't have to go back," Landon said smoothly. "You're staying here with Marcus, Winnie, Marnie and Twila. The rest of us will handle the situation."

"Even Aunt Tillie?"

Landon nodded. "Especially Aunt Tillie. She's going to be very interested in our excursion today. Speaking of that, where is Aunt Tillie?" Landon glanced around the room. "I can't believe she's missing bacon."

"She's in her greenhouse," Marnie replied. "She seems agitated. I thought it was because Annie went missing yesterday and she was still riled up, but now I'm starting to wonder if she suffered the same dream Bay had."

"Now there's something I didn't see coming," I muttered, rolling my neck as I stood. "I didn't consider that. We need to find her and get this party started. I think it's going to be a long day."

"Then let's do it," Bay said, pushing herself to her feet and snagging a slice of bacon from Landon's plate. "Come on, Romeo. We'll need your expertise to get through this."

Landon snagged the back of Bay's shirt before we headed toward the greenhouse. "Tell me about that bacon cake you mentioned. That sounds ... intriguing."

Bay rolled her eyes. "There's no such thing as a bacon cake."

"I think if you put your imagination behind it you'll come up with a different answer."

Bay blew out a sigh and shook her head. "Seriously?"

Landon nodded.

"Fine. I'll figure out a way to make you a bacon cake. Are you happy?"

Landon leaned over and kissed the tip of her nose. "For now. I'll be happier when we find this woman in the woods."

"That makes both of us," I interrupted, drawing their attention to me. "If we do it today, I'll make you a bacon cake. How does that sound?"

Landon's eyes flashed. "That sounds like I have a new favorite witch."

Bay scowled. "Oh, well, that hurts."

Landon grinned as he kissed her cheek. "She'll be my favorite only until the bacon cake digests. I promise."

Even though they had a cute quality that often made me want to puke, I couldn't focus on Landon and Bay today. "Let's get moving. I want to finish this. Annie needs us to finish it."

Landon sobered. "We're going. We're not going to leave that area until we find the woman who did this. I promise you that."

EIGHT

We found Aunt Tillie in her greenhouse. She paced back and forth in front of one of her potting benches, her coat clutched around her, muttering to herself. I couldn't quite make out what she was saying, but I knew she was concentrating because she didn't bother looking up when we entered.

"What are you doing?" Landon asked.

"What?" Aunt Tillie finally jerked her head in our direction. "Oh, I'm making up my battle plans for the day. World domination is just around the corner. You should duck and cover before it's too late."

Landon's lips twitched as he regarded her. "Your battle plans? Are you going to war?"

"Someone took Annie. Of course I'm going to war." Aunt Tillie shook her head, as if trying to discard the heavy thoughts plaguing her, and moved toward a batch of herbs on the bench. "I'm going to cast a modified locator spell to find the person we're looking for."

"It's a woman," Bay volunteered. "Annie told us a little bit over breakfast. She's still shaken up, but she said she walked out of the store on her own and then a woman grabbed her in the alley and took her to the woods. That explains the extra set of footprints we thought we found … and the discarded doll we thought was so weird."

"She blames herself," I added. "She thinks she was taken because she did something bad."

"Well, that's just ridiculous," Aunt Tillie sputtered. "If that was the rule someone would be showing up to take me every single day."

"Oh, that sounds like the best Christmas gift ever," I teased, smirking. My spirits elevated once Annie started talking, and I was feeling much better about myself. My babysitting talents still left a bit to be desired, but I couldn't worry about that now when I had other things to contend with. "I'll keep that in mind for my Santa list this year."

Aunt Tillie made a face and extended her finger in warning. "Don't worry about Santa's list. You're on my list."

"I'm fine with that. I only want things to go back to normal."

"They can't until we find whoever is in the woods," Landon pointed out. "I didn't want to push Annie too far in case she retreated again, but I'm guessing whoever is out there isn't mentally balanced. Annie described a shack essentially, not a house. That means this woman is living a rough existence."

"But why take her at all?" Bay asked, rubbing the back of her neck. "If you're living that kind of life, why add to your troubles? Keeping a child under those conditions wouldn't be easy."

"Which makes me think that grabbing Annie was an impulse rather than a well thought out plan," Landon said. "This woman saw her and took her. She obviously couldn't keep control of Annie, because she escaped."

"But why take her?" Bay pressed. "What possible reason could this woman have to take her?"

"Annie already told us why," I answered. "She said the woman lived alone and was lonely. I'm willing to guess that whoever it is suffers from mental illness or has some sort of personality disorder."

"That doesn't mean it's okay to take our kid," Aunt Tillie barked, causing me to smile. I hadn't seen her this agitated since someone tried to steal her pot stash a few weeks ago. This was a different kind of anger, though. This was the sort of anger that could consume a person if they weren't careful.

"No one is saying it's okay," Landon said, holding up his hands in a placating manner. "We're merely saying that it's a situation that needs to be dealt with. If that woman is mentally unbalanced we can get her help."

"Oh, I'm going to help her," Aunt Tillie growled. "I'm going to put a boot up her behind and help her over a cliff."

Landon ran his tongue over his teeth as he regarded her. "You can't kill her," he said after a beat. "We need to focus on finding her, but when we do, you have to let me take over. Do you think you can do that?"

Aunt Tillie didn't hesitate before answering. "No."

Landon growled. "We need you when we go out there, but I can't risk you killing someone in front of me. We don't know what happened yet. Other than being frightened, Annie wasn't physically harmed. You can't uncork a big bottle of vengeance until we know what's going on."

"Who told you about my big bottle of vengeance?" Aunt Tillie deadpanned.

"I know what you're doing." Landon leaned over so he was at eye level with Aunt Tillie. "I'm not saying what happened here is right. It's pretty far from all right. That doesn't mean this woman is a criminal mastermind. I need you to remain calm when we find her."

"You seem pretty convinced that we're going to find her," Aunt Tillie mused, avoiding Landon's pointed comment. "Why is that?"

"Because I know you ... and Bay ... and Thistle," Landon replied. "You won't stop until we have the answers we're looking for. I want to make sure we don't make a mistake in our zeal to find the woman who took Annie.

"We would all die for her," he continued. "We all love her. That doesn't mean we can do something stupid when we get out there."

Aunt Tillie's expression was challenging when she locked eyes with Landon. "Fine. I won't fly off the broom handle. I'll react in a calm and rational manner."

Landon made a rueful face. "We both know that's a load of crap. Promise me you won't kill her until I can ask a few questions. That's all I ask."

"Fine." Aunt Tillie moved to the bench and swept the herbs she'd been gathering into a plastic bag. "You know, I don't really make a habit of going around killing people. Torture is more my style. I enjoy torturing people. It wasn't hard to make you that promise, so don't go patting yourself on the back for convincing me to do it."

"Yes, well, you're a woman of your word," Landon explained. "You might do some kooky stuff that drives everyone crazy, but when you say you'll do something, you mean it. I'm worried that things will get out of hand, that you might lose your cool when we get out there. I want to make sure that doesn't happen."

"And you naturally believe I'll keep my word?" Aunt Tillie was clearly surprised.

Landon bobbed his head. "I do. You're loyal. You can't help yourself, because at your core you're a good person."

The corners of Aunt Tillie's mouth tipped down. "I think that's the meanest thing you've ever said to me."

Landon snorted. "We leave in five minutes. We'll pick up Clove at the lighthouse on the way." He moved toward the door, but Bay stilled him with a hand on his arm.

"Where are you going?"

Landon smiled. "I'm going inside for a care package. I need bacon for the road."

Bay scowled. "Answer truthfully. If there's a fire, will you save me or the bacon?"

Landon didn't waste time before answering. "Bacon can't walk by itself. Your legs aren't broken."

Bay made a disgusted face. "That's what I thought."

Landon smiled as he gave her a quick kiss. "Meet me out front in five minutes. If you're not there, I'll leave without you."

"**IT'S COLD** and wet out here."

Clove wrinkled her nose as she picked her way through the underbrush and struggled to keep up with Landon and Bay. They were at the front of the group, while we brought up the rear, with Aunt Tillie sandwiched between us.

"It's the woods in the fall," I said dryly. "What did you expect? Did you think you could wear a bathing suit and get away with it?"

Clove scalded me with a dark look. "I don't need your attitude."

"Obviously you do," I shot back. "You've been complaining since we picked you up. I'm sorry Annie being kidnapped has been such a hardship on you."

Clove balked. "That's not what I said."

"Isn't it?"

"I ... um ... I'm sorry." Clove struggled to find the correct words as she rubbed her mitten-covered hands across the front of her coat. "I didn't sleep well last night. I wasn't trying to offend you or anything. I know that Annie going missing was hard on you."

"It was hard on all of us," Aunt Tillie corrected. "She's safe now, though. We're going to make sure she stays safe."

"That's right," Landon confirmed. "There will be no killing."

"I already agreed, Copper," Aunt Tillie snapped. "Stop being a kvetch. We don't have room for two of them in our group today." She sent Clove a pointed look. "If Landon is going to be the kvetch, you have to take on a new persona. A woman can only put up with so much, and two kvetches is my limit."

Clove mustered a slit-eyed glare as she crossed her arms over her chest. "I don't know why I put up with so much abuse from this family."

"I think you like it because it plays to your martyr complex," Aunt Tillie said, unruffled. "Still, you mentioned you didn't sleep. Did you have nightmares?"

I shifted my eyes to Clove, curious. "Yeah. Did you?"

"I ... ." Clove chewed her bottom lip, conflicted. "I'm afraid you'll laugh, but I did have nightmares. I was lost in the woods and I heard someone following me. They were ... whispering ... or something. I think I might've been projecting Annie's ordeal onto myself or something."

"We all had the dream," Bay offered, her hand clasped tightly in

Landon's as we moved toward the spot where we found Annie the night before. That's where Aunt Tillie would unleash her spell. "We all woke at roughly the same time."

"Really?" Clove was understandably intrigued. "Did Annie wake up?"

"She slept through it," I replied. "She was tucked in between Marcus and me the entire night."

"That must've made the romance difficult," Clove mused.

"No one was in the mood for romance," I said, annoyed. "We wanted to take care of Annie, and that's what we did."

"I was just joking," Clove muttered. "Sheesh."

"I think you'll find everyone in serious moods this morning," Bay offered. "Until we deal with the Annie situation, no one wants to take a chance and have a little fun."

"Speak for yourself," Landon interjected. "I had a riotous good time with my bacon this morning."

Bay snickered. "Riotous?"

"I saw it on television this morning," Landon admitted. "It was in a movie review. Someone said that new sex movie was a 'riotous good time' and it stuck in my head."

Bay knit her eyebrows. "Sex movie?"

"That one where they tie each other up and use a leather riding crop to spank each other," Landon replied. "We should totally see that, by the way."

Bay still looked confused, so I filled in the gaps for her. "He's talking about one of the *50 Shades of Grey* movies."

Realization dawned on Bay. "Oh. Eww!" Bay smacked Landon's arm. "We're not playing any perverted games like that. The bacon fetish is weird enough."

"We'll see." Landon squeezed her hand and smiled before ceasing his forward momentum and glancing around a small clearing. "This is where it happened, right? This is where she found us."

I followed his gaze and nodded. "She came through the bushes right here." I moved to the spot and knelt, running my finger over the stark footprints. "We still have no idea what happened to her shoes."

"I forgot about that," Landon admitted, rubbing his chin. "I assume that the woman took Annie's shoes because she figured she wouldn't risk running away barefoot. Annie didn't realize how sick she could make herself by doing it, so it wasn't a very good tactic. We're lucky that Annie wasn't lost outside by herself for the entire night because she might've lost a few toes otherwise."

Aunt Tillie snorted derisively. "I would never have allowed that to happen."

Landon challenged her with a look. "You can stop frostbite with magic now, can you?"

Aunt Tillie merely shrugged, her smile enigmatic. "I am the most powerful witch in the land," she reminded him. "I'm capable of a great number of things."

"Including finding this woman, right?" I asked, drawing Aunt Tillie's gaze to me. "You brought the ingredients to cast a spell. You're going to lead us to the woman who took Annie. That's what you said." For some reason, returning to the spot where we found Annie heightened my sense of unease. I couldn't fathom how close we'd come to losing her.

"I said I would find her and I meant it." Aunt Tillie's expression was odd as she looked me up and down. "I don't know how I missed it, but you're still being consumed with guilt even though I thought you'd shake it off during the night."

"I am not," I protested, averting my gaze. She has a way of seeing into people's souls, and that was the last thing I wanted to grapple with. "I'm ... fine."

"No, you're not fine." Aunt Tillie's voice was almost kind as she moved closer to me. "You didn't lose Annie. She wandered away and then someone took her. That's not on you."

"Was it on you when you lost me in the woods?" I challenged.

"Of course not."

I didn't believe her. "Really? If I'd never been found, are you telling me you'd have been fine with that?"

Aunt Tillie held her hands palms up and shrugged. "I had two other kids to replace you." She winked, but the amusement was fleeting. "Mouth, you were never going to be lost in the woods forever. I was always going to find you ... just like you were always going to find Annie."

"But I didn't find Annie," I reminded her. "She found us. We didn't do anything but happen to be in the right place at the right time."

"I'm going to step in here," Landon said, shuffling closer. "That's not what happened. You heard Annie this morning. She heard our voices. That's how she knew which direction to run. If we weren't out here she would've been wandering around on her own until ... ."

"But ... ."

Landon shook his head and made a clucking sound with his tongue. "You didn't do this. Annie didn't do this either. We need to work on her guilt issues when we get back. It was a perfect storm of events. There's no need to shoulder blame because it's no one's fault."

"Oh, the woman who took her is at fault," Aunt Tillie countered. "She's at fault, and I'm going to crush her like a really ugly bug."

Landon made a face. "Didn't we have this discussion?"

Aunt Tillie's face turned from menacing to angelic in the blink of an eye. "We did. And I was totally serious about doing what you asked."

"Great." Landon shook his head and glanced at the plastic bag. "It's time to put your spell together. We need a trail to follow. I would rather not meander around forever without knowing in which direction we should be heading."

"I'm on it." Aunt Tillie's forehead creased with concentration. "You don't have much patience, do you?"

"That's rich coming from you," Landon shot back.

"Yes, but I'm old, so people can call my lack of patience quirky," Aunt Tillie pointed out. "When you're impatient it's annoying. When I'm impatient it's cute."

Landon didn't look convinced as he shifted his eyes to Bay. "Is that true?"

"I don't find either of you cute when you're impatient," Bay answered. "In fact, I'm feeling impatient right now. It's cold. Can we save this discussion for when it's over and we're sitting in front of a fire?"

"Is there bacon when we're in front of the fire?" Landon asked.

Bay rolled her eyes. "Yes."

"Sold." Landon squeezed her shoulder before moving closer to Aunt Tillie. "Let's do this. What do you need?"

"Space and five minutes of quiet," Aunt Tillie replied. "The spell will be ready and working before you know it."

Landon was understandably dubious. He'd seen more than one backfiring spell since falling in love with Bay. "That will be a nice change of pace."

NINE

"This way."

Aunt Tillie took the lead once she enacted the spell. The ball of light – which was usually blue or white under normal circumstances – was purple today. She added a little something special to the ingredients, although I had no idea what.

"So tell me about the time you lost me in the woods," I instructed, falling into step with her. "How did it happen?"

"I was supposed to be babysitting. I told you that you couldn't have pineapple juice even though you really wanted it," Aunt Tillie replied, her gaze focused in front of her so she didn't accidentally stumble. "You decided to teach me a lesson and hide. It backfired a bit."

"I was gone a long time, though," I prodded. "You must've panicked at some point. I mean … you told my mother. On any other day you would've bribed me and lied about it. Sure, you said you tried to bribe me after to smooth things over, but you had to be worried."

"I was worried enough to tell the truth," Aunt Tillie admitted. "Is that what you want to hear?"

"I … don't know. I want to hear the truth."

"The truth is I was going to let you stew out there until you'd had enough and walked home on your own," Aunt Tillie said. "You've always had a stubborn streak. It's annoying."

"People say I get that from you."

"That's why it's annoying." Aunt Tillie flashed a smile. "You always fight the most with the one you see in the mirror."

I couldn't be sure, but that sounded like an insult. "I don't look anything like you. Clove is the one who resembles you."

"I heard that," Clove barked.

"You should be so lucky to look like me," Aunt Tillie shot back. "I'm so awesome to look at I could be a model ... and not one of those fake ones on *America's Next Top Model* either. I could be a real one."

"Yes. You could do it professionally," I drawled. "If you wanted to leave me in the woods, how did you end up looking for me?"

"Your mother noticed you were gone," Aunt Tillie answered. "I overestimated her attachment to you, and it backfired on me."

I furrowed my brow, confused. "You overestimated her attachment to me? She's my mother. Of course she's attached."

"I love your mother, but let's not lose our heads about her capacity for thinking," Aunt Tillie said. "She's screwy. She loses track of time and people. Quite frankly, I'm surprised she didn't lose you ten times when you were a kid. You were generally too smart to get lost, so you saved yourself there."

"So ... what? Did she notice I was gone and you had to 'fess up or something?"

Aunt Tillie nodded. "That's pretty much what happened. She pitched a fit. I found you. You cried. You whined. You threatened to make me pay. It was a normal day in the Winchester household."

"Did I ever make you pay?"

Aunt Tillie grinned despite the serious situation. "I believe there was an incident with some shaving cream, a whoopee cushion and some chocolate sprinkles."

I shook my head. "I have no memory of this."

"That's probably because I planted a suggestion for you to forget it," Aunt Tillie supplied. "You spent three days trying to pay me back and got more and more daring with each attempt."

"So you modified my memory?" I was horrified.

"You know that's not possible," Aunt Tillie chided. "I merely planted a hypnotic suggestion that you forget the trauma. I gave you caramel apples – your favorite – to anchor it. Within twenty-four hours you were back to yourself. After that, when you threatened retribution it was for normal stuff."

"But ... that's not fair," I protested. "You messed with my head."

Aunt Tillie didn't look perturbed by the charge. "Uh-huh. And what happened to that teacher who caught you skipping school when you were fourteen and threatened to call your mother?"

My cheeks colored as her weighted gaze landed on me. "I ... how did you know about that?" I remembered the incident well. My middle school math teacher caught me screwing around on smoker's corner and threatened to call my mother. Rather than deal with it, I did the same thing Aunt Tillie did: I used a bit of magic to suggest my teacher forget where she saw me. In truth, memory spells are frowned upon. In practice, I might've cast one or two over my tempestuous teenage years. Never for big things, mind you, but I was a master at getting out of little things for a time.

"Because I'm not an idiot and you had a guilty conscience for days," Aunt Tillie replied. "I thought it was kind of funny. For the record, I removed the suggestion and then told your teacher we already knew."

I stilled. "You lied for me and kept me from getting punished? That sounds nothing like you."

"The guilt was punishment enough," Aunt Tillie countered. "That's your biggest fault. It's not the mouth or the snarky attitude – although those give me constant headaches. The guilt is another thing. You take too much on your shoulders occasionally. It's not healthy."

"But this was my fault," I reminded her. "I was supposed to be watching Annie. I failed Belinda."

"You can't watch one person every moment of every day," Aunt Tillie argued. "Annie made the first mistake, and we need to be clear on that when we talk to her. Once she's settled, she needs to see that she did wrong, but that she wasn't taken as a form of punishment.

"This woman – this devil who is going to wish she never met me – she did wrong," she continued. "She's the one who needs to pay."

"No killing," Landon called out. I hadn't even realized he was listening to the conversation.

"I'm not a murderer," Aunt Tillie barked.

"I'm just reminding you of your promise," Landon said, inclining his chin toward the sphere. "It's moving east."

"Then let's follow," I said. "It's cold, and I want to get this over with."

"I'm pretty sure that can be said for all of us," Aunt Tillie said. "We're almost there. I can feel it."

"**WHAT IN** THE ... ?"

Landon extended his hand as we crested a hill, instinctively pushing Bay behind him as a small house popped into view. I was expecting a shack, to be honest. The way Annie described it made me think of a small hunting lodge or something equally tiny and decrepit. The dwelling in front of us wasn't overly large but it certainly wasn't a shack. That didn't mean it looked like a nice place to live.

"What a hole," Aunt Tillie muttered, narrowing her eyes as she stepped to the right and glanced around the side of the house.

"It looks as if the roof is caving in," Clove noted. "It hasn't been painted in years. The front porch is sagging. Look, there's a driveway. How could someone have a driveway out here when there are no roads?"

I followed Clove's finger with my eyes, the sound of rushing water helping things slide into place. "This is the Black River," I said. "There is a road out here. What's it called again? Kettledrum Road, right? It's dirt and you can barely get up and down it in the winter. I don't think they bother clearing it after it snows any longer."

"How can someone live out here if they don't clear the road in the winter?" Clove asked. "We get, like, eighty feet of snow every year."

"We get closer to twelve feet of snow," Aunt Tillie corrected. "You're always such an exaggerator."

Clove crossed her arms over her chest, miffed. "That's not true. I'm an honest person."

"Yes, but you exaggerate," Aunt Tillie said. "You can't seem to help yourself. It's in your nature … and it's not a lie to you because you convince yourself it's the truth."

Clove narrowed her eyes. "You take that back. It's not true."

"Listen, kvetch, I don't have time to deal with your issues," Aunt Tillie said, brushing past Clove and focusing on the house. "We have a kidnapper on the premises, and Thistle's guilt is almost enough to eat me alive. We'll deal with your issues next week."

Clove's mouth dropped open as she turned to me. "Can you believe she said that to me?"

"She's not wrong," I shot back.

"She's really not," Bay added. "Focus on the house, Clove. We'll talk about your kvetch tendencies later."

"You're all on my list," Clove snapped, extending a finger. "Live in fear."

Aunt Tillie chuckled and patted Clove's wrist. "Thanks for that. I needed a good laugh."

"I'm serious."

"That's what makes it even funnier," Aunt Tillie said. "So, copper, how do you want to handle this? I was thinking you could go around the back and I'll kick in the front door and scare her in your direction."

Landon's expression was incredulous. "You didn't really expect me to agree to that plan, did you?"

"It's a totally good plan," Aunt Tillie complained. "I've got great hostage negotiation skills. I could do it professionally."

Landon made a disgusted face. "What hostage?"

"Oh, you're absolutely no fun," Aunt Tillie complained. "Tell me, oh wise one, what's the best way to deal with this?"

"Well, I was thinking that I could go up to the door and knock," Landon said, adopting a patronizing tone. "I know that's a little wacky and outside of the box, but I think it might work."

"Ugh. You're so boring." Aunt Tillie made a face that would've been comical under different circumstances. "You cannot be on my team when the zombie apocalypse hits. You're too much of a rule follower to survive."

Landon scowled. "I would rock the crap out of the zombie apocalypse. I would be Daryl Dixon."

"Oh, I'm Daryl," Aunt Tillie said. "You can be … Eugene."

"Eugene?" Landon was affronted. "I'm nothing like Eugene."

"You have the same haircut."

Landon crossed his arms over his chest and locked gazes with Bay. "I do not have a mullet. Tell her I don't have a mullet."

"I love your hair." Bay took on a placating tone as she patted his forearm and glanced at me. "I'm thinking you and I should go to the door and handle initial introductions."

"I think that's a good idea," I said, pretending I didn't notice the furious look on Aunt Tillie's face. "We're the calmest ones here."

"What about me?" Clove whined.

"You have to babysit Landon and Aunt Tillie," Bay said, skirting Landon's hand when he playfully attempted to swat her rear end. "Someone needs to make sure they don't eat too much sugar or pull each other's hair or something."

"Ha, ha," Landon huffed, shaking his head. "You're not going up there alone. I'm the FBI agent. I'll knock on the door."

"You do that," Aunt Tillie agreed. "While you're attacking from the front, I'll handle the back. She won't get away from me."

"I just said … ." Landon was close to losing his temper but he didn't get a chance to lay down the law because the front door of the cabin popped open. Everyone shifted their eyes to the front porch – to the woman standing on it with a blank look on her face – and my heart fell to my stomach when I recognized her.

"Is that the woman from the store?" Clove asked, confused.

I nodded, grim. "That's her. Cripes. I should've realized it was her. I forgot all about her visit. I … we knew she was off and just let her go."

"You know her?" Landon asked curiously, keeping one eye on the woman and the other on Thistle. "How?"

"She stopped in at the store before Annie went missing," I explained. "She was ... out of her mind. She kept asking for juice. I called Chief Terry and told him she was acting strange and headed toward the market, but then I forgot all about her."

"I'm guessing Terry did, too," Landon said, rubbing his chin. "Well, I don't suppose anyone knows who she is?"

Clove and I shook our heads in unison while Bay merely looked contemplative. Aunt Tillie, on the other hand, took a bold step forward.

"Don't kill her," Landon warned.

Aunt Tillie ignored him. "Are you Sandra Bates?"

The woman's eyes flashed when they landed on Aunt Tillie, a brief moment of recognition flaring before the dullness of confusion settled over her vacant eyes. "I don't know you," she barked out. "I don't know you and I won't fall for the Devil's tricks. Begone, demons!"

Aunt Tillie pursed her lips as she narrowed her eyes. Landon warily watched her for a moment, waiting until he was sure she wouldn't attack before moving closer. "Mrs. Bates, my name is Landon Michaels. I'm with the FBI. I have a few questions to ask you about a little girl who went missing yesterday. Do you happen to know something about that?"

Sandra perked up. "Abigail? Did you find Abigail?"

Landon was understandably confused. "Her name is Annie Martin. She says a woman grabbed her behind the Main Street stores yesterday afternoon, took her to a house, and then held her until she had no choice but to flee without shoes. We found her in the woods last night."

Sandra's eyes flashed wild. "You found Abigail? Where is she?" The woman hurried down the steps, almost tripping over her long skirt as she closed the distance and stood in front of Landon. "I want Abigail right now!"

Landon remained calm despite Sandra's potential meltdown. He never moved his eyes from her face. I took the opportunity to study the woman up close, my stomach twisting when I recognized the disheveled state of her clothing. She was in a terrible position and apparently she didn't even know it because her mind was gone.

"We need to do something for her," Clove said, her voice low. "She clearly needs help."

"We'll do something," Landon said, although his expression was conflicted. "I think I need to call for an adult social worker. I haven't been inside of the house, but if it's anything like the outside, this place isn't fit for a human being to reside in."

"You can't take me from my home." Sandra lashed out, catching Landon's cheek with the palm of her hand as she smacked him. "Where is Abigail? You took her. I know you did!"

Landon didn't react out of anger. Instead he remained calm – incredibly so – and carefully locked his fingers around Sandra's wrists as he kept her stationary in front of him. "Ma'am, we're here to help. I promise we won't leave without helping you. I cannot allow you to strike me again, though. I need you to remain calm."

"I'll call Chief Terry," Bay suggested.

"That's a good idea," Landon said. "We'll need help … and then someone is probably going to have to come out here and condemn this place."

"Wait a second," Aunt Tillie interjected, catching me off guard. "I think we need to have a talk about that before we do anything."

"And why is that?" Landon asked, confused.

"Because I know her," Aunt Tillie replied. "There's more to this story and … well … it's a sad story."

"Does that mean you don't want bloody vengeance any longer?" I asked.

"It means that maybe no one is to blame this go-around," Aunt Tillie answered. "Sometimes things just happen."

"Oh, well, I can't wait to hear this," Landon muttered.

"That makes two of us," I said. "Talk, old lady. What do you know?"

TEN

"Her name is Sandra Bates," Aunt Tillie started. "She went to school with your mothers. I believe she was in the same year with Twila, but I could be wrong about that. She was in there somewhere, though."

"I don't ever remember seeing her before," Bay said. "I had no idea this house was even out here."

"That's because the Black River is slow-moving and mucky," I offered. "There was no reason to swim out here, so there was no reason to visit this area. We did all of our partying at the Hollow Creek and the woods surrounding the house."

"I wasn't sure she was still in the area," Aunt Tillie admitted. "She was ... troubled ... for a long time."

"I'll need more than that," Landon prodded. "What does 'troubled' mean? Is she dangerous?"

"Only to herself," Aunt Tillie said, the sympathetic expression on her face knocking me for a loop as she moved closer and studied Sandra's wrists. A number of long scratches marred the white skin, and they were etched over long-healed scars that ran along the veins vertically. I knew exactly what that meant. "That's why I thought she was out of town. She was in an adult living center in Bellaire for years.

"Her mother died about five years ago," she continued. "She was locked up because she was a danger to herself for a time. I'm wondering if the funding ran out once the money passed on with her mother, so perhaps they just cut her loose."

"Was this ever her home?" Landon asked.

"It was." Aunt Tillie bobbed her head. "Her mother lived here until her death. She was something of a shut-in. She had some crazy tendencies."

"No offense, but just a few weeks ago I saw you wandering into the forest with a chainsaw and a whistle," Landon reminded her. "You'll have to do better than that."

Aunt Tillie rolled her eyes. "Sandra Bates was an only child. Her father, Luther, was a nice man, but he died when she was about three or so. Her mother, Madison, was one of those conspiracy theory nuts."

"You once told me that the police were out to create a slave nation and use senior citizens to do it," Bay reminded her.

"That's a real thing," Aunt Tillie challenged. "Do you want to hear the whole story or not?"

Landon nodded. "We do."

I risked a glance at Sandra and found her staring at Aunt Tillie with wide eyes. I had no idea if she understood what we were saying, but she was fixated on my great-aunt.

"Sandra always went straight to school and came straight home when she was a kid," Aunt Tillie supplied. "Her mother never allowed her do to anything. I always felt bad for her. Because she was overprotected, she did what a lot of lost young women do and married the first man who showed her any attention.

"He was a total deadbeat," she continued. "His name was Chris Jamison and he had a huge rap sheet by the time he was twenty. He married Sandra, knocked her up, and took off."

"I'm guessing that would be Abigail," Landon mused.

"Abigail." Sandra almost sounded piteous when she said the name.

"Because this place is so far removed from society and had no running water, someone reported Sandra's living conditions to the state and said the house wasn't fit for habitation," Aunt Tillie explained. "The state came in and took Abigail. I guess Sandra never got her back."

"That's sad," I said, my stomach clenching. "That doesn't explain why she took Annie."

"It doesn't," Aunt Tillie agreed. "But this is an isolated life. She hasn't had company for a long time and she obviously has no regular visitors to alleviate the loneliness. The loss of Abigail must've hurt her beyond reason."

Landon cautiously released Sandra's arms and kept his eyes on her as he reached for his phone. "We can arrange for an adult social worker. I'm not sure she can stay out here."

"Wait." Aunt Tillie stilled Landon with a hand on his arm and glanced at me. "We might be able to do something."

Landon's eyebrows rose. "What?"

"Just a little something," Aunt Tillie hedged. "That won't fix the issues with the house, though. We'll need more help for that."

"We have help," I said. "We have Marcus, Landon, Sam, Chief Terry ... all of us. We have help. We can fix this place up if you can handle the rest."

"I don't understand what's happening," Landon said. "Are you telling me you can cast a spell to solve mental illness?"

"No, and I would never suggest anything of the sort," Aunt Tillie replied. "I'm saying that we can ease the loneliness and see if it helps. It's not a forever fix – and she might need regular medication when it's all said and done – but now that we know she's out here ... ."

"Okay, I'm willing to try it," Landon said. "But if it doesn't work we have to call for professional help."

"I can live with that."

Landon knit his eyebrows. "Why are you being so easy to deal with ... especially after what happened with Annie?"

"Because I think suffering from loneliness is probably the worst thing in the world," Aunt Tillie replied, not missing a beat. "I may get agitated with the witchy wonders – all six of them – but I'm never lonely. Imagine living out here for years with no one to talk to."

Landon opened his mouth to argue and then snapped it shut. "Do your best. If you fix this, I'll give you free rein on whatever illegal operation you're running this week."

Aunt Tillie snorted. "Like I need a free rein. I have you running in circles when it comes to my side businesses."

"Perhaps that's merely what I want you to think," Landon suggested.

Aunt Tillie made a derisive sound in the back of her throat. "Keep telling yourself that." She turned a set of kind eyes to Sandra. "I think we should take a walk. I have a story I want to tell you."

"Is it about Abigail?" Sandra looked hopeful.

"It's about reclaiming your life," Aunt Tillie replied. "I wouldn't rule out a visit from Abigail one day, though. Come with me."

I watched Aunt Tillie go, a mixture of love and respect welling inside of me. "She never ceases to amaze."

"That's her gift," Landon said. "Come on. While she's doing that, let's start making a list of things to do around the house. We've got a lot to fix here."

"Let's do it."

TWO DAYS later Sandra seemed a different person, although she was still skittish around big groups of people. The men did their best to give her a wide berth as they finished renovations on the house.

She had a new roof, new carpet, fresh paint and a promise to fix the sagging front porch as soon as the weather allowed. The plumbing was in the process of being updated – as was the electrical system – and Chief Terry worked it out with a local church group to bring Sandra regular deliveries so she wouldn't be left alone for long stretches. She also had a standing invitation to dinners at The Overlook, although she didn't appear keen on being surrounded by that many people at one time.

There was only one thing left to do.

"I don't want to see her." Annie stubbornly jutted out her lower lip as she held Marcus' hand and followed him toward the house. We'd explained what happened – and why Sandra wasn't ultimately a bad person – but Annie refused to believe it. She'd gotten most of her feisty nature back and was now milking her ordeal for all it was worth. That essentially meant a never-ending stream of desserts every night. Belinda returned the following day, and I figured it was time to put Annie in a difficult position – whether she wanted to be in one or not.

"She's a nice woman," Marcus said. "She was lonely and made a mistake."

"She was confused," I added. "You've been confused before. You know how that is. Do you think that should be held against you forever?"

"But she kidnapped me," Annie protested. "It's her fault I was lost in the woods and almost died."

"Oh, geez." Aunt Tillie made a face as she sauntered past. She had a large houseplant in her hands. The day was cold but not oppressively so, and even though fall was officially here the sun shone brightly as the red leaves tumbled from the trees. "You've been hanging out with Clove too much. You didn't almost die."

"I did so," Annie fired back, annoyed. "I heard you talking. My feet could've fallen off if you didn't warm them up with magic."

Aunt Tillie arched an eyebrow, Annie's tone clearly grating. "I warmed your feet because they were cold. You were hardly in danger of losing them."

"That's not how it felt."

"Listen, junior mouth, you're being a kvetch. It's not an attractive quality."

Annie narrowed her eyes. She was used to Annie Tillie taking her side no matter what. "But ... ."

"No." Aunt Tillie cut off whatever argument Annie was about to muster with a firm shake of her head. "Sandra had a lot of bad things happen to her over the years. She was sad and confused. She took you because she thought you were someone else. She didn't hurt you."

"My feet froze!" Annie's voice bordered on shrill. "She's bad."

"You're the one who wandered out of the store," I reminded her, keeping my voice gentle and low. "You're not to blame for any of this, but you shouldn't have done that. Sandra couldn't have taken you if you'd stayed with us."

Annie looked positively mutinous as she glared at me. "How can it not be my fault if you're saying it's my fault?"

I shrugged. "Life is full of conundrums."

"I don't know what that means." Annie let loose with a growl as Landon grew closer. "Landon agrees with me, don't you?"

Landon stilled. "About what?"

"That this lady is bad and we shouldn't be helping her."

"Actually I don't agree with that," Landon argued. "I think she's misunderstood and made a mistake. I don't think she's bad. I think she deserves a second chance. You've had a few second chances, haven't you?"

"I'm not bad."

Landon poked her stomach, but Annie refused to smile despite his best efforts. "No one thinks you're bad. You've done some naughty things, though."

"It's okay to be naughty," Aunt Tillie offered. "That's how I live my life ... on the naughty list."

"Don't tell her that," I ordered, shaking my head. "You'll give her bad ideas."

"She already has bad ideas," Aunt Tillie said. "Annie, you need to suck it up and be brave. I know you had a really rough day when all of this went down, but we fixed it. It won't happen again."

Annie didn't look convinced. "How do you know that? Did she promise to never take me again?"

"She doesn't remember taking you in the first place," I replied. "She was confused. I told you that already. Aunt Tillie did a little thing so she's not confused any longer."

"She did?" Annie was intrigued. "Like ... a spell?"

Aunt Tillie shook her head. "You can't mess with someone's memories with a spell," she clarified. "That's not good. You can, however, give a person in pain a suggestion here or there to clear the way to getting better."

"I don't know what that means." Annie was frustrated. "I don't want to be taken again."

"You won't be," Aunt Tillie said. "You're safe. You were safe that night because I was going to find you no matter what."

"She's right," Marcus said, squeezing Annie's hand. "We'll always come looking for you. You're part of our family. You never give up when you have a family."

"So are you saying that when I'm eighteen and legal you'll come for me and dump Thistle?"

Annie's question took me by surprise and Marcus barked out a laugh before he thought better of it. Even Aunt Tillie looked amused.

"You need to find your own man," I said, extending a finger in mock warning. "Marcus is mine."

"He's mine," Annie corrected. "He just doesn't know it yet. I'm going to woo him as soon as I'm old enough."

"Woo?" I cocked my neck and stared at her. "Who taught you that word?"

"Aunt Tillie." Annie pointed for emphasis. "She told me Landon is wooing Bay, and a lot of the time it's a big woo-woo time because he's so sappy."

"Thanks for that," Landon said dryly.

"You're welcome," Aunt Tillie said, smiling.

"They are sappy," I agreed. "They're family, though. You're family. We're family. Sandra is now kind of an extended arm of the family."

"But she won't kidnap me, right?" Annie was adamant that someone promise her that, so I did.

"No one will take you," I said. "We'll fight whoever tries."

"And we'll win," Aunt Tillie added. "You know I don't like losing, so that won't be a problem."

Annie heaved a sigh, resigned. "Fine. I'll be nice."

"That's good," I said, lifting my head when I heard a car door slam and glancing toward the unfamiliar vehicle at the end of the rutted driveway. The blonde who got out appeared uncertain. "Who is that?"

"That is Abigail Prescott," Landon replied, smiling. "I found her through court records. She was raised three towns over and was legally adopted by a wonderful family when she was eight. She remembered her mother, though, and she's keen on seeing her."

"You found her?" Aunt Tillie looked impressed. "That was nice of you."

"I'm a nice guy."

"You're 'The Man,' but you're not too bad," Aunt Tillie said, her eyes lighting up when Sandra appeared on the porch and stared at the woman. "She recognizes her."

"She does," Landon agreed. "I'm going to facilitate a nice meeting between them. Does anyone want to come?" His gaze was pointed when it landed on Annie.

"As long as no one kidnaps me, I'll come," Annie said, gripping Marcus' hand tighter. "I need my boyfriend with me."

"Oh, you're laying it on a little too thick," I teased, amused.

"He's a good boyfriend," Annie said. "I can't bear to part with him."

I shook my head. "Where did you hear that phrase?"

"That's what Aunt Tillie said to her bottle of wine last night," Annie answered. "She said he was a good bottle of wine and she couldn't bear to part with him."

Aunt Tillie averted her gaze and found something interesting to stare at on the other side of the house. "I'm sure I didn't say that."

"We all need to pay more attention to the things we say," Landon said, shaking his head. "Come on, Annie. I'll be your boyfriend today, too."

"You can't be my boyfriend," Annie said, although she took his hand. "You're only supposed to have one boyfriend. Besides, Bay would cry if you left her."

I was pretty sure I should be offended. "What about me? Wouldn't I cry if Marcus left me?"

Annie's grin was impish. "All's fair in love and war. Besides, Marcus is too nice for you, and he's going to wise up to your fresh mouth eventually."

"Who told you that?"

"Who do you think?" Landon asked, chuckling when Aunt Tillie scampered toward the house.

"You'd better run, old lady," I called out. "I'll be coming after you before the end of the day."

Aunt Tillie didn't look perturbed in the least. "I look forward to it. I'll see you on the battlefield."

"And may the best witch win," Annie said, giggling. "I have a feeling I know who that's going to be."

Aunt Tillie beamed. "That's because I've trained you well."

LANDON CALLING

A WICKED WITCHES OF THE MIDWEST SHORT

ONE

"Michaels, what are you still doing here?"

I jerked my head up, shaking off the remnants of a daydream, and fixed my boss Steve Newton with a friendly smile. "I wasn't doing anything," I hedged. "I was just ... running through a mental to-do list and you caught me."

That wasn't a lie. It wasn't exactly the truth, either.

"Uh-huh." Steve didn't look convinced as he perched on the edge of my desk. "Were you thinking about your girlfriend? You can tell me. I think it's cute."

I scowled, drawing my eyebrows together and shaking my head as I leaned back in my desk chair. Even though I fought the urge, I couldn't stop my eyes from flicking to the photo on my desk. It featured my favorite blonde – Bay Winchester, her big smile and mischievous eyes staring back at me, causing my lips to curve – and was a particular favorite of mine. I was in the photograph, too, of course. I stand next to her, my arm slung over her shoulders, and I stare at her profile. She's the focal point of the photo, and now my life. I have no problem admitting that to myself. On the flip side, when other people make fun of me it still grates a bit.

My name is Landon Michaels and I'm an FBI agent. I work out of the Traverse City office in northern Lower Michigan, and while I originally thought I would use my position as a stepping-stone to bigger cities, that's no longer the case. I've found I'm happy here and happy with my blonde. Hell, I'm even happy with the work I do. I'm not sure how it happened, but I'm content. I know. It boggles the mind.

"I was not thinking about my girlfriend," I lied, averting my gaze. It wasn't a complete lie. I'd been thinking about my girlfriend's family – which isn't nearly as weird as you might think – so I didn't feel bad denying my boss's charge. "I don't care what you think, I'm not whipped."

"I don't believe I used that word." Steve's lips twitched. "But now that you mention it, how are the arrangements going for your big move?"

A few weeks ago, after a particularly tough undercover assignment that resulted in Bay being considered a murder suspect, I pulled the trigger and demanded my boss allow me to move to Hemlock Cove. I'd been toying with the possibility for months, trying to figure a smooth way to broach the subject with Steve that wouldn't make me look like a wimp. But the time spent away from Bay turned out to be too much. I didn't want to leave my job, but I needed to be close to her. Steve ultimately agreed that there was no reason I couldn't live in Hemlock Cove – which is only forty-five minutes from Traverse City – while keeping up my duties at the regional office. I was officially a few weeks from giving up my Traverse City apartment and moving to Hemlock Cove. I couldn't wait … although I had no intention of admitting that to Steve.

"Pretty well," I replied. "Thistle is moving in with Marcus as soon as the construction on his stable is completed. We'll all be living with each other for a month or two – which will be a nightmare – but once she's out, Bay and I will have the guesthouse to ourselves."

Steve pursed his lips, amused. "Doesn't it bother you that you'll be living on your girlfriend's family's property?"

"Should it?"

Steve shrugged and held his hands palms up. "It would bother me.

From what you've told me, the big house is full of busybodies. What if they ... I don't know ... barge into the guesthouse and see you naked?"

It was an interesting question, one I'd considered myself. "They do happen to barge in quite often," I conceded. "I can live with it. They generally only do it when they're feeling persnickety."

"The way you describe it, that's pretty regularly."

"I'm fine with it," I said, rolling my neck. That was mostly true. The older generation of Winchesters could be a righteous pain, but I was willing to put up with almost anything as long as I could share a roof with Bay. "You're staying at the inn this weekend. You'll see that they don't have enough time to focus on the guesthouse. They've got plenty of things to keep them busy when it comes to The Overlook."

Steve snorted, amused. "Yeah. Why did they name it that again?"

The Overlook was the inn Bay's mother and aunts operated in Hemlock Cove, which happened to boast a huge tourist population. This coming week, the town would also be full of law enforcement officials for a big conference. Everyone wanted an environment that wasn't too large so we could run a murder-mystery scenario and test a few new gadgets. Hemlock Cove fit the bill, full of inns and good restaurants. Plus, it would keep me close to Bay for days, so I was more than happy to steer the selection committee in that direction when the opportunity arose.

Fine. I'm whipped. I can admit it ... to myself, at least.

"The original property has a big bluff, and the house overlooks it," I answered automatically. I'd heard Bay tell the story so many times I'd lost count. "Bay and her cousins tried explaining about *The Shining*, but it didn't change anything. It's kind of funny, but the tourists seem to love it because they believe they named it that on purpose. Most people forget about the name as soon as they sit down and sample the food."

"The food is amazing," Steve agreed, moving away from my desk. "I'm looking forward to dinner there tonight."

I swallowed hard, surprised. "Tonight? I thought you weren't arriving until tomorrow."

Steve's amusement was obvious as he met my conflicted gaze. "Do you have a problem with me arriving tonight?"

Yes! I have a big problem with it. Of course, I can't admit that. He's my boss, after all. He's also allowing me to break a rule and move in with my girlfriend, so I can't exactly make my disdain regarding his plan known. "No problem," I replied, hoping I sounded blasé enough. "It's just ... I'm not sure I'll be at the inn for dinner tonight. Bay might've made alternative plans."

In truth, Bay probably didn't make alternative plans. We always ate dinner with her family when it was possible because they are amazing cooks. And Bay harbors a lazy streak when it comes to domestic tasks. I'm fine with that, because most days I prefer her attention on me and my needs instead of cooking. Wait ... did that sound sexist? That won't go over well out loud, so I'd better watch myself.

"You don't have to worry about entertaining me," Steve said, chuckling. "The place is going to be full of agents and cops. I'm looking forward to meeting new people and eating some of that wonderful food. I don't expect you to act as my tour guide."

"You don't?" I couldn't help but be dubious. "Good, because I have other plans."

"I'll bet those plans are blonde." Steve shook his head as he smirked. "I don't care how much time you spend with Bay. Go nuts. You still have to put in appearances at all of the classes. You know that, right?"

"I do know that." I had to put in appearances. That didn't mean I needed to stay for the duration of each class – or even half the duration – before making my escape. I'd already worked it out in my head. "I won't let you down."

"Oh, you're such a lovesick puppy," Steve taunted, grinning. "If I catch you making out with your girlfriend I'll embarrass you mercilessly."

Somehow I figured I could live with that. "I'll see you at the inn later. I have a few things to finish up here, and then I have to roll over to the apartment and grab a few boxes. I've been moving things in shifts."

"The next few days should be fun," Steve said. "I can't wait to see what those feisty women cook up while I'm there."

I kept my smile in place even as my stomach rolled. Feisty is one way of describing them. Batshit crazy is another. "Be careful what you wish for," I intoned. "You might be surprised what those women can cook up with minimal effort and one crazy great-aunt to fuel them."

"I'm looking forward to it."

Surprisingly enough, so was I.

I EXPECTED LOUD VOICES, even some shouting, when I let myself into the guesthouse two hours later. Instead I found Bay napping on the couch, a blanket tucked around her waist.

Sometimes she looks like an angel. Only when she's sleeping, though. She has a devilish streak. Thankfully it's nowhere near as pronounced as the ones her family members have. I carried the boxes I brought into her bedroom and stacked them against the wall before returning to the living room. I found Marcus standing by the kitchen counter.

In addition to being Thistle's boyfriend, Marcus owns the local stable. He's a calm guy – he would have to be to put up with Thistle's mouth – and I enjoy his company. Bay is so close with her cousins Clove and Thistle that it borders on codependency, something else I've learned never to mention. I've gotten used to it in the time Bay and I have spent together, but it's still something of a distraction if I'm having a bad day. I was in a good mood, so the Winchester women and the havoc they wreaked when feeling codependent was a far-off worry … for now.

"When did you get here?" Marcus asked, keeping his voice low as he poured a glass of juice from the refrigerator. "I didn't hear you arrive."

"Just got here," I replied, glancing back to the couch and making sure Bay was undisturbed. "I was going to wake her, but there's no reason to just yet."

"Yeah, she's had a long day."

The way Marcus said the words piqued my suspicion. "What do you mean? Did something happen? Please tell me there are no ghosts or evil spirits running around. That won't fly with a bunch of cops here the next few days."

Hemlock Cove had rebranded itself as a paranormal destination several years ago to draw in tourists. Most of the town's residents are normal people pretending to be witches, warlocks and whatever other freaky thing they can think of that might draw in paranormal enthusiasts. The Winchesters, however, are real witches. They have magical powers and curse one another when the mood strikes. Everyone involved in their world works overtime to protect them. So when Steve initially suggested holding the conference in Hemlock Cove I fought him. Once I resigned myself to it, I recognized the multitude of possibilities the situation presented. I remained mildly nervous, but enthusiastically embraced the selection committee members' questions when they started asking about Hemlock Cove attractions.

"No ghosts that I'm aware of," Marcus replied, tucking a strand of his shoulder-length blond hair behind his ear. "It's been a quiet couple of days."

"Good." I shifted my eyes to Bay. She looked peaceful. "Why did she have a long day?"

"Aunt Tillie."

Ah. I should've seen that coming. Tillie Winchester is the matriarch of the Winchester clan. She's in her eighties and calling her "tempestuous" would be a generous way to describe her. There's no problem she's not in the middle of and no family fight she doesn't enjoy stirring up. "What'd she do now?"

"Just being herself," Marcus shrugged. "It's November and the temperature is dropping, so she can't spend a lot of time outdoors. That means she's indoors constantly, and … well … you know how that goes."

"She's driving everyone crazy," I surmised, nodding. "That's hardly out of character."

"Definitely not," Marcus agreed. "She's so bored she's taken it upon herself to 'help' Clove and Thistle at the shop." He used air quotes around the word "help" and grimaced. "It's driving Thistle insane."

I couldn't help but smile at the mental image. Clove and Thistle own a magic shop on Main Street. Bay works as the editor (and newly christened owner) of Hemlock Cove's weekly newspaper, The Whistler. It's a small town, so there was a lot of overlap when it comes to articles and retail work, so Bay often volunteers to help her cousins during busy periods. "What does that have to do with Bay?"

"Thistle got fed up and suggested Aunt Tillie help Bay with this week's edition of The Whistler," Marcus explained. "I don't think it went over very well."

I cringed as I considered the possibilities. "I'm guessing not," I said. "Did Bay get the paper out?"

"She did, but there was some fighting at Hypnotic afterward," Marcus replied.

I arched an eyebrow, surprised. "Bay and Aunt Tillie?"

"There's no sense fighting with Aunt Tillie, because she always wins," Marcus said matter of factly. "It was Bay and Thistle. Bay accused Thistle of sending Aunt Tillie after her. Thistle denied it, even though it was obvious to everyone she did. There were some threats regarding dirt and making people eat it. They went outside to get dirt, but the ground is too hard to scoop up without ruining fingernails. You know, normal stuff."

I barked out a low laugh, frowning when Bay shifted. She was waking up. I had hoped she'd rest a bit longer before dinner. I had big plans for her after, and she'd need her strength.

"Sounds like a normal day," I said, glancing around. "Where's Thistle?"

"Napping in the bedroom," Marcus answered. "Actually, she's not napping. She's complaining about Bay accusing her of things she didn't do – which she did do and won't admit to. And her mouth is dry. I said I'd get her some juice."

I grinned. I couldn't help myself. "You're a good boyfriend."

"They'll be fine once they make up," Marcus said, waving off my compliment. "I think the idea of everyone's living arrangements changing is causing a little fur to fly."

"I thought everyone was excited about the changes?" I'm not insecure, but I've noticed the occasional worried look on Bay's face since we decided to move in together. It makes me nervous. "I thought we agreed this was best for everyone."

"It's not that." Marcus' gaze was keen, as if reading my mind. "Bay is massively excited about you moving in. Yesterday I heard her wondering if you might want to change around the living room. She sounded a little giddy when she thought about redecorating from scratch. She's excited."

I felt marginally better. "So what's the problem?"

"The distance from one another. They've always been together, except for when Bay lived down in the city. I get the feeling that wasn't a good time in any of their lives. She's looking forward to living with you, but I think she'll miss Thistle."

"C'mon, they fight like crazy," I said, pointing out the obvious.

"They also love like crazy," Marcus reminded me. "It'll be okay. We'll have a short adjustment period, but look how fast they got used to Clove's absence. Bay will have her hands full decorating here with you, and Thistle will have her hands full decorating the barn house with me. It'll be fine."

"You're pretty calm considering everything going on," I noted. "You don't seem nervous at all."

"I'm nervous," Marcus countered. "The excitement outweighs it, though. I want to plan my future with Thistle, and this is the first step. On the other hand, Bay and Clove are important to her. It's a good thing they're not going anywhere."

"It is," I mused, watching as Bay's fingers twitched. "I like knowing they're all there for each other. Even though I'll be living here, that doesn't mean I won't be out of town from time to time. I like knowing she won't ever be alone."

"None of them will ever be alone," Marcus pointed out. "The family is growing."

"The family." It was weird to say the word, yet I realized that I'd considered the Winchesters – even Aunt Tillie – my family for some time. Moving in with Bay wouldn't change that. "That's a nice way of looking at it."

Marcus smiled as he clapped my shoulder. "I'm going to cajole Thistle out of her bad mood. You might try to do the same with Bay."

"That's my plan."

Marcus snorted. "Are you going to do it with kisses?"

"Whatever it takes."

"We'll give you a few minutes alone before coming out," Marcus offered. "Then we need to head up to the inn. I think they have a big dinner planned."

"Sounds like a good idea. I'll see you in ten minutes or so."

"Good luck with your blonde."

"Good luck with your … what color is Thistle's hair today?"

Marcus grinned. "Blue. She was agitated with her mother, and Twila hates it when she dyes her hair blue."

"Ah, the trials of the Winchester women," I intoned, my heart filling as Bay lifted her head. "They're difficult, but I wouldn't trade them for anything."

"I'm right there with you."

TWO

The walk to the inn seemed longer thanks to the cold, but I was grateful for it because Bay takes a while to become cognizant after waking. She sleeps hard – sometimes snoring loud enough to wake the dead, which is frightening considering the fact that she can see and talk to ghosts. I generally find her waking period enjoyable because I can talk her into almost anything thanks to a muddled mind and a lack of patience. Because dinner is served promptly at seven, however, I couldn't waste time letting her wake naturally.

"You look grumpy," I said, capturing her hand and squeezing it. "I heard you had a rough day."

Bay shot a dark look over her shoulder, glaring at Thistle as her cousin and Marcus trailed us. "I'm sure you heard her side of things."

"I heard what happened," I clarified. "I know that she sent Aunt Tillie to help you put out this week's edition and things got ugly. I'm sorry for that, but … it's done. There's no need to dwell on it."

"I did not send Aunt Tillie to The Whistler," Thistle countered. "Why would I do that?"

"I heard it's because Aunt Tillie has been helping you around

Hypnotic," I replied. "I'm guessing that wasn't easy and you needed a break. I think anyone would've done what you did."

Bay was affronted. "Hey!"

I held up a finger to quiet her. "Most people would admit they did it, though," I added, my gaze pointed as I pinned Thistle with a hard look. On most days I don't mind her company, but there are moments when I have to fight the overwhelming urge to shake her.

"I didn't do it!" Thistle's face flushed with color as Bay swiveled.

I caught Bay's arm before things could get out of hand. "Sweetie, I know you're upset, but do you really want to ruin our night? We both know what Thistle did. Can't that be enough?"

"Not until she admits she's evil," Bay snapped. "Do you have any idea what it's like to work with Aunt Tillie? She wanted to write her own editorial about how Mrs. Little should be banned from town and how every restaurant should be a 'no kid' zone except for one hour each day."

Laughing wouldn't help, but I couldn't stop myself. "I'm pretty sure that's illegal."

"Not in her world," Bay muttered. "She used to tell us her truck was a 'no kid' zone when we were little and threaten to leave us by the side of the road in the middle of winter."

"Yes, that was always delightful, because Clove believed her every time and turned on the waterworks," Thistle interjected. "It was pathetic."

"Clove turned on the waterworks to get her way," Bay corrected. "I don't think it was because she really believed Aunt Tillie would leave us."

"That's true," Thistle conceded. "Clove cried about everything for a time when we were kids. It worked for her, too."

I sensed a thawing in the temporary freeze and almost heaved a relieved sigh. I managed to contain myself, though, because neither of them would play nice if they thought it reflected poorly on their ability to be proclaimed "victor" for the evening. "I think we should enact a 'no Aunt Tillie' zone," I suggested. "I think that would be best for everyone's mental health."

"I agree with that," Thistle said.

Bay flashed a genuine smile as I led her up the back steps and into the inn. Her relaxed attitude lasted for a moment or two – right until she saw Aunt Tillie sitting on the couch in the family living quarters watching *Jeopardy* – and then the anger returned to her eyes. I didn't miss the hot flush washing over her cheeks.

"It's Detroit, you idiots," Aunt Tillie barked at the television, not bothering to look up. She was dressed relatively normal – for her, at least – in simple cargo pants and a "Flip the Witch Switch" shirt. The ensemble made me smile when I saw her socks as she rested her feet on the coffee table. They were bright orange and had monsters on them. Some things never change.

Aunt Tillie scowled when Alex Trebek announced the answer was Chicago. "That's such a load of crap. Don't they have fact checkers?" As if sensing us for the first time, she shifted her eyes to the entryway and smirked. "You have sleep lines on your face, Bay."

Bay frowned as she rubbed her cheek. "Do I?"

"You're beyond cute," I replied, kissing her cheek before scalding Aunt Tillie with a dark look. "Do you have to cause problems?"

"That's what she does," Thistle interjected. "She sits around dreaming up ways to cause problems. She's a professional."

"Oh, suck it, mouth." Aunt Tillie narrowed her eyes as she looked Thistle up and down. "That blue color washes you out. You should go with richer, earthier tones."

"You suck it," Thistle shot back, annoyed. "You're a pain in the butt. Like … a big pain. You're like a hemorrhoid."

Bay snickered. "That was so weak."

"I just woke up," Thistle protested. "You know what I hope, old lady? I hope now that we're going to have an inn full of cops and FBI agents that you screw up in front of one of them and they lock you away."

As far as arguments go, this was one of the tamer ones I'd witnessed in the Winchester household. Thistle and Bay were off their games, so I expected things to pick up when their minds were firing on all cylinders. What I didn't expect was the shocked look that flitted over Aunt Tillie's features.

"What do you mean?" Aunt Tillie asked, leaning forward. "What cops? What FBI agents?"

Uh-oh. I sensed trouble. Clearly Bay and Thistle did, too, because their eyes gleamed with twin doses of mischief as they exchanged a quick look.

"You don't know," Thistle said after a beat, rubbing her hands together. "You don't know who's visiting this week. Our mothers didn't tell you."

"That has to be on purpose," Bay noted. "They knew she'd have a panic attack, so they kept it quiet until it was too late."

"And it's officially too late tonight," I said. "My boss should be here for dinner."

"Oh, this is too good." Thistle looked like an evil cat preparing to pounce. "You're in for a rude awakening, old lady. The cops are coming for you."

"I don't know what that means," Aunt Tillie said, resting her hands on her knees as her eyes bounced between faces. "What does that mean?"

"Do you want to tell her, or should I?" Bay asked Thistle.

"Oh, let me do it," Thistle pleaded. "I've been waiting for a moment like this for decades. This might be the one that actually kills her."

"Go ahead." Bay slipped her hand into mine and rested her head against my shoulder. The color was back in her cheeks. I didn't want to admit it, but being evil did wonders for her skin. She almost glowed. "Lay it on her."

Thistle was gleeful as she stepped forward. "The FBI is hosting a special investigative techniques event in Hemlock Cove this week," she said. "Police officers and agents from all across the state will be in town. A lot of them will be staying here. In fact, every room is booked, and it's all cops and FBI agents."

"You're lying." Aunt Tillie's voice ratcheted up a notch. "There's no way that's true."

"Oh, it's true," Thistle said, grinning like a crazy woman who just found out there was a sale on invisible friends. "For the next few days, Hemlock Cove and this inn are going to be filled to the brim with cops. So stick that in your straw and suck it."

Thistle was haughty as she strolled across the room and disappeared through the door that led to the kitchen. I had to hand it to her. It must take a lot of stamina to look that full of herself given Aunt Tillie's history of cursing her nieces for insubordination.

"She's lying, right?" Aunt Tillie swiveled and fixed her eyes on Bay. "She's making that up to tick me off. That's the only explanation I can accept."

"I'm sorry." Bay's voice was devoid of emotion as she patted Aunt Tillie's arm. "I guess it's going to be a rough few days for you, huh? Total bummer."

I pressed my lips together to keep from laughing as I prodded Bay toward the kitchen. Aunt Tillie looked furious, and I didn't want to be caught in a room with her when she popped a cork on her homemade wine. Instead of reacting out of anger, though, Aunt Tillie seemed desperate as she grabbed Marcus' wrist.

"Tell me this isn't true!"

Marcus looked caught. "I ... ." He cast a pleading gaze in my direction. "Are you going to help me?"

I shook my head as I marched Bay toward the kitchen. "It's every man for himself. If it's any consolation, you sacrificed yourself for a good cause."

Marcus glowered at me as I disappeared through the doorway. "I won't forget this."

If I were in his position, I wouldn't forget it either.

The kitchen bustled with activity, but Thistle's smugness managed to survive the change in audiences with little variation. Apparently she couldn't wait to tell her mother and aunts that she had lit Aunt Tillie's fuse.

"Oh, she knows," Thistle said, grabbing a radish from the salad bowl and popping it into her mouth. "She's very excited, too."

"Why would you tell her that?" Winnie, Bay's mother, looked

furious as she stared down her niece. "There's a reason we kept that a secret."

"No offense, but how long did you think you'd be able to keep up that ruse?" Bay challenged. "Some of the guests arrived today, and the rest hit town tomorrow. She was going to find out eventually."

"You don't know that." Marnie, Clove's mother, shook her dark head and made a clucking sound in the back of her throat. "Aunt Tillie doesn't pay attention to the guests. I believe she once likened them to ants and herself as the person who stomped on the ant pile. She could very well have gone the entire week without knowing that cops were converging on the inn."

That seemed unlikely. "She's not an idiot," I pointed out. "One of the demonstrations is being held here. You agreed to it."

"What demonstration?" Twila asked, her eyes dark as they settled on Thistle's blue hair. Twila picked hues to dye her hair according to the Ronald McDonald, scale so it was always funny when she lectured her daughter on her color choices. "That color is hideous."

Thistle ignored her. "Yeah, what demonstration is being held here?"

"It's a fake murder investigation," I supplied. "We have a new device that's aimed at gathering evidence. It involves personal scanners – which we got a huge grant for – to get fingerprints while the victim is still on scene."

"That sounds ... delightful," Marnie said, making a face. "Will there be fake blood?"

"Of course there will be fake blood," Twila said, her eyes flashing. "People love fake blood. Do you have an actress to play the dead person?"

I shifted uncomfortably. I recognized the gleam in Twila's eyes. She fancied herself a budding thespian – or perhaps an overlooked one, I really can't be sure – and I sensed trouble. "We're going to have one of the younger agents pretend to be dead for the demonstration."

"Oh, now, that would be silly," Twila said, pressing the back of her hand to her forehead and reminding me of a scene from one of the soap operas my mother watched when I was a kid. "I'd be happy to serve as your murder victim."

"Um ... ." I glanced at Bay for help, but she was steadfastly avoiding eye contact. Her message was clear: You're on your own. "I don't want to take time away from your busy day." That sounded plausible, right?

"Oh, please take her," Marnie grumbled.

Twila ignored her sister and remained focused on me. "How will everyone learn if you're taking away someone's ability to focus on the crime scene? I'm doing you a service."

I heaved out a sigh. "I'm not in charge. My boss is. I believe he checked in tonight. You'll have to ask him."

Twila smiled at the suggestion. She grabbed a platter of vegetables and moved toward the swinging door that separated the dining room and kitchen, an added swing in her step. "His name is Steve, right?"

I nodded. "Yes. Make sure he knows it was your idea and not mine, okay?"

Twila winked. "You don't want him to think you're playing favorites. I get it."

I waited until she was gone to focus on Bay. "This won't end well."

Bay giggled and gave me a hug. "You're a good man for letting her do this. That's one of the reasons I love you."

Even now, after we'd been saying the words for months, she still had the ability to wow me with three little words every time she uttered them. I cupped the back of her head and pressed a soft kiss to her mouth. "I love you, too."

"Oh, puke," Thistle muttered. "You two are sickening."

"Then don't look," I suggested, grabbing Bay's hand. "We're going to the table. I want to see how Steve reacts to Twila's request."

Winnie seemed genuinely amused at the turn of events. "We'll be right behind you."

Steve sat wide-eyed at the middle of the table as Twila explained why she'd be the perfect person to play a dead body, even going so far as to list her community acting credits. I had to bite the inside of my cheek to keep from laughing as I led Bay to our usual seats.

Steve darted a desperate look in my direction as he continuously nodded and made "uh-huh" sounds whenever Twila took a breath – which wasn't often – and when she finally wrapped up her argument he appeared lost. "I guess that would be okay," he said finally, dragging out the words as if he expected someone to swoop in and save him from the inevitable. "If you want to be the dead body, I don't see any problem with it."

"Yay!" Twila hopped up and down as she clapped her hands, and then hurried back to the kitchen.

"I only heard the tail end of that, but you're going to regret agreeing to it." Terry Davenport, Hemlock Cove's chief of police, smirked as he took a seat between Steve and Bay. He graced Bay with a wide smile. "Hello, sweetheart."

"Hello, honey," I tossed back, grinning when he scowled. Terry has a unique relationship with the Winchester family. He's especially fond of Bay. For a long time he was the only father Bay, Clove and Thistle had during their childhood years. I wasn't surprised to see him at dinner. "Anything interesting going on around these parts?"

"Only if you find it interesting that Thistle tried to throw Aunt Tillie out of Hypnotic's front window earlier today," Chief Terry replied. "Thankfully she didn't, and Aunt Tillie headed to The Whistler, so I didn't have to issue public nuisance citations."

"Thankfully?" Bay arched a challenging eyebrow. "There was nothing thankful about that situation."

Chief Terry chuckled. "Well, at least no one died."

"Yet," Bay muttered.

"I'm looking forward to getting a chance to see more of the town," Steve said, reaching for a slice of warm bread. "I've only spent time here in passing. It's a lovely place."

"You're only saying that because you haven't spent any time with Aunt Tillie yet," Bay pointed out. "You'll change your mind after that."

"On the contrary. I find her delightful."

"Give it time," I said. "I ... ." I snapped my mouth shut, forgetting where I was in the conversation as Aunt Tillie picked that moment to flounce through the door. She'd changed her outfit, now sporting camouflage pants and a combat helmet. Her shrewd eyes bounced around the table.

"Good evening, Mrs. Winchester." Steve's smile was amiable. "I'm so happy you're here. I'm excited to stay at the inn and get to know you better."

"Save it," Aunt Tillie barked. "I know your game."

Steve was understandably confused. "What game?"

"You can't arrest me without a warrant, and there's no judge in three counties who will sign a warrant," Aunt Tillie said. "I made sure of that."

"You probably shouldn't be admitting that to law enforcement representatives," Bay said dryly. "I'm pretty sure they frown on paying off judges."

Aunt Tillie snorted. "Paying off? I would never stoop so low."

"I saw you bribe the mailman with wine to lose that catalog with all of the Halloween decorations a few weeks ago," Bay reminded her.

"Yes, but that had ghosts and monsters that talked – something Twila would not have been able to stop herself from buying – and it was too irritating for words," Aunt Tillie said. "That was a public service."

"Whatever." Bay rolled her eyes. "I'm pretty sure no one has any interest in arresting you."

"Don't be so hasty," Chief Terry said, grinning as Aunt Tillie scowled. "I'm not ruling it out."

"Me either," I teased, ignoring the hateful expression on Aunt Tillie's face. "The first thing you learn when you become an agent is that you can't labor under preconceived notions. You have to be open for anything ... even arresting senior citizens."

Aunt Tillie's mouth dropped open. "I am not a senior citizen. I'm middle aged!"

Aunt Tillie's in her eighties, but could easily pass for a spry ninety-year-old. "I forgot. I apologize."

"Why would we want to arrest you?" Steve asked, genuinely curious.

"Don't worry about it," Bay warned. "It could be a variety of reasons. They shift from day to day. It's better to pretend you have no idea what she's up to."

"I see." Steve seemed amused. "I think this is going to be a fun week."

"Then someone has slipped acid into your wine," Aunt Tillie shot back, her eyes flashing. "I want to make everyone aware that I know what's going on, and I won't stand for it. There will be no nonsense in my house!"

Thistle picked that moment to walk into the dining room, amusement licking the corners of her mouth. "And there go my plans for the week. I love a good bout of nonsense."

Aunt Tillie narrowed her eyes as she glanced between faces. "Be forewarned. You're all on my list."

Oh, yeah. This is going to be a great week.

THREE

My favorite part of the day is waking up with Bay. It may sound schmaltzy, but there it is. I love the quiet of the guesthouse. I love the way she makes cooing noises right before she wakes up. I also love how warm and cuddly she is when burrowed beneath the covers and pressed close to my side. In those few moments before I have to pour coffee into her to get her going, the day has endless possibilities.

"Good morning." Bay snuggled closer, resting her head on my shoulder. "How long have you been up?"

"Not long." I stroked the back of her head. "How did you sleep?"

"Hard."

I smiled. "You always sleep hard unless something is bugging you. I guess that means you're no longer annoyed with Thistle."

"Just for the record, I'm always annoyed with Thistle." Bay ran her finger down my cheek, scratching my morning scruff. "I am looking forward to seeing how Aunt Tillie deals with the influx of law enforcement, though. It's bound to be entertaining."

"I'm kind of looking forward to that, too," I admitted. "She doesn't have any pot plants in the greenhouse, does she?"

Aunt Tillie's pot proclivities were well known in certain circles.

The last thing I needed was some overzealous rookie wandering into the greenhouse and deciding to bust her.

"I checked. There's nothing in there. She can't grow anything this time of year anyway. She has her wine supplies out there and looks to be cranking up to make another batch, but I figure people would have to be desperate to bust her for that."

"I guess we're lucky that Noah isn't staying here," I teased, referring to a junior agent from my office. He'd visited Hemlock Cove a few months ago and suspected Aunt Tillie in a series of murders. He'd left in a huff, and I hoped he'd never return. Recent events conspired to make sure that wasn't a possibility.

"Speaking of Noah, do you know where he's staying?"

"At your father's inn."

Bay frowned. Her relationship with her father wasn't always easy, but they were slowly edging toward reconciliation. After leaving Hemlock Cove when she was a child, Jack returned with Clove and Thistle's fathers and opened a competing inn. So far, everyone appeared to at least pretend to get along. Er, well, everyone except for Aunt Tillie. She was still ticked off. She idled at irritated, though, so it was no big loss.

"It will be fine," I said, snuggling Bay into the crook of my arm. "There's nothing hinky going on out there. It's safer to keep Noah there. Your father knows to keep an eye on him."

"I still can't help but worry a little bit." Bay jutted out her lower lip and fixed her sea-blue eyes on me. "Aunt Tillie is a pain, but I don't want her in jail. Worrying about going to jail is another story. She's going to be hilarious."

"I can already picture it." I kissed Bay's upturned mouth and gave her a long hug. "We should probably get ready and head up to the inn. Everyone will be arriving for the first demonstration soon. I'm dying to see how Twila plays her part."

Bay barked out a laugh. "She'll be the only dead body to win an Oscar ... ever."

"That's what I'm counting on." I playfully smacked her rear and then rolled out of bed. "Just think, in a few weeks this place will be ours. We'll be able to decorate and set it up however we want. You're excited, right?" It was a pointed question, but I couldn't stop myself from asking it.

"I am excited," Bay confirmed. "Are you?"

"Yes."

"You know it's going to be a long couple of weeks sharing a roof with Marcus and Thistle, right?"

I nodded. "I like Marcus. He won't be an issue."

"And Thistle?"

"We can always send Aunt Tillie after her when we need a break."

Bay giggled as she followed me. "I like the way your mind works."

"Right back at you."

THE INN BUSTLED with activity when we arrived. I took the opportunity to introduce Bay to several of my co-workers, keeping my hand at the small of her back as I showed her off. Most of the other agents were friendly, but I dreaded introducing her to Chris Wilson, and held off as long as possible. Ultimately I had no choice.

"And this must be the famous Bay." Chris is one of those guys who believe he's heavy on charm when he's really heavy on smarm. He has perfectly coifed blond hair and insists on wearing a suit even in a casual environment. He fancies himself the best agent in the office, even though my case record – and weekly workload – is double his. Yeah, he really irks me.

"I am," Bay said, nodding as I rested my hand on her hip. "And you are?"

"Oh, I'm sorry." I remembered my manners, but just barely. "This is Chris Wilson. We work together out of the Traverse City office."

"I'm sure Landon talks about me all of the time," Chris said.

"Not really." Bay was either oblivious to the chill between us or opted to pretend she didn't notice. I leaned toward the latter, because she's insightful and almost always notices when there's an underlying current of tension. "Should he have mentioned you?"

"You're funny." Chris forced out a laugh, but I could tell her answer irritated him. "You don't have to pretend that you've never heard of me. Landon and I are in competition all of the time at the office. I'm sure he's mentioned me."

"I don't see the need to bring office politics home," I offered. "There's no need to discuss you once I leave the office, because I rarely think about you when I'm away from that environment." Bay's conflicted eyes danced between Chris and me. She heard the edge in my voice, so I adjusted my tone. "When I'm here, I want to focus on her."

"And for obvious reasons." Chris' smile was wide as it landed on Bay. "She's quite pretty, isn't she?"

"She's also right here and can hear you when you talk about her," Bay interjected. "I'm not deaf ... or an idiot."

"Of course you're not." Chris attempted a soothing voice, but his eyes were icy when they locked with mine. "I didn't mean any offense."

"That's exactly what you meant," Bay muttered, shaking her head before turning to me. "I'm going to check on breakfast. If that's okay, I mean."

"You don't have to clear your schedule with me," I said. "Be careful of Twila. She's behind the couch pretending to be dead. I saw her there a few minutes ago. I don't want you to accidentally trip and hurt yourself."

The warning was enough to make Bay smile, which was exactly the reaction I wanted.

"Thanks for the tip."

I watched Bay go, making sure she was out of earshot before letting my smile slip and focusing on Chris. "Don't say anything to upset her. I won't be happy if you do."

"There's no reason to get worked up, Landon." The way Chris said my name made me want to punch him in the face. "I'm not after your woman. You don't have to worry."

"Oh, I'm not worried," I offered. "Bay wouldn't look at you twice."

"Then why warn me away?"

"That wasn't for her benefit. That was for your benefit."

"What? Is she going to bite me? I might like that."

He was trying to get under my skin ... and it was working. "Have I introduced you to the rest of Bay's family? Here's Thistle. You'll really like her."

I grabbed Thistle's shoulders as she moved to pass through the crowd – she still looked half asleep because it was early – and shoved her in Chris' direction.

"What the ... ?" Thistle scorched me with a look. "Do you want me to kick you?"

Chris snorted out a laugh. "I like her already."

"This is Chris Wilson," I said. "We work together."

Thistle was clearly unimpressed. "Lucky you."

"Oh, I really like her," Chris said as if Thistle wasn't there. "The blue hair is a nice touch, although ... the color kind of washes you out. Have you considered an orange or a red?"

Thistle narrowed her eyes to dangerous slits. "Really?"

I'd already won and I knew it, but I opted to push her over the edge. "He wants Bay to bite him ... and not in a sarcastic way. He thinks she'll like it."

"No, what I said was that I would like it," Chris corrected. "You don't listen very well for an FBI agent."

Thistle was off faster than a beagle on the scent of fresh bunny. "Do you think that's funny?"

Chris was taken aback by Thistle's tone. "I didn't mean any offense."

"Oh, I don't mean any offense either," Thistle shot back. "Have I introduced you to my Aunt Tillie? She's going to love you."

Chris offered Thistle a saucy wink. "All women love me."

Thistle turned to me with an incredulous look on her face. "Doesn't the FBI mentally screen you guys before setting you loose with guns?"

I couldn't stop myself from laughing. "I guess he slipped through the cracks."

"Ha, ha. You're a funny twosome," Chris muttered, annoyed. "Do you have something going on with both of them? The blonde and the blue-haired chick, I mean. You seem pretty comfortable with both, after all."

I almost snapped and punched him. "Don't ever say anything like that again."

Thistle stopped me with a hand on my arm. "He's only trying to irritate you."

"It's working," I gritted out.

"That's why he keeps doing it," Thistle said. "By the way, I wasn't lying about introducing you to Aunt Tillie. I think this is going to be the perfect meeting of minds."

Chris rubbed his cheek and smiled, showing his teeth in an ingratiating way. "I look forward to it."

"Great. Here she is now." Thistle caught Aunt Tillie's arm as the matriarch tried to sneak through the crowd.

Aunt Tillie's eyes flashed when she realized she'd ceased moving forward and was instead being dragged in the opposite direction. "You're on my list," she sputtered, anger flaring.

"This dude is about to bump me down a spot," Thistle said. "This is Chris Wilson. He works in Landon's office and he's a tool. Get him."

And with that, Thistle grabbed my arm and yanked me away from Aunt Tillie and Chris, who eyed each other as if they were a pair of heavyweights at the weigh-in before a ten-round bout.

"What are you doing?" I asked, confused.

"That guy is a jerk, and Aunt Tillie needs a jerk to focus on," Thistle replied, not missing a beat. "This will work out best for everyone concerned. Er, well, except for that Chris guy, of course. But no one cares about him. Trust me."

I momentarily felt bad, but the feeling didn't last long. I figured Aunt Tillie would be the one left standing. And the likelihood of her actually murdering Chris in front of so many witnesses was slim.

I found Bay sitting alone at the table and took the empty seat next to her, grabbing her hand and giving it a squeeze. "Are you okay?"

"Why wouldn't I be okay?"

"Aren't you the one who told me that answering a question with a question was a deflection technique?"

"Didn't you just answer my question with a question?"

I grinned as I leaned over and smacked a kiss against her cheek, lowering my voice. "Are you okay?"

"I'm fine." Bay's smile seemed legitimate, which made me feel a tad better. "You don't have to worry about me. I know how to deal with jerks."

"You do. I believe when we first met that I was undercover as a jerk."

"And just a few weeks ago you were a jerk again," Bay pointed out, causing me to frown as her eyes lit up. "It's okay. He didn't upset me."

"Then why did you leave?"

"Because I see no reason to put up with people like that," Bay replied. "I grew up with people like that, people who think they're better than others or somehow golden. I don't want to waste my time when there are so many other things I could be doing."

"Like what?"

"Well, for starters, we have fresh doughnuts." Bay grabbed the plate at the center of the table and slid it in my direction. Someone had gone all out and made fresh cake doughnuts, one of my favorite morning offerings at The Overlook.

I grabbed a chocolate-covered one and immediately bit into it, moaning at its warmth. "Oh, these are fresh!"

"Cop food," Bay teased.

"Funny girl." I flicked the spot between her eyebrows. "Just don't pay any attention to Chris. He's going to go out of his way to talk to you because he knows it will irritate me. I told him you wouldn't be remotely interested in him because you already hit the FBI jackpot with me. He'll take that as a challenge instead of a reason to shut down his attitude."

"You don't have to worry. I'm fairly happy with the FBI agent I have."

"Fairly?"

"I would be happier with half your doughnut."

That was a tough call. I loved her, but … c'mon, the doughnut was still warm. "Why can't you grab your own?"

"Because I want to save room for breakfast," Bay replied. "They're making bacon, eggs, hash browns, corned beef hash, biscuits, sausage gravy ... ."

I groaned again and broke the doughnut in half. "You had me at bacon."

"I saw that coming." Bay pressed a quick kiss to my lips and then smiled when she heard a familiar voice make a disgusted sound behind us. She swiveled in her chair and beamed at Chief Terry. "Good morning."

"Good morning." Chief Terry affectionately patted her shoulder before taking the seat next to me. "You two seem to be in a lovey-dovey mood despite being surrounded by cops."

"We're always in a lovey-dovey mood," Bay supplied. "Are you attending some of the workshops?"

"A few, if I can spare the time," Chief Terry replied. "I have all of my officers attending the events so we're covering everything. I'm actually here because I have a real case and wanted to see if Landon might go for a ride along with me. That way I won't have to pull anyone from a workshop."

"I can do that," I said, my interest piqued. "What's going on? You're not going to make me search the greenhouse, are you?"

Chief Terry chuckled, shaking his head. "No, but speaking of that ... ."

"It's handled," Bay interjected. "Don't worry about it."

"I can't help but worry when it comes to this family. I'll take your word for it," Chief Terry said. "I have a missing person report I want to check out. Procedure doesn't allow me to do it alone because I have to make an unauthorized entry into the house."

"Who's missing?" Bay asked, licking her fingers to get the remainder of the frosting off.

"Donna Emery."

Bay pursed her lips. "The woman who owns the yarn store?"

"You have a yarn store?" I learn something new about Hemlock Cove every day. "Who buys yarn?"

"Knitters."

"That was a dumb question," I muttered. "Who reported her missing?"

"Her sister," Chief Terry answered. "She lives two towns over. Hasn't heard from Donna in three days. The store is closed. I figure it can't hurt to look."

"I'll go with you," I said. "The first demonstration is on the fingerprint scanner. I already know how to use it."

"I'll go, too," Bay offered. "If she's dead and something remained behind ... ."

Chief Terry nodded curtly. He clearly didn't want her mentioning ghosts in front of a roomful of police and FBI agents. "That's fine."

"Can it wait until after breakfast?" I asked. "They've gone all out – and there's bacon."

Chief Terry snorted. "That's fine. It's probably nothing, but I want to be sure."

"Cool." I squeezed Bay's hand and lapsed into silence as I watched the enthusiastic officers and agents chat.

Chief Terry was the first to speak again. "Why is Twila pretending to be dead on the floor?"

"She's our victim," I answered. "We're going to demonstrate the equipment on her."

"Okay, but ... why is she dead now?"

Bay giggled. "I can't believe you even asked that question."

"Forget I did," Chief Terry said, turning back to the table. "I need some coffee and ... hey, doughnuts!"

"Cop food," Bay repeated the lame joke as Chief Terry guffawed.

"You're still my favorite, kid," Chief Terry said. "Now hand me a doughnut so you stay that way."

FOUR

"Why didn't you tell me about Chris Wilson?"

The doors were barely shut on Chief Terry's department vehicle when Bay asked the question. From the passenger seat, I glanced over my shoulder and focused on her pretty face. She didn't seem upset, but she was good at putting on a brave face when necessary.

"What should I have told you?" I asked after a beat. "It's not exactly if we're friends."

"I know, but you tell me about the other people you work with," Bay pointed out as she fastened her seatbelt. "I complain all of the time how I hate working with Brian Kelly – thankfully that's essentially over by the end of the year – and you listen. You never once said, 'Hey, I work with a total tool, too. I get it.' I'm just kind of curious why."

"I ... ." I wasn't sure how to answer. Thankfully Chief Terry swooped in and gave me a moment to think.

"Who is Chris Wilson?" he asked.

"He's a jerk who wants me to bite him," Bay answered, pressing her fingers to the heating vent in the back as the engine roared to life.

Chief Terry furrowed his brow as he glanced over his shoulder. "Are you cold? Where are your gloves?"

I couldn't help but smile at the concern in his voice. Even though he hadn't been my biggest fan when I decided to pursue Bay, I'd always had a great fondness for the man. He doted on Bay to distraction at times, and he was equally good with Clove and Thistle. He seemed to understand their particular needs at any given time and reacted accordingly. He was a good man, and even though she didn't know it, Bay needed a little doting today.

"I have gloves in my pocket," Bay replied, making a face as she giggled. "There's no reason to get worked up. I just like warm air blowing on me."

"Hot air. I guess that's why you ended up with this one," Chief Terry said, jerking a thumb in my direction. "He seems to have an endless stream to share with anyone who will listen."

Bay snickered as I shook my head.

"Don't encourage him, Bay," I warned. "It will only make him play to his audience longer."

"Whatever." Bay focused on Chief Terry. "Chris Wilson is that blond guy Landon works with. I think Landon is in competition with him, even though he doesn't want to admit it."

I narrowed my eyes. "I am not in competition with him."

"That's not how it seemed to me."

"There can't be a competition if I've already won," I explained. "I'm a better agent, so I've won there. I also go to bed with you as often as possible, so I've definitely won there."

"Oh, so sweet," Bay cooed, amused.

"Oh, so wrong," Chief Terry mimicked Bay's voice as he cuffed me. "That's my little sweetheart. Don't talk about doing ... those things ... with her."

I couldn't stop myself from smiling at Terry's discomfort. "Would it help if I told you we do nothing but read books together when we're in bed?"

"Yup." Chief Terry focused out the windshield as he navigated the road. "That's exactly what I want to hear."

"That's not true," Bay protested, earning a stern look in the mirror from Chief Terry.

"It's true in my world, missy," Chief Terry barked, shaking his head for a moment until returning his attention to me. "So this Chris Wilson guy gets under your skin, huh? Why is that?"

"He doesn't get under my skin." I focused on the blurring trees outside my window, Chief Terry didn't stare at my profile too long. I would surely crack if he did.

"Bay, why does this Chris Wilson guy get under Landon's skin?" Chief Terry called out.

"I'm not sure," Bay answered. I could feel her eyes on the back of my head. "Landon was in a good mood until he saw Chris. Then he hit on me ... but in a backhanded way, as if I wasn't a real person, simply Landon's girlfriend. That agitated Landon."

"That irritates me," Chief Terry said. "He didn't touch you, did he?"

Bay shook her head as I finally tore my eyes from the scenery. "If he touched her he'd be dead," I said. "Don't worry about Chris Wilson. He's a douche. I already handled the situation by introducing him to Thistle and Aunt Tillie."

This was apparently news to Bay, who gave a delighted laugh and clapped her hands. "Did you really?"

I nodded. "I thought he deserved it."

"That's thinking on your feet," Chief Terry said, amused. "How did Aunt Tillie take the introduction?"

"She's convinced every cop in town is here to arrest her, so she's hyper-vigilant," I replied, watching as Chief Terry turned off the main drag and headed into a residential neighborhood. "Part of me is entertained by how annoyed she is. The other part is worried she's going to do something stupid."

"I can see that," Chief Terry said, his expression thoughtful as he glanced in the rearview mirror and searched for Bay's gaze. "Are you excited about moving in with this ruffian, Bay?"

It wasn't his smoothest transition, but I knew Chief Terry was interested in getting Bay's take on the situation. I told him about the change in living arrangements a few weeks back. At the time, he'd accepted it without complaint because Bay had just been through an ordeal and he didn't want to make things worse. Now that she was fully recovered, he felt safe to probe.

"I am excited," Bay confirmed, bobbing her head. "We're going to decorate together and everything. I'm going to make Landon move furniture."

I smiled. "I'm going to do it shirtless so she swoons."

Chief Terry scowled. "That right there – your insistence on making everything with my sweetheart sexual – is why I don't like spending time with you, Landon. You know that, right?"

I shrugged, unbothered. "I'll close up my apartment in about two weeks, and then I will officially move into the guesthouse."

"But Thistle and Marcus will be there for a spot of time yet," Chief Terry pointed out. "How is that going to work?"

"I thought they'd sleep in Thistle's room and we'd sleep in Bay's room," I answered.

"Our room," Bay automatically corrected, catching me off guard.

For some reason the simple clarification warmed my heart. "Our room."

"So freaking sappy," Chief Terry muttered, shaking his head. "I know you're going to have separate bedrooms. But won't there be a lot of fighting?"

"There's always a lot of arguing in that house," I replied. "I'll put a line of tape down the middle if Bay and Thistle get out of hand."

Bay was offended. "Hey! I never get out of hand."

"It's rare for you to fly off the handle," I conceded. "It does happen when you're upset, though, and you're bound to get upset with that many people spending that much time under one roof. Don't bother denying it."

Bay turned to Chief Terry for help. "I don't get out of hand." Her voice was plaintive as she searched Chief Terry's kind face. "Tell him."

"She doesn't get out of hand," Chief Terry automatically offered, causing me to scowl.

"You always take her side," I said. "It's annoying."

"That's because I'm always right," Bay said.

"She is," Chief Terry agreed.

"And we're done with this conversation." I focused on the small bungalow in front of us as Chief Terry parked his vehicle. "What can you tell me about this Donna Emery?"

"She's in her thirties," Bay answered. "She owns the yarn store. She seems nice, but a little … um … particular about the type of people she hangs out with."

"What does that mean," I asked, turning in my seat so I could study Bay's face. Her cheeks were redder than they should be. "Do you have an issue with this woman?"

"No, it's not that," Bay replied hurriedly. "It's just … well … ."

"Let me take this one," Chief Terry suggested. "Donna is extremely religious. I mean … extremely religious. She goes to church services on Sunday and Wednesday nights. She goes to a Christian reading group on Mondays. She's extremely devout."

I wasn't sure where he was going. "Is that bad?"

"Of course not," Bay answered. "It's just … people in town are convinced we're real witches."

Things slipped into place for me. "Oh."

"Yeah." Chief Terry shot me a knowing look. "Donna is a nice woman who gives her time freely to help the elderly. She even runs a donation program for new mothers. She's a good woman."

"She just happens to hate witches," Bay supplied.

"Did she ever say anything to you?" I asked. "How does she know you're a real witch?"

Bay snorted. "Everyone knows. They pretend not to know, but everyone knows."

"They suspect," Chief Terry corrected. "Don't get all … melancholy. No one cares what Donna thinks."

"And what does she think?" I asked. "You still haven't told me."

"She thinks Aunt Tillie is the Devil and that she's training us to take over the world so we can end civilization as we know it."

Bay's answer was so absurd I could do nothing but laugh. When she didn't join in, I realized she was serious. "She said that to you?" I was incredulous.

"She's never attacked us or anything." Bay said the words as if that was supposed to make me feel better. "I hope nothing bad has happened to her."

"Still, why are you here?" I asked. "You don't need to put up with this for a woman who treats you in a derogatory manner."

"That doesn't mean I can't help," Bay replied. "Good deeds are in the doing, not the saying."

"Oh, that was almost poetic, sweetie," I teased, "but I don't believe it for a second. I think you wanted to get away from all of the cops and agents. You're just as squirrelly around them as the rest of your family."

"I am not," Bay protested, her eyes widening. "I happen to love cops and agents."

I crossed my arms over my chest and waited.

"Well, I love you and Chief Terry," Bay hedged.

"And we love you," Chief Terry said, smirking at her conflicted expression. "Well, at least I love you. I'm not sure about this lug."

I managed to drag my eyes from Bay and focused on Chief Terry. "Why do you always have to make things worse? Sometimes you remind me of Aunt Tillie."

Instead of being offended, Chief Terry pressed his hand to his heart and mimicked Aunt Tillie's voice to perfection. "That's the meanest thing you've ever said to me."

Bay laughed so hard she was still shaking when I helped her out of the vehicle. I took a moment to feather my fingers over her cheek and rested my forehead against hers.

"You're okay, right?" I kept my voice low.

Bay patted my shoulder. "Landon, you're more upset about him than I am. He didn't hurt my feelings. What he said didn't bother me in the least."

"But ... you walked away."

"I smelled fresh doughnuts. I'm a glutton, not a coward."

Her simple answer was all I needed to relax. "Good." I pressed a quick kiss to her mouth. "There will be more of that when I'm not on the job."

Bay grinned. "Good to know."

We followed Chief Terry to the front door, my gaze wandering to the pile of newspapers accumulated on the front porch.

"That doesn't look good," Bay mused. "This is at least four days' worth of The Detroit News. How long did her sister say she'd been missing?"

"She said she hadn't talked to her in at least three days," Chief Terry answered. "I might have to do a more formal interview and pin down that information."

"What can you tell me about her?" I pressed. "I know she owns the yarn store, but does she have any children? What about a boyfriend?"

"She was married," Bay replied. "I think it lasted about three years. They met at the church and were very ... pious."

"Yeah, I heard it that time," I said, extending a finger "You didn't like this woman. Admit it."

"I'm pretty sure it would be wrong to admit something like that when she might be missing." Bay tilted her head as she scanned the side of the house for hints of movement. "I don't see anything yet, but that doesn't necessarily mean anything."

Bay can see and talk to ghosts – something that threw me for a loop when I discovered her powers not long after we started dating. I was attracted to her from the moment I saw her at the opening of a corn maze in late October of the previous year. I was undercover with an unsavory group of bikers, and she let her mouth get away from her. At the time, I didn't realize it was a family trait. Still, I couldn't get her out of my head.

I kept running into her, and each time she was doing something goofy, like talking to herself or wandering around a cornfield at night. When I learned the truth I took a step back. I still don't understand why. It wasn't the magic that upset me as much as the lying she did to cover things up. Still, after giving it some thought, I realized she didn't have a choice. She didn't know me well enough to risk her entire family. With Winchesters, trust is earned, not freely given.

When I came back into her life after a small break, I never looked back. Now, a year later, I can't imagine life without her. People call me schmaltzy and co-dependent. I don't care. She's what I want. Hemlock Cove is where I want to make my future. This place, these people … this is home now.

"Where did you go?" Chief Terry asked, narrowing his eyes. "Were you thinking about that douche you work with?"

"He was thinking about me," Bay teased, grabbing my hand. "Didn't you see the moony look on his face? He only gets that look when he's thinking about me."

"You're so smart," I teased.

"Oh, geez." Chief Terry pinched the bridge of his nose and stared at the sky. "Sometimes I think someone up there … or even right here in Hemlock Cove … is testing me. You, Landon Michaels, are my test."

"What did I do?" I asked, confused.

"You made my little sweetheart happy."

"Shouldn't that put you in a good mood?" I challenged.

"You're also a pervert," Chief Terry added.

"Can't win them all." I gripped Bay's hand tighter. "Let's see what we can find here and then go from there. I already don't like the newspapers on the porch, but that's hardly proof something nefarious happened."

"Agreed," Chief Terry said, his expression turning somber. "Let's see what we can find. We don't have probable cause yet to enter the house if we don't see something suspicious through the windows, but there's nothing stopping us from searching the grounds. Bay, if you see anything or anyone … ."

"You'll be the first to know," Bay finished. "Let's do this."

FIVE

By the time we got back to the inn we were no better off than when we had started. The house was quiet, no sign of Donna, yet everything was still around the house so we had no reason to enter. Bay walked the property perimeter twice, even peering through the windows in hopes of seeing a ghost as she made her slow progression around the house. But there was nothing there for her witchy powers to suss out.

The Overlook's foyer buzzed with activity when we entered, people practicing using the new fingerprint scanner on Twila. She was in her element – even though she was playing dead – and reveled in the attention as everyone maneuvered around her prone body. Bay effortlessly stepped over her as we passed, not bothering to look down as we made our way to the dining room.

Steve sat at the table with Winnie and Marnie, the trio enjoying coffee as they chatted. I didn't miss the dark look on Chief Terry's face when he caught sight of the women who generally spent their time fawning over him. They barely looked up when we approached, their attention trained on Steve.

"There you are," Winnie said, finally flicking her eyes to Bay. "I expected you back sooner. Did you find Donna?"

Bay shook her head. "The house is quiet and empty."

"She's probably at church," Marnie suggested. "Did you try looking there?"

"No, that never occurred to me," Chief Terry deadpanned, causing Marnie to arch an eyebrow as he sat on the chair next to Steve. He gave my boss a long appraising look and then rolled his eyes. "I don't suppose I could get a cup of coffee?"

On a normal day Marnie and Winnie would've jumped to their feet to be the first to serve him. Today neither one of them so much as shifted on their chairs.

"The pot is right there," Winnie said, waving down the table. "You know where the mugs are."

Bay pressed her lips together and darted an amused look in my direction. She realized what was happening right away. Truth be told, even though she would hem and haw and make disgusted noises as she mimed barfing, I knew Bay would relish the thought of Chief Terry getting together with her mother. He was already a father in her heart. Being able to legally call him that would simply be a bonus. For his part, Chief Terry refused to make a move on any of the battling Winchester sisters no matter how hard they pressed him. I was pretty sure he didn't want to risk offending anyone, which meant none of them would get the chance to be happy. It was something I filed away to discuss with him at a later date, when curious witches weren't loitering around every corner.

"I guess I do," Chief Terry grumbled as he grabbed three mugs from the stack on the buffet and tipped them over so he could pour coffee for everyone. He shoved mugs for Bay and me in my direction when he was finished and proceeded to glower at an oblivious Steve.

My boss appeared fascinated with the witchy women sitting across from him – even though he had no idea they were really witches. "So, you raised Bay, Clove and Thistle as sisters even though they're cousins, huh? That was probably smart on your part."

"They're all exceedingly close," Winnie said.

"Sometimes too close," Chief Terry muttered.

"How can they be too close?" Steve asked, legitimately curious.

"Because they find more trouble together than when they're apart. When they're together they find a lot of trouble," Chief Terry replied after sipping his coffee.

"I'm pretty sure that was an insult, but I'll let it slide," Bay said. "Are there any more doughnuts?"

Winnie smiled and nodded. "I saved some of the ones with sprinkles for you. They're in the kitchen."

"Yay." Bay pushed herself to a standing position and glanced at me. "Want one?"

"Are you really going to share your doughnuts with me?" I couldn't help but be surprised. We're one of those couples that tend to hoard our favorite foods – even from those we love best. It's unattractive, but ... there it is.

"You shared your doughnut with me this morning."

"I'll share another with you now," I said. "I don't want to eat too much before dinner. I'm guessing your mother and aunts have something special planned."

"We do," Marnie confirmed. "Prime rib."

Chief Terry groaned. "My favorite."

"Well, you're invited," Winnie said, wrinkling her nose as she carefully looked him up and down. "You're always invited for dinner."

Bay briefly locked gazes with me before disappearing into the kitchen. I smiled as I watched her go, not realizing that Steve was staring at me until I'd spent a good thirty seconds watching the kitchen doorway. "What?"

"You're so whipped," Steve teased, shaking his head. "I wouldn't have believed it unless I saw it with my own eyes. It's ... so cute."

I scowled as I warmed my hands around the mug. "I knew having this conference here was a bad idea," I grumbled.

"Oh, you need to act all proper in front of your boss, but it's fine to be schmaltzy and romantic in front of me," Chief Terry complained. "Why is that?"

"Because I enjoy bugging you," I shot back.

"So cute." Steve's grin was wide enough it almost swallowed his face. "So, ladies, what did you think of Michaels when you first met him? Did you fall in love with that hair and smile at first sight like almost every woman who comes in contact with him?"

"Excuse me?" Chris Wilson picked that moment to join the conversation, settling on the other side of Chief Terry. His gaze was pointed when it landed on Steve. "I'm the office heartthrob. Everyone knows it."

"Only in your own mind," Steve shot back, smiling at Bay when she returned with a doughnut. "I was just asking your mother and aunt what they thought of Landon when they first met him. What did you think? Did you swoon right away?"

"I thought he was a jerk," Bay replied, causing Chris to laugh. The sound was beyond irritating.

"I was undercover," I reminded Steve. "She was supposed to think I was a jerk."

"You're very good at being undercover," Bay teased, breaking the doughnut in half and giving me a share of it.

"Where's my doughnut?" Chris asked, winking. "I'd love to share a doughnut with you."

"Is there something wrong with your eye?" Aunt Tillie asked, appearing on the other side of the table. "You keep opening and closing it … like you have a twitch or something. You might want to have that checked."

Chris' smarmy smile turned upside down as Aunt Tillie sat at the end of the table – the opposite end from where she usually sat – and stared at him. She didn't bother to blink – which was creepy on its own – but she also steepled her fingers and lowered her neck so she could be really overt as she stared. I couldn't help but enjoy the way she made Chris shift in his chair.

"I only share my doughnuts with Landon," Bay said, pursing her lips when she saw Chief Terry's pout. She broke off another chunk and handed it to him. "And Chief Terry."

Winnie smiled at the interaction, amused. "I don't know what Bay thought of Landon when she first saw him, but I know what I thought. He saved us that night. He was on the ground and took a bullet to save my family. I loved him from the start."

I widened my eyes, surprised. "You did?"

"I knew you'd be with us forever after that, even though I was a little worried you might break Bay's heart," Winnie said, her eyes taking on a far-off look. "When you kept showing up and making Bay smile each and every time, never once going out of your way to hurt her feelings, I wanted to keep you forever."

"Oh." Steve made a cooing sound as Chris rolled his eyes. "You're a real prince, aren't you, Michaels? Like from a fairy tale."

I'd once spent an entire night locked in a fairy tale with Bay and her cousins – and it hadn't gone well – so I couldn't stop myself from making a face. "I'd rather be an agent than a prince."

"You're both," Bay said, sucking the frosting off her thumb and making me grin.

"Here comes the schmaltzfest," Chief Terry muttered when I leaned closer to Bay.

I remembered that my boss and a guy I truly disliked were present before my lips touched hers, and regained control of my emotions. I focused my attention on Steve. "How are the demonstrations going?"

"Well, everyone seems to like the new scanner," Steve replied, his expression thoughtful as he darted a look in the direction of the foyer. "Twila keeps demanding that everyone not disturb the scene of the murder as they're scanning, so that's been a bit of a thing."

Bay snickered as she grabbed her coffee. "That sounds like her. If you get lucky, maybe she'll fall asleep and you can train your men on how to approach a snoring dead person."

"Bay," Winnie chided, shaking her head. "That's your aunt."

"That doesn't mean I can ignore the snoring," Bay pointed out.

"Isn't that the truth," Aunt Tillie grumbled, narrowing her eyes at Chris as he did his best to pretend she wasn't staring at him. "Whenever I pictured 'The Man' coming into my house with an army of soldiers, this isn't what I saw in my nightmares."

Chris ran his tongue over his teeth as I bit the inside my cheek to keep from laughing. "And what did you see?" he asked.

"Death at the end of a sword," Aunt Tillie replied, her tone ominous. "Your death. My sword."

"Aunt Tillie." Winnie extended a warning finger – which Aunt Tillie promptly ignored – and wagged it in her elderly aunt's face. "Stop trying to scare the guests."

"He's an FBI agent," Aunt Tillie said. "He says he's the best FBI agent in the Traverse City office. If that's true, he shouldn't be afraid of me, right?"

Winnie looked caught, her eyes narrowing as she focused on Chris. "Are you really the best agent in the office?"

"No." Steve and I answered in unison, even mustering twin snorts of derision. Chris answered in the affirmative at the same time.

"I am the best agent," Chris barked. "I've solved every case that landed on my desk."

"So has Michaels," Steve pointed out. "He's also solved twice as many as you. And he's not a pain when he's at the office."

"That's because he's barely at the office," Chris argued. "He's always in Hemlock Cove with his ... girlfriend."

I didn't like the way he said "girlfriend." It was the same tone I used when I said "murderer."

"I think you're just jealous," Aunt Tillie mused, resting her chin on her palm as she continued to stare at Chris. She's a master when she wants to unhinge someone, and she was homing in on Chris. I couldn't muster much sympathy because ... well ... it was darned funny.

"Why would I be jealous?" Chris sputtered, his annoyance obvious.

"Because Landon has found balance," Aunt Tillie replied, refusing to back down. "He's found a happy medium where he's not all about the job. He loves his job – and he's good at it, don't get me wrong – but the job is not everything to him.

"Landon is happiest when he has his feet on the table, one hand on Bay's thigh and the other hand full of bacon," she continued. "He likes to solve cases and help people, but he wants to be more than that."

I hated to admit it, but she just described my ideal Friday night. "That sounds like a plan for this weekend," I teased, poking Bay's side. "Make sure you stock up on bacon."

"Will I get more loving than the bacon?" Bay challenged.

I nodded. "Always."

"Oh, geez," Chris muttered. "This is such crap. Everyone knows I'm the best field agent in this region. You're just yanking my chain."

Noah Glenn, the junior agent determined to catch the Winchesters doing something nefarious so he could arrest them, picked that moment to burst into the dining room. Instead of entering through the foyer, he came from the kitchen. That was a big no-no in the Winchester house. Only family was allowed past the dining room door.

"Speaking of someone who's definitely not the best agent in the office," Aunt Tillie grumbled.

"There you are," Noah hissed, his eyes landing on Aunt Tillie. "You thought you could fool me, didn't you?"

"You'll have to be more specific," Aunt Tillie replied, blasé. "I'm pretty sure I could fool you ninety-nine out of every hundred times. Still, you might get lucky once or twice. Even fools are right during a blue moon."

"What were you doing in the family living quarters?" I asked, my temper getting the better of me.

Noah at least had the grace to look abashed when he shifted his attention to me. "I ... got lost."

"You got lost?" I had my doubts. "It's an inn, not a maze. The family living quarters are off limits to guests."

"What's your deal, Michaels?" Chris challenged. "What are you hiding back there?"

"I'm not hiding anything," I answered. "It's a sign of respect. That's Winnie, Twila, Marnie and Aunt Tillie's private space. You shouldn't be back there."

"But ... ." Noah's eyes were wild. "I was following her." He extended a finger in Aunt Tillie's direction. "She was outside running around and acting crazy. She wanted me to follow her."

I shifted my eyes to Aunt Tillie, conflicted. "I thought you were inside bothering Chris."

"Oh, she's been bothering me," Chris muttered.

"I'm a multi-tasker," Aunt Tillie supplied. "I can outsmart two Feds at the same time without missing an episode of *Jeopardy* or my stories in the process. I'm just that good."

Steve barked out a laugh. "And what was she doing outside?" he asked, genuinely curious. "Is she running an evil drug cartel under everyone's noses?"

While I would hardly consider Aunt Tillie's pot field big enough to fund a cartel, the question hit a little too close to home. As if sensing my discomfort, Bay squeezed my knee under the table to offer reassurance.

"She's doing something weird out there," Noah replied. "I'm serious. She had a big stick and a whistle."

Steve snorted. "I see. Well, we should probably convene a task force to make sure she doesn't get out of control with that whistle."

I exchanged a quick look with Chief Terry. He laughed easily at the joke but appeared mildly worried.

"It wasn't a stick," Aunt Tillie argued. "It was a broom."

"A broom?" Steve asked, confused.

"Yes. I'm a witch."

I felt Bay tense, so I slipped my arm around her waist. I had no idea what Aunt Tillie's master plan consisted of, but she was clearly in the mood to mess with Chris and Noah. On a normal day I'd applaud her efforts. This felt like a slippery slope, though.

"That's right," Steve said, nodding. "Everyone in Hemlock Cove is a witch, right?"

"Kind of," Winnie replied, her eyes dark as they landed on Aunt Tillie. "It's part of the tourist draw."

"I'm the wickedest witch in the Midwest," Aunt Tillie said, lowering her voice to a conspiratorial whisper as she leaned closer to Steve. "Everyone should live in fear of me."

"I know I certainly do." Steve clearly thought it was a joke, his easy smile telling me that he thought he was playing along with an act. Chris and Noah were different stories. They looked legitimately suspicious.

Thankfully for everyone, Twila picked that moment to rise from the dead and stomp toward the table.

"What's wrong with you?" Marnie asked, focusing on her sister. "Is acting harder than you thought?"

"The acting is fine," Twila replied. "I'm good at it. The lack of respect is another thing."

"Who isn't respecting you?" Steve asked, sobering.

"All of them." Twila planted her hands on her hips. "They're over there talking about a potential missing woman when they have a fake dead body right here. Do you know how rude that is?"

Steve opened his mouth to answer, but I cut him off with a shake of my head. I was used to the chaos in the Winchester house.

"I'll talk to them," I offered. "I'm sure it will be okay."

"We'll see about that," Twila huffed. "I'm off to fix my makeup. I'll be back for scene two in twenty minutes."

Everyone watched her go, silence wafting over the table for a few moments. Steve was the first to speak.

"What the heck is scene two?" he asked, confused. "I didn't even know there was a scene one."

I shrugged. "I guess we'll find out in twenty minutes."

SIX

After coffee and a kiss – one she laid on me in front of my boss and co-workers – Bay took off for town, leaving me to enjoy my conference without disruption. Here's the thing: She's definitely a distraction, but I prefer being distracted. I never realized exactly how boring a room full of law enforcement officials could be until I heard eight different guys try to tell the same monotonous joke.

I really couldn't wait for Bay to get back. Then I could come up with an excuse to get out of the rest of the demonstration and slip away with her to the guesthouse for some alone time. That was the plan anyway.

"You miss her, don't you?"

Steve's voice jolted me as I leaned against the wall, my arms crossed as I watched Twila gag and flail about. It was her fifth death performance of the day – as far as I could tell, at least – and they were becoming progressively more theatrical.

"Who? Twila? She's right there." I pointed for emphasis. I knew he meant Bay, but I had no intention of opening the door for potential teasing.

"She's a trip," Steve said, smiling. "I like all of them. I can see why you're always so eager to get over here every weekend."

Something about his tone set my teeth on edge. "I always complete my work before I leave for the weekend."

"You do," Steve agreed, bobbing his head. "In fact, you work twice as hard while you're at the office. It's so you can enjoy this place without having the job vie for your attention. That's not always possible, but you manage it as often as you can. I get it."

"I love this place," I admitted, glancing around. Sometimes the big inn felt as much like home as the small guesthouse. "I love every woman in this house."

"Even Aunt Tillie?"

I smirked. "Even Aunt Tillie," I replied. "She's not as bad as she seems."

Steve cocked a dubious eyebrow. "Oh, really?"

"Sometimes she's even worse," I conceded. "But sometimes she's ten times better. She's a mystery, that woman. She's a complete and total pain in the butt most of the time, but she's also loyal and loves her girls more than anything."

"I see that about her." Steve matched my stance as he leaned against the wall. "She has a different relationship with everyone, though. I've been watching her. I like to take those dormant profiling skills of mine out for a walk every now and then."

"Oh, yeah? And what have you surmised?"

"That Winnie is the bossy one," Steve answered. "She's the oldest sibling, and she likes to tell her sisters what to do. She also carries more weight on her shoulders than the rest."

"I'd say that's fairly accurate."

"Marnie is the middle sister and likes egging everyone on," Steve supplied. "She loves her family, but she's got attitude sometimes. Twila is the youngest sister, her head in the clouds. She's allowed to be that way because everyone spoiled her, and they continue to do it even though she's an adult."

"She's a bit flighty, but lovable," I said, grinning as Twila flopped to the floor.

"As for the younger girls, Bay is the oldest and the most grounded,"

Steve continued. "She brightens up a room when she walks in. She certainly brightens you up. She's also extremely thoughtful."

"She's an angel." I didn't bother hiding my smile.

"I don't have a good read on Clove because she's not around as much," Steve said. "She's busy with her boyfriend, but she likes being with her family, so she's never gone long. She's the buffer between Bay and Thistle's more ... prickly ... personality."

"Thistle is more than prickly," I confirmed. "She's the future Aunt Tillie, although if you say that to her she'll murder you in your sleep."

Steve snorted. "Yes, they're a lot alike and enjoy fighting. I've noticed that, too."

"I'm not sure what you're getting at," I said after a pause.

"I'm merely stating that you found yourself a wonderful family," Steve said. "Chris doesn't want to believe it because no one could ever put up with him long enough to build a family. But you're doing the right thing. You're not focusing on the job to the detriment of your relationship. You're putting your relationship first while still doing the job. That's why you won't burn out."

For some reason, his words caused me to puff out my chest a bit. "Thank you."

"Now, speaking of your relationship, I believe that's your blonde coming this way. She looks happy to see you, and I know you're happy to see her. Try not to be too obvious when you sneak out with her in front of the other agents." Steve patted my arm and smiled before walking away.

I greeted Bay with a quick hug and kiss, ignoring the stares of my fellow agents and remaining focused on her face. "I missed you."

"I was gone for three hours," Bay pointed out. "I told you I'd be back in plenty of time for us to have dinner together."

"You did indeed." I grabbed her elbow and tugged her toward the library. "I was thinking we could have a drink while this thing breaks up. How does that sound?"

"Nice, but ... don't you have to stay?"

"I'm the best FBI agent in the land," I reminded her. "I don't have to do anything I don't want to do."

Bay appeared intrigued by the suggestion. "A drink sounds good," she said after a moment. "Something light, though. I don't want to risk getting drunk when there's so much potential for arrest around every corner."

Her smile was mischievous as I directed her toward the library, ignoring everyone who glanced in our direction and pretending I didn't notice the way they looked at us when we paused next to Twila's limp body.

I didn't care about the stares. At first I merely told myself that was true, ignoring the unsettled feeling in the pit of my stomach. However, it only took a few moments to realize I meant it. "You're cute. If you pick up your feet and walk into that room so we can have a little privacy, I'll show you how cute."

Bay effortlessly stepped over Twila. "Dinner will be ready in a half hour, and Mom says there's no fake blood at the table," she called out to her aunt. "Give yourself time to get cleaned up. You don't want to miss the prime rib."

Twila slapped her hand on the floor. "I'm dead, Bay! You're ruining my performance!"

"Sorry."

I grinned as I pulled Bay into the library and shut the French doors. I could see Chris staring in our direction from the other side of the foyer. I shut the blinds and flopped on the couch, letting out a loud groan. "Oh! You have no idea how happy I am to be alone with you ... even if it's only for five minutes."

Bay arched an eyebrow, intrigued. "Did you really miss me that much?"

I tucked a strand of flaxen hair behind her ear and shrugged. "See, this puts me in an awkward position. I did miss you. I always do. It's not just that, though. It's ... all of this."

"You don't like your co-workers?" Bay's eyes were keen as she settled next to me.

"I like most of them fine." I linked my fingers with hers and rested our joined hands in my lap. "I just ... bringing them here was a mistake. When Steve first suggested it, I thought it was a bad idea. I worried everyone would find out the big secret."

"I can see that."

"Then I realized that was stupid because it was only for a few days and you guys have hidden your abilities in front of guests for a long time," I added. "Then I got excited because I thought it would be like a vacation week for me and extra money for your mother and aunts. I'm already up on all of the techniques and new gadgets, so attendance isn't mandatory for me.

"I thought I could sneak away and spend afternoons with you," I continued. "I thought we could take naps and get a jumpstart on living together."

"And that hasn't exactly happened," Bay surmised. "We've got a missing woman, that Chris Wilson douche, Noah, Aunt Tillie, Thistle … . In other words, it's a normal weekend with added stressors."

I couldn't stop myself from laughing as I slipped my arm around her waist. "I guess. I just … I don't like worrying. Now I have to worry about Chris hitting on you and Noah getting himself in trouble with Aunt Tillie. That's on top of the missing woman – who may not be missing – and it's just … a lot."

"Well, I can't help you with Noah and Aunt Tillie," Bay said. "She'll do what she's going to do. Noah clearly hasn't learned his lesson. He needs to get his butt kicked Winchester style so it sets in."

"Winchester style, huh?"

"It's quite a sight to behold."

"I believe you." I brushed a kiss against her brow. "What about Chris hitting on you? Do I have to worry about that?" I already knew the answer, but her incredulous expression was worth any potential embarrassment attached to asking the question.

"I don't like blondes," Bay said. "Otherwise you'd be in real trouble."

I chuckled as I rubbed my fingers over the back of her neck. "I'll keep that in mind." We lapsed into amiable silence for a moment, the sound of voices moving toward the front door telling me today's demonstrations were about to end. There were enough cops and agents in the area that we had to split up and make reservations at three different inns. Only The Overlook's registered guests would be staying for dinner, and I couldn't help but be relieved about that.

"So, what did you do with your afternoon?" I asked, changing topics. "Did you work at the newspaper office?"

"For an hour," Bay replied. "Then I went to Williamsburg."

"What's in Williamsburg?"

"Donna Emery's ex-husband."

I stilled, surprised. "I thought you said she was religious."

"I did."

"Doesn't that mean divorce is frowned upon?"

"Yes, but I don't think that's our place to judge," Bay chided, tapping her finger against my chin.

"That's not what I was doing," I argued. "I'm just trying to understand. You guys started talking about Donna when we were in the car, and then we got sidetracked."

"Don't we always?" Bay's eyes were full of mirth as she squeezed my hand. "Anyway, Tim and Donna Emery divorced about three years ago. They met at church and were big pillars of the community. Then he started having an affair with the woman who ran the church's daycare center and ... well ... I'm sure you can figure out the rest."

"Yes, you've connected the dots brilliantly," I said. "So Tim Emery had an affair. Was he caught or did he own up to it?"

"He admitted it, but only after half the town saw him in a few parking lots," Bay answered. "The car was always bouncing ... and his wife wasn't in the passenger seat."

It was sad, but I couldn't stop myself from snickering. "I'm guessing that gossip traveled fast given the size of Hemlock Cove."

"You have no idea." Bay shifted so her legs rested over my thigh. She seemed eager to tell her story. "So Mrs. Little found out and told everyone. She was on the church's elder board – I think that's what it's called – and enjoys ruining people. That's exactly what she tried to do to Donna.

"She tells Donna the truth and Donna doesn't believe it at first," she continued. "Tim lies for a couple of weeks, but then finds out that

Julie Woods, the daycare worker, is pregnant. He then admits to Donna that he has been having an affair and he wants a divorce."

"How did that go over?"

"Not well," Bay answered. "Donna contested the divorce and this went on and on for what felt like forever. It was years before the divorce was officially settled. Donna refused to sit for mediation and fought the entire process.

"That, of course, caused Julie to freak out, because she didn't want her kid to be born out of wedlock," she continued. "She was still attending church regularly, if you can believe that. Anyway, she started saying horrible things about Donna, and they had a few public showdowns."

"It sounds like Hemlock Cove's version of *General Hospital*, huh?"

Bay nodded. "Eventually a judge pushed through the divorce because he thought it was best for Donna's sanity. He was very sympathetic and awarded her a huge settlement. He said that Tim had to pay alimony until Donna remarried."

I rolled the idea through my mind. "Donna isn't the type to remarry, because she's ultra-religious and believes she's supposed to be with Tim forever."

"Exactly. It was like a giant 'screw you' to Tim. He had a meltdown and tried to appeal, but as far as I know he's paying alimony for life. He moved to Williamsburg and switched churches. He's a real estate agent, so he doesn't exactly make boatloads of money."

"Uh-huh." I rubbed my chin. "He has a lot of motive to make Donna disappear."

"Does he?" Bay tilted her head to the side. "I don't think he can get out of alimony if she's missing. I think all of those funds go into an account unless a body is found. If a body is found, he'll be the primary suspect."

"You have a point." I shifted so her head rested on my shoulder. "Did you talk to him?"

"I talked to Julie. She said she's glad Donna is missing, but that she and Tim had nothing to do with it."

"Do you believe her?"

"She seemed ... angry in general," Bay replied. "I have no authority to ask questions, though. I think it would probably be smarter if you asked the questions."

"I'll do it tomorrow if she doesn't show up between now and then. Good tip, sweetie."

"I'm full of good things," Bay teased. "In fact ... ."

Whatever flirty thing she was about to say disappeared from her lips as Twila threw open the library door and stalked inside.

"You look pretty good for a dead woman," I quipped, working overtime to keep from laughing at Twila's furious countenance.

"Oh, you're such a comedian," Twila deadpanned. "Do you have any idea how much work it takes to lie on the floor all day?"

That had to be a trick question. "I can honestly say that I don't know the answer to that question."

"Well, it's tough," Twila barked, heading for the drink cart. "It's also a thankless job. Do you know that when I got off the floor they didn't even bother applauding? I mean ... I wasn't expecting a standing ovation or anything. Random applause would've been nice, though."

I bit my lip and buried my face in Bay's neck so Twila couldn't see that I was laughing. Bay patted my shoulder as she stared down her aunt.

"I'm sorry you've had such a rough day," Bay said. "Dying is never easy."

"Oh, trust me. I know."

"Still, we have prime rib. And you didn't have to slave away in the kitchen all day," Bay pointed out. "That should make you happy."

Twila tilted her head to the side, conflicted. Finally she heaved out a heavy sigh. "I guess you're right. Still, it's tragic not to be revered by the little people when you've put on a performance that transcends time."

I lifted an eyebrow, dumbfounded. "Transcends time?"

"Just go with it," Bay prodded. "I'll always remember your performance, Twila. It's seared in my memory."

Twila beamed. "And that's why you're my favorite." With that, she seemingly forgot the drink she'd been jonesing for moments before and strode out of the room.

I watched her go, a mixture of amusement and weariness warring for top billing in my head. Then I turned my full attention to Bay. "You're my favorite, too."

Bay giggled. "Right back at you."

SEVEN

*B*ay was warm and cuddly when I woke the next morning. I did my best to ignore the clock on the nightstand as it taunted me with impending work, opting to remain where I was for as long as I could. She was conscious – but just barely – and she rubbed her cheek as she took a few moments to focus.

"What time is it?"

"We have a few minutes." I rubbed my thumb over the back of her neck. "I'm going to carve out some time to go talk to the ex-husband with Chief Terry this morning. I have to lead a demonstration this afternoon, so I need to do it before then."

Bay lifted her eyes, intrigued. "You didn't tell me you were going to lead a demonstration. What is it about?"

I chuckled. "Nothing that would entertain you. It's on interrogation techniques."

"Will Twila be your acting subject for that one, too?"

"I hadn't considered it, but probably not," I replied. "She wouldn't hold out for very long. It would be more effective if I tried to use it on Aunt Tillie."

"She'll curse you if you try."

"That's why I have no intention of trying." I pressed a kiss to Bay's forehead and stretched. "What are you doing today?"

"A little work at the newspaper office. Then I plan to question some of the regular customers at the Yarn Barn."

"The Yarn Barn?"

"That's the name of Donna's store."

"Oh, well, the name fits Hemlock Cove," I said, shaking my head. "What do you expect to find out from the patrons?"

"Maybe nothing."

"And maybe something?"

Bay shrugged and averted her gaze, smooth, as if she was simply scanning the room as she enjoyed waking. She wasn't fast enough for me to miss the look of determination on her face, though.

"Sweetie, you don't have to get involved in this," I reminded her. "You were at the house. If Donna's ghost was around, you would've seen it. She probably just took off for a few days to clear her head."

"Do you really believe that?"

"I have no reason not to believe it right now," I replied. "You said it yourself, Bay, the woman has been going through some personal issues. Her husband left her for another woman. She's extremely religious and believes she married for life. It might've been too much for her to bear when she finally accepted the fact that her husband felt otherwise."

Bay rolled so she was half on top of me and I had no choice but to meet her gaze. She looked fierce, which made me uncomfortable – I had the feeling the expression meant she was going to find trouble rather than run from it. "You think she killed herself, don't you?"

It was a simple question for which there was no good answer. I opted for honesty. "I don't know. I don't know her. If she was really that upset, though … ."

"But she's extremely religious, and suicide is a sin," Bay pointed out. "She wouldn't kill herself."

"I hope not." I really meant it. "She could've gone away for a few days to clear her head and not told anyone. We don't know yet. There's no law against an adult voluntarily disappearing."

"But you don't think she took a vacation, do you?"

"I ... don't know, sweetie." I framed her face with my hands and marveled at the high cheekbones and inquisitive eyes. She made my heart flip without even trying, which is a schmaltzy thing to think or say, but ... well ... there it is. "If she committed suicide, would she leave a ghost behind?"

"Generally not," Bay replied. "Most ghosts stay because there's something unfinished to focus on, or they were yanked out of their lives so violently they didn't have a chance to grasp what was happening to them. A suicide knows what's happening. They embrace death."

"Most women commit suicide with pills, or occasionally slitting their wrists in the bathtub," I mused, keeping my hands busy as I rubbed her shoulders. "Do you know why that is?"

"Because they worry about who is going to have to pick up the mess," Bay answered automatically. "Men usually opt for a gun and don't care about the mess. Women want to either leave no mess or contain it."

I couldn't help but be surprised. "How did you know that?"

Bay grinned. "Aunt Tillie and I watch a lot of crime shows on the nights you're in Traverse City."

"Pretty soon there will be no nights in Traverse City." I kissed the tip of her nose. "I want you to be careful if you chase this Donna story. We don't know that anything happened, but if it did ... ."

"If it did, odds are that it's the old husband or new wife," Bay finished, her pragmatic side taking over. "If that's the case, I'm already a target because I drove to the house yesterday."

I didn't want to admit it, not even to myself, but she was right. "Don't wander off alone, okay? Be careful."

"I'm always careful."

I scowled. "Be a lot more careful than that."

"Okay, but I might need some motivation," Bay teased, her eyes flashing. "Like, for example, you might want to remind me what I'll be missing if I find myself in trouble I can't get out of."

"What did you have in mind?"

"I'm so glad you asked."

I HAD AN extra spring in my step as I followed Bay into the inn an hour later. We were five minutes late, but it was well worth the dirty looks as we took our regular seats at the table. Winnie glowered at us even though the rest of the table barely noticed our arrival. There was one other exception.

"You two look happy and sweet." The sneer was obvious in Chris' voice as he watched us get settled. "You obviously weren't studying the new tactics, like the rest of us."

"Oh, he knows all of the tactics," Bay intoned, causing me to smirk. "He doesn't need to study them. They come naturally to him."

"Bay!" Winnie was scandalized and chastised her daughter with a firm headshake, which Bay ignored.

"You're just jealous because the only one interested in seeing your tactics is Aunt Tillie," Bay added. "You should be terrified of what happens when she decides she's seen enough, by the way."

"Bay!" Winnie's voice grew deeper and full of warning.

"Leave her alone," Aunt Tillie ordered. "She's right."

"I think Aunt Tillie is following me because she likes me." Chris winked at the elderly witch, eliciting an eye roll so pronounced I briefly thought it could whip a tornado out of thin air. Aunt Tillie can control the weather when she feels like it. "I find her charming, so I like the attention."

"I so want to put my broom in his behind," Aunt Tillie muttered, forcing me to bite the inside of my cheek as I reached for the platter of toast.

"He might think that's your version of flirting," Bay suggested. "I … ." She broke off, causing me to lift my eyes and follow her gaze. She stared at the potted plant by the doorframe. It took me a moment to realize someone was standing behind it and staring in our direction.

"Who is that?" I asked.

Steve swiveled to see what drew our attention and frowned.

"That's Noah. He's using the new surveillance tactics from the packet I handed out last night to watch Tillie."

I pursed my lips. "I see. Um ... he knows we can see him, right?"

"Obviously not," Aunt Tillie replied. "He's like a cat hiding under the floor rug. He thinks if he can't see us that we can't see him. Don't make direct eye contact. I'm dying to see if he'll lose interest in spying and lift his leg so he can groom himself in public. It will be a fascinating display."

Steve's mouth dropped open at the visual. "I ... um ... ."

"You'll get used to it," I said, patting my boss's arm before turning to the day's schedule. "I have an errand to run with Chief Terry, but I'll be back in plenty of time for my demonstration."

"Speaking of that, where is Twila?" Bay asked, glancing around. "Landon is going to put his interrogation talents on display. I thought she'd make a perfect guinea pig."

"She's probably still upstairs pouting," Marnie replied. "That's where she was when I left her last night. She was having a meltdown because no one respected her acting talents. She was on the floor for an entire day, for crying out loud. I've never heard about anyone winning an Oscar for playing dead."

I chuckled. "It's just as well. I'll make do with the recruits. As for you, sweetie, remember what I told you. Be careful while you're out and about today. I'll be in touch if I find something."

"I promise I'll be careful," Bay said. "I also promise to be back in time for your demonstration. I'm excited to see you acting as an instructor."

I lowered my voice so only she could hear. "If you're lucky, I'll teach you a thing or two later."

"I heard that," Winnie barked. "Don't make me separate the two of you."

"Just ignore her," Aunt Tillie said. "Go back to watching the cat. It's kind of fun. I can practically see his whiskers twitching. It's so much better than watching the random winker blink his way through life." Aunt Tillie jerked her thumb in Chris' direction.

Chris scowled. "I'm starting to think you don't like me, Ms. Winchester."

"That makes you a terrible investigator," Aunt Tillie shot back. "I've been obvious about my dislike for you from the moment we met. Now ... wink at your pancakes. They can't get indigestion from being close to you."

TIM EMERY DIDN'T LOOK SURPRISED when he opened the door and found two law enforcement representatives on his doorstep. He ushered us inside, giving his new wife a reassuring smile before leading us into the living room.

Julie Emery – she made a point of correcting me when I referred to her by her maiden name – offered to get us coffee and then disappeared from the room.

"Do you know why we're here?" Chief Terry asked, leaning back in one of the chairs organized around the coffee table and resting his hands on his knees.

"I had a feeling you'd show up when Julie told me about Bay Winchester's visit," Tim replied. "I remember Bay from when I lived in Hemlock Cove. She wouldn't have stopped by unless she had a reason. I'm guessing it's true, about Donna I mean. Is she really missing?"

"That's what we're trying to ascertain," Chief Terry answered. "She hasn't been seen in about four days. Her store remains closed. Her friends at the church haven't seen her. Newspapers were piled up on the front porch when we stopped by yesterday."

"What about inside the house?" Tim pressed. "Did you go inside?"

"We don't have just cause to enter yet," Chief Terry explained. "We might have to make an exception soon if Donna doesn't show up."

"And you think I had something to do with her going missing." Tim looked weary and beat down as he rubbed the back of his neck.

"We're not saying that, Tim," Chief Terry countered. "We're saying that Donna is missing and we need to ask a few questions. Do you have a problem with that?"

"No. Ask away."

"Great." Chief Terry shifted his tall frame in the chair. "When was the last time you saw Donna?"

"Saw her? About six weeks ago," Tim replied. "She's been around since then, though."

"What do you mean?" I asked, leaning forward. "Are you insinuating she's been stopping by the house?"

"I'm not insinuating it," Tim replied. "I flat out know it was her. She doesn't bother to hide her tracks when she does it. She's been in the house. She's moved things around. She's ... stolen items of clothing from Julie's closet."

I shifted my eyes to Julie as she carried a tray laden with coffee mugs, sugar and creamer into the living room. "She stole your clothes?"

"She took a jacket and a skirt," Julie replied carefully. "She took two pairs of shoes."

"How can you be sure?"

"Because she wears them," Julie answered, smoothing her skirt. "When the jacket went missing I thought I'd just misplaced it. You know how that goes. I drove myself crazy looking for it, but then I attended a church retreat in Traverse City two weeks later.

"I wasn't expecting Donna to be there," she continued. "We moved to put a little distance between Donna and ourselves. She never went to the Traverse City retreat. She used to always go to the one in Gaylord. That's why we decided to base ourselves close to the Traverse City church.

"Anyway, I went to the retreat and there's Donna," she said. "She knew I'd be there. She marched right up to me – wearing my jacket – and pretended she had no idea what I was talking about when I accused her of breaking into our house."

"Did you file a police report?" I asked. "If she's breaking into your home ... I mean, that would be the first thing I'd do."

"We considered it, but I really don't want to make things worse for Donna," Tim answered. "She's not a bad woman. When I married her I ... it's not that I didn't love her, you understand. I loved her to the best of my ability. But there was no fire there. I thought that was normal.

"Then I met Julie and realized that wasn't normal," he continued. "I know it's probably hard to believe, but I didn't set out to hurt Donna. I really fought my feelings for Julie for a very long time. I know there's a lot of gossip in Hemlock Cove surrounding this situation, but hurting Donna was the last thing I wanted to do.

"Still, at a certain point I realized that I was hurting everyone by not ending my marriage to Donna," he said. "I thought I was doing her a kindness. I thought she could find someone better suited for her. She refused to let go, though. It's been … difficult."

"I wanted to call the police," Julie volunteered, tucking a strand of her walnut-colored hair behind her ear. "We have a small child. We just found out we're going to have another baby in six months. Tim doesn't want to hurt her, but … ."

"I'm guessing you're fine with hurting her." I didn't mean for the words to sound as harsh as they did, but when Julie's eyes flashed I got the feeling I'd hit a sore spot. "I'm sorry. I didn't mean that like it sounded."

"I think you did mean it," Julie argued. "I think you believe I'm in the wrong."

"I try not to judge people," I countered. "I think that everyone ended up hurt. It sounds as if Donna is mentally unbalanced, though. You should've reported her antics to the police."

"Would they have believed me?" Tim challenged. "After I told my story, would they have taken Donna's side? You can sit there and say they would've done their duty, but I feel tremendous guilt where Donna is concerned.

"I keep hoping she'll eventually move on from this," he continued. "I hope she'll find some happiness, some peace. I need her to be all right, because if she isn't … well, it's too much to bear. She needs to find someone to be happy with."

"And if she marries someone else you're off the hook for alimony," I pointed out. "The thing is, from what I've heard, Donna still believes you're married in the eyes of the church, and she'll never remarry."

"No, she'll just bleed us dry," Julie grumbled.

I narrowed my eyes as I studied her a moment. She was definitely bitter. But if Donna was breaking into the house and stealing clothing she had a right to be bitter. If she was making it up in an attempt to further hurt Donna that was a different story entirely.

"If she doesn't remarry then I'll pay her forever," Tim said. "I knew that was a possibility when I filed for divorce. I wouldn't kill Donna over money. I'm not that type of man."

"Well, there is another possibility," Chief Terry said. "Donna could've been despondent and killed herself. Perhaps she did, and her body is in the house. Or maybe she did it somewhere else entirely."

Tim balked. "Donna would never kill herself. That's not the way she works."

"Well something is going on," Chief Terry said. "Either she took off alone and didn't tell anybody or something happened to her. I don't see any other options. Either way, we'll be in touch."

EIGHT

"What do you think?"

I waited until we were in Chief Terry's cruiser to ask my question, keeping my eyes on the window and Julie Emery's slim frame as she watched us through the filmy curtains.

"I think there's a lot of bad blood in this triangle," Chief Terry replied. "I'm honestly not sure what to think about it. Tim seemed sincere. And I believe he's suffering a great amount of guilt."

"His wife seems extremely bitter. I wouldn't doubt it for a second if she went after Donna," I said. "The wife definitely has a problem with the alimony payments – and Donna's mere existence."

"I would have a problem with someone breaking into my house and stealing clothing, too." Chief Terry rubbed his cheek as he fired up the cruiser's engine. "Do you think that story is true?"

"Bay said that Donna fought the divorce for as long as she could. That means the kid was born outside of marriage, which is definitely frowned upon in a lot of church circles. If these guys are as religious as Bay makes them out to be ... ."

"Oh, that little group is extremely religious," Chief Terry said. "When the town rebranded itself a few years back, it was that church that put up a fight. They said we were promoting paganism and Satanism.

"Now, a lot of the people in Hemlock Cove are church-going folk," he continued. "Most of them didn't see a problem with pretending to be witches and warlocks in an attempt to make sure the town survived."

"I don't see a problem with it regardless," I supplied. "Still, a messy divorce is one of the top reasons for murder. I can't rule out the husband, but I definitely get a strange vibe when talking to the wife."

"Yeah, and we have no idea if it's because she's paranoid about Donna breaking into the house or if she's antsy because she did something to Donna and we ended up on her front porch," Chief Terry said. "It's a mess."

"What are you going to do?"

Chief Terry shrugged. "There's nothing I can do at the moment. We still don't have probable cause to enter Donna's house. I might be able to talk a judge into giving me a warrant, but I don't see that happening until tomorrow at the earliest. It's far more likely I'll have to wait a full seven days."

"Well, either way, I have a demonstration to run back at the inn," I said. "I have to show off my interrogation techniques. Bay suggested I use Twila, but I figure that's a surefire way to give myself a migraine."

Chief Terry choked out a mangled laugh. "It could be worse. You could question Aunt Tillie."

"That's what I said!"

"Great minds think alike." Chief Terry navigated his cruiser to the main highway. "For now we're stuck. You should focus on the conference. I'll focus on the case. If I get anywhere, you'll be the first to know."

THE MAJORITY of the conference attendees were lounging around the library and foyer when I returned. I greeted a few of the familiar faces with nods as I wound my way through the main floor of the inn.

I found the dining room empty, which was a surprise, and headed toward the kitchen door. That's where Chris stopped me.

"I thought that area was off limits to guests." He tried to play off the comment as teasing.

"I'm not a guest. I'm family."

"So it seems." Instead of giving me free passage into the kitchen, Chris purposely crossed his arms and lounged in the doorframe. "You're very domestic here. You realize that, don't you?"

"You say that like it's a bad thing."

"I think it is for men in our line of work," Chris said. "How do you expect to claw your way to the top when you've got a woman holding you back? Now, don't get me wrong, she's a fine specimen of a woman. But do you think you can get everything you want if she's weighing you down?"

"Bay is everything I want," I shot back, tugging on my limited patience. Now was not the time for a scene. "I don't need to climb to the top of the FBI heap, because I'm perfectly happy here. I like my job. I love Bay more."

"How … sweet."

"I'd think you'd be happy about that." I decided to switch tactics. "You fancy yourself the top agent in the office, after all. Doesn't it help you if I'm not on top of my game?"

"You'd think so, wouldn't you? Maybe I like the competition."

"Do you know what your problem is, Chris? The competition is in your head. I'm not in competition with you." I pushed him away from the door and strolled through, pulling up short when I caught Bay scurrying around the counter. She made a big show of pretending to lean against it – as if she'd been there the whole time instead of eavesdropping on my conversation with Chris – and flashed a wide smile. "What are you doing?"

"Waiting for you," Bay replied innocently, shifting her eyes to her mother. "Isn't that right?"

"She was eavesdropping," Winnie volunteered. "She doesn't like that Chris guy, and whatever he said to you gave her heartburn."

"No one likes Chris," I said, strolling closer to Bay. "You were eavesdropping, huh? Somehow I figured that out before your mother told me. You're not very subtle."

"I wasn't eavesdropping," Bay protested. "I simply heard voices on the other side of the door and decided that it would've been rude to interrupt."

"Uh-huh." I ran my fingers through her hair, smoothing it. "You know that I don't believe what he said, don't you?"

"I'm not sure what he said." Bay averted her eyes. She's ridiculously cute when she's avoiding serious questions. It drives me crazy.

"I have everything I want, Bay. If I wasn't happy, I wouldn't be here."

"Oh, is that what he was saying?" Winnie's eyes flashed. "He's a putz, Bay. Don't listen to him. I could've told you Landon was happy. It's written all over his face whenever he looks at you."

Bay flushed with a mixture of embarrassment and pleasure. "I know he's happy."

"Good." I poked her side. "We talked to the husband and new wife, by the way. The husband seemed genuinely surprised and is riddled with guilt. The new wife is another story."

Bay arched an eyebrow. "Meaning?"

"Meaning that she claimed Donna was breaking into their house and stealing her clothes." I launched into the tale, and when I was done Bay made a horrified face. "On one hand I think it's reasonable for the new wife to be bitter. On the other, they never filed a police report. I find that suspect."

"I'm sorry, but if one of your old girlfriends suddenly showed up and started appearing at various places in my clothes, I'd do more than report her to the police," Bay said, grabbing a cookie from the plate on the counter and breaking it in half. She handed half to me, but she didn't release it when I reached for it. "I'd curse the crap out of both of you, just for the record."

I smirked as I took the cookie. "There are no old girlfriends that I was close enough with to warrant that kind of attention," I said, tweaking her nose. "I'd help you curse this imaginary individual if it became an issue. Seriously, though, you would call the police, right? It's not normal to keep that to yourself."

"I don't know." Bay shrugged. "From Tim's perspective, I can see why he didn't call the police. He already looks like a jerk in the eyes of almost everyone he's ever met. I'm sure his family took his side, but the rest of the town? Yeah, they took Donna's side."

"Is that because she's a business owner?"

"And she was the wronged party," Bay replied. "I understand about the chemistry thing. I felt it the minute I met you. But I wasn't married to someone else at the time. Tim did Donna wrong."

"How long is he supposed to pay for it?"

"That's the question, isn't it?" Bay held her hands palms up. "I have sympathy for everyone concerned to some extent, but the fact of the matter is that Donna is missing. Something happened, and we need to figure out what it is."

"Well, for what it's worth, Tim didn't seem to believe Donna was the type to kill herself," I offered. "After listening to the stories, I have to concur. My best guess is that if she really got that desperate she would've taken out the new wife before ending her own life. I've never met the woman, so that's just a hunch."

"Donna isn't a murderer." Bay was forceful. "She may not be perfectly clean in all of this, but I'm sure about that."

"For now, Chief Terry is going to see if he can get a warrant to enter the house. Until then, we're kind of stuck." I finished off the rest of my half of the cookie. "I have a demonstration to give on interrogation techniques. I don't suppose you want to be my test subject?"

Bay's cheeks colored as Aunt Tillie appeared at the bottom of the stairwell and used her hip to edge Bay from the counter.

"Oh, yes, that sounds fascinating," Aunt Tillie drawled. "You can draw the truth out of her with kisses and those little touches you keep dropping on her when you think no one is looking."

I arched an eyebrow. "Touches?"

"You're touch happy," Aunt Tillie shot back. "You can't keep your hands off her. I'm pretty sure it's because you're perverted."

"Well, thank you for that," I said dryly, rolling my eyes. "I think I can ask Bay questions – and get her to provide the right answers – without kisses."

"She'll roll over and give you whatever you want," Aunt Tillie argued. "You need someone stronger, someone immune to your charm. You need ... me!"

My heart dropped at the gleam in her eye. "You can't be serious."

"I've heard several people suggest it to you," Aunt Tillie countered. "I was against it at first – you know how I feel about helping 'The Man' – but now I think it will be a good exercise for those new agents and cops. It will show them that not everyone can be coerced into a confession."

I pinched the bridge of my nose in an effort to fight off an imminent headache. "You want me to use you as my interrogation subject? That sounds nothing like you."

Aunt Tillie slapped my arm with enough force to jolt me. "It sounds exactly like me. I love a fun afternoon of games and messing with 'The Man.' I think you're worried you can't break me."

I narrowed my eyes as I stared her down. "You think I can't break you?"

"I know you can't."

"You're on." I knew the words were a mistake the moment they left my mouth.

Aunt Tillie's smile was smug as she flounced toward the door. "I'm looking forward to it. By the way, if anyone runs into Twila, tell her I'm the new star of the show. I'd rather she finish her crying before I see her next."

"Speaking of Twila, where is she?" Bay glanced around the kitchen. "I haven't seen her since last night."

"Oh, she's around," Winnie said, waving her hand dismissively. "She's probably pouting. Her performance didn't go as intended. Now, Aunt Tillie's performance?" She fixed her somber eyes on me. "You're going to be at her mercy in front of a group of colleagues. I hope you know what you're getting yourself into."

"I'm perfectly aware it's going to be a mess," I said. "I'll win, though. Have faith."

"It's a good thing you're handsome," Winnie said, patting my cheek. "You're not very bright sometimes, but your looks make up for it."

Bay giggled maniacally as I shook my head.

"Are you turning on me, too?" I asked.

"No. I have total faith in you." Bay rolled to the balls of her feet and kissed my cheek. "I'm still running to town to question some of the Yarn Barn customers this afternoon, but I'm totally going to watch some of your performance beforehand. I can't wait."

That made one of us.

AN HOUR later I sat in one dining room chair and Aunt Tillie sat in another, facing me. We moved the chairs to the foyer so we could have room for onlookers to group around and get a gander at the show. I didn't miss the smug look on Chris' face when he caught sight of my interrogation suspect.

"Oh, geez," Chris muttered. "He's going to terrorize a grandmother into giving him answers. How terrifying is that?"

"You have no idea," Thistle said, appearing at the edge of the circle and catching my gaze. "I heard you were doing this. Sucker!"

I ran my tongue over my teeth, annoyed. "I have everything under control."

"That's what makes you a sucker," Thistle said, picking her way through the crowd until she was situated next to Bay. "Well, go on. I'm dying to see how this goes."

"Okay, here's the situation," I said, raising my voice to a level that demanded attention. "Tillie Winchester is being questioned about the disappearance of her husband. He's been missing for three days and we're trying to ascertain what became of him.

"It's important to remember when going into a situation like this that preconceived notions are the enemy," I continued, gripping my knees as I got comfortable in the chair. "You want to make the person you're questioning comfortable, ask them open-ended questions, and hope they'll volunteer information."

"Stop yapping and start doing," Aunt Tillie ordered. She looked bored as she lounged in her chair. "My stories start in three hours. If you haven't broken me by then, you'll have to concede defeat."

"If I haven't broken you by then I'll be in the corner crying my eyes out," I muttered. "Do you remember the dossier I gave you on your background? You have to follow that for answers. You can't answer as yourself."

Aunt Tillie rolled her eyes. "Lay it on me."

"Okay, let's get started." I sucked in a centering breath. "Ms. Winchester, when was the last time you saw your husband?"

"Do you mean saw, as with my eyes, or saw, as with my other senses?"

The question caught me off guard. "What do you mean?"

"Well, I'm psychic." Aunt Tillie was prim as she smiled. "I can see him with my sixth sense even now when I close my eyes."

I furrowed my brow and stared at her. "That wasn't in the dossier."

"There was no rule about not being psychic," Aunt Tillie pointed out. "I know. I checked."

"She has a point," Steve offered. "Her reaction is legitimate. Witnesses say off-the-wall stuff all of the time. I think you should go with it."

Off-the-wall stuff? There was no doubt things would get worse before they got better. "Fine," I gritted out, locking gazes with Aunt Tillie. "If you want to do things the hard way, we'll do them the hard way."

"Oh, I love it when things are hard." Aunt Tillie knew exactly what she was saying. She even preened when the rest of the room guffawed. "Bring it on."

"It will be my pleasure."

NINE

Three hours later I wanted to crawl into a hole and die.

"Stop mentioning your visions," I barked, my temper wearing thin. "You most certainly didn't see your husband dancing on a toadstool in a tutu with Miss Universe. And they weren't hanging out with talking goats."

Aunt Tillie smiled serenely. "That's what I saw."

"I just … ." I pressed the heel of my hand to my forehead and focused on Steve. "Well, this was a waste of time."

"Speak for yourself," Chris chuckled. "I'm having a ball."

Aunt Tillie shifted her predatory eyes to him. "You think you can do better?"

"I think I would've broken you three hours ago," Chris answered, not missing a beat.

"Then take a seat." Aunt Tillie gestured toward my chair.

It took me a moment to realize this was the outcome she'd been working toward all afternoon. I slowly got to my feet and relinquished the chair, anxious to put distance between Aunt Tillie's evil ways and myself. "I think that's a great idea."

Chris seemed surprised by my capitulation. "You're leading this demonstration."

"Yes, but we often approach interview subjects in pairs," I said, fighting to keep my voice calm. "I've obviously struck out. I think it might take a different face to break her."

"That's a very good idea," Steve said. "Chris, you're up."

Chris was caught, and he knew it. He had to save face in front of the other agents and officers, so he squared his shoulders and took the offered chair. "Let me show you how it's done."

"We're all on pins and needles," I said, moving toward the back wall.

"Be careful," Noah urged. "She's tricky. Trust me, I know."

"You'd think a two-year-old was tricky," Aunt Tillie shot back, leveling her gaze on Chris. "Come and get me, big boy."

"Fine." Chris heaved out a sigh. "When did you first know you were psychic?"

"I was born with the gift. It comes and goes, though."

"I see. When was the last time it came?"

"When I got a mental picture of you in a clown costume a few minutes before you sat down across from me. It came quite quickly. I can sense … fear."

I pressed my lips together to keep from laughing, glancing around in an effort to find Bay in the crowd. Despite my agitation and weariness, I didn't want her to miss the show. In fact, there was no one I'd rather share it with.

I found Thistle sitting in a chair in the opening between the dining room and hallway, her eyes on Aunt Tillie as the elderly witch turned Chris into a slobbering mess.

"There are times I really hate that woman," Thistle noted. "But there are times I really love her. This is one of those times."

"Yeah? I'm torn. I'm tired, but looking forward to this." I glanced into the empty dining room. "Where's Bay?"

"She said she was running into town to question some regular Yarn Barn shoppers," Thistle replied. "I'm sure she'll be back soon."

"I hope so." I rolled my neck until it cracked. "I think I'm going to the kitchen for a snack. I never thought questioning a senior citizen could take so much out of me."

AMANDA M. LEE

Thistle snorted. "She's not a normal senior citizen."

"Definitely not," I agreed. "Still ... I'm freaking tired. I want my Bay to make me feel better."

"Oh, you're so gross." Thistle shook her head. "You can take a nap in the family living quarters if you're so inclined, but I'm sure she won't be gone long. She was having a good time watching the interrogation, but she wanted to hit town and be back before dark."

"Well, I'll wait for her in the foyer. I don't want to miss Chris being brought to tears."

"None of us do," Thistle said, leaning forward anxiously in her chair.

"**THAT IS** the most evil woman known to man."

Chris was unnaturally pale as he accepted a glass of orange juice from Winnie two hours later, his hands shaking as he tried to hold the glass steady.

"She has certain ... talents," I corrected, leaning back in the dining room chair and glancing toward the front door. Bay hadn't yet returned, and I was starting to worry.

"She's evil," Chris hissed, causing Steve to chuckle. "Evil."

"Yeah, you barely scratched the evil surface with Aunt Tillie," Thistle said. "That's what you get for opening your big mouth, so I don't have a lot of sympathy for you."

"No one asked you," Chris growled.

"Hey, this is her house," I warned, pointing a finger. "Don't talk to her like that."

"I thought she lived in the guesthouse with your girlfriend," Chris challenged.

"She does, for now. This is still her home. She doesn't need your attitude."

Thistle widened her eyes. "Oh, you're standing up for me? You must be exhausted."

"It's probably temporary insanity," I conceded. "I ... where did

Aunt Tillie go? Is she snoozing after her long afternoon of torturing law enforcement? That probably took a lot out of her."

"She took off out the back door," Thistle replied. "She said she needed a break because all she could smell was bacon when she walked into the house. You know ... because it's full of cops."

"Ha, ha," I intoned, shaking my head. "If this place smelled like bacon I'd never leave. You haven't seen Bay, have you?"

"Are you lost without her?" Chris taunted.

I ignored him. "Shouldn't she be back by now?"

"You'd think so," Thistle answered. "I'm not sure, though. I ... here comes Aunt Tillie."

I turned my head in the direction of the door and found Aunt Tillie standing there, a bohemian scarf wrapped around her neck, her eyes flashing as her chest heaved.

"Uh-oh," I muttered.

"Uh-oh is right," Thistle said. "Prepare for something ugly. I have no idea what, but it doesn't look good."

I sucked in a breath and forced a bright smile. "Is something wrong?"

"Perhaps she got one of her psychic flashes," Chris suggested.

"That's exactly what I got," Aunt Tillie snapped, her annoyance flaring. All of the visitors not staying at The Overlook had left twenty minutes ago, so only overnight guests remained. I was mildly thankful for that, because this looked to be a doozy of a meltdown. "I had a psychic flash that I was going to put a boot in someone's behind. Do you want to take one for the team?"

Chris made an incredulous face as he shifted his eyes to me. "Is she serious?"

"She appears to be," I said, sighing as I straightened. "What's the problem?"

"Someone has been in my greenhouse," Aunt Tillie replied. "I believe strict instructions were left when everyone checked in. My greenhouse is off limits!"

"That was made clear," Steve said, his eyes alert as he glanced between faces. "Did someone go into the greenhouse without permission?"

A dozen people shook their heads.

"Are you sure?" Steve pressed. He got the same response. "They say they weren't in the greenhouse. What makes you think someone was inside?"

"I have my ways," Aunt Tillie muttered, her narrow eyes scouring individual faces. "What happened to Agent Genital Wart? He's been following me around for days. He probably let himself into the greenhouse when I was playing interrogation games with you lot."

"Who is Agent Genital Wart?" Steve asked, confused.

"Noah," I replied. "She gave him that lovely name when he tried to arrest her for murder."

"You've been arrested for murder?" Chris' eyebrows flew up his forehead. "I guess that shouldn't surprise me, but ... sheesh. Did you torture the people questioning you that day, too?"

"Ask him." Aunt Tillie jerked her thumb in my direction. "If anyone sees that little maggot, tell him I'm looking for him. I'm going to bring the fire when I find him. He shall know the burn of my fury."

"So ... what? Are you going to curse him with hemorrhoids?" The words were out of Thistle's mouth before she realized her mistake. She scrambled to cover quickly. "Along with being psychic, she likes to curse people." Thistle laughed, playing it off as a joke. Everyone except Steve – and me – joined in. I fidgeted nervously in my chair. Steve looked mildly intrigued.

"I'll curse him with worse than that," Aunt Tillie growled, prowling around the table, clenching and unclenching her fists as a series of what I'm sure were purely awful revenge scenarios played out in her storming brain. "He'll wish he'd never met me."

"He's already there," I said, drawing her attention to me. "What makes you think someone was in your greenhouse?"

"Because I set up a security system and someone tripped it."

"You have a security system on the greenhouse?" Steve asked. "Does the system have electronic sensors that go off when someone enters?"

"It's not that kind of security system." Aunt Tillie made an annoyed face. "Good grief! I know someone has been in my private space. Isn't that enough for you people?"

"What do you have out there that you're so worried about?" Chris asked.

That was a pretty good question. Bay said she searched the greenhouse and discarded all of the contraband, but that didn't mean Aunt Tillie wouldn't drag in more of it if the mood struck.

"Don't worry your pretty little head about it," Aunt Tillie replied. "It's my stuff. It's my space. It's my … ."

"Oh, I know what's going on," Thistle broke in. "Someone drank your wine, didn't they?"

Aunt Tillie swiveled quickly, locking gazes with her favorite nemesis. "Was it you, mouth?"

"I didn't steal your wine," Thistle replied. "I know better than drinking it out there anyway. It's cold enough that the wine would give you a false sense of warmth even as you're dying of hypothermia."

"What's the deal with the wine?" Steve asked, leaning closer. "Why would anyone keep wine in a greenhouse?"

I cleared my throat, uncomfortable. I was hoping to avoid that question. "She … um … makes it herself." She also grows marijuana during warmer months, but there was no way I could admit that. "It's quite strong. The family has a lot of funny stories that revolve around Bay, Clove and Thistle stealing the wine when they were teenagers."

"She makes it herself?" Steve was understandably intrigued. "That sounds interesting. Is it good? Have you tried it?"

"I have tried it." I didn't think it was possible to feel more discomfort. I was wrong. "It has a bit of kick to it."

"How much kick?"

"One glass is enough to give you a hangover," Thistle supplied. "It's good stuff, though. That doesn't mean I've been in your wine, Aunt Tillie. And, for the record, I can't imagine any of these people trying to lay claim to your wine. They're here for a purpose."

"Yeah, to spy on me and steal my wine!" Aunt Tillie stomped her foot for emphasis, drawing everyone's attention. "Mark my words, I

AMANDA M. LEE

will find the party responsible and make him or her cry like a little girl!"

"Well, we're certainly looking forward to that," Steve said brightly, smiling as Aunt Tillie made a growling sound and turned away from the table.

Bay jolted as she walked through the swinging door, giving Aunt Tillie's retreating form a wide berth as she tugged off her mittens and glanced at me. "What was that about?"

"Someone has been in her greenhouse and she's on the warpath," Thistle answered. "She's not a happy camper. She won't admit it, but I think someone has been at her wine."

"Well, that would explain the mood." Bay pressed her cold hand to my neck. "It's going to be a good night for a fire. I think we should build one when we get back to the guesthouse."

"I'm up for that," I said, grasping her fingers. "Where were you? I was starting to worry."

"I told you I was going into town to question the Yarn Barn patrons," Bay replied, blasé. "Did you forget? How did your interrogation go, by the way?"

"Pretty much as you'd expect," I answered. "I gave up after three hours. Chris took over for another two. She outlasted both of us."

"She didn't outlast me," Chris sniffed. "I took pity on her and thought it best if I gave her a breather."

I snorted. "Sure you did. That's why you were crying when she finished with you."

"I wasn't crying," Chris snapped. "I … had something in my eye. It must've been the smoke from the fireplace."

"Oh, yeah, that was it," Thistle intoned, grinning. "I've had smoke in my eyes so many times where Aunt Tillie is concerned that I've lost count. It's a terrible thing."

Chris scalded Thistle with a dark look. "I'm done talking to you."

"It's my lucky night."

I ignored the snarkfest and fixed my full attention on Bay. "Did you get anywhere?"

"Not really," Bay replied. "Everyone I talked to said Donna was acting normal the last time they saw her. She didn't mention closing up the store. She didn't mention going on vacation. Also, she got a big delivery this afternoon. It was just sitting in front of the store."

"Did you do anything with it?"

"I thought that would be overstepping my bounds," Bay replied. "I called Chief Terry, and he took the delivery. He left a note on the front of the store and said it would be at the department."

"That was probably smart. Well, did he mention anything about the warrant?"

"He said the judge would sign one tomorrow if Donna hasn't shown up by then."

"That's something, at least."

"Yeah." Bay bit her lip. She looked nervous, as she does when she's hiding something from me.

I narrowed my eyes, instantly suspicious. "What did you do?"

"What makes you think I did anything?" Bay's blue eyes widened with faux innocence, and I knew right away that I was on to something.

"Son of a ... !" I grabbed her hand and tugged her toward the kitchen. "We'll be right back," I called over my shoulder. "We're just going to ... flirt and stuff."

"That's not how it looks to me," Chris shot back. "It looks to me as if you're going to yell at her."

"Looks can be deceiving," Bay retorted, shrinking when she saw the dark look on my face. "But maybe not in this case."

I waited until we made it into the kitchen to ask the question a second time. "What did you do?"

"You're not going to like it," Bay muttered, averting her eyes and scratching her cheek. "You're going to be mad."

"I figured that out myself." I crossed my arms and waited.

"Well, if I tell you, do you promise not to yell?"

"No."

"Do you promise not to yell really loud?"

"No."

Bay blew out a frustrated sigh. "I guess it was worth a shot."

I caught her chin with my hand and forced her eyes to me. "What did you do?"

"I let myself into Donna's house and took a look around," Bay admitted. "There were no signs of a struggle and no dead body. There's no ghost. Everything is clean and in its proper place. How much do you hate me?"

The air escaped my lungs with a whoosh and I had to tug on every bit of my limited patience to refrain from blowing up. "That's so much worse than I expected."

Bay's eyes flashed. "You still love me, right?"

"I'll have to give it some thought."

TEN

"What were you thinking?" I worked overtime to hold my temper in check as Bay's eyes widened and her cheeks puffed out. I wasn't in the mood for an argument, but pretending that what she did was acceptable wasn't an option.

"I thought that knowing if there was a body inside the house would be helpful." Bay shrank away a bit, almost as if she expected me to explode.

"Bay, that's illegal. You know that."

"But ... ."

I shook my head. "Forget the legalities for a moment," I said. "What if someone was inside? What if Julie really did kill Donna and she went back to check something and ran into you? What if someone else was hiding in the house?"

"But no one was there." Bay has a stubborn streak. The way she crossed her arms over her chest told me this wouldn't be easy. "I'm perfectly fine. See. This is me, and I'm standing in front of you."

"After committing an illegal act and putting yourself in unnecessary danger." I didn't snap at her, even though that was my initial inclination. She doesn't respond well to bellowing, and I'm no fan of upsetting her. She has a weird insecurity streak that gives me heartburn at times.

"But ... at least we know she's not dead," Bay hedged.

I licked my lips as I stared at her, frustrated. "I think we should take a walk outside," I said finally, earning a surprised look from Winnie and Marnie as they worked on their dinner preparations. "We'll finish talking about this when we're away from prying ears."

Bay didn't look thrilled at the prospect. "Is that because you want to make sure no one can hear me scream?"

I refused to smile, even though her defiant expression tempted me to give in and embrace the unintended hilarity. "No."

"Is it so you can more easily hide my body?"

"No."

Bay blew out a sigh, one I'd heard multiple times when she was dealing with irritating family members. "Fine. I'm not in the mood to be yelled at."

"That's delightful," I said, grabbing my coat from the chair in the corner of the room and ushering her toward the back of the inn. "I'm not in the mood to yell. I think this will work out well for both of us."

"Good luck, dear," Winnie called out, amused.

"Thanks so much, Mom," Bay drawled.

"I was talking to Landon."

I ignored Winnie's dig and made sure Bay tugged on her mittens and hat before following her outside. She looked adorable in the knit cap, but she was clearly spoiling for a fight despite her words to the contrary only moments before. I remained silent until we were on the back patio, sucking in a steadying breath as I stared at the moon.

"There's a full moon tonight," I noted.

Bay followed my gaze. "Yeah. It's pretty."

"Maybe that's why you're acting like a crazy woman."

Bay's mouth dropped open. "I am not crazy. I was doing you a favor."

"Don't pretend you were doing me a favor," I countered. "That's unfair to both of us. You were curious and couldn't stop yourself. At least admit that much."

"I ... fine." Bay made a low growling sound in the back of her throat. "I was doing it for me. That doesn't mean I wasn't doing it for you, too."

"I know. You have a good heart." I brushed my knuckles over her cheek. "You have very bad self-preservation instincts. It worries me. I'd appreciate it if you'd work on that."

Bay narrowed her eyes, suspicious. "I ... that's it? You're not going to yell?"

"Does yelling work?"

"No."

"Then I'm not going to yell. I need you to be careful, though. What happened today was bad. You got lucky. You can't break into someone's house simply because you're curious, sweetie."

"You clearly didn't grow up with Aunt Tillie," Bay muttered, swinging her body back and forth to generate warmth. "That was one of the first things she taught us."

"Well, if you're going to keep it up I suggest learning her masterful interrogation techniques," I said. "That's the only thing that will keep you out of jail if I catch you breaking into someone's house again."

Bay's mouth dropped open. "You can't be serious. You would arrest me?"

"If I thought it would save you, yes, I would arrest you."

"That's so mean."

"I like to think of it as love," I countered. "I love you enough to put you in jail. Don't worry, though. You wouldn't have to do much time. And I'd arrange conjugal visits."

Bay rolled her eyes even as she laughed. "You're really too kind."

"I do my best." I drew her to me and kissed her cheek. "I'm not joking about being careful, Bay. You need to do better."

"I thought I was," Bay muttered, although she didn't pull away from me.

"You didn't think you were doing better, and we both know it," I challenged. "You knew you were wrong. That's why you slipped away and didn't tell me what you had planned. And before you look me in the face and lie, I know you planned it before you left the house, so don't bother denying it."

"I ... didn't really plan it," Bay hedged. "I merely kept it open as a possibility."

"Oh, well, that makes it so much better." I exhaled heavily and shook my head. "You're work, woman. Has anyone ever told you that?"

"Just you ... every weekend."

I grinned as I pressed a kiss to her forehead. "You're just lucky that Aunt Tillie sucked out all of my energy and I have no inclination to fight. I feel like an old man after she raked me over the cauldron."

Bay giggled, relaxing against me. "She was funny about her greenhouse, wasn't she? I heard the tail end of her meltdown when I was coming in. What do you think is going on there?"

"I think it's probably Noah. He's an idiot for taking her on," I answered. "I guess since we're out here, we might as well take a look."

"You only want to get me in a private spot so you can spank me for being a bad girl." Bay's eyes lit up as she hopped down a step and held out her hand. I took it and let her lead me toward the greenhouse. "Just be warned that I'll pout if you try to punish me."

"That doesn't mean it won't be worth it," I teased.

"I agree."

We lapsed into comfortable silence, the cold air whipping past us and causing me to draw her close. "Winter is almost here. It used to be my least favorite season, but now that we're moving in together and there's a fireplace in the guesthouse, I think it's going to be my favorite season."

Bay smirked. "Me, too. We can spend entire weekends doing nothing but sitting in front of the fire. Of course, that means I'll have to learn to cook so I can feed you."

"That's what pizza is for, sweetie."

"I love the way your mind works."

I stilled by the greenhouse door. "Right back at you." I pressed a kiss to the corner of her mouth before playfully swatting her rear end.

"You're still in trouble. I simply don't have the energy to deal with the situation until I've had food and sleep."

"Duly noted." Bay was happy as she pushed open the greenhouse door. That feeling lasted only a split second as a compact figure scampered from the closest bench and disappeared into the darkness at the back of the building. "Did you see that?"

I nodded grimly. "Someone's in here."

"I guess Aunt Tillie was right."

"She always is," I muttered. "That's unbelievably frustrating. I don't suppose this place has a light, does it?"

"It's right here." Bay moved to the right. I kept close to her until she flipped a switch, flooding the room with light. That's when my gaze fell on a face I recognized, although it wasn't one I expected.

"What the ... ?"

Donna Emery, a mug of coffee clutched in her hand, offered us a rueful expression. "I can explain."

"That would be great," I said. "I just questioned your ex-husband about your potential murderer today. I'd love to hear why you're hiding in a greenhouse and not dead."

Donna licked her lips, unsure. "I don't know where to start."

"I suggest the beginning."

"I DIDN'T SET out to do this," Donna said, wringing her hands. The greenhouse wasn't nearly as cold as I expected, and I remained suspicious as to what Aunt Tillie was doing out here earlier. "I thought I'd be able to get Tim back if he thought I was missing. I didn't expect the FBI to get involved. I thought eventually Chief Terry would question Tim and that would be enough for him to come looking for me. You have to believe that."

"I don't understand," Bay said, her voice gentle. "You disappeared to make your ex-husband go looking for you??"

Donna nodded. "I thought he would realize he made a mistake when I turned up missing. I thought he would realize after a few days that I wasn't showing up around his house and he would worry."

"Donna, you've been stalking Tim and Julie." I was careful to keep my voice even. "You've been breaking into their home, stealing Julie's clothing and acting like a psychopath."

Donna clearly didn't like my interpretation of evidence, because she twisted her face into a harsh expression. "He's my husband!"

"Not any longer." I adopted a gentle but firm tone. "I understand the divorce was hard on you, but this is not the way an adult deals with a situation. Whether you want to admit it or not, Tim has moved on."

"But we pledged forever to one another," Donna said, her lower lip trembling. "We were supposed to be together forever."

"But Tim changed his mind," Bay countered. "He found someone else. That sucks for you, but he made a decision that changed your life. You have no choice but to live with it."

"He can still change his mind and come back," Donna said, crossing her arms over her chest. "He can still make things right."

"He has a child with his new wife," I prodded. "He has another child on the way. He's not leaving Julie. He's not leaving his children. You need to accept that."

"But … ." Donna looked broken at the news that Tim had another child on the way. "He never wanted children with me."

"That's probably because he knew that there was something wrong with the marriage from the beginning," Bay supplied gently. She appeared sympathetic but resolute as she took an uncertain step toward Donna. "How did you end up out here?."

"I was watching Tim's house because I wanted to see how he would react when he found out I was missing," Donna admitted. "I was there yesterday when you showed up. I listened from outside the window as you told Julie what was going on.

"After you left, she seemed almost … giddy," she continued. "I waited until she told Tim what happened. I expected him to rush out and race toward the house. I was going to follow him there so we could make up."

"And that didn't happen," I said, my heart rolling at the woman's pain.

"No." Donna looked almost pitiful as her face fell. "He said that was terrible and then proceeded to eat dinner and watch television with Julie and his son. He didn't even bother calling to see if I was okay."

"Wasn't that the final clue you needed to move on?" Bay asked.

"I guess not," Donna answered. "I came out here because I wanted to talk to Bay, but the place was packed. Then I realized it was packed with police officers and FBI agents, and I panicked.

"I followed Tillie out here because I hoped she could get you for me without causing a scene. But some FBI guy was following her," she continued. "I didn't know what else to do, so I hid out here. I hoped you'd make your way out here eventually."

"Well, here I am." Bay forced a bright smile. "What do you want me to do for you?"

"I ... ." Donna broke off, uncertain. "I wanted you to get a message to Tim. I wanted you to tell him where he could find me. I ... you don't think he'll come, do you?"

"No." Bay firmly shook her head. "I think that Tim is where he wants to be. However much that sucks for you, it's time to move on and pick a new path. It's not okay for you to terrorize Tim and Julie. They did wrong by you – both of them – but it's time to be the bigger person. You have the strength to do that. I have faith."

I shot Bay an appraising look. She's good at calming people. I often forget that, because she's also good at riling me up.

"I don't know how to do that," Donna admitted. "I ... ." She shrank back in fear when the greenhouse door opened and Aunt Tillie hopped inside. She had a broom in one hand and a knife in the other.

"Ha!"

"Oh, don't kill me!" Donna wailed. "Have mercy on me!"

"What the ... ?" Aunt Tillie looked disgusted – and a little disappointed – when she realized who we were talking to. "Donna Emery? I thought you were missing."

"She followed me here and then freaked when she saw all of the cops," Bay supplied.

"Oh, well, I can understand that reaction." Aunt Tillie lowered the knife and broom. "But you don't have to hide out here. It's cold. And I have all of the law enforcement officials bowing at my feet. Isn't that right, Landon?"

"Yes, that's exactly what I was thinking," I deadpanned, rolling my eyes.

"You must be cold out here," Aunt Tillie said. "Why don't you come inside and we'll all have dinner. Then we'll talk about whatever it is that's bothering you."

The offer surprised me. Aunt Tillie isn't known for taking pity on others. "That's nice of you."

"Yes, well, I'm feeling powerful today," Aunt Tillie noted. "I took down two FBI interrogators and lived to tell the tale."

I scowled. "That's mean of you."

"My benevolence comes and goes," Aunt Tillie said, grinning.

"I'm really not all that cold," Donna admitted. "I've been drinking your wine. I hope you don't mind. It kept me warm all night and day."

"That's why it's here," Aunt Tillie said, narrowing her eyes when she saw the open bottle. "I could actually use a belt of that before we go inside. All of those cops are giving me heartburn."

"That's funny because you're giving me heartburn." I found myself shuffling behind her. "I want some wine, too."

"I think we should all have some wine," Bay suggested. "We still have two days of this to deal with."

"At least I'm no longer missing," Donna said, giggling.

"Yes, that is a bonus," I said, tossing my arm over Bay's shoulder. "Okay, we can finish off that one bottle of wine, but then we have to go inside and pretend we're not drunk. Does everyone understand the plan?"

Bay and Donna nodded solemnly while Aunt Tillie smirked.

"I like the way you think." Aunt Tillie tapped the side of my head. "You're a crappy interrogator, but you're a good boyfriend for my niece."

"Be careful, that almost sounded like a compliment."

"You almost earned it," Aunt Tillie said. "I heard you two on the back porch. You didn't even yell a little bit when she told you she broke into Donna's house. That's progress."

"You broke into my house?" Donna wrinkled her nose.

"I was trying to see if there was a body inside," Bay protested.

"Oh, well, I guess I understand that." Donna took a long swig of wine and coughed. "That's some good stuff."

"Hand it this way," I ordered. "I ... ." I didn't get a chance to finish because another figure stormed out of the darkness, hands on hips, and fixed me with a dark look. "How many people are hiding in this greenhouse?"

"That's a good question," Aunt Tillie said, looking Twila up and down. "Why are you out here?"

"Because I've been hiding all day," Twila snapped. "I thought being a missing person was the only way to get any attention ... just like Donna. Clearly I was right. You finally found me. Congratulations."

"Did we know you were missing?" I asked, confused.

Twila shot me a disgusted look. "You're so not funny." She flounced toward the door. "I'll meet you inside for dinner. Don't get too drunk. I can't wait to see Marnie and Winnie's faces when they realize I'm fine and not dead in a ditch somewhere."

I leaned forward and watched her stride toward the inn. She had a purpose in her step. "Seriously, did we know she was missing?"

"I thought she was upstairs pouting all day," Aunt Tillie replied, unbothered.

"Oh, well, that should make dinner a disturbing affair," Bay muttered. "Pass me the wine."

"Me first." I kissed her nose before drinking a huge gulp of the wine, my cheeks immediately beginning to warm. "Come closer," I whispered.

Bay grinned and did as instructed, grabbing the wine from my hand. "Are you still angry?"

"Not so much."

"Do you still want to have a fire?"

"Bay, I want to do everything with you." I watched as she took a long drink of the wine, and then I snatched the bottle back. "That starts with getting drunk and getting through the rest of this conference. After that, I'll follow wherever you lead."

"That's the best answer I've heard all day." Bay grinned, causing Aunt Tillie to groan.

"Give me that wine," Aunt Tillie ordered. "If I have to watch you two fall all over each other I'll need a case of this stuff."

"Let's take it one bottle at a time," I said. "As long as Noah and Chris are here, we'll need a hidden stash."

"I have three cases in the other room," Aunt Tillie said. "We're covered."

"And that's why I love you, too," I offered.

Aunt Tillie stilled, clearly surprised. "You're not nearly as bad as I thought you'd be when I first met you."

"And how does that make you feel?"

"Relieved." Aunt Tillie grinned. "Now I don't have to hide a body."

And just like that, things were back to normal. "I think we're all relieved about that. Do you know what would make this wine even better?"

Bay and Aunt Tillie didn't hesitate when they answered in unison. "Bacon."

"You've got that right."

I DREAM OF TWILA

A WICKED WITCHES OF THE MIDWEST SHORT

ONE

FIFTEEN YEARS AGO

"Okay, here are the lists."

My sister Winnie was all smiles as she slipped four sheets of paper in front of me. She's an organized person – which I admire, because no one ever called me organized with a straight face – but the fact that she made lists to keep me on task was beyond annoying. When she makes lists for herself I like it. This, though, this was just ... too much.

"You made me lists?" I did my best to remain calm as I swiped a hand through my short-cropped red hair. This month I picked Island Sunrise as my color choice. It's a bit too tame for me – the red's more muted than the Lucille Ball color I generally go for – but it's fine until I have time to touch it up.

"Of course I made you lists." Winnie's face was hard to read, a mixture of blandness marked by occasional flashes of worry. "I'm leaving you home for an entire weekend with three teenagers and Aunt Tillie. They'll eat you alive if I don't give you lists."

I was pretty sure that was an insult disguised as sisterly concern. "Uh-huh. You have four lists for me."

"You have four people to take care of."

She had a point, still … . "Three of them are children and one acts like a big child. I'm sure I can handle a weekend babysitting four kids."

"I heard that." Aunt Tillie, the woman who raised my sisters and me after my mother's death, breezed into the room with a gardening shovel in her hand. She didn't look happy about being abandoned by Winnie and Marnie for the weekend, which surprised me. Winnie was always ordering her around like she was one of our girls. I expected Aunt Tillie to be excited at the prospect of freedom.

"I wasn't whispering." I did my best to look bossy – channeling my inner Winnie, if you will – but Aunt Tillie didn't look worried in the least. That was enough to put me on edge. "Just tell Winnie you'll be good this week and she'll be on her way."

I thought that would be enough to appease Aunt Tillie. She hates Winnie's bossy nature, even though she taught Winnie to be bossy. As the oldest of three sisters, Winnie often takes it upon herself to tell my sister Marnie and me what to do. As the youngest sister, I often take it upon myself to pretend I don't hear what she's saying. It's a balancing act that's about to go out of whack because Marnie and Winnie are leaving town for the weekend. Which means I'm in charge. Me. Twila Winchester. I'm the boss of the world this weekend.

I'm really looking forward to it, in case you missed that little detail. I'm never in charge. I can't wait to rule the roost … and take stock of kingdom … and … um … whatever other stuff people in charge get to do when they put on the crown. Wait, what was I doing a few seconds ago?

As if reading my mind, Winnie cocked a challenging eyebrow and stared me down. "Are you even listening to me?"

That's a trick question, and I know better than to answer it. "I was simply saying that Aunt Tillie has promised to be on her best behavior," I offered, reminding my oldest sister of a conversation we had almost a month ago. Was it really that long ago? Time spent with my sisters often feels endless. "She won't be an issue."

"I'm not especially worried about her being an issue," Winnie admitted, taking me by surprise. "I'm worried about you being an issue."

Now wait just a curse-casting minute. "Me? How am I the issue?"

"Are you really asking that question?" Aunt Tillie asked, catching my niece Bay's attention as the teenager slipped into the room. Bay's blue eyes met Aunt Tillie's brown and held for several beats before the blonde teenager broke eye contact and flipped her gaze to her mother.

"What's going on?"

Winnie shifted to face her daughter, and I realized that Bay was about to get the same earful meant for me. No wonder the kids – we each have a daughter living under this roof, and they treat each other as sisters rather than cousins (which isn't always a good thing, mind you) – always hide from Winnie when she puts on her "listen to me" face.

"We're leaving town for the weekend." Winnie said the words with more gravitas than necessary. "We'll be gone for days."

Bay blinked slowly as she blew a bubble with the purple gum she chewed and waited for it to pop before speaking. "I know. I'll miss you terribly." Bay's face was solemn, but I didn't miss the hint of mayhem lurking beneath.

"No one needs your sarcasm," Winnie said, wagging a finger in Bay's face. "You're not funny."

"I thought you were funny," Aunt Tillie interjected, grinning when Winnie gave her a dirty look. "What? She's getting really good with the snark. She's almost a full-fledged teenager. She only needs a few more weeks of practice."

"I am a teenager," Bay corrected, tilting her head to the side as she shifted her hips from one side to the other. She wore cutoffs thanks to the warm temperatures, and it occurred to me that her legs had somehow grown really long when I wasn't looking. She was almost a woman ... and that was a frightening thought. "I'm fourteen. I've been a teenager for a year and a half now."

"Being a teenager isn't a matter of age," Aunt Tillie corrected, her expression pointed. "It's a state of mind. Why do you think I'm forever young?"

"Mom says it's because you're allergic to the word 'responsibility' and you don't want to listen to reason," Bay answered automatically.

Aunt Tillie was blasé. "Oh, whatever. You could learn oodles from me, and we both know it."

"Yes, well, I don't want her learning oodles from you," Winnie interjected, grabbing a tissue from the box on the table and holding her hand in front of Bay. "Spit."

Bay knit her eyebrows, confused. "What?"

"Spit," Winnie repeated, shaking her hand for emphasis. "The way you snap that gum is massively annoying. We've talked about this. I can't stand it."

Bay opened her mouth to argue and then snapped it shut when Aunt Tillie gave her an almost imperceptible shake of the head. Something was definitely going on between them, which didn't bode well for me if they were plotting. Instead of fighting with her mother, Bay forced a smile and spit out the wad of gum.

"Better?"

"I don't think things will be better until you hit the age of thirty but I'll take what I can get." Winnie forced a bright smile before turning her attention back to me. "So, we were talking about the lists, right?"

Unfortunately we were. I was starting to believe the lists conversation would never end, that Winnie would simply talk through the weekend and miss the cooking seminar that she and Marnie insisted on attending so they would know something about cooking for large groups when we opened our own inn. I was under the impression that you just made more food for those people, but Winnie and Marnie seem to think otherwise.

Whatever. I'm looking forward to their absence. That's all that matters. Twila is in charge, people! It's going to be a great weekend. Wait ... Winnie's lips are moving. That means she's talking. Crud. I forgot what we were talking about again.

"The thing is, even though it's summer break all of the girls have schedules to stick to," Winnie said, drawing me back into the conversation. "Thistle has summer camp down at the town square."

I narrowed my eyes. "I know that Thistle has summer camp. She's my daughter." Thistle is more akin to what I imagine the offspring of

Medusa and Satan would be like – on a bad day. But she's still mine. I love her ... most of the time. "She's taking an art class. I know all about my daughter's art class."

Winnie crossed her arms over her chest, clearly annoyed with my tone. "I wasn't suggesting you didn't know about Thistle's art class."

"Great. I guess we have nothing to argue about."

"You two will always find something to argue about," Aunt Tillie argued, gesturing for Bay to move out of the way so she could flick on the television. "That's what you do. Bay, go into the kitchen and pour me a glass of iced tea."

Bay made a face. "I'm not your slave."

"Do it or I'll enchant a flyswatter to smack your bottom blue all weekend. How much fun does that sound like?"

Oh, that's right, we're also witches. I probably left that part out. It's not important this weekend, because I'm the boss and as the boss I'm ordering that no one perform any magic. It causes too many problems. No magic, no problems. See, I have it all under control.

"You're mean when you want to be," Bay grumbled as she stomped toward the kitchen. "One of these days I'll enchant a flyswatter to go after you. We'll see how you like it."

"It won't be this weekend, so you can shut up about it and get my iced tea," Aunt Tillie ordered. "Make sure you put a fresh lemon wedge in it, too."

"Oh, whatever." Bay rolled her eyes and disappeared from the room. Frankly, I was glad to see her go. I love her, but she's taken on some of Winnie's less-favorable mannerisms ... like general bossiness and thinking she's always right.

Wait ... what were we talking about again?

"Twila, are you even listening to me?" Winnie's eyes flashed as I shifted in her direction.

"Of course I'm listening to you," I snapped. "You were just insulting me and suggesting I didn't know that my own daughter has art classes in the town square."

"I didn't suggest that at all." Winnie looked as if she was about to lose her temper. I couldn't be bothered to care. Shouldn't she be gone already? "I was merely going to ask what Bay and Clove do while Thistle is at her art class."

I stilled, the question catching me off guard. "Wait ... what?"

"That's what I thought." Winnie's expression turned from falsely benign to triumphant. "That's the whole point of this conversation. And why you need lists, Twila."

I blew a raspberry as I pushed my hair away from my forehead. The house, which always felt small when we were all inside, suddenly felt inordinately compressed as Winnie sucked up all of the oxygen in the room. "I know what Bay and Clove are doing while Thistle is in her art class."

"Really? What?" Winnie crossed her arms over her chest, a clear challenge to the authority I was due to claim – that was if Winnie ever left the house, of course.

"They ... um ... ." I darted a panicked look toward the kitchen door in the hope that Bay would swoop in and rescue me. Instead, Aunt Tillie did the dirty deed, stunning everyone.

"Bay is spending her afternoons at the newspaper office helping William Kelly," Aunt Tillie volunteered. "He's paying her as an intern, but she's really doing busy work and listening to him yammer on and on about stuff that's not really important, given the state of the newspaper industry today."

Winnie narrowed her eyes to dangerous slits. "It's good for Bay. She wants to be a reporter."

"She should pick a more dependable occupation," Aunt Tillie argued. "That one will never get her anywhere but trouble. Trust me. I know things."

"Yes, well, I am impressed you know where Bay is spending her days this summer," Winnie admitted. "I had no idea you knew."

"I knew it, too," I offered.

Winnie made a face only a sister could love – and when I say that, I mean only our other sister could love her right now. She's honestly on my last nerve. She's so perfect ... and bossy ... and she never forgets anything. She's so ... Winnie. It makes me want to punch her. What?

It's her fault. I'm the innocent victim here. Wait ... what were we talking about again?

"What about Clove?" Winnie prodded. "What is she doing with her afternoons this week?"

That had to be a trick question. As far as I could tell Clove was doing nothing other than drooling after boys and eating ice cream – not necessarily in that order – and she wasn't focused on anything other than her rampaging hormones.

I licked my lips. "Well ... ."

"Clove isn't doing anything but stalking that Fitzgerald boy," Aunt Tillie snapped. "She was supposed to get a summer job, but she decided to become a pint-sized *Fatal Attraction* wannabe extra instead."

"Exactly." I bobbed my head. "She's a ... wait ... what?" I snapped my eyes to Aunt Tillie. "Clove is a stalker?"

"I'm not a stalker," Clove announced, arriving at the bottom of the stairs and scalding me with a dark look. "I can't believe you'd say that about your favorite niece."

"I'm her favorite niece," Bay corrected, strolling back into the room with a glass of iced tea in her hand. "I'm the good one who never gives anyone trouble."

Aunt Tillie snickered as she accepted her iced tea. "You're not the good one. You're simply the one who is better at hiding things when you're bad. Clove is a poor liar – although she can cry on a whim, and that can come in handy – and Thistle doesn't care enough to bother thinking up a lie. You're merely smarter than the other two. That doesn't make you the good one."

"Leave her alone," Winnie ordered, waves of annoyance rolling off my sister and cascading through the room. "She's not the one I'm worried about this weekend."

"If you're worrying about me, don't," Aunt Tillie supplied. "It's supposed to be hot. The only trouble I plan on finding is in a bottle. Oh, and I might take the girls to the lake for a swim. That's it."

"Believe it or not, I wasn't talking about you either," Winnie said, her eyes drifting toward me. "I'm most worried about Twila."

"Oh, well, that makes perfect sense," Aunt Tillie said, brightening. "She'll screw everything up. Everyone knows it."

I risked a glance at Bay and Clove and found them solemnly nodding.

"Hey!"

Winnie ignored my outburst. "If you run into trouble, Twila, we're only a phone call away."

"Don't worry about that," Aunt Tillie said. "I'll be here to make sure everything is fine. You can count on me to fix whatever mess Twila dreams up. Don't I always?"

"Hey!"

Winnie and Aunt Tillie went on talking as if I wasn't even in the room.

"The girls know their schedules, and they've been relatively good for weeks," Winnie said. "That means they're due for mischief. The problem is, you've been good for a full ten days, which means you're due for a round of mischief, too. If both of those bouts coincide, Twila will be in over her head, and that hardly seems fair."

"Hey!"

No one bothered to look in my direction.

"Am I suddenly invisible?"

Aunt Tillie shook her head, her eyes never moving from Winnie's face. "I said I'd be good. Why don't you ever believe me?"

"Maybe because she's met you," Bay suggested, offering up a prissy smile.

"You're on my list, junior Miss Bossy," Aunt Tillie barked. "You probably don't want to push things too far."

"Oh, whatever." Bay heaved a sigh before focusing on her mother. "Everything will be fine. We promise to be good for Aunt Twila. You have nothing to worry about."

"We promise to be angels," Clove added, batting her eyes. "Would we lie to you?"

Winnie extended a finger and narrowed her eyes. "No stalking that poor Fitzgerald boy while we're gone. You've turned him into a nervous wreck. His mother is convinced that you're in heat or something."

"I don't know what that means, but I don't stalk people." Clove jutted out her lower lip. "I think I'm being persecuted. Wait ... that's the correct word, right? Witches back in the olden days were persecuted, right?"

Bay nodded. She had the best vocabulary of all the girls. "Yeah. That's the right word."

"I'm still persecuted," Aunt Tillie noted.

"Okay, fine." Winnie threw up her hands. "I trust you all to be good and not make things too rough for Twila." She handed the sheets of paper to me and forced a smile. "I wrote down the emergency numbers so you have everything in one place. If you get into real trouble, call Terry."

Terry Davenport, Walkerville's top cop, was accustomed to frequent stops at our house.

"I'm more than capable of taking care of three children and one demented old lady for a few days," I barked. "I've got everything under control."

"Okay, well ... good luck."

I rubbed my forehead as Winnie grabbed her suitcase and shuffled toward the door. I followed her progress, finally locking gazes with Aunt Tillie, who glared in my direction. "What?"

"Demented old lady?"

"It was a figure of speech."

"Yeah? Figure you're now on my list."

Bay giggled as she wiggled her hips and did a little freedom dance. "Live in fear."

Aunt Tillie grinned. "You're definitely the smartest of the group."

TWO

"Dinner is served."

I slid the platter of pasta toward the center of the dining room table and smiled at my young charges.

"It's on time and everything. For those of you keeping notes – and I know who you are, Bay – you can tell your mother that not only was dinner on time the first night it also was nutritious and delicious."

Bay didn't look remotely embarrassed as she jotted something down in the notebook she'd taken to carrying. "For your information, these notes aren't about you."

"Oh, really?" I cocked a dubious eyebrow. "What did you just write down if it wasn't about me?"

"I'm working on a list of things I want to do over the summer." Bay delivered the response with a steady expression, but I knew she was lying.

"That was better," Aunt Tillie noted. "You squared your chin a little too fast, though, as if you were offended. What have I been telling you guys about getting offended?"

"Don't get offended, just get even," Clove automatically answered, reaching for the tongs at the center of the table so she could dole out the pasta.

"Very good, Clove." Aunt Tillie beamed. "You parrot things back with the best of them. But you need to work on your lying. You're so bad at it that it's getting embarrassing."

Wait a second .... "You're teaching them to lie?"

"Not very well," Aunt Tillie replied, blasé. "What is that ... thing ... in the middle of the sauce, by the way? It doesn't look like meatballs."

"It's vegetarian," I answered, my mind busy. "It's eggplant, cauliflower, broccoli and onions. Why are you teaching them to lie?"

"I don't like broccoli." Aunt Tillie wrinkled her nose. "If the Goddess had meant for us to eat vegetables she would've made them taste better than meatballs."

"Why are you teaching them to lie?" I repeated, refusing to let my aunt derail the conversational train. "Also, broccoli is better for you than meatballs. Meatballs will clog your arteries and give you a heart attack. Heart attacks can kill you."

Aunt Tillie rolled her eyes until they landed on my daughter Thistle, who sat at the end of the table glaring at the vegetarian pasta. "See, the mouth clearly agrees with me about vegetables and meat not being interchangeable."

"Thistle happens to love vegetables. Don't you, sweetheart?"

Thistle poked her fork into a hunk of onion. "No mushrooms?"

Aunt Tillie snorted. "Yes, she's clearly thrilled with your dinner choice. Who wants to order pizza ... with meat?"

Bay and Thistle raised their hands in unison while Clove continued to stare at the vegetables.

"Thistle, I thought you liked vegetables," I challenged. "You eat fresh tomatoes and green beans from the garden every single day. That means you like vegetables."

"I like certain vegetables, and only in moderation," Thistle said, adopting an annoying tone that I was fairly certain she picked up from Winnie in an effort to annoy me. "You always say that we should only do things in moderation."

"You do say that," Clove echoed. "You can only drink in moderation."

"And when you're over twenty-one," Bay added, wrinkling her nose as she used her fork to comb through the pasta.

"You can only eat in moderation if you don't want to be fat," Clove added.

"You can only have sex in moderation if you don't want to be considered a sex fiend," Thistle interjected, causing me to snap my head in her direction. "I don't know that one from personal experience, but I'm looking forward to finding out if it's true."

"I know what you're doing," I snapped, sucking in a deep breath to calm myself. "You're trying to say things to see how upset you can make me. I know the game you're playing, Thistle, and it won't work."

"I have no idea what you're talking about," Thistle said, her face twisting with sadness. "Is that really what you think of me?"

I balked. "Well … ."

"That right there was much better," Aunt Tillie interjected, waving her fork in Thistle's direction. "Did you see how she did that, Bay? She lied with a straight face, didn't get defensive and never once acted as if she was saying anything untruthful. Very good, Thistle!"

I pressed the heel of my hand to my forehead as I absorbed the latest Winchester family wrinkle. "Okay, um, why are you teaching them to lie?"

"Because it's a very important skill, and because they're witches," Aunt Tillie replied. "I mean … think about it. They can perform magic. Sure, they only dabble now and can't do very many things, but that will change as they get older. When that happens they run the risk of being discovered. I want to make sure that doesn't happen."

I didn't realize I was gaping until I caught sight of Thistle and Bay mimicking me out of the corner of my eye. "So you're teaching them to lie in case one day, far down the road, they might need to lie to someone about being a witch?"

Aunt Tillie nodded. "I was too late teaching you guys to lie. We've paid for that several times since. I don't want to be too late with these guys."

"You weren't late teaching us," I argued. "We simply don't feel the need to lie all of the time. If you're careful from the start, girls, there's no need to lie." I flashed a sugary smile that caused everyone else at the table to roll their eyes in unison.

"I'm happier knowing how to lie," Bay said, clicking her ink pen before writing something in her notebook.

"Now what are you writing?"

"I'm just making a note to remind myself that I promised Mom I'd weed the side garden tomorrow," Bay answered without hesitation.

"Much better!" Aunt Tillie clapped approvingly. "You didn't blink at the wrong time. You didn't swallow and let her know you were making it up. You even added in that little part 'for my Mom,' and that means people will be less likely to call you on your subterfuge. That was a vast improvement."

Bay preened under the compliment. "Thank you."

"I can't believe this is happening." I lowered my forehead to my palm as I rested my elbow on the table. "You can't offer them lessons in lying. That is just ... ."

"Ingenious?" Aunt Tillie prodded.

"All kinds of wrong," I snapped, my temper getting the better of me. "Seriously, what are you even thinking?"

Aunt Tillie ignored my outburst and returned her attention to the pasta. "So ... where did we land on the meatballs?"

"You're eating those vegetables and you'll like it," I barked.

"I love vegetables," Clove enthused, dishing a huge heap of pasta onto her plate. "I love that Aunt Twila took time out of her busy day to cook us a nutritious and delicious meal. I feel so lucky."

Gratitude washed over me. "Thank you, Clove." Finally someone appreciated me. It wasn't my aunt or daughter, but at least it was someone.

"That was better, Clove, but you lacked sincerity in the delivery, and the last part – the part where you added 'I feel so lucky' – was way too much. Sometimes less is more." Aunt Tillie smiled as she leaned back in her chair. "So ... where did we land on the pizza?"

"Fine!" I tossed my napkin in the middle of the table and hopped to my feet. "You guys are going to do what you want anyway ... so do it. I don't care."

"That's great," Aunt Tillie said, refusing to give in to my meltdown. "We're going to order pizza, breadsticks and wings. I need you to give me some money to pay the delivery guy."

I narrowed my eyes until they were nothing but slits. "Do whatever you want."

"What are you going to do?" Aunt Tillie asked, watching as I stomped toward the stairs that led to the second floor.

"I'm going to take a bath."

"That sounds good." Aunt Tillie refused to engage in an argument. "You need to relax. That will help. I'll handle dinner. That's the least I can do."

I gestured toward the table. "I handled dinner!"

"Okay, I should probably rephrase that," Aunt Tillie said. "I'll provide a dinner they'll actually eat. How does that sound?"

I couldn't find the words to answer so I merely growled as I stomped up the stairs. The last thing I heard was Thistle talking to Aunt Tillie.

"She's going to murder you in your sleep if you keep doing stuff like this."

Aunt Tillie snickered. "Just watch and learn, little mouth. I've got everything under control."

AFTER AN HOUR in the tub, steaming hot water allowing my steaming temper to abate, I almost felt human again. I dressed in jogging pants and a sweatshirt, and made my way to the main floor, intent on eating my leftover pasta and getting to the bottom of the lying classes before bed.

I still had several days to be in charge – and they were going to be great days – and I wanted to make sure this little issue didn't become a big thing under my watch. If Aunt Tillie wanted to continue her lying lessons when Winnie and Marnie returned and could deal with the outcome that was one thing. I wasn't going to let this situation get out of hand on my watch.

No way.

No how.

Nuh-uh.

I was halfway down the stairs when an ear-splitting scream rocked the house and I jerked my attention to the main floor. I hurried down the stairs and raced into the living room, to find Clove gasping for breath next to the bay window at the front of the house while Thistle and Bay tried to calm her.

"What's going on?"

"There's someone outside," Clove said, holding her hand to her chest, her face red. "There's someone looking in the window ... peeping!"

I stood still, waiting for Aunt Tillie's critique on Clove's lying abilities before responding. I risked a glance toward Aunt Tillie's favorite chair and found it empty, which caused me to furrow my brow and take a step closer.

"Is this a game?"

"Of course not." Clove looked scandalized. "Why would I lie?"

"You didn't really just ask that, did you?" I pushed past her and shoved the curtain out of the way so I could look outside. I wasn't expecting anyone to be there, but the deepening darkness wouldn't have allowed me to see anything even if a peeper really was present. "There's no one out there."

"You don't know," Clove challenged. "There could be a stalker out there. It's too dark for you to see."

"And she would know about stalkers," Aunt Tillie said, breezing into the room. "What's going on?"

"Clove says there's a peeper outside," Thistle answered, throwing herself on the couch and resting her feet on the coffee table. "Like she has anything anyone would want to peep at."

Aunt Tillie snickered as Clove bristled.

"I have stuff." Clove ran her hands over her mostly flat chest. "I have good stuff. And a lot of people want to look at it."

"Yeah, perverts," Bay muttered.

"Don't worry, Clove," I said, patting her shoulder. "You don't have stuff yet, but you will. You're built like your mother. That means you're going to get the most stuff."

Clove wasn't completely mollified, but the snarky look she sent Thistle was full of meaning. I don't have half the "stuff" Marnie had, so odds are Thistle would end up with my curve-light body. Of course, now was not the time to point that out.

"Ha, ha, mouth," Aunt Tillie laughed, clearly enjoying herself. "She's basically saying you'll be flat your entire life."

"I was not saying that!"

Thistle's expression darkened. "I hate all of you sometimes."

"Join the club," I snapped. "There are days I want to lock all of you in closets and pretend you don't exist. Yeah, I said it. I'm not sorry either. If one of you starts crying I'm not going to apologize. Bay, what are you writing in your notebook?"

Bay shrugged. "I have no idea what you're talking about. I'm not writing anything."

"Oh, that was inspired." Aunt Tillie nodded approvingly. "We haven't even gotten to that lesson and you're already teaching it to yourself. You guys are the best students ever."

"What lesson?" Thistle asked. It was fairly obvious she didn't want to know for her own edification but because Bay was receiving praise. Thistle wanted to beat Bay at her own game. She just needed someone to identify the game for her.

"The 'deny-no-matter-what' lesson," Aunt Tillie answered. "There's going to come a time in your lives when no lie – no matter how brilliant and shiny – will save your bacon. Ooh, we should've gotten bacon on the pizza. I didn't even think about it. I love bacon. Wait … what was I saying?"

I must get that particular scattered gift from her. There can be no other explanation.

"Oh, right, I was talking about denying you're up to no good even when you're caught in the act," Aunt Tillie said, regaining her train of thought. "There's going to come a time when no lie will be good enough to get you out of trouble. When that happens, girls, deny you're doing anything and pretend the other person is crazy. This won't work for the first minute or so, but if you keep it up eventually people will get so annoyed with you they'll forget what they're suspicious about."

"Don't tell them things like that," I chided. "You're corrupting them."

"They're witches. They need a little corruption." Aunt Tillie hunkered down and stared out the window. "So ... we think a peeper was out here?"

I'd almost forgotten Clove's freakout. "Oh, yeah, is this one of the games you're playing with the girls?"

"I have no interest in playing peeping games with girls," Aunt Tillie answered, her expression serious. "I don't roll that way."

"Gross." Bay made a face. "Clove swears she saw someone on the porch looking in through the window. It wasn't part of a game."

"I'm not making it up," Clove said. "I honestly saw someone staring in the window."

Part of me didn't believe her. I couldn't, after all. They were playing a lying game, for crying out loud. The other part couldn't ignore the serious expression on her face. She was a tiny girl, and even though she was thirteen, she was small for her age. There were days I looked at her and believed she was eight. No joke.

I heaved a sigh. "Okay, Clove, tell me exactly what you saw."

"I wasn't really looking at anything," Clove explained. "I was thinking about Alex Fitzgerald – he's really cute, you know – and I was deciding how I was going to visit him without looking like a stalker tomorrow when I happened to look through the window. That's when I saw him."

"Him?" I arched an eyebrow. "You're sure it was a him? Did you recognize the face?"

"I'm only sure it was a him because he was tall," Clove replied.

"Everyone is tall compared to you," Thistle said.

"I understand that, but it was a guy," Clove said. "He was as tall as Officer Terry."

I pursed my lips. Terry Davenport was a big man. If the person Clove saw was that big there could be no mistaking someone being on the front porch. I made my decision on the spot. "Did you see which direction he headed in?"

Clove pointed straight out, in the direction of the main road on the other side of the driveway. "That way."

"Okay, well … ." I flicked my eyes to Aunt Tillie, uncertain. "I should probably go check things out."

"You probably should," Aunt Tillie agreed, nodding.

I wasn't keen on the idea – and I kind of hoped she'd try to talk me out of it – so I couldn't hide my disappointment. "Oh. You want me to go?"

"I think it's a swell idea."

"Fine," I gritted, out, squaring my shoulders as I moved toward the door. "If I die out there because there's really a peeper I expect you to take care of the girls until Marnie and Winnie get back. Oh, also, I want a really big funeral with a lot of weeping guests."

"Oh, geez." Aunt Tillie made an exaggerated face. "Hold on. We'll go with you."

"We will?" Thistle looked upset at the prospect. "What if we all die?"

Aunt Tillie shrugged. "Then we'll die together. That, too, is the Winchester way."

Well, at least I wouldn't die alone. I had that going for me.

THREE

"You stepped on my foot."
"I did not."
"You did, too."
"I did not."
"You both stepped on my feet, and I don't like it."

"You know what I don't like? I don't like little girls making noise when we're supposed to be sneaking around the woods." Aunt Tillie walked to my left and as I attempted to tune out the girls' squabbling she opted to engage with them. "We've been through this before. When sneaking through the woods, what is the most important thing?"

"Don't step on a rake because you'll knock yourself out," Clove answered. I couldn't see her in the dark as I made my way down the driveway, but I could make out a small shadow near the ditch and I swear I heard an eye roll in her voice.

"That is a good rule," Aunt Tillie confirmed. "Laugh all you want, but that's happened to me twice."

"Some might call that karma," I noted.

"No one is talking to you," Aunt Tillie said. "While the rake rule is very important, girls, that's not the rule I was talking about. I taught you a very important rule just two weeks ago when we were spying on Margaret Little. What was it?"

"If she's naked, close your eyes," Clove replied.

"If she's doing something evil, call Officer Terry and tattle," Bay answered.

"If she's happy, make sure she's crying before leaving the house … even if you have to kick her or smack her around with a baseball bat to do it," Thistle supplied, grinning as the moonlight poked through the clouds.

Wait a second … . Something occurred to me. "When did you take them to Mrs. Little's house to spy on her?" I asked, racking my brain for a night when Aunt Tillie voluntarily spent time with the girls. "I don't remember you taking them anywhere."

"That's because we sneak out of the house sometimes when you're drinking your wine and pretending you don't have sisters or a daughter," Thistle said. "Don't worry about it. We rarely get in real trouble."

Oh, well, in that case … . "Clove, do you see anything that reminds you of the face you saw staring into the window?"

Clove is usually the most congenial of the girls, but that wasn't on display tonight. "Yeah. You see that tree over there? It was that tree I saw. My bad."

"No one needs your snark, young lady," I chided. "It was a simple question."

"It was a stupid question." Aunt Tillie was seemingly unbothered by the fact that we were wandering around in the dark looking for a potential window peeper. "First, if we saw anyone out here it would obviously be the man we were looking for. We don't have an overabundance of men running around on our property after dark."

"Mostly because they're afraid you'll shrink their junk," Bay interjected.

"Do you even know what you're saying?" I challenged.

Bay nodded. "Men think with their penises, and if their penises are too small they go crazy."

I shook my head and glared at Aunt Tillie. "Did you tell her that?"

Aunt Tillie ignored the question. "Where was I?"

"Second," Clove prodded.

"Right." Aunt Tillie bobbed her head. "Second, if Clove saw someone out on this property while we were walking around she'd start screaming and annoy the living crap out of all of us."

Thistle snickered as Clove scalded Aunt Tillie with a dark look. "She'd definitely be annoying the crap out of us."

"I hate everyone in this family," Clove muttered.

"You'll have to get in line with that one," I said. "I'm pretty sure I hate everyone more than you do."

"That's not even possible. I ... hey, what is that?" Clove lost interest in her familial hate and pointed toward a bevy of lights flickering in the field at the end of the driveway. They weren't electrical lights, but the warm illumination of multiple lanterns. "Is that a ... party?"

I wasn't sure how to answer. It seemed ludicrous that anyone would be partying at the edge of our property without me knowing it. Of course, when I was younger we used to party in this field all of the time. We also had picnics here ... and picked flowers in the summer ... and did cartwheels as our mother looked on and applauded. That was long before she died, of course.

"It does kind of look like a party, doesn't it?" I flicked my gaze from face to face as several sets of expectant eyes moved in my direction. The people in the field were dressed in flowing clothing and looked as if they'd run away from a renaissance festival. They even had a gypsy caravan wagon. It was ... surreal. "This isn't a dream, right?"

"Yeah, like we would dream about trespassers having a bonfire party on our property," Aunt Tillie muttered, tilting her head to the side as she locked gazes with an older woman sitting next to the bonfire. The woman, long silver hair pulled back in a loose bun, regarded us with unveiled interest. She didn't say anything or ask the people flitting around the field to stop dancing (or whatever it was they were doing). Instead she merely stared ... and waved.

"What is she doing?" Bay asked, confused. "Is she smiling at us?"

"What did I tell you about trusting people who smile before they even meet you?" Aunt Tillie queried.

"They're hiding something and will probably try to steal your wallet or your virtue," Bay answered automatically.

"Don't tell her things like that," I snapped, my eyebrows flying into my hairline. "You'll make her suspicious of people, and that's no way to live her life."

"She needs to be suspicious of people," Aunt Tillie countered. "She's gifted. People will try to use that gift at some point, and she needs to be wary of users."

"Yes, but if she's too wary she'll close herself off to people," I argued. "She doesn't want that."

"Don't worry about that." Aunt Tillie's lips curved as she spared a glance for Bay. "She'll find her place ... and person ... eventually. I don't want her becoming a doormat before it happens."

I never know what to think about Aunt Tillie when it comes to the girls. Most of the time she acts agitated and annoyed when spending time with them, but she also enjoys warping their minds to her way of thinking. The girls are eager to do it because Aunt Tillie seems fun and magical when you're thirteen and fourteen and believe the world revolves around you. Aunt Tillie is in her late sixties and believes the world indeed does revolve around them, so the girls think she's on their side.

The true problem is that Aunt Tillie is on their side more often than not. Even when she's agitated and wants the girls to shut their mouths and stay out of her stuff, she's still their biggest fan. It's ... odd. She yells and screams and teaches them horrible things, but she loves them beyond reason. There's no other way of looking at it. She wants them to succeed no matter what ... even when she wants them to fail because they're working against her.

Wait ... what were we talking about again?

"Welcome." The elderly woman sitting in the central spot next to the fire slowly got to her feet, her eyes busy as they bounced between faces. "Can I help you? Are you lost?"

"That's weird," Aunt Tillie said, planting her hands on her hips. "I was just about to ask you the same question."

"Oh, I'm not lost," the woman said. "I always know where I am."

Aunt Tillie narrowed her eyes, her stance defiant. I wasn't sure if it was meeting someone close to her age who appeared to have the same attitude or the fact that she really didn't like trespassers that bothered her. She was clearly agitated, though. "I know where you are, too. You're on my property."

"Your property? I thought this property belonged to the Goddess."

Oh, well, that was interesting. Of course, she looked to be a true believer given the caravan wagon. "You believe in the Goddess?"

"Don't you?"

I nodded without hesitation. "My name is Twila Winchester. This is our property. It looks as if you're just passing through, so you're welcome to stay."

"I didn't agree to that," Aunt Tillie said dryly. "In fact ... were you just looking through our living room window?"

I'd forgotten all about that. We were only out here because Clove thought she saw someone staring at her from the other side of the glass. If the campers decided to take a look around their surroundings and ended up at the house, that could explain a few things. "Did you come up to the house?"

The woman nodded, seemingly unbothered about being caught. "We wanted to see if we were alone. I felt a presence I couldn't explain. Jonathan here went to see if he could find something. He found you ... which explained everything."

I shifted from one foot to the other, uncertain. "I see." I really didn't see.

"I'm Cherry Brucker," the woman announced. "I'm the greatest fortune teller in the world."

The tightening in my chest eased as a few things slipped into place. "Oh, well, that sounds fun. Doesn't that sound fun, Aunt Tillie?"

"Fun?" Aunt Tillie apparently had the exact opposite reaction. "That doesn't sound fun at all. And what kind of name is Cherry?"

"What kind of a name is Tillie?" Cherry challenged.

"It's a family name," Aunt Tillie barked. "A very fine family name, for that matter. I'm not named after a fruit. A bad fruit at that."

"I like cherries," Thistle said, shifting closer, her eyes keen as she looked Cherry over. "You read fortunes?"

Cherry smiled and nodded. "I do."

"I hate cherries, but I think Cherry is a fine name," Bay offered. "It's better to be named after fruit than herbs."

"That's definitely true," Thistle agreed.

"Your names are perfect for your personalities," Aunt Tillie argued. "For example, thistles are prickly. I don't know a pricklier person than you."

"I do," Thistle muttered just loud enough for everyone to hear. "You."

"I can't hear you, mouth." Aunt Tillie held up her hand to silence Thistle as she focused on Cherry. "So … what? You guys are a fortune telling crew?"

"We're part of the Moon Lake Renaissance Troupe," the man Cherry identified as Jonathan volunteered. "We do more than tell fortunes. That's Cherry's main job."

"And what are you doing here?" I asked.

"We broke off from the rest of the group because we had a short side job," Jonathan replied. "We're supposed to meet up with everyone else in St. Ignace in about a week, but we're heading to Traverse City first. We were traveling through the area when Cherry insisted on stopping. She said this place had special energy."

"Oh, well, it does." I felt more relaxed after hearing that the ten people camping in my backyard really were with a renaissance festival. I happen to love renaissance festivals. I think they're tons of fun … and who doesn't like grog? I'm a witch. Grog is right up my alley. "So you're here just for the night?"

"Probably," Cherry hedged. "We have two days before we have to be in Traverse City, so we might stay more than one night. If that's okay."

"That's fine."

"Wait a second." Aunt Tillie wrinkled her nose, her displeasure evident. "This is my property. I didn't say they could stay. I'm the one who makes the final decision."

"Why can't they stay?" Bay asked, sitting in the chair across from Cherry and smiling when the woman grabbed her hand and flipped it over to study the palm. "I think they're neat."

"And they have a really cool wagon," Thistle added. She wasn't nearly as interested in the people as she was in the ornate green wagon. "Do you live in here?"

"Not generally," Cherry answered, running her index finger over Bay's lifeline and causing Aunt Tillie to scowl. "We do when we're traveling, but we often stay in hotels. The weather right now is wonderful, so everyone is fine camping for a few nights."

"Especially here," Jonathan enthused. "This is a great piece of land. And the house ... well ... from what I could see, the house is beautiful. It's a Victorian, right?"

"It is," I confirmed, smiling. "We had a simple homestead at one time, but over the years it was enhanced until it became what you see today."

"Well, it's beautiful."

"Uh-huh. Were you looking through the window in the living room?" I could hardly let that slide. I had three young teenagers (one was technically still a tween) under my care. I couldn't let a potential pervert just wander around without at least questioning him.

"I saw the house," Jonathan replied. "I took a closer look and stepped on the front porch. I was going to knock and then I heard some raised voices – I identified a few of them as children – so I didn't want to interrupt. I was going to come back up and introduce myself, but I wanted to wait until you were done ... um ... yelling."

"We weren't yelling," Clove said, her interest pointed toward one of the women dancing in the field. "That's just the way we talk to each other."

Well, she wasn't wrong. "It's fine if you want to stay for the night – even if you want to stay for another night or two after that – but don't sneak around the house. It makes everyone nervous."

"I assure you that wasn't my intention," Jonathan promised, holding up his hands. "I simply didn't want to interrupt a family moment."

"We're always having family moments, so don't let that be a concern." I smiled as Jonathan laughed. "It's fine."

"I didn't agree to that." Aunt Tillie's anger was palpable, but I refused to play her game.

"You'll live." I smiled as Cherry pointed to a spot on Bay's palm. "Do you see something?"

"I do," Cherry said, bobbing her head. "This child is going to have a very interesting life."

"We already knew that," Aunt Tillie muttered, folding her arms and pursing her lips. "She's a Winchester. All Winchesters have interesting lives."

"Yes, but this child is unique even for your bloodline," Cherry said, her finger busy as it moved across Bay's palm. "Do you see this? Your lifeline has a hitch here. That's a point in your life where you'll have a choice to make. It will be a big one."

Bay leaned forward, intrigued. "Will I make the right choice?"

"It's not that kind of choice," Cherry replied. "It won't be a case of what's right or wrong. It will be a case of what's right for you at the time. You have greatness in you, child, but when this decision comes the option will be for safety or adventure. You won't have a bad life either way, but one choice could mean terrible things for those around you."

Wherever I thought the fortune talk was going, that wasn't it. "I … what are you telling her?"

"Do you mean I'll kill my family?" Bay furrowed her brow. "Is that what you're saying?"

"Of course not," I automatically answered. "That's not what she's saying."

"That is what I'm saying," Cherry argued. "You have a mark on you, Bay. You could bring greatness to those you love or sadness. It's not your fault. It's the mark."

"So I'm … cursed?" Bay looked horrified at the prospect.

"You're not cursed," Aunt Tillie argued, grabbing Bay's arm and dragging her away from Cherry. "Sometimes I feel cursed when I'm with you, but that's hardly the same thing."

Bay didn't look convinced. "But she said … ."

"Ignore what she said." Aunt Tillie's gaze was unfathomably dark as it landed on Cherry, the warning emanating from her obvious. "She doesn't know what she's talking about. Come on. I've got the stuff to make s'mores up at the house. Let's see how much sugar we can eat tonight. How does that sound?"

Thistle quickly lost interest in the wagon. "Awesome. Are we going to stalk Mrs. Little when we're done?"

Aunt Tillie shrugged as she pointed Bay toward the house. "The night is young and so are we. The possibilities are endless."

"It was nice meeting you all," I said, falling into step behind my aunt and nieces. "If you need anything, don't hesitate to come up to the house."

"Yes, well, thank you." Jonathan bobbed his head. "Your hospitality means a great deal to us."

My eyes briefly landed on Bay, and I couldn't help worrying about the way she stared at her hand and refused to smile. "Don't mention it."

FOUR

"Okay, I have blueberry pancakes and bacon. Is everyone okay with that this morning or should I start taking orders and pretend I'm running a restaurant?"

I was still mildly irritated the next morning that no one ate the vegetable pasta from the night before. In general, I'm a happy person. I like being a happy person. My sisters are not bright and shiny people. They're crabby people ... and they blame the kids and Aunt Tillie. My entire goal this weekend is to make sure that I remain an upbeat person despite having to monitor the four immature Winchesters.

"Who doesn't like pancakes?" Clove enthused, digging into her mountainous breakfast.

"No one who I want to spend any time with," Thistle replied, drowning her pancakes in butter and syrup. "Pancakes are awesome ... especially your pancakes, Mom."

My cheeks colored with pleasure. Thistle wasn't one for doling out compliments. "Oh, well, thank you."

"That was very good," Aunt Tillie said, nursing her mug of coffee as the girls inhaled their pancakes and bacon. "She didn't see it coming, and you totally distracted her, Thistle. This is one of the few times your mouth is a gift."

"My mouth is always a gift," Thistle shot back, breaking a slice of bacon in half as she cast a sidelong look in Bay's direction. Unlike everyone else at the table, my blonde niece looked morose. "What's wrong with you?"

"Nothing," Bay replied hurriedly, shaking her head as she dragged her attention to the plate in front of her. "I love pancakes and bacon, and I think Aunt Twila makes the best pancakes of everyone – and I'm not just saying that to be a suck-up like you, Thistle."

Aunt Tillie snorted. "She did sound like a bit of a suck-up, didn't she? The problem is that you're an unlikable person, Thistle. It's not a bad thing. You make it work for you. I make it work for me, too, which is why I recognize it in you. The older you get, the more you'll have to watch yourself, because people won't believe it when you say nice things."

"Don't tell her that," I scolded, lightly cuffing the back of Aunt Tillie's head as I moved around the table to get a better look at Bay. She appeared pale, shadows under her eyes. I couldn't help but wonder if she was ill. "Sweetie, is something wrong?"

I didn't wait for an answer, instead pressing my hand to her forehead and earning a pronounced eye roll.

"I'm not sick," Bay muttered, slapping at my hand. "I'm just ... tired."

"Didn't you sleep?"

"She was up all night," Clove answered, her expression thoughtful as she stared at her cousin. "I think she's upset about what the gypsy lady said."

"I don't think you're supposed to say 'gypsy,'" I corrected. "I think that's a slur – like if you say the N-word or the S-word."

"What's the S-word?" Thistle asked, her gaze bouncing between Aunt Tillie and me. "I can only think of one S-word, and I didn't know that was a slur."

"I can actually only think of one S-word, too," Aunt Tillie admitted. "What is the S-word, Twila?"

Uh-oh. Now I was caught. "Oh, well, it's something that people – obnoxious people, mind you – call Hispanic individuals."

It took Aunt Tillie a moment to realize what I meant. "Oh. Okay, I'll give you that one."

"I still don't know what the S-word is," Thistle complained.

Aunt Tillie waved off Thistle's dour mood. "I'll tell you later."

"You will not," I snapped, moving my hands to Bay's cheeks even as she struggled against my efforts. "The longer the girls go without hearing words like that, the better."

"She's probably already heard it," Aunt Tillie argued. "She simply doesn't realize it."

"There's nothing wrong with that." I pulled my hands from Bay's face and stared down at her. "You don't have a fever."

"That's because I'm not sick." Bay made small shooing motions with her hands to get me to back up. "Stop being a kvetch."

Aunt Tillie beamed at Bay. "You used that word correctly. You slapped her back without being overtly rude. Good job." She rewarded Bay with an extra slice of bacon from her plate. That seemed unusual – Aunt Tillie isn't known as much of a sharer – until I realized Aunt Tillie was as worried about Bay as I was.

"Anyway, what was I talking about?"

"How we shouldn't use the word 'gypsy' because it's a slur," Clove answered. "What other words are slurs? Besides the N-word and S-word, I mean."

"The I-word for Native Americans but not people from India," Bay answered, showing off her big brain and making me smile. The girl looked weary and worn, but she still had her sense of humor.

"That's a very good one, Bay." I took a step toward my chair. "You're very smart and didn't offend anyone. Good job." I figured if Aunt Tillie could reward the girls for lying and covering up their misdeeds I could fight some of her efforts and praise the girls for saying the right things. I would beat Aunt Tillie at her own game.

"The C-word is definitely a slur, though," Bay added, catching me off guard.

"The C-word?" My eyebrows flew toward my hairline. "How do you know the C-word?"

"I hear Mom use it all the time," Bay replied without hesitation. "She called Aunt Marnie the C-word yesterday before they left, and she called you the C-word when you didn't bake the bread like you promised last weekend."

Anger churned through my stomach. "So she called me the C-word?" This was the first I'd heard about that. "I can't believe she taught you that word. That is the worst word in the English language."

"It's not really a slur," Aunt Tillie noted. "I guess it is when you're talking about women."

"I thought it was a slur for witches," Bay argued.

I stilled, legitimately confused. "What C-word are you talking about, Bay?"

"Crone."

"Oh." Relief washed over me. "That C-word. Yeah, you shouldn't use that word when talking about witches. That's definitely true."

Bay scratched her cheek, her expression unchanged. "What C-word did you think I was talking about?"

"I ... um ... that's the C-word I thought you were talking about."

"No, you acted like I was talking about a really bad word and then seemed relieved when I said I meant crone. That means you thought I was thinking of another C-word."

Aunt Tillie grinned like a sugar addict in a lollipop factory as she bobbed her head and cut up her pancakes. Otherwise she remained silent.

"Are you going to help me?" I prodded, my frustration bubbling over.

"I think you're doing a fine job on your own."

I felt the exact opposite. "Aunt Tillie, I think you should help me. That only seems fair because I cooked breakfast." What? That's a totally even tradeoff.

"Fine." Aunt Tillie blew out a sigh and leaned over, whispering something to Bay and causing the teenager to giggle. When she turned back to me, her eyes were dark and challenging. "There. I told her. Are you happy?"

"Not even close," I seethed. "I didn't want you to tell her what the other C-word was. I simply wanted you to distract her."

"Oh." Aunt Tillie didn't appear bothered by the screw-up. "Well, you should've been more specific." She patted Bay's wrist as I scowled and stalked toward my chair. My breakfast was surely cold by now. My family was even colder.

"I just ... hate this family," I muttered under my breath.

"Join the club," Thistle said, smiling serenely as I shot her a dirty look. "No, seriously, we've started a club. It's usually us against you guys, but if you're willing to pay a year's worth of dues in advance we might let you in."

"Eat your breakfast, Thistle," I snapped, using my fork to cut into my pancakes so hard it screeched against the plate. "So, what is everyone doing today?"

"I have day camp," Thistle reminded me.

"I know."

"I have to type up some calendar stuff for Mr. Kelly," Bay said. "He said I could do it here and email it in."

"Oh, well, that sounds productive." I couldn't help but be impressed. "You're typing up things that will actually be printed in the newspaper?"

"Just calendar stuff."

"Still, that's a big deal, Bay. Good for you. Do you still want to be a reporter when you grow up?"

Bay nodded, although the sadness was back and lurking around her eyes. "If I ever grow up and don't hurt other people, I mean."

Her words confused me. "What do you mean?"

"She's moping about what that woman said to her last night," Thistle explained, grabbing her glass of juice and slurping half of it down before speaking again. "She thinks she's going to kill us all."

I knit my eyebrows, trying to remember exactly what Cherry said to Bay. I don't have the best memory. I find dwelling on the past counterproductive, so I don't put a lot of effort into remembering things.

Clearly Bay was exactly the opposite. I already knew that about her, of course. She held on to things longer than she should – just like her mother. It was annoying and a great way to bring down a good day. I opened my mouth to tell her just that, but Aunt Tillie took over the conversation before I could.

"Don't worry about that woman, Bay," Aunt Tillie ordered, taking me by surprise with her vehemence. "She has no idea what she's talking about, and there's no reason to get worked up about it. She's a fake and a fraud, so you don't need to do anything but ignore her."

"Well, that's taking it to an unnecessary level," I said. "You don't know that she's a fake."

"I do, too." Aunt Tillie was adamant. "She told Bay a bunch of nonsense last night and got her all worked up. She didn't see anything in Bay's palm. People's futures aren't written on their palms."

"They're not?" Bay looked almost hopeful as she pinned Aunt Tillie with a weighted stare. "Are you sure?"

"I'm positive," Aunt Tillie replied. "Bay, the line on your palm is set at birth, but your path changes with each decision you make. Each fork in the road is not set years before you reach it. It's up to you to decide where you'll end up. What that woman said to you … well, it's a crock of crap, and someone needs to smack that woman upside the head to teach her a lesson."

"Aunt Tillie!" I shot her a warning look. "Violence isn't the answer when you disagree with someone."

"Since when?" Aunt Tillie sniffed. "If I didn't have violence and magic to settle scores, then I'd have nothing to use as a weapon."

"You have a gun," Thistle pointed out.

"And a whistle," Clove added.

"And they're fun to use when I'm bored," Aunt Tillie said. "That doesn't mean other types of violence aren't fun, too."

"Stop telling them that," I hissed, leaning forward. "You're making matters worse."

"No, you're making matters worse," Aunt Tillie snapped. "Bay is clearly upset because of what that woman told her. She doesn't look as if she got any sleep last night. She has more lines around her eyes than you do ... and that's saying something."

Hey!" My fingers inadvertently flew to the corners of my eyes. "I still get carded at the bar. I look young."

"Oh, puh-leez." Aunt Tillie let loose a theatrical sigh. "The only reason that guy at the bar in Gaylord carded you is because he knew he'd get a big tip out of it. You almost passed out you were so excited, and then you gave that kid a sixty-dollar tip on a twenty-dollar tab. He probably uses that line on every middle-aged woman he meets because he knows it works."

Well, that had to be the meanest – and patently untrue – statement I'd ever heard. "You're dead to me."

"Oh, well, I'll try to refrain from crying because I don't want to add to the lines at the corners of my eyes," Aunt Tillie drawled, shaking her head. "That's hardly our biggest problem today."

Problem? How did we get from the fact that Aunt Tillie was making up lies about me having crow's feet to a problem? That hardly seems possible. "What problem do we have?" I challenged, my temper getting the better of me. "As far as I can tell, everything is great. Thistle is going to camp. Bay is working. Clove is ... doing whatever Clove is supposed to do. I forget."

"I'm wandering around town to see if I can find Alex Fitzgerald, and then I'm going to figure out a way to make him buy me an ice cream cone," Clove supplied.

"See, Clove has her day planned."

"Yes, Clove is spending the day stalking a boy," Aunt Tillie shook her head. "That seems a fine way to waste time."

"I'm not stalking him," Clove whined. "That's a mean thing to say. I'm just ... hoping to run into him."

"That's stalking." Aunt Tillie held up her hand to cut off Clove when the girl looked ready to mount another argument. "I'm done talking to you right now."

"Fine." Clove got to her feet and shuffled away from the table. "I'm going to grab the newspaper from the porch so I can see if anything is going on today downtown. But when I get back we're going to have a long talk about what is and what is not stalking."

"I believe you've shared that conversation with your mother several times," I pointed out. "Shouldn't you know what stalking is by now?"

"Which is exactly why I know I'm not guilty of it."

That seemed unlikely given the fact that I knew she spent four straight hours hiding in bushes to watch Alex Fitzgerald play basketball shirtless in the high school parking lot earlier in the week. "I don't have time for this argument."

"None of us do," Aunt Tillie said, ignoring Clove as she flounced out of the room. "We have to focus on those con artists you allowed to stay on our property. They're our biggest problem."

"How are they a problem?" I argued. "They seem like nice people and they're staying, like, two nights. How is that an issue? It's not as if they're threatening us."

"Take a look at Bay's face," Aunt Tillie snapped. "Tell me she doesn't look threatened. The poor girl is freaking out."

"I'm not freaking out," Bay argued. "I'm fine."

"See, she's fine."

"She's not fine." Aunt Tillie rolled her eyes to the ceiling. "Sometimes I feel as if I'm talking to a particularly dull wall."

"Join the club," Thistle intoned.

"Thistle, don't add to this madness," I snapped, wagging a finger. "That little troupe isn't hurting anyone. They're simply passing through. They're no threat to us."

"They told Bay she was going to make a choice that resulted in members of her family getting killed," Aunt Tillie exploded. "How is that not a threat?"

"I ... well, that was weird," I conceded. "It's probably part of the show they put on, though. No one wants to hear boring things about themselves. I'm sure she didn't mean to upset Bay."

"Then you're even dumber than you look," Aunt Tillie huffed. "The woman is a grifter. I could tell the moment I laid eyes on her. She tells people what they don't want to hear and then conveniently comes up with a way to make sure the bad thing doesn't happen – perhaps she can lift curses or tell Bay which path is the right one to choose – but only if we give her money."

"She didn't ask for any money," I pointed out.

"Yet. She didn't ask for any money yet. That doesn't mean it's not coming."

"That doesn't mean it's coming either," I argued. "Bay is a child. She doesn't have any money."

"No, but she's sensitive in her own way and that's why Cherry Brucker – that's an absolutely stupid name, by the way – targeted her," Aunt Tillie said. "She took one look at Bay and knew she could manipulate her. And look. It worked. Bay didn't sleep and looks like death warmed over."

"Thanks," Bay said dryly. "I feel so loved."

Aunt Tillie ignored her. "That woman is a con artist, Twila. You never should've allowed her to stay on our property."

"Oh, you're so overdramatic." I sighed. "She's not doing anything, and she'll be gone within a day or two at the most. What could possibly happen?"

As if on cue, Clove picked that moment to wander back into the dining room. She had an odd look on her face. "So, I don't want to panic anyone, but the back door is open."

"Open?" I furrowed my brow. "Like … unlocked?"

"Like someone left it completely open and I think there's probably a killer in the house," Clove replied, her eyes solemn.

Oh, well, good. That will keep everyone calm. The idea of a killer in the house won't panic anyone. Wait … I live with four people prone to dramatic fits. Everyone will panic.

FIVE

"There's probably someone hiding in the pantry with a knife." Thistle's eyes sparkled with excitement rather than dread. "He's waiting in there to pick us off one by one, and he'll probably start with Mom because she's in charge. We'll be easy pickings after that ... and we'll die quickly. Well, except for me, because I'm the strongest. I'll be the lone survivor."

Bay slid a haughty look in Thistle's direction. "I've seen enough horror movies to know that you'll be one of the first to die when the guy jumps out of the pantry and starts hacking. Do you want to know why?"

"Probably because you convince yourself of things that aren't even remotely true," Thistle fired back.

"No, because cocky people always die in horror movies. Masked killers don't like them." Bay looked blasé, but I didn't miss the gleam in her eyes.

"She's not wrong," Aunt Tillie said. "But I doubt very much that anyone is hiding in our pantry. It makes no sense."

I couldn't help being relieved. "Thank you for being the voice of reason, Aunt Tillie." There's a sentence I never thought I'd say. Whew.

Things were looking up this weekend. Aunt Tillie and I were actually on the same side.

"That pantry is far too small for a full-grown man," Aunt Tillie said. "He wouldn't be comfortable in there long enough to wait us out. He's probably in the front closet. There's room to sit down there."

I narrowed my eyes. "What?"

"Ooh, you should go check, Aunt Tillie," Thistle said, her excitement growing. "Do it right now, otherwise Clove will cry."

"I'm not going to cry." Clove was defensive, but I didn't miss the way her eyes watered. She was definitely the girl most likely to freak out under this roof. Bay is sensitive, too, but in a different way. If someone was really hiding in the front closet, Bay and Thistle would beat him to death with a baseball bat, Aunt Tillie cheering them on the entire time, while Clove hid under a table and cried. That's simply the way they were built.

Aunt Tillie ignored Clove's potential meltdown and planted her hands on her hips as she faced off with Thistle. "Why do I have to check the front closet?"

"Because you're the bravest of us all," Thistle replied solemnly.

"That wasn't even remotely believable," Aunt Tillie argued. "You just lost some ground there, mouth."

Thistle stuck out her tongue and frowned. "Fine. I think you should go first because you're the oldest and you've already lived a full life. While the guy is stabbing you we'll have plenty of time to get away."

"Ooh, I like that plan," Clove enthused.

"You're both on my list," Aunt Tillie snapped.

"There's no one in the closet," I said, moving to the doorway that led from the dining room to the back porch so I could look for myself. The door in question was closed. "Are you sure it was open?"

"Wide open," Clove confirmed. "It was cold out there, too, which makes me think the door was open for a long time."

I pursed my lips and glanced between the door and the dining room table. "Where's the dog?"

Sugar, the girls' Christmas gift from several years ago, was a regular fixture around the house. He slept with the girls every night – taking turns hopping from bed to bed even though he was strictly forbidden from sleeping on the furniture. He followed them around when they played outside. He slept in front of the fireplace during the winter. He was a good dog.

He was also a dog I hadn't seen all day. He generally hung around my feet when I cooked, hoping to catch scraps or errant ear rubs. Sugar could smell bacon from an entire acre away. So ... where was he?

As if reading my mind and not liking what I was thinking, the girls moved together and glanced around, their eyes busy as they searched for signs of their canine friend.

"When was the last time anyone saw him?" I asked, hoping I sounded calmer than I felt. "I think I saw him last night when you girls were going up to bed."

"He slept with Bay," Thistle said, her face dark and serious. "He knew she was upset, and he slept with her."

"Okay." That was at least something. "Was he still in bed with you when you woke up?"

"I ... no." Bay shook her head. "He was already gone when I woke up."

"Clove and Thistle, did you see Sugar this morning?"

Thistle shook her head. "No."

"I didn't see him this morning," Aunt Tillie offered. "He usually waits for me by the front door and then I take him out on the front porch with me while I drink my first mug of coffee. When he wasn't there this morning I assumed he was with the girls."

"I guess that means we need to find him." I abandoned my breakfast and stood. "We need to break into teams."

"We definitely do," Aunt Tillie agreed. "Everyone who wants to be on the winning team should come with me."

I scowled as all three girls scrambled to follow her toward the back door. "Wait ... you're leaving me alone?"

"We'll find the dog," Aunt Tillie said. "Trust me. We'll find the dog. You stay here and ... check the closets."

There was something about her expression I had trouble reading, so I waited until the girls were gathering their shoes in the living room to speak. "Do you think something happened to Sugar?"

"I think something weird is going on," Aunt Tillie clarified. "The door was open. The dog is gone. We have squatters on our property ... and they're close. I didn't believe that stupid story they spouted last night about checking to see if someone was in the house. They were watching us."

"Don't say things like that in front of the girls," I warned, extending a finger. "You'll make them paranoid and you're paranoid enough for all of us."

"It's not paranoia if someone really is out to get you," Aunt Tillie noted. "We have an open door and a missing dog. Someone is clearly out to get us."

She had a point, still ... . "Just find the dog," I ordered. "If something happens to that dog the girls will be inconsolable."

"They're not the only ones," Aunt Tillie muttered. "I like the stupid mutt, too. I swear to the Goddess, if anyone hurt that dog I'll rain down fire and brimstone and make the guilty party cry."

"Well, that sounds ... lovely."

"And then I'll kill him or her," Aunt Tillie added, her expression grim. "I'll rip someone's head off if that dog is hurt."

"That sounds less lovely. Just ... find him."

I WAS A NERVOUS wreck as I wandered the house, double-checking all of the hidden jewelry caches and electronics to see if anything was missing. Everything seemed in place. I wasn't sure that should make me feel better or worse.

I found myself checking the front and back doors regularly for signs of Aunt Tillie's return with the girls – and hopefully the dog – but every scan came up empty. They'd been gone long enough that I couldn't help being upset.

"Where the freaking freak of a freak are they?" I muttered, losing my temper long enough to kick the couch leg. At the exact moment I made contact there was a knock on the front door.

I widened my eyes, surprise and worry colliding. For one brief moment I thought I'd open the door to find Terry Davenport waiting for me, bad news on his lips. Instead, when I pulled open the door, I found Cherry Brucker standing on the porch with a small satchel in her hand.

"I ... um ... what are you doing here?" I fancy myself polite most of the time, but all thoughts of welcome flew out of my head when I locked gazes with the woman.

"I need a place to stay."

"You ... need a place to stay?" I didn't bother hiding my confusion. "I thought you were traveling to Traverse City."

"That's what I thought, too," Cherry said. "Then I woke up this morning and everyone in my troupe was gone. They stole everything – even my wagon."

The information was difficult to absorb, especially given the fact that I hadn't seen my young (or old, for that matter) charges in more than two hours. "They stole your wagon and just left you?"

Cherry nodded. "I should've seen it coming."

She was psychic so I wanted to agree. Instead I merely held my hands palms up and shrugged. "I ... um ... well ... ."

"Is something wrong?" Cherry adopted a quizzical look that didn't make it all the way up to her eyes.

"Actually, yes." I saw no reason to lie. "Our dog is missing – and the back door was ajar when we woke this morning. Someone tried to get into the house while we were sleeping – so I have a few things on my mind."

"A few things other than a houseguest, right?" Cherry flashed a rueful smile. "I don't want to intrude. I know that you're really busy. I saw you with your children last night, and ... that's a lot to deal with, even with your aunt's help. Three girls almost all the same age ... that's so much."

"Oh, they're not all mine."

Cherry stilled. "I knew that." She said the words, yet her expression said otherwise. "Of course I knew that. They're your ... ."

"Nieces," I supplied. "Bay and Clove are my nieces. They belong to my sisters."

"Oh, well, that's good. They seem close."

"They are close."

"And where are your sisters now? Are they dead?" Cherry's face twisted with sympathy. "They are dead, aren't they? Oh, you're such a good woman for taking in your sisters' children."

For a psychic she wasn't very good at gleaning things with her mind. Of course, I was so distracted I wasn't giving her much to work with. "My sisters are at a cooking class for the weekend. We all live here together. We plan to turn this into a bed and breakfast soon. Then, in a few years, we'll build an inn. We need to learn a few things before we launch our own business."

"Oh, of course." Cherry moved her satchel from one hand to the other and shifted her hips so her weight leaned left rather than right. "I read most of that last night. I must've forgotten."

"Well, you've had a trying day." I didn't open the door further to make room for Cherry even though she gestured several times for me to do just that. "What are you going to do now that you've been left behind?"

"Well, I was hoping to use your phone." Cherry forced a tight smile. "I need to place a few calls."

"Oh, of course." I felt like an idiot, so I stepped back, allowing Cherry entrance. "Just out of curiosity, how did they take off without you realizing it?"

"They drugged my bourbon." Cherry looked angry as she shook her head and dropped her bag on the floor by the door. "They drugged my bourbon and I fell asleep next to the fire. The next thing I knew it was daylight, everything was gone and my hip really hurt from sleeping on a ground."

That sounded terrible. "I'm sorry. I don't understand how they could do something like that."

"That makes two of us." Cherry rubbed her hip, her eyes busy as they moved around the house. "This is a really nice place. You're very lucky. It's so ... roomy."

"It doesn't feel roomy most days. I have two sisters, one daughter, two nieces and an aunt who can suck all of the oxygen out of an entire house in thirty seconds flat."

Cherry chuckled, her eyes flashing. "Yes, your aunt is very ... colorful."

"That's one way of looking at it." I flicked my eyes back to the door and sighed. "They should've been back by now."

"They're out looking for a dog?"

"The girls have a dog. Sugar. They love that dog beyond reason. No one has seen him since he went to bed with Bay last night. She woke and he was gone, and now ... no dog."

Cherry didn't look worried about my predicament. "I'm sure the dog will show up."

"I certainly hope so. Of course, if he doesn't I'll never live it down. I will always be the one who let something bad happen to the dog the first night she was left in charge. That would be exactly like me."

Cherry's expression was blank. "I'm sure the dog will be absolutely fine. In fact ... yes ... the dog is not only alive, but about to walk through that door."

I wasn't sure I believed Cherry was a genuine psychic, but I found myself staring at the front door with unbridled anticipation all the same. And then, right on cue, the door opened and Sugar raced inside. The mutt's tongue lolled out the side of his mouth and he happily scampered through the living room and headed straight toward the kitchen.

Cherry beamed, her chest puffed out. "I told you."

"You definitely told me." I was fairly impressed with Cherry's magical show. "That was ... pretty good." I kept my smile in place as the girls – followed by Aunt Tillie – filed into the house and widened their eyes when they saw we had a guest. "Look who came up for a visit."

"Why is she here?" Bay's blue eyes widened to comical proportions and she looked anything but happy. "I don't want her here."

"Bay," I scolded, shaking my head. "That is not how we talk about guests."

"I'm sorry, but I don't want her here," Bay repeated. "She's ... weird."

"I think she's kind of fun," Thistle countered. "She tells the future and she makes you and Aunt Tillie mad. What's not to like?"

Bay elbowed Thistle hard enough that she knocked the air out of her cousin's lungs. "I'm going to make you eat dirt."

"And I'm going to sit on your head and watch," Aunt Tillie added, her eyes nothing but narrow slits of anger as she focused on Cherry. "Why are you in my house?"

Cherry forced a smile for Aunt Tillie's benefit. "It's a long story, but ... I need a place to stay for a night or two."

"Oh, really? They have some wonderful inns on the other side of town," Aunt Tillie said. "I'm sure we can arrange for you to get a ride to one of them."

"I'd love to stay at an inn," Cherry said. "It's just ... I can't. My troupe packed up in the middle of the night and they took my wagon and purse. I have no money."

"But you do have a bag, I notice." Aunt Tillie gestured toward the satchel on the other side of the door. "How did that happen?"

Cherry shrugged. "I guess they didn't want to leave me with nothing to my name."

"Uh-huh." Aunt Tillie didn't look convinced. "So they took your wagon and purse – and you didn't wake up while it was happening – and they left you to your own devices? Is that what you're saying?"

Cherry nodded. "I apologize for putting you out, but if I place a call I should be able to get someone from the renaissance festival circuit to come and pick me up. It probably won't be today, but .... I generally wouldn't ask, but I'm really caught."

She wasn't the only one who was caught. I felt caught, too. "It's only for a night, Aunt Tillie," I prodded. "We can make room for one night."

Aunt Tillie rolled her eyes so far I thought she'd overbalance and smack into the side of the couch. Instead she shook her head and rested her hand on Bay's shoulder. "Do whatever you want. I know you're going to do it regardless. Keep in mind, however, that I'm in charge here and I'll be watching our new guest as if she's a thief and I have the only set of sterling silver candlesticks in the county."

"I'm not sure what that means," Cherry hedged. "Does that mean I can stay?"

I forced a smile for Cherry's benefit even as Aunt Tillie prodded Bay toward the kitchen. "Of course you can stay. It would be uncharitable to lock you out in the cold."

"I would be smart," Aunt Tillie grunted. "Come on, girls. Let's check on Sugar."

"Where did you find him, by the way?"

"He was locked in the garden shed," Bay answered, her voice small as she gave Cherry a wide berth. "He's okay other than being thirsty."

"And we're going to keep him that way," Aunt Tillie added, her voice tinged with warning as she locked gazes with Cherry from across the room. "Now that I know what's going on I'll be able to better prepare for what's to come."

Cherry didn't blink as she met Aunt Tillie's gaze. "And what's going on? Did I miss something?"

"Probably," Aunt Tillie answered. "You should know I don't miss things, though. I never miss things."

"That's right." Clove bobbed her head. "That's why she uses a shotgun instead of a rifle. It makes it much easier not to miss things."

I didn't miss the way Cherry's smile faltered as Aunt Tillie's lips curved.

"Yes, well, she rarely brings out the gun, so there's no need to worry." I ran my tongue over my lips as I gestured for Cherry to look in my direction. "I'll show you where the phone is. I'm sure you want to make a call."

Cherry blinked several times in rapid succession, swallowed hard and then nodded. "Yeah, I definitely need to make a call."

SIX

Cherry was a lovely houseguest, full of stories and energy. She went out of her way to engage the girls and me while giving Aunt Tillie a wide berth. I thought things were fine until Cherry announced that she wouldn't be able to catch a ride with her renaissance festival cohorts until the following day at the earliest. She had to wait for a confirmation call as well.

I was okay with that – the house is huge, after all – but I thought Aunt Tillie's head would pop off her neck there was so much steam pouring out of her mouth. She wasn't happy in the slightest, which left me with a dark feeling in the pit of my stomach.

"So, how long has your family lived here?" Cherry sat in the living room drinking a glass of iced tea as I put together the weekly shopping list and kept one eye on Aunt Tillie. She kept running in and out of the room, whispering something to the girls before leaving again. At present only Thistle remained in the living room with me. Bay and Clove were off doing something with Aunt Tillie.

That couldn't be good. Aunt Tillie whines and complains that the girls are always up to mischief, but she often encourages them to engage in trouble.

"Oh, well, the property has been in our family for a really long time," I explained, forcing myself to focus on Cherry even though I was fairly certain potential mayhem lurked somewhere in the house. "I can't remember the exact year – I've never been good with history – but our ancestors bought the house. It started as a one-room cabin, and the surrounding area was for farming."

"Oh, wow. That sounds exciting." Cherry's eyes sparkled. If she sensed something else was happening, she didn't show it. Despite her prognostication about Sugar's return, I was back to wondering whether or not she was a complete and total fraud.

"I didn't know them or anything," I offered. "That was before my time."

"Barely," Thistle quipped, earning a dark look from me before turning her attention back to the bookshelf she pretended to peruse. She made sure not to get too close to Cherry, but she kept a rather obvious eye on the woman's movements. Occasionally she'd poke her head into the kitchen for a few seconds before returning to the books. It was all very suspicious.

"How did the house grow to be this big?"

"Oh, well, it passed through generations of Winchesters, and each generation added something to the house. At one point it was transformed into a modified Victorian, with the bulk of the original homestead taking up the back area of the house."

"And now you're going to turn it into an inn," Cherry mused, seemingly impressed. "That is a massive undertaking."

"We've been working toward this goal for a very long time," I explained. "We love cooking, and the idea of running our own business is something we've dreamed about since we were little girls."

"Still, it must be an expensive undertaking," Cherry prodded. "How will you afford the construction and everything?"

"Oh, well ... ." I shifted uncomfortably on my seat. That was a very direct question, one I'm sure Aunt Tillie would have an absolute fit about if I answered. "I let Marnie and Winnie handle the business stuff. I'm just here to cook."

That wasn't entirely untrue. Cooking and baking are two of my favorite ways to spend time. I'm not interested in the business side of things – that's why I'm going into business with Winnie and Marnie, after all – so I don't pay much interest to the things my sisters say. I do a lot of nodding and smiling until they grow tired of repeating things to me and stomp off in a huff. Hey, it might be passive aggressive but it works for me.

Wait ... what were we talking about?

"And Marnie and Winnie are your sisters?" Cherry's expression was friendly, yet there was something about the way she asked the question that set my teeth on edge.

"They are," I confirmed, nodding as Thistle fixed the back of Cherry's head with an odd look before scampering toward the kitchen. "I'm the youngest, so I let them battle it out for business supremacy. I'm much more interested in cooking."

"That's because you're a nurturing soul." Cherry's smile was so wide it almost swallowed her entire face. "You're a giving person and you're an absolute joy to be around. Your sisters might be the public face of the business, but you'll be the heart."

Something about her words calmed me, soothed the frazzled nerves that so often took me over these days. "Oh, well, thank you."

"That's why I'm here."

"Why are you here?" I didn't notice Thistle ease back into the room until the question was already out of her mouth. She didn't so much as spare a sidelong glance for me as she stared at Cherry.

"I got left behind by my group," Cherry replied, adopting a mournful expression. "I should've seen it coming."

"You're supposedly psychic, so that makes sense," Thistle agreed, resting her hands on the couch arm as she shifted from one foot to the other. "If you can see the future like you say you can, why did you get left behind?"

"I can't see everything," Cherry clarified. "Can you imagine how busy one person's head would be if they saw everything in the world?"

I laughed. "Is that how it works? You only have so much room in your head? I can see that being the case. There are days when I feel as if I don't have enough room for one more thing. That if someone even opens his or her mouth to say something to me I might fall over from too much information rattling around in there."

The sound of raucous snickers assailed my ears from the other side of the kitchen door, and when I glanced over my shoulder I saw several shadows moving in the crack between the floor and the bottom of the door. That meant Aunt Tillie was eavesdropping with Clove and Bay. I wasn't surprised, but I had no idea what she hoped to accomplish by doing ... whatever it was she was doing. Seriously, what does that evil woman have planned for the rest of the day? It can't be good.

"It's not that I have only so much room in my head as much as it is that thousands of things are projected in my direction every second of my life and I can't absorb everything that's out there." Cherry was solemn. She either didn't notice the people laughing in the next room or didn't care. I wasn't sure which option I preferred.

"I have special exercises I do every day so I'm strong enough to keep the voices out," Cherry continued, seemingly oblivious to the fact that Thistle was murdering her with hateful stares every time she crossed behind the couch and three other people were giggling about twenty feet away, the only thing separating us a thin door and my ability to pretend I don't hear things. "I make mistakes, of course, but when I drop my barriers I get inundated with visions and whispers. It's an ... uncomfortable gift."

"I know someone who can talk to ghosts," Thistle announced, taking me by surprise with her fortitude. "She can see them, too. People say that's the most uncomfortable gift."

"Those would be people who don't understand my gift," Cherry countered. "It's only my sheer force of will and the strength in my heart that allow me to stand upright and move forward daily."

I pressed my lips together to keep from laughing at Cherry's earnest expression. Even I couldn't fall for that one. Still, I mustered a bit of faux sympathy. "That must be quite terrible for you."

"It is." Cherry's expression was almost comical. I was glad I invited her into the house for the laughs alone.

Thistle, however, clearly felt differently. "You managed to read

Bay's hand last night and tell her bad things, but you couldn't see that the people you were staying with were going to steal your stuff and leave you in the middle of the night. Your magical psychic powers didn't tell you that was going to happen, huh? What good is your magic if it's so lame?"

"Thistle!" I leaned forward, horrified. "You have better manners than that."

"I really don't," Thistle said dryly.

"I've taught you better manners than that," I clarified. "Don't be a ... whatever it is you're being."

Thistle narrowed her eyes and opened her mouth, what I'm sure was a right saucy comeback on the tip of her tongue. Instead she darted her eyes toward the kitchen door for a beat and then heaved a sigh. "You're right. I'm being mean. I'm sorry for being rude, Ms. Brucker."

The apology stunned me. Cherry either fell for it or decided it wasn't worth fighting about.

"Don't worry about it, dear." Cherry waved off the apology. "I find the whims of children delightful. I'd never change them for anything. They're refreshing ... and honest. Plus, well, their minds aren't fully developed, so I don't have to work as hard to construct strong mental barriers when they're around."

Thistle wrinkled her nose as she ran what Cherry said through her mind. "Wait a second ... ."

I hopped to my feet in an effort to cut off what I was sure would be a screeching diatribe. "It doesn't matter, Thistle. In fact, why don't you go into the kitchen and help your great-aunt and cousins do ... whatever it is they're doing."

"They're ... cleaning the cupboards," Thistle said, averting her eyes when I scorched her with a disbelieving look.

"Really? Aunt Tillie, Bay and Clove are cleaning the cupboards? On a Saturday?"

"That could totally happen." Thistle maintained the premise even though she clearly didn't believe it.

"Aunt Tillie will punish you for that pathetic lie," I offered, smirking as Thistle grimaced.

"Aunt Tillie has her mind on other things," Thistle advised, her eyes briefly landing on Cherry before flicking back to me. "She'll be fine with my lapse."

"Whatever." I didn't have time to deal with obnoxious kids when we had a houseguest. "I need you girls to go up to Marnie's room and make sure everything is clean so Cherry has a comfortable place to sleep tonight."

Thistle balked at the order. "She's spending the night?"

"She is."

"Do you really think that's a good idea?" Thistle didn't bother apologizing to Cherry this time. She clearly didn't care that the woman might find her rude. Thistle was rude ... and often on purpose. That was probably never going to change. She didn't get that particular trait from me, of course. Aunt Tillie taught her that ... and it was one of my least favorite things about her.

"I think that Cherry has been lovely to spend the afternoon with, but you're being an obnoxious brat," I replied. "You know better than treating company like this. Really, Thistle, what has gotten into you?"

I thought Thistle would show grace under pressure and offer another lame apology. Instead she merely shook her head. "Someone was in our house last night, and you invited this woman to stay here even though it was probably her. If you expect me to like that ... well ... then you're as crazy as she is."

I strode forward and grabbed Thistle's elbow, mortified. "You take that back, young lady," I hissed, lowering my voice. "That was a terrible thing to say."

"I won't take it back." Thistle moved to yank her arm from me but my grip was too tight. "I'm not sorry. Something could have happened to Sugar. He could've died or ... got lost ... or been taken."

"He wandered outside." I tugged on my limited patience and reminded myself that the missing dog had upset all the girls. Thistle was clearly still coming to grips with that panic. The dog was a family member to the girls. They would've been brokenhearted had something happened to him. "No one hurt Sugar."

"And we're going to make sure that he's not hurt," Thistle pressed. "He's a dog. He's a good dog, but he's friendly to everyone. Someone walked in the house last night and locked Sugar in the shed. What if we hadn't heard him? What if we'd never thought to look for him there? He could've starved or died without water or something."

"I think you're being a bit dramatic," I argued. "The dog is clearly fine. No one was in the house. I checked the house while you girls were gone. No one was in here, and nothing is missing. Honestly, I checked."

Thistle wasn't ready to let it go. "If no one was inside, how did Sugar get outside?"

"I don't know," I replied. "Maybe we didn't latch the door properly when we came in last night. Everyone was excitable – Bay was in a bad mood and you girls were trying to perk her up. We could've easily forgotten to latch the door properly."

"We came in through the front door last night," Thistle pointed out. "We locked the back door after dinner. In fact, we checked on the back door before we went for our walk because Clove said she saw someone outside and we didn't want to leave the house unlocked."

Crap. She had a point. I'd forgotten all about that. "Well, that doesn't necessarily mean anything," I hedged, racking my brain for something that would explain the open door. "Sugar is very smart. Maybe we didn't latch the door as well as we thought and Sugar somehow opened it and let himself out. Did you consider that?"

Thistle shot me a "well, duh" look and rolled her eyes. "Seriously? Sugar has never opened doors before. Why would he get out of bed? He was sleeping with Bay. You know how he is. He doesn't usually get up until Aunt Tillie gets up. Then she lets him outside and drinks coffee with him on the front porch. He was already up and gone when Aunt Tillie got up."

"Listen, I know you're upset but … ."

"I'm not upset, but I'm not stupid either," Thistle countered, holding up her hands to stop me from yelling. "Someone was here and opened the back door. That's how Sugar got out. That's how Sugar got locked in the shed. You don't have to believe it. I believe it."

"Thistle, you're being rude," I said. "How many times have I told you about being rude?"

"Obviously not enough," Thistle muttered, crossing her arms over her chest.

"It's perfectly okay," Cherry interjected, offering me a friendly smile. "The girl is upset. She loves her dog. She has a right to be upset."

"Yes, well ... she still knows better than talking to adults that way."

"It's fine." Cherry struggled to a standing position, draining her iced tea before leaving the glass on the table and focusing on me. "I will clean up the room I'm staying in myself, if that's okay. I want to rest for a little bit before dinner."

That seemed odd given the fact that Cherry had supposedly been drugged and spent the better part of the morning passed out, but I didn't see any reason to argue. "Oh, well, sure. It's up the stairs ... the third door on the right."

"Great." Cherry beamed as she moved in that direction. When she reached the bottom of the stairs, she stopped and stared. "Um ... do you know what happened to my bag?"

"No. I ... ." Crap. Something occurred to me and swiveled to glare at Thistle, who was already moving toward the kitchen with a clear purpose. "Where do you think you're going?"

Thistle didn't answer, instead disappearing through the door and leaving me with a perplexed houseguest.

Oh, well, this weekend clearly wasn't going how I envisioned.

SEVEN

"Wait right here."

My legs were surprisingly unsteady as I lurched in the direction of the kitchen. What seemed to be harmless eavesdropping with the potential for future mayhem had quickly swung toward the dark end of the spectrum.

"I don't understand." Cherry sounded more confused than suspicious. "I swear I dropped the bag right here when I came in. Where would it go?"

That was a very good question. Of course, I already knew the answer. "I'm sure it was simply moved by accident. I'll find it." I pushed through the swinging door separating the kitchen from the rest of the house, frowning when I saw four figures scurrying toward the door to the back porch. They didn't even bother glancing in my direction. I didn't blame them. I was about to lay down the law.

"What do you think you're doing?" I meant for the question to come out in a booming voice. Instead I merely sounded weary.

"We're not doing anything," Clove answered, spinning fast enough that her hair flew out in an arc and caught on her lip. "In fact, I'm really sad that you would dare ask us something like that when we're clearly going through a traumatic ordeal."

Oh, what a load of crap. All of the girls have specific abilities, but Clove can flip the martyr switch without taking time for a long breath. She can also muster tears out of thin air, which she did now.

"I feel sick to my stomach because you'd accuse us of doing something bad," Clove added. "In fact ... I'm starting to feel weak because your love gives me strength. I just ... it's awful."

Clove let loose a blubbering sigh and turned her head so she could bury it in Bay's shoulder. I had to give her credit for a masterful performance. Anyone who didn't know her would think she was genuinely upset.

I was not most people.

"Cut the crap, Clove," I ordered, annoyance bubbling up when her tear-free face popped up from Bay's shoulder. "I know for a fact that you're not sitting here mourning my lack of faith in you. I don't have time to deal with your crap."

If Clove is the master of martyrdom, Thistle is the master of turning a situation around and going on the offensive. She learned the technique from Aunt Tillie and refined it a bit to fit her age. It was fairly impressive. That's the tack she took now.

"You don't have time for our crap?" Thistle arched a dubious eyebrow. "Have you ever considered that we don't have time for your crap? No? Oh, I can tell by the look on your face that the answer is no. Well, let me tell you something, Mom. We're so very tired of your crap that we can't stand it.

"You let a stranger in our house after it was broken into and our dog went missing," she continued, her voice gaining strength with each charge. "That woman is bad news, and you just let her in our house. Shame on you!"

I stared at Thistle a moment, the feeling coursing through me hard to define. On one hand I was proud that she could spout that nonsense without cracking a smile. On the other I was completely terrified. She wasn't even thirteen yet (close, but not quite) and the fact that her evil little mind could work that fast was terrifying. Seriously, what will she be like at sixteen? At twenty? Ugh, I wonder if her powers of persuasion will grow as she ages, like Aunt Tillie. That would be a good swift kick in the ... .

Wait, what were we talking about again?

"I don't have time to play this game with you, Thistle," I snapped. "On my list of things to do this weekend, watching you practice your Aunt Tillie impression is fairly low."

"And what's on your list?" Bay challenged, taking her turn to argue. I was mildly curious about how she'd choose to attack. She has a penchant for watching a situation and picking the exact right way to ensure she wins. She gets that from Aunt Tillie, too, but she's somehow stronger and more thoughtful when she does it. I don't know how to explain it.

"Well, for starters, I have to put together a grocery list for the week," I replied, crossing my arms over my chest. I was just as ready to argue with her as she was with me. "You know how important shopping is around here."

Bay rolled her eyes. "You guys buy the same stuff every week. Why not just use the list from last week, switch things around and add chicken instead of beef or something? That way Mom and Marnie will think that you did all the work, but it will only take you five minutes."

My mouth dropped open at the suggestion. I wanted to be offended, but it was actually a good idea. "Well, I didn't think about that. Thanks for the idea. That's hardly the only thing I'm focusing on right now, though. In fact ... ." I tilted my head so I could see around the island and grabbed Cherry's open satchel from the floor. "What are you doing with this?"

Instead of answering, Aunt Tillie pasted an innocent expression on her face. "Why would you possibly think we have anything to do with that bag? That's an ugly bag."

"Totally," Clove agreed. "It's brown. You know how we feel about brown bags."

I honestly had no idea how any of them felt about brown bags. Personally, I preferred a little color when it comes to clothes and bags, but that's neither here nor there. The color of the bag had absolutely nothing to do with the question.

"Why is that bag in here?" I asked, my voice firm. "Why are you going through Cherry's things?"

Now it was Aunt Tillie's turn to change tactics, which she did in a manner that surprised even me ... and I thought forty years with the woman had shown me everything she had to offer.

"We believe she's a threat to the family, and we're banding together to fight the threat," Aunt Tillie replied, not missing a beat. "As for that bag, we were going through it to see if she had anything interesting."

I lifted the bag off the floor and kept my gaze focused on Aunt Tillie. "And did you find anything?"

"Not really, but there is a weird box of herbs in there that I'm pretty sure is black magic."

I didn't realize that Cherry had followed me into the kitchen until I heard her feet shuffling against the linoleum. I glanced over my shoulder, forced a bright smile, and held up her bag. "Good news! Someone accidentally carried your bag in here. I found it, and everything is accounted for."

I handed the bag to Cherry with what I hoped was a winning smile. "It's all there." I risked a brief glance at Aunt Tillie for confirmation. "Right?"

Aunt Tillie nodded without hesitation. "Mostly."

I scowled and held out my hand. "What did you take?"

Aunt Tillie found something on the wall to focus on. "Nothing of consequence."

"It's probably the rose petals," Cherry suggested. "She mentioned herbs, but I don't have herbs in my purse. I have a tin with rose petals because I like to scatter them across a pillow before I sleep.

"You see, I sleep in different places quite often, and it's hard not having my own bed," she continued. "By scattering a few rose petals everything smells the same and it feels familiar. It's the closest thing to having my own bed. That's what's in the tin."

"Oh, that's what is in the tin, huh?" I knew I shouldn't allow my inner smugness out to play, but I couldn't stop myself when I saw the disappointed look on Aunt Tillie's face. "Well, that sounds like a lovely tradition. Doesn't it, Aunt Tillie?"

Aunt Tillie was never one to admit defeat, and apparently being caught in the act wasn't about to change that. "I still think she's most likely evil."

"Of course you do."

DINNER WAS A DOUR AFFAIR.

I roasted chicken and vegetables so meal preparation would be easy. Cherry was friendly and chatty – something that threatened to drive Aunt Tillie round the broomstick bend because she kept trying to catch her in lies.

Aunt Tillie started with friendly questions. What is it like to travel with the renaissance festival? Where did you grow up? Do you like performing for strangers?

I was mildly impressed with the way she controlled herself under the inquisition, but the poise didn't last very long because Aunt Tillie started asking more ... um, intricate ... questions.

Do you believe in magic?

Do you take money from people to change their futures?

Do you think it's okay to terrorize a small child to get your own way? No? Then you don't know how to handle children.

Yeah. It was a really weird dinner.

Once it was over, Aunt Tillie gathered the girls and took them upstairs, calling for Sugar to follow and casting a derisive look in Cherry's direction. The look spoke volumes, but the message was clear: Don't mess with my family.

Cherry's reaction was less clear. She waved happily – something that I knew would cause Aunt Tillie to start plotting curses for our houseguest – and blew kisses to the girls as she wished them happy dreams. Once it was just the two of us, Cherry turned the conversation to something more serious.

"Your aunt hates me. Why?"

"It's not that she hates you," I hedged, rinsing dishes before loading them into the dishwasher. "She's simply ... protective and loyal."

"I don't think she's the only one." Cherry grinned as she moved to the table and collected empty plates. "You're loyal to her. I see it in the way you look at her. She drives you crazy, but you'd be lost without her."

"We're a close family," I explained. "We spend a lot of time together. My mother died when we were teenagers and Aunt Tillie raised us. She's always been with us. I can't remember a time when she wasn't telling us how to live our lives."

"My mother died when I was a teenager, too," Cherry said. "You're lucky to have your aunt. I had no one."

"What did you do?"

"I went into foster care for two years and then struck out on my own," Cherry replied. "I joined up with a carnival because I didn't have many options, but my gift made me want to deal with people and a carnival was all I could think of.

"I learned a lot while I was there – mostly about customer relations and the like – but I don't regret traveling with the carnival," she continued. "Eventually I heard about the renaissance festival circuit and thought it was worth a try. That was twenty-five years ago. I've never looked back."

"I bet you're looking back now," I countered. "The people you trusted most, the people you worked with, they took off and left you. Not only that, they stole from you."

"They did, and I definitely should've seen it coming," Cherry said. "But I was distracted."

"By what?"

"The blonde girl."

I stilled. Blonde girl? "Bay?"

Cherry nodded, her expression shifting from mild interest to worry. "She's an interesting girl."

"She is," I confirmed, my stomach squirming. I couldn't decide if Cherry's tone or expression bothered me worse. "You saw something when you looked at her palm last night?"

"I saw myriad things."

"You saw something bad, though. Admit it."

"Nobody's future is completely set," Cherry stressed. "Even in the split second before an accident the driver of a car can change the future by pulling left or right. None of those things are set until they're already in the past. Things happen … and shift … and slide all over the place until they're actually set in time."

I wasn't sure if she meant the words to be comforting, but they were far from it. "But?"

"But Bay is a complicated girl," Cherry replied. "She's bright and funny. She's loyal and happy. She's snarky and strong. She's also … troubled."

"She wasn't troubled before you freaked her out," I pointed out. "She was in a good mood and playing games with Aunt Tillie before that happened. You made her troubled. You made her so troubled the dog understood she was upset and chose to sleep with her."

"And you blame me?"

I shrugged, noncommittal. "I live in a house with three young girls and three grown women. I'm used to mood swings. Trust me. I've seen every mood swing ever invented. What happened with Bay last night was different."

"I didn't mean to upset her." Cherry licked her lips as she handed over two plates. "Sometimes I speak before I think. I didn't mean to upset her. It's just … what I saw in her future … it could be difficult for your family."

"You said yourself that nothing is set in stone until the moment of choice," I reminded her. "Bay is a good girl. She's not my daughter, but I love all of them as if they're my daughters. My sisters feel the same way.

"If I die, I can move on without fear because I know Marnie and Winnie will take care of Thistle and treat her as their own," I continued. "Do you know how I know that? Because that's exactly how I'd be with Bay and Clove.

"The thing is, Aunt Tillie thinks you're a con artist. I can't decide what I think," I said. "I can't see how you think you'd benefit by conning us. You can't steal from us because we have nothing worth stealing, and Aunt Tillie would make you pay if you tried. I can't see anything in this for you.

"But I know that Bay is a good girl. She won't do something that will kill all of us ... or even some of us," I said. "You should probably be very careful where she's concerned."

"You're definitely loyal," Cherry said. "I didn't mean to upset the girl. I simply ... saw something that took me by surprise."

"Well, in this house, we see a lot of things that take us by surprise. We deal with them as they come. We don't live in fear. I won't allow Bay to live in fear."

"I understand that." Cherry forced a smile. "I'll keep it to myself. It's not as if she's suffering because of what I told her."

"Bay may not look like she's suffering, but that doesn't mean she isn't," I argued. "If something happens, Aunt Tillie will make you pay. If it's something really bad, well, Aunt Tillie will go on a rampage."

"That sounds like something to fear."

"Oh, you have no idea." I loaded the last of the dishes into the dishwasher. "So, are you ready to get settled for the night? I think you'll have a long day tomorrow ... what with you leaving and all."

Cherry licked her lips, and I thought she might put up an objection. Instead she simply nodded. "Of course. Thank you so much for your hospitality."

"Don't mention it."

EIGHT

I paced the hallway outside Marnie's bedroom an hour after Cherry retired. When I first decided to put our guest in that room it seemed the most logical choice. Marnie's room was closest to the bathroom and there was nothing in the room worth stealing. I made sure of that – moving my sister's jewelry into my room and making sure to lock the door when I wasn't present.

Still, as the house grew dark and quiet I couldn't help rethinking my decision. It was a bad idea. I should've put Cherry on the couch. Marnie was going to have an absolute meltdown when she returned Sunday evening and found someone else had been sleeping in her bed. When Marnie has a meltdown it usually culminates with yelling … and pinching … and occasionally biting.

Crap. Winnie and Marnie would make sure I was never left alone with the girls again. I couldn't blame them. I'd completely fouled this up.

Now I had a strange woman sleeping under our roof, and Aunt Tillie ready to blow a gasket. That's never a good combination.

Even though I was exhausted I didn't retire to my bedroom. I wanted to – the Goddess knows the thing I needed most was sleep – but I couldn't bring myself to leave the hallway. My mind was filled with a hundred different "what if" scenarios, each one progressively worse than the last.

What if Cherry was a thief who tried to steal the few pieces of jewelry we had that were worth anything?

What if Cherry was worse than a thief, and entered our lives because she wanted to get inside the house to allow her cohorts – who hadn't really abandoned her after all and were merely lying in wait in the trees surrounding the house – inside so they could steal from us?

What if Cherry was unbalanced and that's why her troupe abandoned her? What if she was so crazy she tried to kill us in our sleep?

Worse, what if Cherry's interest in Bay was for something much more nefarious? What if one of the girls disappeared during the night along with Cherry? We might never see her again. Cherry would force her to join the renaissance festival and wear corsets the rest of her life. Now, I like a good corset as much as the next person – they're great for when you have a small bust – but no one wants to be forced into one.

I had just about made up my mind to walk into Marnie's bedroom, roust Cherry from her sleep and kick her out of our lives when the quiet pervading the house was shattered by a shrill scream.

I jolted at the sound, taking a moment to gather my bearings and then racing toward the girls' bedroom at the end of the hallway. I was almost there when Aunt Tillie swooped out of the shadows, her face grim as she pushed open the door and stepped inside ahead of me.

I flicked on the light to find Thistle and Clove standing next to their bunk beds – fists clenched – staring at Bay's bed. For her part, Bay sat up, her fingers clutching the quilt on top of her shaking body, tears streaming down her cheeks. My heart rolled at the expression on her face even as I tried to understand why she was screaming.

"What happened?" Aunt Tillie asked, moving closer to Bay. "Did someone try to get in through your window?"

Bay shook her head, the tears increasing. "I ... ."

"She had a nightmare," Clove offered, taking me by surprise with her fortitude. "She ... saw things."

I flicked my eyes to her and found an unreadable expression on my other niece's face. "What did she see? Did she tell you?"

"She didn't say anything," Thistle answered. "I didn't hear her say anything. I'm not sure how Clove knows she had a nightmare."

"I saw it," Clove supplied. "I saw in her head. I … saw it."

Clove looked as shaken as Bay – almost – so I squeezed her shoulder to offer comfort. "It's okay. Nothing is going to happen. The things Bay is worried about are … ."

"Stupid," Aunt Tillie offered, sitting on the edge of Bay's bed and running her hand over the girl's tousled hair. "Bay, I need you to listen to me."

Bay looked as if the last thing she wanted was a pep talk from Aunt Tillie, but she lifted her eyes all the same. "That woman is running a scam," Aunt Tillie said, keeping her voice low. "She didn't see anything when she read your palm. She's making it up."

"But she has the gift," Bay protested, her voice cracking. "She sees things for a living."

"No, she pretends to see things for a living," Aunt Tillie corrected. "She doesn't see real things. Do you want to know why?"

Bay chewed on her bottom lip and nodded, her cheeks flushed with color.

"The future is determined by an individual's heart, Bay," Aunt Tillie explained. "You have a good heart. That woman doesn't. She doesn't recognize your power. That's on her. Don't let the fear get the better of you."

Bay nodded, her eyes wary and exhausted. "Okay."

"Okay." Aunt Tillie bobbed her head before pushing Bay to a reclining position. She patted the top of the mattress and Sugar instantly sprang up to lie beside Bay, his eyes keen. To my utter surprise, Aunt Tillie leaned forward and whispered something to the dog, resting her hand on his head before patting him three times and taking a step back. When her eyes landed on me they were full of wrath. "That woman is leaving this house first thing in the morning. If you even think of arguing with me you can go with her."

I balked. "I planned on showing her the way out myself."

"She never should've been invited in," Aunt Tillie growled, pointing a gnarled finger at the bunk beds and causing Thistle and Clove to hop into their respective beds without complaint as she passed. "Everything will be fine, girls. I promise. Now ... get some sleep. If you're good and don't give me any grief I'll take you for ice cream and doughnuts in town tomorrow."

"You shouldn't bribe them for good behavior," I chided.

Aunt Tillie rolled her eyes so dramatically I thought she'd knock me over when she swayed. "And that right there is why you're not invited."

Oh, well, that hurt. "I'm not exactly happy with you right now either," I volunteered. "You've been a real pain ever since Marnie and Winnie left. You could've made things easier on me, but instead you made them worse. It's not as if this is my fault."

Aunt Tillie snorted. "Well, it's certainly not my fault. Now ... go to bed. The sooner everyone goes to sleep the sooner we'll wake up and throw out the trash."

"As far as we know, Cherry hasn't done anything to us," I reminded her.

Aunt Tillie spared one more glance toward Bay, who rolled into a ball and let the dog take up a protective stance along her back. "I don't know how you can say that with a straight face. Honestly, I don't care. But it doesn't matter. That woman is out of here tomorrow ... and if you even dare try to argue you'll have all ten spots on my list to yourself."

Now that was a daunting thought.

MARNIE'S BEDROOM was empty when I walked past it on my way to the shower. The door was propped open and Cherry had gone above and beyond in her attempt to make sure that the room didn't look "lived in" when she vacated it. The bed was made, everything discarded on the floor in Marnie's haste while packing was put away. If anything that made the room look completely out of character. I knew Marnie would freak out all the more when she returned to the house in twelve hours.

"Crap."

I showered quickly, wasting little time on pampering of any sort before dressing and heading toward the main floor. I stopped in Marnie's room long enough to mess up a few things – my sister isn't someone to live in a pristine room – and then closed the door before leaving. In truth, I also searched to make sure nothing was missing. Marnie didn't have anything of high value in her room, but everything looked to be in place all the same, which was a relief.

By the time I got to the main floor I was feeling better about things. Cherry was a normal woman in an abnormal situation. That's all there was to it. She was a woman going through a hard patch who had been betrayed by those closest to her. She was a victim, not a user. Aunt Tillie was merely spouting nonsense because she dislikes seventy-five percent of the population – and only tolerates the other twenty-five percent – and the woman likes a little drama with her morning coffee ... and afternoon tea ... and before-bed belt of bourbon.

I pushed open the door that led to the kitchen with a wide smile on my face and an "I told you so" on my lips. I expected to find Cherry nursing a cup of coffee at the table as she waited for her ride. Instead I found a fuming Aunt Tillie and a panicked-looking trio of girls watching her.

"What's going on?"

The question was out of my mouth before I considered how wise it was to utter it given my audience. They looked positively ... manic. That was the only word to describe them.

"You're on Aunt Tillie's list," Thistle answered without hesitation, grabbing an orange from the fruit bowl on the counter and digging her fingernails in to peel it.

"You're going to be homeless by the end of the day," Clove added. "She's kicking you out."

"Worse than that, she's not claiming you as a niece again," Thistle said. "She is keeping Aunt Winnie and Marnie. She says she's going to need them to wreak bloody vengeance." Thistle wrinkled her nose and tilted her head to the side. "Wait ... did I say that right?"

"Wreak," Bay automatically corrected, her eyes wide as she watched Aunt Tillie stalk back and forth behind the cupboards. "She said 'wreak bloody vengeance.' I'm going to guess that wreck will work for what she has planned, too."

As the oldest, Bay has the most expansive vocabulary. She always has. When she was five she sounded like a pint-sized adult and often had to explain words to me. It's freaking annoying. She gets that from Winnie, by the way, because I'm not like that at all.

"Does someone want to tell me what's going on here?" I asked, tugging on my waning patience and forcing a smile for the girls' benefit. I figured they were only acting out of sorts because Aunt Tillie got them riled up before breakfast. That's Aunt Tillie's specialty, after all.

"Your friend robbed us," Aunt Tillie hissed, her eyes sliding to slits as she prowled the kitchen. "She robbed us, and I'm going to make her cry like a little girl."

"Hey!" Clove was offended. "Other people besides little girls cry."

"Not very well," Aunt Tillie shot back. "Do you want me to make you cry, Clove? If so, keep talking to me that way. I'll make you cry and still find that thieving fake fortune teller and rip her innards out through her nose."

I rubbed my forehead as I pictured the scenario Aunt Tillie described. "I don't think that's possible. How would you get a grip on someone's innards from their nose?"

If Aunt Tillie was agitated before she was positively apoplectic now. "Is that really something to worry about?" she barked. "We've been robbed!"

"So you've said twice now." I kept my tone even as I moved between Thistle and Clove. They looked antsy, which meant they were liable to scatter in different directions should Aunt Tillie start barking orders. I took a moment to scan the kitchen and found everything exactly as I left it the previous evening. "What's missing?"

"Aunt Tillie's marbles," Thistle answered, grinning as Aunt Tillie stopped pacing long enough to point at her.

"You're on my list, mouth."

I ignored the potential fight between the two most cantankerous members of the immediate family and instead focused on Clove. She looked relatively settled. "Would you like to translate for me?"

"Where do you want me to start?"

Clove's tone told me I read the situation entirely wrong. She was in the mood to get dramatic, and I'd missed the signs. Well, crap. It was too late to turn back now. "I'd like you to start at the end because I don't have time to listen to a long, drawn-out story."

Clove had the gall to look offended. "I don't tell long, drawn-out stories."

Even though they were agitated, Aunt Tillie and Thistle snorted in unison.

"That's all you do tell, kvetch," Aunt Tillie said. "Don't worry about it this time, though. I'll handle the story."

That sounded like a terrible idea. Clove inherited the inclination to meander at the mouth from Aunt Tillie. That was one thing they had in common. "I don't think … ." I didn't get a chance to finish because Aunt Tillie was already launching into her story and she clearly wasn't in the mood to get straight to the point.

"So, I slept relatively well despite the fact that we had a demon in our midst," Aunt Tillie started. "I think she cast a sleeping curse, because I was determined to stay up all night and it didn't happen."

"Or you simply fell asleep on your own," I muttered.

Aunt Tillie ignored me. "When I woke up this morning the first thing I did was go to Marnie's room. Do you know what I found?"

"That Cherry had made the bed and cleaned up after herself."

Aunt Tillie enthusiastically bobbed her head. "Exactly. Who does that?"

"A polite houseguest."

"A demon, that's who!" Aunt Tillie rubbed her hands together, clearly enjoying her role as storyteller. "Anyway, I was suspicious – and rightly so, because no one makes a bed when they're a houseguest unless they're up to something – and when I came downstairs, I immediately found this … travesty of justice."

I widened my eyes at her tone, dumbfounded. I took another slow look around the room hoping to find what Aunt Tillie was talking about. I came up empty. "What are you even talking about? There's nothing missing from this room."

"Oh, no, Helen Keller? If that's the case, tell me where my mother's silver is."

My heart sank as my eyes flicked to the counter and I realized the silver box was missing. "Oh, no." It wasn't just that the silver was valuable – it was – but it was also an important Winchester keepsake. The silver was one of the few things Aunt Tillie had from her mother. "I ... are you sure?"

"No, the silver got up and walked away by itself," Aunt Tillie drawled, making an exasperated face. "The silver is gone – and I'll bet other things are missing, too – and your little friend is conveniently absent."

"Absent?" For the first time since entering the kitchen I realized Cherry wasn't present. "Where did she go?"

"How the Hecate should I know?" Aunt Tillie exploded. "I'm going to find out, though, and when I do that woman will wish she'd never met me."

"She probably already wishes that," Thistle said dryly, turning her full attention to a quiet Bay, who shuffled closer to the wall phone as we all turned in her direction. "Did you call someone?"

Bay nodded without hesitation and I knew from her expression I wasn't going to like the answer.

"Oh, no. Tell me you didn't call ... him." I felt sick to my stomach. If Bay called the person she always ran to when she was upset or wanted someone to fix her problems I was not only sunk, I'd really end up banished from the family when he told Winnie and Marnie what I'd done.

"I had to call him," Bay protested. "We've been robbed. He's the police. When you get robbed you call the police."

"Oh, no." I pinched the bridge of my nose as I sank into one of the dining chairs. "Why would you do that?"

Bay refused to buckle despite my whining. "Because I want him here."

"It's a bad idea, Bay," I argued. "Call him back and tell him you made a mistake."

Bay folded her arms and shook her head. "He's on his way."

"Oh, crappity crap, crap, crap." I wanted to scream, but I couldn't muster the energy.

"I think it's a good idea," Aunt Tillie announced, taking me by surprise.

"You do?" I was dubious. Aunt Tillie hates 'The Man,' even when he comes in the form of Terry Davenport.

"Of course I do." Aunt Tillie was blasé. "He can help cover up the crime when I murder Cherry Brucker and bury her in the backyard. He knows exactly what to do."

Oh, well, that made perfect sense. Wait … is it too early to start drinking?

NINE

I thought I would have more time to talk Aunt Tillie and the girls off the ledge they were preparing to jump from, but – true to his loyalty to the girls – Officer Terry Davenport wasted no time making his way to the house.

"Officer Terry!" Bay was near tears when he knocked on the back door. She ran to him and dramatically threw her arms around his neck. "I knew you'd come!"

"Of course I came, Bay." Terry looked tired, as if he'd had a late night and Bay's early-morning call woke him from a deep slumber. Unlike most people I know, though, he didn't take out his frustration on my young charge. "Are you okay? Let me look at you."

Terry gripped Bay's arms as he pulled back and looked her over. Her hair was a mess from sleep and she still wore her fuzzy pajama pants and T-shirt. Otherwise she looked fairly normal, other than her puffy eyes. Terry knew the girls well enough to recognize the signs of strain. He ran his thumb over the dark shadows pooling under Bay's clear blue eyes.

"Have you been crying?"

"She has," Aunt Tillie confirmed, slamming a cupboard shut and murdering me with a look that promised retribution once everything was settled. "Blame Twila."

I balked at the look on Terry's face when he swiveled in my direction. "I didn't make her cry."

"It's your fault this happened," Aunt Tillie barked. "You invited that con artist into our home ... and that was after she told Bay that she'd make a decision in the future that might cripple the entire family."

"It was for show," I protested, my stomach threatening to revolt. I hadn't eaten or drunk anything in more than ten hours, yet I felt as if I might hurl at any moment. "It was a game."

"It doesn't look like a fun game to me." Terry planted his hand on Bay's shoulder to steady her. He's attached to all the girls, but his relationship with Bay is exceedingly strong. He dotes on her to distraction at times, something she knows and uses to her advantage. "Why is she crying? It's summer and she's fourteen. She's supposed to be happy."

This time Aunt Tillie's derisive snort was pointed at Terry, which offered me a moment of relief.

"Oh, please," Aunt Tillie scoffed. "She's a teenager. All teenagers have more hormones than brains. They turn into monsters for four years and are intolerable until they turn eighteen and move out of the house."

Terry's scowl was pronounced. "She's an angel."

"I'm an angel, too, right?" Clove cozied up to Terry's other side and he slipped his arm around her diminutive shoulders.

"Of course you are," Terry soothed. "You're almost always perfect."

"Oh, geez." Aunt Tillie gave in to her inner crone, kicking the cupboards as hard as she could. "You're not helping, Terry. I know you love them, but telling them stuff like that only feeds their egos and makes them unbearable."

"The truth is the truth." Clove jutted out her lower lip. "The truth is we're angels and you punish us for no reason most of the time."

"Oh, I didn't say that," Terry muttered, releasing Clove and rubbing his chin. "You're simply not evil. I think that was my point."

"That's not what you said, but it doesn't really matter," Thistle argued. "They want to be angels so you'll tell them they're angels because you hate it when we cry – even when Clove fake cries."

Clove was offended. "I do not fake cry."

Now it was Terry's turn to snicker. "Oh, sweetie, you fake cry all of the time. It's fine. That's part of your charm."

Clove's frown slipped, but she didn't look entirely happy. "I hate this family sometimes."

"Join the club," Aunt Tillie said. "Now that we have an actual police officer here, though, I want to file a formal complaint."

"We don't know anything about her," I pointed out. "How can we file a complaint if we don't know anything about her?"

"About who?" Terry asked, smoothing Bay's hair. "Who are you talking about?"

"Oh, I don't want to file a formal complaint against Cherry Brucker," Aunt Tillie countered. "I want to file one against you, Twila."

"Me?" I could feel the heat climbing my cheeks when Terry's gaze slid in my direction. "What did I do?"

"You're an idiot," Aunt Tillie replied simply. "That's got to be a felony."

Oh, well, that was the frosting on the top of a very bad doughnut day. "I'm an idiot? How can you possibly think this is my fault? I'm the victim here … of you and her."

"Oh, whatever." Aunt Tillie clearly wasn't in the mood to bolster my spirits. "You invited her into this house even though I told you it was a bad idea. You let her stay even though Bay was clearly upset. This is on top of the fact that the dog went missing and the back door was suspiciously open after we found those freaks on our property. This is entirely your fault!"

"I don't believe in killing family members, but I'm considering making an exception in your case," I shot back.

"Okay, that will be enough of that." Terry stepped away from Bay, extending his hands to keep Aunt Tillie and me from clawing each other's eyes out. "I want someone to explain what's going on right now."

Aunt Tillie opened her mouth to do just that, but Terry cut her off with a shake of his head. "Not you. I want someone who isn't riding the crazy train to tell me."

I shot Aunt Tillie a haughty look and smiled. "Thank you."

"I wasn't talking about you either," Terry said, tilting his head to the side as he met Bay's mournful gaze. "You tell me what's going on, sweetheart. I want to know what has you so upset."

"Oh, well, that figures," Aunt Tillie muttered. "He always turns into a huge mountain of whipped cream when it comes to her."

Terry is a strong bear of a man. He does melt whenever Bay bats her eyelashes. Most of the time it's cute. Occasionally it's insufferable. This would be an example of the latter.

"Well, it started the night before last when someone was peeking into the house and Clove caught him," Bay started. She kept on point as she recited the story for Terry. She told the story in a balanced manner that had me believing Terry would take my side before it was all said and done.

I couldn't have been more wrong.

Terry's eyes were on fire as he turned on me a few minutes later. "What were you thinking?"

Well, so much for me being large and in charge for the first time. I had a fairly good feeling I was never going to be the authority figure in the house again. Strangely enough, I was fine with it. Who needs that level of responsibility?

"**I'M JUST ... SO** annoyed with you people."

Terry was still complaining an hour later as we walked him to the clearing where we first met Cherry and her renaissance festival pals. The clearing was relatively clean, only a few random indentations from where the wagon stood two days before serving as proof that we'd had overnight guests.

"This really isn't my fault," I complained, scuffing my feet against the dirt driveway as we walked. "I don't understand how you believe this is my fault."

"Because you invited the crazy woman into your house even

though you knew she was a loon," Terry shot back, risking a glance over his shoulder to make sure the girls still tailed us. He'd been reluctant to leave them behind given the break-in. He insisted they change into real clothes before leaving the house. Now he couldn't stop checking to make sure all three of them were okay. "You know, Twila, I usually find you funny and enjoy your company. You screwed up this time, though."

Terry's dark mood was enough to ruin my day. "All I wanted was to be in charge for a weekend and prove I could do the same things Marnie and Winnie do daily. I didn't even get five minutes of peace before things fell apart. Maybe they are right. Maybe I am helpless."

"Oh, geez." Terry pinched the bridge of his nose. "Stop feeling sorry for yourself. This isn't about you. You're the adult here. This is about the girls."

"No, this is about Bay," Aunt Tillie corrected, her eyes keen as she studied the field. "Something isn't right here."

"There's a lot that's not right here," Terry countered. "This isn't just about Bay. I care about the other two just as much, so don't even try to make this into a thing."

Aunt Tillie snorted. "Terry, in general I have absolutely no use for police officers. You know it. I know it. Heck, everyone in Walkerville knows it. I haven't bothered to hide my feelings."

"And here we go," Terry muttered, shaking his head.

Aunt Tillie ignored him. "But I like you. I don't like you because you're a cop. I don't even like you because you do random Mr. Fix-It things around the house. I like you because you sit and listen to those girls chatter on for hours at a time and you never look bored.

"You're the type of man who loves with his whole heart and never feels embarrassment," she continued. "You love the girls and go out of your way to protect them."

Terry was taken aback by Aunt Tillie's kind words. "Oh, well, thank you."

"I'm not finished," Aunt Tillie snapped. "You favor Bay. Pretending otherwise is insulting to everyone, but especially Thistle and Clove. There's no reason to feel guilty about it. You don't mistreat Clove and Thistle. You've merely bonded with Bay. Admit it."

Terry wasn't the type to crumble in the face of adversity. "I love them all. Bay simply ... needs me more."

"And that's exactly why she called you this morning," Aunt Tillie said. "My first instinct was to hunt down Cherry Brucker, kill her, reclaim my goods and bury her in the backyard. I would've gone on with my life without a second of guilt."

"I don't really think you should tell a police officer that," I offered. "I think he can lock you up for intent."

"She's not wrong," Terry intoned. "Is there a point to this diatribe, Tillie? If not, I have work to do."

"There is a point," Aunt Tillie said, dropping her voice. "Bay called you because she wanted you. That means she relies on you. You're a part of this family whether you like it or not."

"I like it when it has to do with them," Terry said, jerking his thumb in the girls' direction. They were fixated on the spot where the wagon stood forty-eight hours ago. "There are times I want to snatch them up and rescue them from you lot."

"You know you would get stuck with Thistle in that equation, too, right?" Aunt Tillie pressed. "You wouldn't just have angelic Bay and the occasionally leaky Clove to contend with. You'd have Thistle's mouth, too."

Terry paled at the notion. "Fine. I'll settle for being their hero when they're sad and in trouble. That's what I want to do today, but ... I need more information. What direction did Cherry flee? How long has she been gone? Did you hear any vehicles last night? Is anything else missing besides the silver?"

"I locked up all of the jewelry because Aunt Tillie had me convinced Cherry was evil," I offered. "Then I decided Aunt Tillie was crazy and I was overreacting. That was before I found them all freaking out in the kitchen this morning."

"I wasn't freaking out," Aunt Tillie argued. "I was swearing vengeance. That's very different."

"Yes, well, let's focus on this Cherry Brucker, shall we?" Terry's weariness returned as he ran a hand through his hair. "I doubt very much that's her real name. Do you know anything about her?"

"Just that she's with the renaissance festival and they're supposed to pick her up today," I answered.

"What renaissance festival?"

That was a good question. "I ... um ... don't think she mentioned it. I can't seem to recall if she did."

"I think they said that they were going to the Upper Peninsula next," Aunt Tillie offered. "That might help. I seem to remember her mentioning Moon Lake Renaissance Troupe I think, although I could be making it up in my head."

"It might be of some help if it's the correct name," Terry conceded, "but only if they're really connected to a legitimate renaissance festival. Have you guys considered – even for a moment – that the entire group is a bunch of grifters and this is the way they operate? They could run the same scam in different towns across forty-eight states."

"Why forty-eight?" I asked, legitimately curious. "Why not fifty?"

"Because they can't pull that wagon across Canada or the ocean to get to Alaska and Hawaii," Aunt Tillie snapped.

"Oh." That totally made sense.

"This is why people think you're an idiot," Aunt Tillie muttered, shaking her head. "I swear. I am at my limit with you this weekend."

"I'm sure she feels the same about you," Terry said dryly, shaking his head as he straightened and looked to the east side of the field. "Where are the girls?"

For the first time in several minutes I realized the younger set had stopped chattering, which was very unlike them. "I ... don't ... know." I scanned the area, my eyes narrowing when they landed on a thick crop of bushes close to where the girls stood a few moments before. "Are they over there?"

Terry didn't answer, instead striding in that direction. His anger was evident, but it wasn't fury fueling him at this particular moment. It was fear. He was worried about the girls. That should've been my first clue that things were more serious than I realized.

I chased after Terry, picking up my pace as he turned the corner and walked behind the bushes. He was bent over when I caught up. I didn't see him right away and careened into his backside.

"What the ... ?"

I flailed backward, hitting the ground hard enough to knock the breath out of me as Aunt Tillie joined us. She looked amused when she saw me on the ground.

"Graceful."

"Stuff it," I muttered. I expected Aunt Tillie to have a comeback handy, but when she didn't immediately lob it I flicked my eyes back to her and found her staring at something on the ground on the other side of the bushes. When I turned my full attention there, I found Cherry Brucker cowering as Thistle, Bay and Clove stood across from her. Bay and Clove had their hands clenched at their sides, but Thistle brandished a big stick and wagged it in front of Cherry's face.

"Well, well, well," Aunt Tillie huffed. "Look what we have here. You girls found yourself a thief. Good job!"

"Thistle, put down the stick," Terry ordered, knitting his eyebrows as he took in Cherry's terrified appearance. "You must be the fortune-telling thief who stole the family silver. I see you didn't run very far."

Cherry scowled, finally moving her eyes from a threatening Thistle and focusing on us. "Who are you?"

"You're psychic," Terry challenged. "Shouldn't you already know that?"

"She's a fraud," Aunt Tillie reminded him. "She doesn't know anything. Now ... give me my silver." Aunt Tillie grabbed the box Cherry sheltered on her lap. The fortuneteller put up only a token fight before releasing it. She looked positively furious.

"I am not a fraud," Cherry argued. "I'm a psychic."

"You're in big trouble is what you are," Terry countered. "Not that I'm not happy about you being too stupid to run – it honestly makes my job easier – but what are you doing here? Why didn't you flee when you had the chance?"

Cherry scowled, her eyes dark as they flicked to Aunt Tillie. "Ask her. I'm pretty sure she knows why I didn't manage to get away."

Aunt Tillie's expression turned from evil to innocent. "I have no idea what she's talking about."

"Oh, geez! I'm pretty sure I don't want to know what's going on here. Thistle, put down that stick!" Terry grabbed the stick and jerked it away from a furious Thistle. "You'll poke out someone's eye."

"I'm fine with that," Thistle said. "Give it back!"

"No." Terry made a face. "Does someone want to tell me what's going on here?"

"We're all doomed," Cherry wailed, widening her eyes. "We're all about to die!"

"Oh, well, that was fairly pathetic," Terry muttered. "While we're waiting to die, though, I think I'm going to take you into custody." He bent over to grab Cherry's arm, but she fought the effort.

"We're all going to die," Cherry screeched. "Evil is coming!"

"This is the same crap she pulled on Bay," Aunt Tillie argued. "It's a bunch of nonsense."

"I bet it works on kids," Terry's anger was back. "I heard what you said to that girl. I haven't decided what I'm going to charge you with concerning that, but I'll come up with something."

"Yeah, and then we'll stab you with a big stick." Thistle made a move for her stick, but Terry held it over his head.

"I think you'd better start talking now, Ms. Brucker. If you don't … you're going to find yourself in trouble."

"Oh, we're already in trouble," Cherry said, her gaze landing on Bay and causing my niece to shuffle from one foot to the other. "Evil is almost here."

Terry narrowed his eyes, his patience completely frayed. "And I'm done messing around. You're under arrest."

The relief spreading through my chest at Terry's words didn't last long. Everything was going to be okay. I was sure of it … until I heard the unmistakable sounds of a wagon, accompanied by people talking, and realized the renaissance people were returning.

It was only then that I recognized we weren't quite yet safe.

TEN

"What is that?"

Terry straightened his frame and stared over the bushes, his eyes widening when the caravan loitered into view.

"Those are the other renaissance festival folks," I supplied. "They were here the first night and then disappeared by the next morning."

"Leaving Sticky Hands Cherry behind to steal my silver!" Aunt Tillie barked.

"That's not a very good nickname," Clove said. "You should come up with something cuter than that. How about Big Butthead Brucker? That sounds better."

"It does have the alliteration," Bay agreed, shifting a bit closer to Terry as she eyed the approaching festival workers. She didn't appear to be in the mood to show off her vocabulary. "Do robbers usually travel in packs like that?"

"Not that I've ever seen outside of the big city, sweetheart." Terry absently stroked her hair, his eyes never moving from the incoming visitors. "When it happens in the city they usually have motorcycles."

"I've been thinking about getting a motorcycle," Aunt Tillie said. "I'd look totally badass on one."

"Would you get a tattoo?" Thistle asked. "Bikers always have tattoos."

"I don't feel the need to follow trends," Aunt Tillie replied. "I set my own trends. I don't need a tattoo. I'd simply wear a combat helmet."

"Oh, that would look totally cool," Thistle drawled. "No one would laugh at an old lady on a motorcycle wearing a combat helmet. You'd totally set trends."

"You're on my list, mouth."

"What else is new?"

"Stop talking, Thistle."

"Both of you stop talking," Terry ordered. "We need to pull it together here. We have a gang of ... renaissance festival workers ... approaching. Do you have any idea how intense this could get?"

The workers looked as confused as us, which bolstered my courage. They're renaissance festival workers, for crying out loud. How dangerous could they be? I puffed out my chest and moved around the bushes, drawing Jonathan's attention as he hopped down from the wagon and fixed me with a quizzical look.

"Is something wrong?"

"Oddly enough, I was just about to ask you that myself." I was thankful my voice didn't crack. I sounded stronger than I felt. "What are you doing here?"

Jonathan's expression was blank. "Picking up Cherry. We agreed to meet here before separating yesterday morning. We had an errand to run and she didn't want to leave. She said she would be camping here."

Oh, well, that was interesting. "I see. The thing is, she told us you abandoned her and she had no choice but to stay with us until she called for someone else to pick her up."

"She also said that you stole her stuff and drugged her," Thistle added, moving around Terry and gesturing with her fingers. "Give me my stick."

Terry wordlessly handed it to her, which surprised me. Of course, he might've been worried a fight was about to break out and wanted her armed with more than her mouth.

Thistle brandished her stick, shaking it at Jonathan to make sure he stared in her direction. "We don't like you people. We think you're bad ... and stealers."

"Thieves," Bay corrected, shaking her head. "Sometimes I think you say stuff like that just to bug me."

"That's a little cousin's job," Terry supplied. "She's only doing her job to the best of her ability."

Bay made an exaggerated face. "Are you taking her side?"

"Oh, honey, I have no idea," Terry said, causing me to bite the inside of my cheek to keep from laughing at his frustrated expression. "I wasn't really listening. This entire thing is making me uncomfortable."

Bay wasn't about to be ignored. "Why?"

"Because this woman is a thief who said some horrible things to you. I don't want to wander too far away from her, but there's a lot more people over there, and they're wearing frilly shirts in the middle of a field and I think it's odd they're pulling a wagon through here. Don't you think that's weird?"

Bay held her hands palms out and shrugged. "Why don't we just ask them?"

"That's a great idea, Bay," I enthused. I wasn't keen to agree with her as much as I was eager to put this behind us. "We should just ask them, Terry. I think that's our best option."

"Oh, well, you would surely know better than me on that front," Terry boomed. "I'm only a police officer."

I blew out a sigh, relieved. "I'm glad you agree. I'll take it from here. I am in charge, after all."

For a moment I thought Terry would put up an argument, but a glance at Cherry had him changing his mind. "Fine. Go nuts. Handle this yourself. Just ... be careful if they try to grab you or something."

"Don't worry about that," Thistle offered. "I have a stick."

"Oh, well, good."

I ignored Terry's tone and approached Jonathan with what I hoped was a friendly look. "So, we're having a bit of a thing over here. I don't expect you to understand it ... unless you're a part of it."

"I don't know what you're talking about," Jonathan admitted. "We ran to Traverse City and did the job we were contracted for early – they called to see if it was possible and we were happy to get it out of the way. Cherry insisted on staying behind because she felt that she was needed here."

"I see." I risked a glance at Cherry and found her cheeks coloring as she stared at the horizon, searching for something only she could see. "Does she do this often? Say that she sees something in her visions and make an excuse to separate from you guys, I mean."

"Um, I don't know." Jonathan looked legitimately confused. "She likes time to herself. She says that's when the visions flow clearest."

"She says our thoughts flood her mind and give her a headache," a woman, a cute blonde with a blasé expression on her face, added to the conversation. "I think she's just talking to hear herself talk, but I don't get a vote."

"I don't doubt that," Thistle muttered. "Her boobs are hanging out of her top."

"What does that have to do with anything?" I asked.

"You can't vote when your boobs are hanging out of your top. Aunt Tillie told me."

Aunt Tillie refused to avert her gaze despite my heated glare. "What? That's a thing."

"You need to stop telling them stuff like that," I hissed. "They believe it when you say certain things. It's going to cause them to grow up warped."

Aunt Tillie didn't look bothered by the assertion. "You invited a thief who mentally terrorized Bay into our house. I think the girls prefer my brand of knowledge over your brand of charity."

"Oh, whatever." I rolled my neck until it cracked, something occurring to me. "You probably shouldn't talk about someone else's boobs, Thistle. That's rude."

"I agree, Chief Terry said, focusing on Jonathan. "Go back to the morning you left this woman here. Why did you do it?"

"Because she said it was important that she have time to clear up her visions," Jonathan answered. "It happens about once a month when we're traveling. We're used to it."

"And you were always going to return and pick her up?" I asked.

Jonathan nodded. "We're actually three hours late. We were supposed to be here before the sun – the sun messes with Cherry's visions and forces her to sleep in the wagon while we're traveling – but we got held up in traffic."

"Huh. I guess that makes sense." Things slipped into place for me. "Um, just out of curiosity, does Cherry always return with a special gift when she takes one of these sojourns?"

Jonathan immediately bobbed his head. "She's a people person. People pay her with gifts because she doesn't want to deal with anything as crass as crash … well, unless that's all the people have to offer. She doesn't want to be rude and turn down gifts even though she would do what she does for no compensation."

"Yeah, I think she might be putting one over on you." I shared a knowing look with Terry. "She's a thief, not a psychic. She doesn't earn gifts from people. She waits until they fall asleep and then steals from them."

"Oh." Jonathan didn't look particularly surprised. "I wondered if it was something like that. I couldn't see people parting with antique jewelry like that, but … hey, I wasn't there."

"Well, you're here now," Terry said, straightening. "Ms. Brucker is being taken into custody. And you'll be expected to answer some questions before being allowed to leave."

"Okay, sure." Jonathan exhaled heavily. "I don't suppose we could camp in your field while that's going on, could we?"

He had to be kidding. When I flicked my eyes to Aunt Tillie I found her watching me with hateful eyes. She was waiting for me to fail, even though I'd clearly learned my lesson.

"I don't see why you can't stay," I answered after a beat. "Just keep in mind that the girls and Aunt Tillie will be watching the entire time, and they'll stab you with sticks if you screw up."

Jonathan wasn't bothered by my answer. "That sounds like a normal stop for us. Thanks."

TERRY TOOK CHERRY into custody and questioned the rest of the festival workers before declaring them "stupid but not dangerous." Terry was diligent while grilling Jonathan – especially about looking in the window of the house and whether or not he let Sugar out and locked her in the shed – but Jonathan denied knowledge of the dog at all and Terry cut him loose.

By the time he made his way back to the house it was almost time for dinner – Marnie and Winnie were due to arrive at any moment – and he was more than happy to join us for a Sunday meal. I couldn't help but worry it would be my last meal when my sisters heard what happened, but I couldn't dwell on that just yet. I still had questions.

"Did she admit to putting Sugar in the shed?" Bay asked, sitting on the footstool between Terry's feet as he got comfortable and sipped his iced tea.

"She's bucking for a deal – and claiming that her psychic powers allow demons to invade her brain occasionally and those demons steal – so she hasn't admitted much," Terry replied. "She did it, though, honey. I managed to get most of the story from her between bouts of psychic visions."

"She saw things?" Bay tilted her head to the side, her long blonde hair cascading over her shoulder as she considered what Terry told her. "Did she see what's going to happen to me?"

"No, honey, she didn't." Terry turned serious. "She never saw what was going to happen to you."

"Terry is right, Bay," I prodded. "She was putting on a show. You of all people know that no one's future is set in stone. You're a good girl. You'll stay a good girl. You can't worry about things like this, because you can't control them."

"That was very well said, Twila," Terry offered, causing me to beam, "but that's not why she shouldn't worry about it."

My smile slipped. "Excuse me?"

"That woman was a fraud, Bay," Terry pressed. "She doesn't see the future. She made that up because it was her way in. She miscalculated when she came across your family. She thought you'd automatically believe what she said. She thought that you girls made Twila and Tillie especially vulnerable.

"What she didn't realize is that you girls made Twila and Tillie more protective," he continued. "Other people might've been dazzled by her, sweetheart. Other people might've been sold on her act. Your family is too strong for that, though."

Bay pursed her lips. "But she has the gift. That's what she said. I have a gift, too, although I'm not supposed to talk about it in front of you because Mom says it makes you uncomfortable."

"I'm not ever uncomfortable around you, Bay," Terry pressed, causing my heart to warm as he soothed her shredded emotions. "I love you very much."

"You love us, too, right?" Clove always opted to be needy at the worst time.

Instead of chiding her, Terry winked in affirmation. "I love you all," he confirmed.

"Except me," Aunt Tillie interjected.

"Except Aunt Tillie." Terry scooted forward a bit on his chair, making sure Bay's eyes remained on him. "You have a gift. It's something real. It's something inside of you. Ms. Brucker was faking a gift because she wanted to be special. You're already special.

"You have the best heart of anyone I know, Bay," he continued. "Yes, Clove, before you ask, you have a good heart, too. You're not going to hurt anyone, Bay, because it's not in you. Do you understand what I'm saying?"

Bay nodded, solemn. "You're saying Thistle doesn't have a good heart." She cracked a smile to let Terry know she was kidding before ducking her head to avoid Thistle's cuff.

"Knock that off," Terry ordered, grabbing Thistle's wrist to still her. "Believe it or not, you're a good girl, too. You have a wonderful heart … it's just buried really deep because you like pretending to be the villain."

"I am the villain," Thistle countered. "I don't pretend anything."

"You're not fooling me." Terry released her and smiled when the

I DREAM OF TWILA

corners of Thistle's lips curved. "See. I knew you had a good heart. Only someone with a good heart wouldn't be able to keep a straight face."

Thistle fought to erase her smile, but failed. "Fine. I'm a good girl."

I giggled at her downtrodden expression. "You're all good."

"You are," Terry agreed. "I don't want you worrying about what that woman told you, Bay. She was making it up. She's ... evil."

"And not evil like Aunt Tillie," Thistle said. "She's bad evil, not fun evil."

"You've got that right." Aunt Tillie sat on the couch and rested her feet on the coffee table. "Speaking of evil, Winnie and Marnie just pulled into the driveway. What are you going to tell them about this weekend?"

I raised my eyebrows. "I don't think I have much of a choice. I have to tell them the truth."

"You always have a choice," Aunt Tillie countered. "Everything is back to normal. The girls are safe, the dog is home and those derelicts in the field promised to leave first thing in the morning. You don't have to tell the whole truth if you don't want to."

"That's a nice offer." It really was. "I don't think that's the message I want to send the girls, though. I screwed up. I need to own up to it."

"Ugh. Sometimes I think we're not even related and you stole me at the hospital or something," Thistle rolled her eyes. "We'll lie for you. It will be fine."

I pursed my lips as I risked a glance at Terry and found him frowning.

"You're not going to lie," Terry argued. "Twila made a mistake, but it was an honest one. There's no reason to lie."

"Aunt Tillie says there's always a reason to lie," Clove countered.

"Yup, I'm taking you all to live with me," Terry muttered, shaking his head. "I'm your only hope. I can feel it."

"You are." Bay giggled as he poked her side.

The sound of doors closing and conversation at the front of the house caught my attention. I squared my shoulders as I readied myself for a big battle. Winnie and Marnie would be furious. There was no doubt about that. They wouldn't care about my reasons for doing what I did. They would only care about what happened.

They'd yell and scream.

They'd threaten me with any number of curses.

They'd never let me live it down, bringing it up over and over again until they finally broke me and I cried.

Wait ... what was I thinking about again? Oh, right.

Winnie walked through the door, a bright smile on her face. "How is everyone? I was worried for some reason, but you all look fine."

"Everything is great," I said, forcing a smile. "Absolutely nothing bad happened and everything went exactly according to schedule."

"Oh, geez!" Terry slapped his hand to his forehead and stared at his lap.

I puffed out my chest and smiled as I locked gazes with Aunt Tillie. I expected her to be proud. She was anything but.

"That was pathetic," Aunt Tillie announced. "I'll expect you in class with the girls tomorrow morning. You'll be the class dunce if you're not careful, because these girls are ready to do laps around you."

Well, crap. I slid my eyes to Winnie and found her glaring. She didn't know what had gone wrong, but she definitely knew things didn't run smoothly.

I took a step away from her and held up my hand in a placating manner. "I'm going to start running now."

"That's probably a good idea."

No, it was a great idea. I'm so over being in charge.

HOW AUNT TILLIE STOLE CHRISTMAS

A WICKED WITCHES OF THE MIDWEST SHORT

ONE

FOURTEEN YEARS AGO

"Watch the road!"

I honestly didn't mean to screech – I didn't think it would do much for my great-niece's nerves as she navigated my truck through the downtown streets – but I couldn't stop myself when Bay pointed her blond head toward the ornate Christmas display in front of the Gunderson Bakery and made little sighing noises.

"I am watching the road," Bay barked back, gripping the steering wheel tightly. She was fifteen (going on thirty given the way men looked at her) and she'd just gotten her learner's permit. Her mother wanted to take her out on backwoods roads to teach her to drive, but I thought that was a terrible idea. You don't learn to be a responsible driver by avoiding road hazards. Heck, that's half the fun of being a driver. If you can't swerve at the very last second to miss a construction barrel, why even bother risking the roads? Of course, it had been a while since I taught anyone of a certain age how to drive, so I might've forgotten a few things about the attention span of the standard teenager.

"You're making her nervous, Aunt Tillie." Clove, her brown hair secured safely under a combat helmet as she shared a seatbelt with her cousin Thistle in the middle of the truck bench, stared out through the windshield. "She's more likely to make mistakes if she's nervous."

"Oh, really?" Clove irritates me to no end at times. She's a valuable asset when I need someone to fake cry and get us out of a jam, but she's something of a whiner and I'm pretty sure she's going to be a complainer as an adult. I hate complainers – unless I'm the one complaining, of course. I'm an excellent complainer. I could do it professionally. Hey, that's something. Do they have professional complainers? Wait, that's a politician. I have no interest in being a politician.

"Yes, really." Clove bobbed her dark head. "I read it in the books Bay brought home after her driver's training class. The more nervous she is, the more likely she is to be involved in an accident and die in a fiery crash."

"Aren't you just a little ray of sunshine," I muttered, risking a glance at Bay and finding her blue eyes wide as she tightened her grip on the wheel. "Calm down, Bay. There's hardly anyone downtown, the roads are dry, and there's no reason to panic."

I didn't want to give credence to Clove's suspicions, but I was quickly regretting offering to help teach Bay to drive. Her mother had thought it was a terrible idea, but I overruled her. My nieces – Winnie, Marnie and Twila – were stuck home baking Christmas cookies, and I volunteered to attend the emergency Walkerville Township meeting that my arch nemesis Margaret Little called. Before you give me attitude, yes, I have an arch nemesis. When trying to picture Margaret, you should think of me as Batman and her as Killer Croc. She has scales and everything. What? I'm not making it up.

Because we were coming to town anyway and I needed something to entertain my great-nieces – it's much harder to do since they turned into teenagers and became afflicted with the Great Eye-Rolling Influenza of 2002 – I figured a short road trip was a great way to spend the afternoon. That was before the Great Eye-Rolling Influenza took over the day – again. Sadly, it appears there's no cure. Eventually the symptoms will dissipate and be hardly noticeable.

That's like six or seven years away, though. For now, we simply must struggle through the epidemic.

"The parking lot is behind the building, Bay." I kept my voice even so she wouldn't think I was attacking and smiled when she double checked the rearview and side-view mirrors before hitting her turn signal. She'd clearly been reading the manuals. I shouldn't have been surprised that she was so focused. That's simply how she does things, with an eye toward the details.

For me, Tillie Winchester, details are something I find easy to gloss over. Even though I'm a witch by birth and a superhero by trade – sometimes I'm a super spy, high fashion model and private detective by trade, too, for the record – the details were unnecessary. I never needed to focus on the details unless … . "Bay! Look out for Terry!"

Bay managed to park the truck without hitting Terry Davenport, Walkerville's favorite police officer. Her expression was rueful when she slid the truck into park and killed the engine. Terry was on the other side of the door before she could open it.

"What's going on?" Terry scorched me with a dark look. "Are you drunk or something, Tillie? It's illegal for Bay to drive."

Well, if he was going to take that tone. "Show him, Bay," I prodded.

Bay, her eyes sparkling, unfastened her seatbelt and dug in her pocket. She returned with the laminated learner's permit and slapped it into Terry's hand. "I'm officially a licensed learning driver now."

Terry's mouth opened but no sound came out.

"Look at him. He's speechless. That's how horrible this entire thing is." Thistle, my third great-niece, made an exaggerated expression as she unfastened the seatbelt she shared with Clove. "He understands this is the first sign of the apocalypse. He knows Bay will screw it up and kill us all."

Terry was close with all the girls, but his relationship with Bay was strongest. After their fathers departed several years ago – barely mustering the energy to send gift cards for Christmas – Terry picked up the slack. He was a wonderful father figure. Even though he was a police officer – something that generally made my skin itch – he was a good man. I liked him a great deal.

Terry realized fairly quickly that Thistle was needling Bay, and he found his voice. "Bay will be a fine driver." He returned the learner's permit to Bay and forced a smile. "You are. You just need to pay better attention. You almost hit me when you pulled into the parking lot."

"I didn't mean to." Bay was earnest. "This truck just feels … big."

Terry studied my Ford with a critical eye. "That's because the truck is older than you." He helped Bay down from the driver's seat, holding my gaze for an extended period before reaching for Clove. "Maybe you should learn on a smaller vehicle first."

"Hey, I'm the one teaching her," I argued. "This is my vehicle. She'll be fine."

Terry didn't look convinced. "How about I make some time this weekend to take you out?" he suggested. "We can make a day of it. I'll ask your mom to pack a picnic and we'll go out to some of the quieter roads behind the mill and you can learn out there."

"Can we come?" Clove asked.

"Well … ." Terry looked caught.

"He doesn't want you with him, Clove." For some reason, I was feeling mischievous. Terry couldn't stand it when any of the girls felt neglected or left out. He crumbled faster than one of Marnie's cookies. "He likes Bay, best so you're not invited."

Terry balked, his cheeks flushing with color. "That's not true. It's just … I think Clove and Thistle will be distractions. Bay needs to learn how to drive without distractions. It's a big responsibility."

"I think you're making a bigger deal out of it than necessary," I countered. "She's learning how to drive, not perform brain surgery or anything. Although, I was watching *General Hospital,* and they have a new bar owner who moonlights as a brain surgeon on the weekends. I've been thinking that's something I might like to consider."

Terry rolled his eyes, momentarily reminding me of the girls. "Yes. I think that's a wonderful idea. I can't wait to see what kind of person would trust you to operate on his or her brain."

"It would be a smart person."

"Whatever." Terry patted the top of Clove's head in a placating manner. "Bay needs to learn to drive without distractions. I promise to take you and Thistle out on your own when it's your turn to learn, too. I'm not playing favorites."

"But Bay is your favorite, right?" Thistle scowled as Terry helped her down from the truck, wrinkling her nose as she yanked off her protective football helmet, which my great-nieces were required to wear when riding with me, and tossed it on the floor of the vehicle. "We all know it."

"Right now she's definitely my favorite," Terry replied. "Overall, though, I don't have a favorite."

Clove and Thistle exchanged dubious looks as they moved toward City Hall. They were unconvinced – as was I.

"You don't have favorites, huh?" I cocked an eyebrow. "You're a terrible liar. Has anyone ever told you that?"

Terry made a growling sound deep in his throat. "You make me so very tired."

Bay, ever the teenage flirt, tugged on Terry's arm and lowered her voice. "I'm still your favorite, right?"

Even though he tried to pretend otherwise, Terry cracked a smile. "Always."

I watched him pat her head before shaking my own and turning to the situation at hand. "Do you know what this cockamamie meeting is about?"

Terry remembered we were here for a reason and sobered. "No, but I'll bet it's not good."

"I'll bet it's something stupid," I said, falling into step with Terry as we walked to the building. "Everything Margaret does is stupid."

Terry didn't argue with the statement, which was wise. "I guess we'll find out relatively soon, huh?"

That was an unfortunate reality.

THE MEETING ROOM WAS PACKED, Margaret standing at the front of the room lording her power over the simple-minded residents. Her gaze met mine and something sizzled between us, an animosity born through years of battle and hatred ... or maybe I simply had acid reflux from the greasy lunch I ate before leaving with the girls.

"She doesn't look happy to see you," Thistle noted.

"That's probably going to be the high point of my day. How sad is that?" I directed the girls toward a spot at the back of the room, picking a row of chairs that had easy access to the exit should we want to escape early. Terry sat with us, taking the chair next to Bay, and whatever he told her caused her to break out in a wide smile. Terry wasn't known for being sarcastic and snarky, but he could pull it out when the occasion called for a bit of mocking.

"I'd like to bring this meeting to order." Margaret didn't have a gavel – which I'm sure was something she wanted to correct – so when everyone kept talking amongst themselves rather than acknowledging her she made an obnoxious throat-clearing sound. "I said, I would like to bring this meeting to order!"

Her bellow was enough to end conversation and bring everyone's attention in her direction. Margaret forced a smile, one that made it look as if she was doing us all a favor for even being here, and then clapped her hands together.

"So, I know you're all probably wondering why I called this meeting," she started.

"Aunt Tillie says it's because you crave attention and think it gives you power," Clove supplied helpfully.

"Clove." Terry shook his head in admonishment. "Don't make things worse."

"And don't make this meeting last one second longer than it has to," Thistle added. "They're showing *A Charlie Brown Christmas* tonight. If you make me miss it I'll make you eat the dirt in Mom's kitchen plant."

Hmm. "That's on tonight?" I was torn. On one hand, irritating Margaret was always entertaining. If Clove interrupting her resulted in a frustrated Margaret, the world would be a better place thanks to the girl's efforts. On the other hand, who doesn't love *A Charlie Brown Christmas?*

"I was just repeating what Aunt Tillie said." Clove jutted out her lower lip and folded her arms across her chest, earning a warning look from Margaret.

"Let's just see what she has to say," I said after a beat. "Hopefully she won't be long-winded."

"Since when isn't she long-winded?" Thistle challenged.

"Good point."

Margaret scalded me with a dark look as she ran her tongue over her lips. My presence at the meeting had to be driving her insane. That's the only reason I agreed to attend when Winnie suggested it.

"Are you done talking?" Margaret asked pointedly.

"For now." I adopted a faux sweet tone. "You may continue, Margaret."

Margaret's expression promised future mayhem – which was good, because I'm often bored during the long winter months in northern Lower Michigan – but she refused to engage in a public battle when she was supposed to be the voice of reason. I knew that, which was exactly why I always tried to goad her into a public battle. Just for the record, I never want to be thought of as the voice of reason.

"Earlier today, I was contacted by a representative from the Longfellow Juvenile Detention Home," Margaret explained. "As everyone is probably aware, the facility is located about thirty-five minutes away in Gaylord. It burned to the ground last night."

A low murmur rippled through the crowd, and for the first time since entering City Hall I was officially interested in what Margaret had to say. That right there was a Christmas miracle.

"It seems that they only have placements for a small number of the teenagers who were being housed there. They want us to open our homes to some of them." The way Margaret wrinkled her nose made it clear how she felt about the suggestion. "I had numerous conversations with the representatives and I explained why I wasn't comfortable with having a bunch of – troubled youths – in Walkerville. I mean, our residents must take priority, right? That didn't stop them from asking for help. Apparently they must be desperate."

"What's the problem?" I spoke before I realized I was going to do it. It wasn't just that I knew my opinion would irritate Margaret. No, really. I also couldn't quite wrap my brain around Margaret's stance. "They're kids. They've lost their home right before Christmas. Why wouldn't we want to help?"

"They're not kids," Margaret shot back, her temper flaring. "They're ... hoodlums."

A few of the women sitting close to the front of the room nodded as they bent their heads together. They clearly agreed with Margaret. I believe anyone who agrees with Margaret must be brain damaged – or just outright evil – so I opted to dig my heels in.

"I still don't understand," I pressed. "They're kids."

"They're kids who have been arrested."

"Not for violent crimes, though, right?" I looked to Terry for confirmation.

Terry nodded. "The kids who are in that facility are there because most of them come from troubled homes," he said. "They've gotten into general mischief and the like – some vandalism and maybe a stolen car here or there – but that's not the reason they're in the home. They're in the home because their parents either couldn't or wouldn't take care of them. I don't think calling them 'hoodlums' is exactly fair."

"And what do you know about the situation?" Margaret challenged.

"Just what I've heard through my position as a police officer – you know, where I investigate crimes," Terry replied dryly. "I'm not saying that the kids won't cause a spot of trouble, but I think holding things that are out of their control against them is unfair."

"Yes, well, nobody asked you." Margaret's tone was dismissive. "While I respect Terry's position and opinion, I think that he's overlooking something very important: This is a family-oriented town. We care about our families. Keeping them safe and not exposing them to dangers that could be avoided is our primary concern."

"So why are you even bringing this up?" Terry challenged, his voice taking on an edge that I didn't often hear.

"Because it's a town matter and it should be a town decision,"

Margaret huffed. "I'm not queen. I can't decide for everyone. I thought everyone should be aware of the issue so they can decide for themselves."

I'd heard enough. "Come on girls." I prodded Clove, Thistle and Bay to stand. "This is absolutely ridiculous."

"Did you say something, Tillie?" Margaret narrowed her eyes, practically daring me to take her on.

"I said this is ridiculous," I repeated, unruffled. "You just said this was a family-oriented town in one breath and then tried to dissuade people from helping at-risk kids with another. That's not what a family-oriented town would do."

"They're dangerous."

"No, you're dangerous," I countered. "You're a terrible person. If you can't see those kids need help – that this is the time of year when we should all want to help – then I feel sorry for you." I realized what I said when it was too late to take it back. That didn't mean I couldn't modify it.

"Actually, I don't feel sorry for you," I corrected. "I think you're a petty and foul individual. I'm not going to let you sway my decision. If I can help those kids – and I will be making calls as soon as I get out of here to find out – I'm totally going to offer up my help.

"It's the Christmas season, after all," I continued. "We're supposed to give of ourselves for others. That's what I'm going to do."

"Then you'll be the only one," Margaret snapped.

I scanned the room with a weighted gaze, internally crowing when I saw that at least a few residents – although not nearly as many as I would have liked – were clearly thinking along the same lines. "I guess we'll have to see about that, won't we?"

Margaret folded her arms over her chest, determined. "I guess we will."

"Now can I say something mean about her?" Clove whispered.

I nodded.

Thistle stilled Clove with a hand on her arm. "I've got it. You might not be mean enough and we've only got one shot at this." She turned to face Margaret head-on. "You look like a plucked chicken when you dance naked in front of your mirror every morning."

I pressed my lips together to keep from laughing.

"How do you know I dance naked in front of my mirror?" Margaret was incensed as she pinned me with a murderous gaze. "How could you possibly know that? I mean … I don't do that. Why would you think I do that? Don't tell people I do that. I'll sue if you ever say anything of the sort again."

I knew exactly how Thistle knew. It was the same way I knew. We did a little harmless spying when the weather cooperated. There was nothing wrong with it.

"I'm not backing down from this, Margaret," I called out. "I'll help save Christmas for those kids. Shame on anyone else who won't help."

And with that, I swept out of the room. I know how to make an entrance and an exit, and this was no exception.

I had plans to make calls to place. It seemed Christmas needed to be saved … again.

TWO

It turned out it wasn't hard to offer my help. Terry followed us to the parking lot and supplied the number to the state agency in question. The woman who answered the phone sounded harried – and grateful – and before I even realized what was happening she was making arrangements to drop off three boys at the house.

Thistle, her expression hard to read, stared me down when I disconnected.

"What?"

"Don't you think you should've asked Mom and the aunts about this before you did it?"

Bay is generally the one with a pragmatic streak. She didn't say anything this time. That's how I knew Thistle was only arguing to mess with me.

"It's my property," I reminded her. "I can do what I want with my property."

"It's technically their property, too," Thistle pointed out. "They own half of it together and you own the other half. Once you die, they'll own everything."

"How can you possibly know that?"

"I know things."

"Nothing that could be construed as good," I countered. "Now, get in the truck." I pointed toward the passenger side when Bay moved to get behind the wheel. "I'm driving home. We need to make it there before dark – and in one piece. If we get in an accident before your mother finds out I've added three members to the family things will get ugly."

"But I need to practice," Bay complained.

"Terry is taking you to practice this weekend. You're done practicing today."

Bay's expression was pouty enough that it caused Terry to smile as she moved past him. He patted her on the shoulder before fixing his full attention on me.

"I think what you're doing is great, but I also tend to side with Thistle on this one."

"Ha!" Thistle barked from the middle of the seat, triumphant.

"No one is talking to you, mouth," I barked. "Fasten your seatbelt and shut your hole."

"Fine, but I'm going to do a little dance when I'm right again back at the house," Thistle said. "This is totally going to blow up in your face."

I wanted to argue but feared she was right. "It'll be fine." Somehow I would make it fine. "Your mothers are giving souls. When they realize we're helping those less fortunate they'll reward me for being so altruistic."

Bay, Clove and Thistle made identical faces of doubt. When I turned back to Terry, his expression mirrored theirs.

"You, too?"

Terry held his hands palms out and shrugged. "The thing is, I don't believe you did this because you were in the giving spirit. I think you did this to get one over on Margaret Little."

That sounded like an insult. "I am full of giving spirit," I argued. "I am so full of giving spirit that … um … they should create a whole other me just so they can fill it with the overflow."

"That sounds like a nightmare," Thistle said. "Heck, that sounds like a nightmare that I've had a time or two. Can you imagine two Aunt Tillies? That's like cruel and unusual punishment."

"Given the things I know you've done over the years – and the stuff I'm sure you're hiding – it seems an apt punishment," Terry argued, although his eyes were kind. "As for having two Aunt Tillies, I think that law enforcement should have a say in whether that's possible or not."

Oh, well, I was getting it from all sides now. I didn't like it. "I don't have to take this abuse."

"It's not abuse," Terry said. "I'm trying to be rational here. Winnie, Twila and Marnie won't be happy when they hear what you've done. I thought you were just going to make an initial call. I didn't realize you were going to volunteer to take kids without running it past them."

"Well, it's done." I hauled myself up into the driver's seat and jammed my key into the ignition. "I think you're wrong about my nieces. They're going to be thrilled when they hear about the very wonderful and Christmas-y thing I've done."

Terry remained dubious. "Good luck."

Sadly, I had a feeling I was going to need it.

"YOU DID WHAT?"

Winnie was positively apoplectic when I told her what had happened. I wanted to drag it out, butter her up, maybe conk her over the head when she wasn't looking so I could tell her she knew about the visit and merely forgot thanks to an injury. Instead, because the boys were due to arrive within the hour I had to come clean right away.

"You weren't there." I fought hard to maintain my temper. "You weren't there and you didn't see what Margaret was doing. She was basically labeling those kids Crips and Bloods. I couldn't have that."

"You mean you couldn't let her win," Marnie corrected. She looked nearly as unhappy as Winnie. "How could you volunteer our home without telling us?"

"Hey, this is my home, too." I switched tactics. "It's Christmas.

Those kids were already going to have a lousy Christmas and then they lost their home on top of everything else. What have I told you about Christmas?"

"It's best to make a list and threaten people if they don't adhere to it if you want to get your heart's desire under the tree," Clove replied helpfully, grabbing a cookie from the counter. The little monster was enjoying the fight, remaining unobtrusive until she found an opening to drive me crazy with her snarky comments.

"Not that," I snapped. "I'm talking about the Christmas season, that giving feeling that's supposed to overtake all of us at this time of year."

"You told us we were supposed to ignore that giving feeling until we're eighteen," Bay said.

"And on birth control," Thistle added.

"And not just pills, but condoms and stuff, too," Clove interjected.

"I said you were supposed to do that with teenaged boys," I shot back, my temper flaring. "That's a very important caveat. Don't you ever listen to a thing I say?"

Bay didn't back down. "Aren't the people coming to our house teenaged boys?"

Oh, well, she had me. I *really* hate that. "Stop talking." I grabbed a cookie from the counter and shoved it in Bay's mouth to cut her off from saying something else that would make me look stupid. "I'm not sorry for what I've done. Those boys need a special Christmas, and I won't rescind the invitation."

"And I think if you'd asked us about it we would've agreed with you," Winnie said. "I don't argue with what you're doing. That's not what I'm upset about."

"So ... what are you upset about?"

"The way you did it."

Oh, now she was just arguing to argue. "I did it just fine," I said. "Those boys will be here in about an hour. We're going to shower them with love ... and family togetherness ... and cookies."

"That should make everything better," Thistle said, wisely keeping to the other side of the counter as she perused the cookie selection while ensuring I couldn't kick her. "Cookies will make the fact that their house burned down all better."

"It doesn't matter," I barked. "They're coming. I'm not going to rescind the invitation, and not just because Margaret would never let me live it down. It's done. Deal with it."

Winnie licked her lips as she pinned me with a dark look, her mind clearly working overtime. "Fine." She heaved out a sigh, resigned. "You're right. We can't turn them away when they get here. We're simply going to have to make things work. How long are they staying?"

"The woman on the phone said a few days. They're working on permanent placements."

"So, the first thing we need to do is find a place for them to sleep." Winnie has an organized mind and there's nothing she loves more than making lists. "I think we'll have to go with the attic guest room. We can grab an extra cot from storage. That room needs a quick cleaning."

I smiled. They were coming around to my side. "Okay. Great. While you guys do that, I'll watch the girls."

Winnie's eyebrows flew up her forehead. "Oh no! You created this mess. You're going to help clean up the mess in the attic as penance. Besides, we'll need the girls to help, too."

"Oh, man!" Thistle made a face. "You know how I feel about cleaning."

"Yes, the same way you feel about being polite." Twila grabbed Thistle's cheek and gave it a good squeeze. "It doesn't matter. You girls are going to be polite and helpful to these boys when they get here. If you're not, well … ."

"There will be dire consequences," Winnie finished, her expression serious. "We have to work together to pull this off. Does everyone understand?"

I understood. That didn't mean I was happy about it. "I still think I should stay down here and watch the cookies while the rest of you get the room into shape."

"Don't even think about it," Winnie hissed, leaning closer. "We're still going to have a talk about this, by the way. We're doing it – but we're also going to have a talk. You'd better prepare yourself."

That sounded ominous. "It's Christmas. I think we should have a moratorium on talks."

Winnie pointed toward the stairs, her expression stern. "Upstairs. Now."

I knew she wouldn't fall for that. Crap! It was going to be a long couple of days.

ROSA WARREN DROPPED OFF DAVID, Michael and Andrew Forrester shortly before six. The woman, who I had spoken with on the phone, looked haggard and exhausted. Winnie picked up on that right away as she ushered the foursome into the house.

"Can I get you something to drink? We have fresh cookies."

I thought for a moment that Rosa would take her up on the offer. Instead, she merely smiled and handed over a stack of paperwork.

"We're in a real pickle right now, especially because of the holidays, and I honestly don't have time," she responded. "I need you to fill this out before I can go."

Winnie didn't as much as blink as she accepted the paperwork. "Sure. Just give me a minute." She disappeared into the kitchen, leaving me with Rosa and the boys.

I pasted a bright smile on my face as I studied the three brothers. "I'm Tillie. Welcome to our home." That was as warm as I got, so I wasn't surprised when the boys merely stared.

"Don't forget your manners," Rosa prodded, elbowing the oldest boy in the ribs.

"Thank you for having us," David gritted out, his dark skin gleaming under the living room lights. Walkerville was a quaint town, although hardly set in the dark ages. Still, there weren't many people of color around. I hoped the boys wouldn't feel out of place because of it.

"Tell me about yourselves," I said, sitting in the chair at the edge of the room.

"We used to live in the juvenile home and now we're here," Michael, the middle brother, answered. "What more is there to tell?"

There was a lot more to tell but I knew they weren't going to immediately open up to me. "That will do for now. My nieces are making a big dinner for you boys. Meatloaf. Mashed potatoes and gravy. The works. We also have fresh cookies."

"Doesn't that sound nice?" Rosa looked between the boys hopefully. "I want to thank you so much for volunteering your home, Mrs. Winchester. When I initially called, my contact for this area didn't give me much hope. She said she would hold a meeting, but I'd pretty much written off Walkerville. Then you called and a bunch of other people called after you so ... thank you."

That was an interesting turn of events. "Other people called after me?"

"At least five other families."

"Well, that's nice." I internally crowed when I pictured Margaret's face once the news filtered down to her. She would have a conniption fit. Good. She deserved it. "I know this won't be easy for you boys, but Walkerville isn't as bad as you think it's going to be."

"Really?" Michael's expression was dubious. "Rosa drove through town. We saw that there's nothing to do here. You don't even have a movie theater."

"We don't," I agreed. "That doesn't mean there's nothing to do."

"Oh, yeah?" Andrew spoke for the first time. He was the youngest and looked frightened compared to his brothers. "What do you do for fun?"

"I plow snow."

Andrew made a face. "What's fun about that?"

"Maybe we'll get some snow and I'll be able to show you," I replied. "We're due for some flurries. Even if you're not up for that, we have a lot of land. You can build snow forts and ... have snowball fights ... and make snowmen."

David snorted, catching me off guard. "We're not five. We don't make snow forts. Do you even know anything about teenagers?"

I met his challenging gaze with an even one of my own. "More than you can imagine. In fact … ." I gestured toward the stairs, urging a reticent Bay, Clove and Thistle to descend. They'd been watching the show from the shadows, and they didn't look happy to greet their new houseguests. "These are my great-nieces." I ran through the introductions. "I'm sure they can find some way to entertain you if you're really bored."

"Oh, sure," Thistle said, rolling her eyes. "We'll take them upstairs and drag out the old dollhouse. I'm sure everyone will have a ball with that."

I flicked her ear, causing her to yelp. Rosa widened her eyes to comical proportions, but remained silent.

"Don't be a pain, Thistle," I gritted out. "This is your home. You're supposed to be welcoming these boys with an open heart and mind."

Thistle made an exaggerated face. "Have you started drinking already? It's a bit early, isn't it?"

I knew what she was doing. She thought she might be able to manipulate Rosa into taking the boys back if the woman thought I was a poor option for a caregiver. Well, that wasn't going to work.

"When I start drinking, it'll be with you right by my side," I warned. "Then I'm going to come up with a chore list that's unique to your … talents."

"Did you hear that?" Thistle turned a set of plaintive eyes to Rosa. "She's crazy. She's unbalanced. I can't believe you're just handing over three impressionable young minds to this old lady."

Instead of reacting with anger or worry, Rosa merely smiled. It seemed Thistle's show managed to do the opposite of what she intended. It put Rosa at ease.

"I see that the boys are in good hands here." Rosa's grin was so wide it almost swallowed her entire face. "I worried they might try some shenanigans, maybe pull a prank or two. They're known for that."

"Oh, everyone in this house is known for that," I said. "You don't have to worry about us falling for it. I'm well aware of how to handle teenage shenanigans."

"I'll bet you do."

Rosa turned her attention to Winnie as my niece returned to the room with the completed paperwork. "Here's my card." She handed it to me. "If you run into problems, don't hesitate to call. I'll be in touch as soon as I know more about permanent placement."

"Don't worry about us," Winnie said. "Everything will be fine here. Trust me."

"I don't have much choice in the matter," Rosa said. "Still … I think things will turn out. Again, I'm unbelievably grateful. You boys, try to behave yourselves. If you don't, something tells me that Mrs. Winchester will know how to handle the situation."

I offered up an evil grimace. "Oh, you have no idea."

David swallowed hard as he met my gaze. "I'm not afraid of you."

Thistle made a clucking sound with her tongue. "You should be. She's going to suck the life out of you like she does us. Welcome to our world."

THREE

Things didn't go exactly as planned with the boys. They were surly, depressed and downright mean throughout dinner. They clumped together at one end of the table and glared while Bay, Clove and Thistle grouped together at the other end and scowled right back. There seemed to be a battle of the sexes brewing, and it was clear that Winnie, Marnie and Twila blamed me for it.

I thought about apologizing – I really should have told them before volunteering the house we all shared, after all – but that seemed like a lot of work, and I hate work. Instead, I excused myself early for bed and left my nieces to deal with the mess.

What? I'm old. They have more energy than I do.

I had no idea how the sleeping arrangements were settled and I was happy to put off finding out until morning. I was in the middle of a fun dream – one in which Margaret Little found herself trapped in her home, a thick sheet of ice cutting her off from the rest of the world as she slipped and fell trying to escape – when a persistent ringing sound woke me.

I remained in bed, staring at the ceiling for a long time, and listened for the sound of footsteps in the hallway. I'd just about convinced myself that I imagined the sound and was ready to return to the dream when my bedroom door opened. I shifted my eyes in that direction and found Winnie staring at me, the hallway light glowing behind her and giving off enough illumination for me to identify her.

"What?" I asked crossly.

"You need to get up." Winnie's voice was calm but firm.

"Why do I need to get up? It's the middle of the night."

"It's almost seven," Winnie corrected. "It's hardly the middle of the night."

I flicked my eyes to the window and groaned. Winters in Michigan mean early nights and late mornings thanks to Daylight Saving Time. I should've realized it was later than I initially thought. "Fine." I tossed off the covers and climbed out of bed, engaging in a series of elaborate stretches as Winnie watched from the doorway. She looked impatient. That didn't surprise me because she always looked impatient, but the look on her face told me something was up.

"What's going on?" I rubbed my cheek as I joined her at the door. Up close, it was obvious that Winnie was fraying at the seams. She looked ready to throttle me. Granted, that's not a new expression, but this time she appeared to be seriously considering it.

"Terry called."

"Whatever Margaret says I did, I didn't. I went to bed last night and didn't sneak out at all. There's no reason to go all … bossy kvetch … on me."

Winnie murdered me with a dark look. "Why is it that I have to hear excuses like that from my aunt? I expect it from the girls. They're getting to that age where they'll be sneaking out soon. But you should be setting a good example."

I blew out a wet raspberry and rolled my eyes. "No one ever had 'she was such a good example' etched on her tombstone."

"I might have it etched on mine."

"You're just saying that to irritate me."

"And you're just saying that to irritate me," Winnie snapped. "We have a situation. I don't have time for your childish games."

"Who are you calling childish?"

"If the beanie cap fits … ." Winnie licked her lips as she stared me down. She's formidable when she wants to be. I raised her that way. I like it when she uses the power on others. I hate it – I mean really hate it – when she attempts to use the power on me.

"Why don't we start this conversation over," I suggested, pushing past Winnie and heading in the direction of the kitchen. "You tell me what's bothering you and I'll tell you how we'll fix it. How's that sound?"

"Is your idea of 'fixing it' going to include you going to bed early and dropping the problem on us?" Winnie challenged as she followed. She was clearly spoiling for a fight.

"I have no idea what you're talking about," I lied, frowning at Twila and Marnie as I shuffled into the kitchen. "I was exhausted last night. I'm old. You know that."

Winnie snorted derisively. "You're only old when you don't want to do something. That's not an option today."

"Well, because I have no clue what you're talking about, I have no idea what my options for today are as of yet." I grabbed a mug from the counter and filled it with coffee. "Why don't you tell me what has your girdle in a twist and we'll go from there."

Winnie narrowed her eyes and resembled something that looked as if it hopped off the pages of a horror novel. "I don't wear a girdle."

"Then what do you use to suck in your stomach?"

"Exercise."

I pursed my lips. "I think I'd rather spend the money on a girdle."

"Girdles aren't really a thing any longer," Twila interjected. "Now they have control top pantyhose and stuff. Girdles are considered torture devices."

Now it was my turn to stare with overt disdain. "Where did you read that?"

"I saw it on a television show."

"What television show?"

"I don't remember."

"Yeah, you need to stop watching crap," I admonished. "When you watch crap, it rots your brain and causes you to say stupid things."

Twila, never the sharpest athame in the set, was blasé. "I don't say stupid things."

"Keep telling yourself that," I muttered, sipping my coffee.

"This conversation has nothing to do with anything," Marnie announced, taking control of the situation. As the middle sister, she always figured it was her job to play peacemaker. When that didn't work, she basically spent most of her time needling her sisters to continue fighting. That's the Winchester way, after all. She can't help herself.

"Most of our conversations don't lead anywhere," I reminded her. "I still don't know what the big deal is. You said Terry called. What's going on?"

"Well, it seems that the Michaelson family took in three of the boys from the home," Winnie replied.

"So what? Good for them. It's probably driving Margaret crazy to know that people in town are helping instead of turning their backs."

"Yes, well ... ." Winnie chewed her bottom lip.

I turned to Marnie. "Will you just tell me what's going on?"

"The Michaelson house caught fire in the middle of the night," Marnie replied. "It looks to be deliberate. The juvenile home also burned down, so I'm sure you can guess what's being said."

I'm slow in the mornings, so it took me a moment to grasp the words. "Wait ... ."

Marnie shook her head to cut me off. "Yes. It looks like there was a firebug in that state home, and now the firebug is in Walkerville. So ... good job." Marnie sent me a sarcastic thumbs-up as I ran my tongue over my teeth and focused on Winnie.

"Just because the house caught fire doesn't mean the kids did it," I hedged.

"It doesn't," Winnie agreed. "But that's not how Mrs. Little will spin the narrative. You know that as well as I do."

Sadly, I knew it better than she did.

"Well, this isn't good."

That was the understatement of the year, of course. What now?

MICHAEL, DAVID AND ANDREW were showered and dressed when they came down for breakfast. They cast a series of suspicious looks my way as they sat at the table. They didn't appear happy about their predicament – I couldn't blame them – and I could practically see their minds working.

"How did you sleep?" Winnie asked, carrying a pitcher of juice to the table.

"Fine, ma'am. Thank you," David answered stiffly.

Oh, geez. These kids were treating us as if we were the enemy. I guess, in their situation, I'd act the same way. Still, we're tons of fun. They should be thrilled to have us as their temporary guardians, for crying out loud.

"Is the room okay?" Winnie is a born nester, and she was determined to get the boys to open up. I thought she was going about the task wrong, but given the chilly pall lingering over the room I figured now wasn't the time to point that out.

"The room was fine, ma'am."

Winnie shot me a dirty look before returning to the counter. "Well, if you need anything … ."

"They don't need anything," I supplied, cutting her off. "They're tough guys. Can't you tell?"

Winnie's look of disgust was right out of her mother's playbook. I loved my dearly departed sister Ginger a great deal, but she was a pain when she decided it was necessary to control my behavior. I could already tell Winnie was going to attempt to do the same. There was no way I would let that happen.

"Look at them," I barreled forward. "They're clearly tough guys. They don't need a bunch of women flitting around and waiting on them. Isn't that right, David?" I chose to address the oldest boy because he was clearly the one who made decisions for the trio. "You guys only care about each other, and we're in your way. If I'm reading you correctly, that is."

David narrowed his brown eyes. "I don't believe we said that, ma'am."

I hate it when people call me "ma'am." It's merely a polite way of saying "old woman," and because I'm still young and hip that's an unbearable insult. "Well, don't worry, David. I'm going to yank that stick out and loosen you up before the end of the day. Just you wait."

Instead of reacting with anger, which I expected, David's lips curved as he fought a smile. If I had to guess, he wasn't used to anyone speaking to him frankly unless it was in a condescending manner. He seemed to like my bold tone. That was good, because I don't know any other way to speak.

"I don't think you should talk to them like that," Twila whispered. "They probably think you're rude."

I offered up a cheeky wink for David because I was sure he'd heard Twila's statement. "I'm going to guess that, much like me, they find joy in being rude. Am I right, boys?"

This time I was sure that David was holding back a smile. "Whatever you say, ma'am."

I narrowed my eyes. "You can't call me 'ma'am.' I'm not big on rules or anything, but I'm instituting that one. I'm too young to be a ma'am."

"But ... ." David shifted a weighted glance to Winnie. "I thought we were supposed to call you ma'am if we weren't comfortable calling you by your first names. That's what Ms. Winchester said last night."

"Oh, you can call them 'ma'am,'" I automatically corrected, gesturing toward Winnie, Marnie and Twila. "They're old of spirit and heart. I'm young and spry, though."

David's grin was sly. "Okay. What should I call you?"

"Tillie is fine."

"And if I'm not comfortable with that?"

"You can call me 'your highness.'"

Michael and Andrew giggled at David's loopy grin. They were already warming to me, which was a good thing. Out of the corner of my eye I saw Winnie work her jaw as if she wanted to admonish me. She obviously thought better of it, shrugging as she turned to the back door at the sound of a knock.

Terry stood at the door, patiently waiting for someone to open it. Winnie was the first to get there, even though Twila made a valiant effort to knock her sister out of the game. Winnie has broader hips, though, and Twila is no match for my oldest niece's determination.

"Good morning," Winnie trilled, beaming. "I'm so glad you're here. You're just in time for breakfast."

Terry, who looked exhausted, brightened considerably. "That's the first good news I've had all morning."

Winnie ushered him inside, patting his shoulder before returning to her breakfast preparations. I kept my eyes on Terry as he eased into the room, scratching my nose as he took in the quiet boys at the table.

"Good morning, boys." Terry was a friendly sort, and even though it was obvious to me that he was tired he didn't hold back his smile when he sat next to David. "How was your night?"

"Pretty boring," Andrew answered. "They don't even have a basketball hoop here."

"It's winter," Terry pointed out. "You couldn't play basketball even if they had a hoop."

"They kept the hoop area cleared at the home," David explained. "We could go out no matter how cold it was."

"Oh. I didn't know that." Terry rubbed his chin. "Well, you'll survive. The Winchesters have a lot of land, and it's not so cold you can't do something outside."

David's expression was unreadable. "Like what?"

"I don't know. What do the girls do?" Terry looked to Winnie for help.

"The girls spend all of their time doing their hair and makeup," I answered. "They're at that age where they're nothing more than empty shells with sarcastic mouths."

"So ... they're you?" Terry teased, smirking when David let loose with a low chuckle. "The girls are fine. Leave the girls alone. Speaking of them, where are they?" Terry took a moment to scan the room. "They're usually greeting me the moment I arrive."

"They're upstairs getting ready," Twila explained. "I think the fact that there are boys in the house means they have to be perfectly made up for breakfast."

"I'm a boy and I'm in the house when I eat with them," Terry argued.

"Yes, but you're not a boy in their age range," Marnie explained.

"Thanks," Terry said dryly. "That doesn't make me feel old or anything."

"You're not old," Winnie argued. "You're ... perfect."

"No, you're better than perfect," Twila said. "You're ... what's better than perfect?"

"Not your brain," I muttered under my breath, grabbing my coffee mug and moving to the table so I could talk to Terry without having to listen to my nieces make fools of themselves. "So what's the word on the fire?"

Terry arched an eyebrow as he slid his eyes toward me. It didn't occur to me that he wouldn't want to talk about the fire in front of the boys until the question was already out of my mouth. Given the look of interest on David's face, though, it was too late to put the potion back in the flask.

"What fire?" David asked, leaning forward.

"One of the homes where some of your friends were staying burned down last night." Terry chose his words carefully. "We're still investigating, but it looks like it was deliberate."

David exchanged a long look with Michael. "Who's staying at the house?"

"Why does that matter?" Terry asked, instantly alert.

David immediately backed down and shrugged, disinterest returning to his features. "It doesn't. I was just curious."

"I don't have names, but I'm heading over there to ask some questions after breakfast," Terry said. "I'm sure I'll know more this afternoon."

"It could still be an accident, right?" Twila asked. She was naïve under the best of circumstances. She never wanted to believe the worst about people.

"I doubt it," Terry replied. "An accelerant was used. That doesn't generally happen when we're dealing with an accident. Also ... ." He broke off and stared at the boys for a moment, obviously conflicted about finishing whatever he was going to say.

"Just tell us," I prodded. "They'll find out regardless."

Terry wasn't convinced. "How?"

"Because the girls are masters at eavesdropping and they have huge mouths," I replied without hesitation. "I know you think Bay can do no wrong, but she's just as bad as the others."

Terry heaved a sigh. "I know you're right. Not about Bay being as bad as the others, mind you, because she's a sweetheart. I know the news will spread around Walkerville like a wildfire."

"So spill it."

"News came down from the state police late last night," Terry said. "The group home fire was also purposely set. Accelerants were used. We're trying to find out if they were the same accelerants, but we're still waiting for reports from the lab.

"Basically, the fire here and the fire at the group home are too convenient not to be connected," he continued. "I think we're dealing with an arsonist ... and apparently we brought that individual to Walkerville."

Crap! I averted my eyes so I didn't have to see the recrimination in his gaze. He was basically saying that I brought an arsonist to Walkerville with my big mouth. Well, that just bit the big one ... and by big one I mean broomstick.

How was I supposed to handle this?

FOUR

Terry directed the conversation to something lighter once he realized the boys were uncomfortable with the questioning. We shared a weighted look – one that promised further conversation later – and then let the discussion turn mild.

The boys would have to be pressed about what they knew, but now wasn't the time to do it. Thankfully for us, the sound of feet pounding on floors directed everyone's attention to the staircase. When Bay, Clove and Thistle descended, they were all made up and dressed for a day of mischief. How did I know? I taught them how to dress when they were going to get into mischief. Let's just say there was a lot of black entering the room.

"There's my girls." Terry beamed when he saw them, tilting his chin up so Bay could kiss him on the cheek as she hurried over. All the girls love Terry, but Bay is especially attached to him. He purposely gives her more attention. They make quite the pair.

"What are you doing here?" Bay asked, snagging the seat next to Terry before Twila could swoop into it. She barely spared her aunt a glance before plopping a napkin on her lap. "Are you here to see me?"

"Not everything is about you," Thistle shot back, earning a

scolding look from Winnie before planting herself on the other side of the table. "What? It's true."

"I never said everything was about me," Bay snapped. "I was just asking if he was here to see me. He's going to take me driving. Wait … is that why you're here?"

Terry was caught and he knew it. "I am going to take you driving, but I thought we would do that this weekend," he said. "I'm actually here because I need to discuss a few things with your mom and aunts."

"He means he's here for adult conversation," Clove said, wrinkling her nose as she grabbed a slice of bacon from the platter on the counter and then giggling as she hopped away from her mother's outstretched arm when Marnie tried to slap her. "We're not supposed to know why he's here."

"Oh, is this like when you came out for some adult conversation about the way we dressed during the summer and how it wasn't very ladylike?" Thistle asked.

"That was not why I came out that day," Terry corrected. "Although, to be fair, I don't think tube tops are appropriate for girls your age."

"It wasn't a tube top," Bay said. "It was a bathing suit cover-up."

"She didn't have a bathing suit on underneath it," Terry pointed out.

"No, but that's because she lost the top at the lake. We still don't know what happened to it."

"How could you possibly lose your top at the lake?" Terry's eyes narrowed on Thistle. "You're too young to lose your top. In fact, you're not supposed to be losing your top until you're thirty."

Thistle and I snorted in unison, although I was the one who earned the dirty look from Terry.

"What?" I challenged. "Like she's going to wait until she's thirty to start losing her top. Her mother started losing her top when she was sixteen."

"I was seventeen, and I didn't lose it," Twila interjected. "Matthew Prince stole my top. That whole thing wasn't my fault. You grounded me for a week because of something I wasn't even responsible for."

"I didn't ground you for a week because the Prince boy stole your top," I argued. "I grounded you for a week because I told you to wear a bra and you refused to. That entire incident wouldn't have been so embarrassing – and you wouldn't have been driven home naked – if you'd bothered to wear a bra."

"I was making a statement." Twila puffed out her chest. "The sixties were all about women taking control of their lives and being strong."

"You need a bra to do those types of things."

"Not really."

"Yes, really."

"Oh, geez." Terry slapped his hand to his forehead. "I can't believe I'm sitting through this conversation."

"Shh." Andrew pressed his finger to his lips to quiet Terry "This is the most entertaining thing I've heard in days. No one talks about bras at the home."

"They shouldn't be talking about them here either," Terry said.

"What kinds of things do they talk about at the home?" Bay was curious as she spooned scrambled eggs onto her plate. "How did you end up there?"

"Bay, I don't think that's an appropriate question to ask," Winnie chided.

"Oh, sorry." Bay cast her eyes down at her plate. "I didn't know I wasn't supposed to ask it."

In typical fashion, Terry fell for the ploy right away. "It's fine." He rubbed her back. "I'm sure the boys will tell you when they're ready."

"It's fine," David said dismissively, his eyes widening when he saw the huge platter of bacon and sausage Winnie slid onto the table. "We can eat some of that?"

Winnie stared at him for a long moment. "You can eat as much as you want."

David looked as if he almost expected it to turn into some sort of trap. "But … what do you want us to do for it?"

"What do you mean?" Winnie was genuinely puzzled.

"I mean … we have chores, right?"

"Oh, well … ." Winnie broke off, uncertain.

"You don't have chores while you're here," I supplied. "Think of it as a vacation."

"Or being Aunt Tillie," Thistle said.

"Watch it, mouth." I extended a warning finger. "It may be the Christmas season – and we all know I'm a total marshmallow when it comes to the holidays – but I will take you down if you get out of hand."

Thistle rolled her eyes. "Whatever."

"I would listen to her," David said, solemn. "She said she's going to yank my stick out. If you're not careful, she might use it to beat you."

I pressed my lips together and found something fascinating to stare at on the wall when Terry's mouth dropped open and he turned an incredulous look in my direction.

"I can't believe you said that to him." Terry was incensed.

"Oh, believe it," Thistle intoned. She was either oblivious to the fact that Terry was about to go off or sticking the needle in further because she enjoyed watching me squirm. I chose to believe it was the latter. "She says horrible things like that all of the time. Once, she told me that I was never going to attract a man unless I learned how to give better lip service. Now, I'm not sure exactly what that means, but I'm pretty sure I saw one of those erotic titles on Cinemax at night and the lip service they were giving isn't something I want to do."

Terry's cheeks were so red I momentarily worried he was having some sort of heart attack or fit. "That's probably a good idea, Thistle. I don't want you to give that sort of lip service either."

"That's not the sort of lip service I was talking about." I adopted a pragmatic tone. "I was merely saying that, with her attitude, she would have to be a much better actress than she is now if she wants to catch a man. Of course, to be fair, I don't think she needs a man. I think she'll be fine on her own."

"I can't believe I'm having this conversation." Terry was so befuddled he could do nothing but rub both of his hands over his cheeks. "Okay, Thistle, you don't have to change to catch a man. If you want to catch a man, that's great. If you don't, that's great, too. Just be who you are."

As if realizing exactly what he'd said, and who he'd said it to, Terry adapted quickly. "Or, if you want to mellow a bit with age, that couldn't possibly hurt," he added.

Thistle made a derisive sound in the back of her throat. "I don't need a man. I'm going to take over the world on my own."

I beamed at her. "And that right there is why you're my favorite sometimes. That was my goal when I was your age, too."

"Oh, I'm going to be much better at it than you are," Thistle replied.

I knit my eyebrows. "You know what? You're on my list."

"What else is new?"

I slid my eyes to the boys and found them following the conversation with rapt attention. They seemed to be enjoying themselves.

"Don't listen to those girls," I offered. "Especially that one." I pointed at Thistle for emphasis. "She's a menace. I'm a good person and I always have good ideas, no matter what they say."

"I'm starting to like you," David admitted. "I thought you were a creepy old lady when I heard we were going to be staying here, but now I'm starting to think that you're crazy, not creepy."

"I'm also not old."

"Right."

"Okay, we're done with this conversation," Terry announced forcefully. He was determined to turn the discussion to something that he could stomach. "What does everyone want for Christmas? That seems a safe topic."

"I want a car," Bay answered instantly.

"Not a chance," Winnie said, ignoring the way her daughter's expression fell. "You can have a car when you earn the money to pay for one."

Bay jutted out her lower lip. "That doesn't seem fair."

"You won't even be able to drive legally for months," Terry pointed out. "Plus, well, teenage drivers are much more likely to die in an automobile accident than adult drivers. I don't think you need a car."

"But … ." Bay broke off, unsure. Terry almost always took her side. He was adamantly against her now, though.

"You don't need a car," Terry repeated. "I'll drive you wherever you need to go."

"What if she wants to meet a boy?" Thistle asked mischievously. "Are you going to wait for her to come back after a hot-and-heavy date? What if she loses her top?"

"That is not going to happen!" Terry's voice hopped an octave. "We're done talking about it. Pick a more realistic gift, Bay."

"I only want a car." Bay's voice was mournful. "I guess I won't have a merry Christmas."

"You can suck it up," I said. "I didn't have my own car until I was forty."

"Yeah, but that was in olden times," Thistle said. "We live in a modern world."

She was in rare form this morning. I had to give her that. "Do you want to take up every spot on my list from now until Christmas?"

Thistle, always in a mood to fight, quieted down. She knew exactly what that would mean for her comfort level during the next week. She swallowed hard. "I was just joking."

"You need to learn the difference between 'joking' and being a pain in the butt," I said. "You can't seem to tell the difference."

"I wonder where she learned that," Terry muttered.

I ignored the dig. "What about you guys?" I forced a bright smile as I eyed the boys. "What do you want for Christmas?"

"Oh, we won't get anything for Christmas." David was matter-of-fact. "We usually get turkey for Christmas dinner, so we're looking forward to that."

Bay's head snapped in David's direction and her mouth fell open. "What do you mean? Why don't you get presents?"

David shrugged, noncommittal. "We just don't."

"We used to before our mom died," Andrew explained, his expression sad. "Not a lot or anything, but we always got something."

He had opened the door, so I stepped through it. "How did your mother die?"

"She was sick," Michael answered. "She was fine one day and then sick the next."

"It was a heart attack," David explained. "The doctor said she'd been sick for a long time, but she didn't know it."

"What about your father?" Terry asked, his expression grave. "Where was he in all of this?"

"He left a long time ago," Andrew replied. "He just took off one day. He never came back to visit or anything."

"Mom said it was good that he did what he did," Michael added. "She didn't say a lot about him, but … I don't think he was a good guy."

"That's okay." Clove patted Michael's hand in a soothing manner. "Our dads aren't around either."

"I don't think it's the same thing," Thistle said. "Our dads at least pretend to call, and we'll have gifts under the tree from them."

"It's not the same thing," Terry agreed. "You girls are lucky. I know you don't always see it, but you're lucky. Not everyone is as lucky as you are."

"Oh, we see it," Thistle said. "We agree we're lucky. We're also unlucky because we have Aunt Tillie."

"That did it, mouth." I balled up my napkin and glared. "Do you want me to get out my list and start crossing off names to make room for multiple runs of your name?"

Michael giggled, genuinely amused. "What kind of list? Is it a chore list?"

"No, but the person who is going to be taking over the list is a total chore," I replied. "As for Christmas, you don't have to worry about that this year. You're going to get gifts."

"We are?" Michael looked beyond pleased … and surprised. That was enough for me to ensure that the brothers had the best Christmas possible.

"You are," I confirmed.

"You don't know that." David was back to being cautious as he held a hand in front of his younger brother. "We're only here for a little bit because they didn't know where else to put us. You don't even know that we'll be here for Christmas."

"You'll be here for Christmas." I was firm.

"The state people are the ones who decide that," David argued, refusing to back down. "They can come in and yank us out – or apart – whenever they want. They've done it before. We only just got back together in this home. They could change it any minute."

"You mean they separate you boys?" Twila was understandably horrified. As worldly as I liked to believe we were, there were some things that we never had to grapple with. Loss of family and an overall support system was one of them. On that front, we were truly blessed.

"We were apart for almost six months before we got placed together in this last home," Andrew said. "Now I don't know what's going to happen to us."

"And all because some of the kids like playing with fire," Michael complained. "That's what happened, right? That's why you asked about the other kids and setting fires."

"We don't know what happened yet," Terry cautioned. "We're still investigating it."

"We're going to be separated again." David was morose. "I always promise them that it's not going to happen again, but it keeps happening. Once I age out of the system, I'm going to get a good job and a house so we can all live together."

"Can you do that?" Bay leaned forward, intrigued.

"I will do that," David answered. "I don't know how ... but I will do that."

"I believe you will." I meant it. "You're still getting gifts for Christmas, and I don't want to hear another word about you guys getting separated again. I'll fix that."

Terry scalded me with a look of incredulity. "You can't promise them that."

"I just did."

"But ... you can't," Terry protested. "You don't have any control over what the state does."

I stood, leaving my breakfast discarded, and crossed my arms over my chest. "Don't ever tell me what I can and can't do. I'll handle it."

"How?" Winnie asked, her face betraying a mixture of curiosity and confusion. "How can you possibly think you'll bully the state into doing what you want?"

"How do I bully every single other person in the world?"

"You'll try to run them down with your plow?" Thistle asked, excited at the prospect. "What? She did that to Mrs. Little last week, although she lied and said her foot slipped off the brake."

"You're definitely getting the whole list treatment," I announced when Terry scowled. "You'll be sorry you ever met me when I'm done."

Thistle's smile was smug. "Ah. I love it when you shower me with love and affection. The Christmas season is the time for miracles, and that's my favorite one."

I narrowed my eyes and leaned forward so we were at an even level. "Keep it up. If you're not careful, I won't let you help me save Christmas."

Thistle blinked several times in rapid succession before giving in. "Fine. But I want to help you bully people. I won't be happy if you leave me out."

And she was back to being my favorite. "You've got yourself a deal."

FIVE

I thought I'd be able to slip out of the house unnoticed, but I got a rude awakening when I hit the driveway and found Bay, Clove and Thistle waiting for me.

"What are you doing here?"

Thistle, her eyes flashing, made a face. "We're here to save Christmas ... just like you."

Now that was a kick in the pants. Despite my promise to let them help, I thought I'd be able to sneak out of the house without anyone realizing what I was up to. I should've known better.

"That's very sweet of you." I gave Thistle an awkward pat on the top of her head. "You're not coming with me, though."

"Oh, we're coming with you ... and don't pet me like a dog. I'm not Sugar."

"Where is Sugar?" I asked, hoping a change in subject matter would distract the girls long enough that I could make my escape. "I haven't seen her all morning."

"She's hanging around with the boys," Bay answered. "They keep slipping her food when they think no one's looking."

"Speaking of food, I've never seen anyone eat as much as they did at breakfast," Clove said. "They must not be worried about getting fat."

"You've never been hungry, Clove," I pointed out. "We always make sure you're well fed. Imagine what it would be like if things were different and you didn't always know when your next meal was coming."

Bay was appalled. "They don't get fed? Are the state people starving them?"

Crap. Sometimes I forget how dramatic teenagers can be. I should've thought about how I phrased that before letting it slip out. Now the girls would spend the next few days plying the boys with endless servings of food.

"The state people feed them," I clarified. "I think they've been in a variety of homes, though, and I'm sure they get specific servings at the home so they can't eat willy-nilly like we can."

"Like you can," Clove said, patting her stomach. "I'm on a diet. I have to look good for the winter dance."

I flicked her ear. "You look fine. And you can't be on a diet around Christmas. It's against the law. You'll end up in jail if you try it."

"I think you're making that up."

"And I think you're a kvetch," I said. "But it doesn't matter. You girls can't come with me."

"If you don't let us come with you we're going to tell Mom and the aunts that you're sneaking around to do something bad," Thistle said. "They'll stop you. Do you want them watching your every move between now and Christmas?"

Holy crud! The little minx was blackmailing me. It wasn't the first time, of course, but it was the first time she was so overt about it. Previously she tried to be sly and pretend she was doing something else. "Are you trying to bully me into doing what you want?" If she thought I would fall for that she was crazy.

Thistle immediately started shaking her head. "I'm not trying to bully you."

"We kind of are," Bay argued. "We're not trying to bully you into doing what we want as much as we're trying to bully you into taking us with you, which you should secretly want."

"Why?"

"Because we want to save Christmas, too," Clove said innocently. "We want to make sure that David, Michael and Andrew have a special day."

"It's not fair that they haven't had one up until now," Thistle added. "You can't keep us out. We won't let you."

"Besides, you're probably going to need us," Bay argued, adopting a pragmatic tone. "I have no idea what you're planning, but I'm sure you'll need diversions."

She had a point. Double crud. Still, to buy time, I continued the debate. "Why do you think I'll need diversions?"

"Because we've spent time with you before," Bay answered without hesitation. "You're going to need us for whatever you're planning. I can already see the way your mind is going. You're thinking of … possibilities."

I stared at her long and hard. "Fine. I'll take you with me under one condition. You have to promise to do what I say. No exceptions, no excuses."

"This isn't going to be like the time that you tricked us into wrapping Mrs. Little's house in toilet paper and then left us to take the rap while you hurried home and pretended to be in bed the entire time, is it?" Thistle asked suspiciously.

She would bring that up. "Probably not."

"Then we agree to your terms." Thistle stuck out her hand, causing me to roll my eyes as I gripped it and shook. "We're all going to save Christmas together this time."

"Great. You know I'm going to be the one doing the heavy lifting, right?"

"You told us you hate physical labor," Bay pointed out. "That means you'll make us do the heavy lifting."

She wasn't wrong. "Just get in the truck." I made small shooing motions to get them to move faster. "We need to get a jump on the day if we're going to get anything done."

"And where are we going?" Clove asked.

I finally managed to muster a smile, and it was one that the girls immediately didn't like. "I'm glad you asked."

"HOLY MOLY!" Thistle's eyes were wide as she sat in the passenger seat and twisted so she could stare into the back of my truck. "I've never seen that many gifts."

Our first stop was Gaylord – almost a full hour away – so I could buy gifts for the boys. It wasn't as easy as buying gifts for the girls, but my trio of manic minions had some helpful ideas, which I was grateful for even though I would never admit it. We put them in the bed of the truck and covered them with a heavy tarp (and a bit of magic so no one would try stealing them when I wasn't looking) before heading to Bellaire.

Now it was time for the second leg of our trip.

"You think they'll like those video game things, right?" I was a little nervous about the gift selection. Putting Bay, Clove and Thistle in charge of anything was akin to dropping a nuclear bomb and praying no one died.

"They'll like it," Bay said. "Although ... will the state let them have that? Will those people keep the gifts if they move the boys around again? How does that work?"

Bay is an inquisitive sort and generally asks more questions than I can answer. Today was no exception.

"I've been wondering about that myself, "I conceded, gripping the steering wheel tightly as I floored it in the passing lane and glared at the huge truck to my right. "It's the speed limit for a reason, bucko! You're supposed to drive the limit, not dip below it."

Bay's expression was speculative when I risked a glance in her direction. "What?"

"That's not what a speed limit is, but it's probably a waste of time to argue about it with you because you're not the type of person to follow a driving manual," Bay replied. "Why are we going to Bellaire?"

"Because that's where the state Families and Services Office for this area is located."

"Oh." Bay tapped her bottom lip, her mind clearly working. "What are we going to do there?"

"I want to talk to them to see what I can do about keeping the boys together," I replied.

"And when they tell you to mind your own business, what are you going to do then?" Bay challenged.

"They're not going to tell me to mind my own business," I countered. "They're going to be interested in what I have to say and then they're going to tell me I'm a genius and they should've thought of it themselves."

Thistle snorted, genuinely amused. "Are you lost in La-la Land or something?"

I hate when she uses that tone. "No. I've been giving it a lot of thought. It's going to work."

"It's not going to work."

"You don't know."

"I know."

Bay held up her hands to quiet us before a fight could break out. "I think we need to focus on finding them a forever home rather than fighting with the state about keeping them together."

Hmm. Despite myself – and the disapproving look she gave me that was right out of her mother's playbook – I was intrigued by the suggestion. "How do you suggest we do that?"

Bay shrugged. "Why can't we find their father? Maybe he's lost or something."

This is where being overprotected and naïve often comes back to bite the girls. "He's not lost. He abandoned his family."

"They didn't really say that," Clove pointed out.

"They did. You guys simply didn't hear it because you didn't understand what they were saying. What happened with your fathers was very different from what happened with their father."

"Still, there has to be a way to give them a home," Bay pressed.

"Wait … ." Thistle narrowed her eyes to suspicious slits. "You're not going to adopt them, are you?"

I snorted. "Don't be ridiculous."

"You're too old to adopt them," Thistle pressed. "Plus, we don't have room in the house."

"Plus they're boys," Clove added. "We don't want boys in the house unless we can date them."

"You need to find different things to focus your attention on besides boys," I ordered, shaking my head. "You're one big hormone these days, Clove, and it's not attractive."

"Whatever." Clove was blasé as she smoothed her hair. "You can't adopt them, though."

"I have no intention of adopting them." That was true. Mostly. "But I want to see if I can make their lives better. We're extremely lucky because we're surrounded by family."

"That doesn't make me feel lucky very often," Thistle muttered.

"Don't push me, mouth," I snapped, shaking my head as I turned toward Bellaire's small downtown area. "There must be a way to keep those boys together. I'm going to find it."

"How?" Bay challenged. "These people we're going to see aren't just going to do what you want because you order them to do it."

"Did you just meet me? That's how I get everything I want."

"This is different." Bay folded her arms across her chest, stubborn. "It won't work."

"Fine, genius. What do you think we should do?"

"I don't know," Bay replied. "I know I want to do something, but I'm not sure what's best."

"Well, since you have no ideas, we'll do things my way," I said. "If you don't like that ... you can sit in the car."

Bay pursed her lips. "I'll think of something."

"You do that." I pulled into the government building's parking lot. "No matter what you say, I know things will work out exactly how I want. It's Christmas. It's the time for miracles. I have things completely under control. Trust me."

"THAT'S NOT POSSIBLE."

The woman behind the desk – her nametag read "Susan" – was firm as she met my gaze.

"What do you mean it's not possible?" I wasn't in the mood to be denied.

"It's not possible," Susan repeated. "I understand that you're coming from a place of love and you really want to help David, Michael and Andrew Forrester, but there's really nothing you can do in this situation."

"I told you," Bay muttered under her breath as she stared at the ceiling.

"Go out in the hallway," I barked, grabbing an arm and shoving her toward the door.

"You're such a giving soul," Thistle drawled, rolling her eyes.

"You go with her." I pushed Thistle so she had no choice but to join Bay on the other side of the door, fixing Clove with a hard look. "Do you want to go with them?"

"I'm good," Clove replied, smiling. "I'm trying to help you guys come up with a solution we all can live with."

"You watch too much television," I muttered, reclaiming my seat in the small office.

"I read that in a magazine," Clove countered.

"Shh." I pressed my finger to my lips before focusing my full attention on Susan. "There must be something we can do. Those boys only have each other. The thing they want most for Christmas is to stay together. I want to give that to them."

"I understand, and it's a wonderful sentiment." Susan's tone was cool and clipped. "It really is. Sometimes reality can't keep up with our hopes and dreams, though. The boys' living situation is fluid – especially now – and we have no idea what will happen one week from now, let alone a year from now."

"But … ." I wanted to reach across the counter and smack her disinterested face.

"I don't see how you can let something like this happen." Clove's voice was appropriately innocent, a hint of a shake creeping in to let Susan know there might be tears. That's why I like the kid and want her with me on missions like this. She knows how to manipulate the crowd. "There has to be a way for David, Michael and Andrew to get what they deserve."

"And what's that?" Susan challenged. "What do they deserve? Why do they deserve it? Do you have any idea how many kids come through our doors? Don't they all deserve a happy ending?

"It's nice that you want to do something, but you don't seem to understand what we're dealing with," she continued. "We have thousands of children in the system throughout the state. Just in this immediate area we have five hundred kids – and half of those kids don't have a home right now.

"We want to do right by them, and heaven knows that we would like to make their lives better, but right now it's all we can do to keep food on the table and roofs over their heads," she said. "We're doing the best we can, but the last thing we need is someone who doesn't understand the situation poking her nose in and trying to fix things for three kids when we have hundreds more in straits more dire than this."

I didn't like her tone, yet part of her argument slipped through the haze and made a bit of sense. Sure, I understood what she was saying. That didn't mean I was going to back down. "Can you at least give me some information on the boys, like if they have any family members in the area?"

"That information is confidential."

One look at Susan's face told me she'd already dismissed me. "Well, I guess that's it then. Come on, Clove."

Clove obediently followed me to the door, stopping when I turned and fixed Susan with a harsh look.

"You might look at it as if I'm only trying to help three kids and you have hundreds to worry about so you can't possibly be bothered, but I look at it differently," I said. "I look at it as you have to start somewhere. Just because there are more kids to help – and that will never change – that doesn't mean you can't help these particular kids."

"Ms. Winchester ... ."

"Don't." I held up my hand to silence her. "I don't expect you to help me. Just so you know, though, I'll do this with or without you."

"What is that supposed to mean?"

"Just sit back and watch. You'll find out eventually." I grabbed Clove by the back of the neck as we exited the office, keeping her close as I scanned the hallway for signs of Bay or Thistle.

"Have you seen them?"

Clove wordlessly nodded and pointed toward the parking lot.

I headed in that direction, pressing my lips together when I found Bay and Thistle loitering by the passenger side of the truck. The whole office meltdown had been part of the plan. I knew from the moment I saw Susan that she wouldn't help. That meant I needed Bay and Thistle to get some much-needed information that I figured Susan wouldn't be willing to share with us.

"Did you get it?"

Bay held up a manila folder and nodded. "I stole it."

Crap. I should've thought this out better. "Why did you steal it?"

"Because there was no way for us to make copies without getting caught," Thistle replied. "Don't worry. We only took the family information from Michael's file and then shoved the rest in David's file so they'll think it's some sort of filing error."

"Oh, well, that sounds smart." I straightened and smiled. "How about we head to lunch and go through the file? Hopefully we'll find something that can help us."

"Okay, but you're buying," Bay said. "I don't want this to be like last time when you told us to order whatever we wanted and then tried to stick us with the bill."

I smiled at the memory. "That was an important lesson for you girls. You should thank me."

"It was definitely an important lesson," Bay agreed. "That's why we're making sure you understand that you're paying."

"I've got it." I poked her arm. "You were smooth in there. You've obviously been paying attention to my lessons."

"Yes, well, when it comes to breaking the law you're the best."

"Oh, I think that's the nicest thing you've ever said to me."

SIX

"I brought ice cream."

I purposely picked a light and friendly approach as I led the girls into the house two hours later. The look Winnie shot me from behind the kitchen counter told me I was in for a rude awakening if I thought my nieces would be willing to simply gloss over my absence.

"Where have you been?" Winnie barked, her temper on full display.

"And a happy afternoon to you, too, niece." I refused to let her draw me into an argument, instead putting the container of ice cream on the counter. "I hope you boys like ice cream, because I got some good stuff."

David, who looked much more relaxed than he had during breakfast, sat next to Terry at the table as his brothers and the police officer worked to put together a model. "We like ice cream."

"Good." I beamed at him. "What did you guys do with your day?"

"Mr. Terry took us for a walk outside, and we gathered wood for the fire tonight," Michael volunteered. "He even showed us the big rocks up on that one hill and said that you guys do freaky stuff out there when it's warm out."

"Freaky stuff?" Winnie turned her accusatory gaze from me to Terry.

"I told you that was a secret." Terry smiled while giving the admonishment, refusing to look in Winnie's direction. "I think he misheard me, Winnie. I said you did some wonderful stuff out on the bluff."

"Only if you're not afraid of seeing old ladies naked," Thistle offered, shrugging out of her coat as she stared at the model. It looked to be some sort of airplane. "That's neat. Where did you get that?"

"Mr. Terry got it," Andrew answered. "You can help us put it together if you want."

"No, she can't," Terry argued. "While Thistle is wonderfully crafty and has steady hands, she also refuses to follow directions. That means the models she puts together never look like they're supposed to."

"You just can't think outside the box," Thistle complained. "I still maintain that castle you got us looked better with the turrets in the center rather than at the edges."

"Only an evil king or queen would've lived in that castle," Terry countered.

"We live with Aunt Tillie. Of course, we gear everything toward evil queens."

Instead of continuing the argument, Terry chuffed out a laugh as he pointed toward something on the plane. "There, David. That's where that piece I showed you a few minutes ago goes."

Bay watched with a conflicted gaze, the folder she stole from the state building in her hand. I'd almost forgotten about it. I needed to hide it before someone asked a question none of us wanted to answer. Bay was distracted by Terry, though, and I had a feeling I understood what was bothering her.

"He still likes you best," I whispered, grabbing the folder from her as I crowded her to the side so we wouldn't garner attention from my nieces. "He's just trying to do something special with them."

"I know." Bay snapped to attention quickly. "I wasn't trying to be a pain or anything."

"I know," I shot back. "I just wanted you to know that you're still his favorite. He's taking you driving this weekend, isn't he?"

"I'm not jealous." Bay's eyes flashed. "I'm just ... watching."

I didn't believe her but now was hardly the time to make a point of it. "Fine." I pressed the folder to my stomach and walked around the counter, flashing occasional smiles when people looked at me while I was doing my best to act innocent. That entailed picturing scenes from *Little House on the Prairie* in my head, causing me to think about running down a hill with a dog. Then it caused me to wonder what would happen if I tripped while running down the hill. Then it made me wonder why anyone would run down a hill. Most of the glances I earned from those gathered in the kitchen were of the blasé sort, but I was relieved when I managed to slide the folder inside without anyone noticing.

Then I realized someone had noticed – and it was the last person in the room I wanted to tangle with.

"What was that?" Winnie asked, pinning me with a hard look.

"What was what?" I asked innocently, resting my hand on top of the ice cream container. "I already told you it's ice cream. Rocky Road. Everyone loves Rocky Road, right?"

"Uh-huh." Winnie wasn't convinced in the least. "What was in the folder you put in the drawer?"

"I think you're seeing things," I replied, avoiding eye contact as I rolled my neck so Winnie couldn't watch my mouth. I whispered a small curse in the direction of the drawer, making it so it would stick should she try to open it, and then pointed at the overhead cupboard. "Bay, can you get down some bowls?"

"Sure." Bay moved to join me, her eyes traveling to her mother when Winnie strode to the drawer and attempted to open it. "What are you doing, Mom?"

"I'm trying to figure out what you girls were up to when you disappeared for the better part of the afternoon," Winnie gritted out as she fruitlessly tugged on the drawer. "We're going to talk about that, by the way."

"Go ahead," I said, snapping my fingers and pointing toward the drawer that held the ice cream scoop so Clove would know to get it.

"I'm not a dog," Clove complained, although she did as I wanted and retrieved the scoop.

"I think Winnie wants to know where you took the girls and why no one bothered to leave a note or inform their mothers where they were going," Terry interjected.

"We forgot," Clove said.

"You forgot?" Terry cocked an eyebrow. "I'm not sure how you could forget to tell your mother you were leaving the house, especially after you've been warned about it so many times. We were about to call for a search with the state police until someone downtown mentioned that they might've seen Tillie's pickup in front of Margaret Little's house – and there was some distinctive yellow snow left behind."

Oh, well … it had to be Beatrice Monroe. She spends way too much time worrying about what other people are doing. She's such a tattletale. "I have no idea what you're talking about," I lied.

"Yellow snow?" David looked amused. "You were out putting yellow snow in someone's yard?"

"Only for part of the time," Bay replied, moving around the counter so she could stare closer at the airplane. "This is cool. You guys have done a lot of work."

"Officer Terry has done most of the work," Andrew said sheepishly.

"No, you've done most of the work," Terry corrected, absently patting Bay's back. "I only supervised."

"He's good at supervising," Bay offered.

"No, he's not," Thistle countered. "I hate it when he supervises. I always end up grounded when he supervises."

"Maybe that says a little something about you," Terry suggested, scorching her with a look.

"I think it says something about you," Thistle countered.

"And what's that?"

"Well … I think you like torturing little kids."

Michael snickered. "Man, you guys are funny. Are you always like this?"

"Unfortunately, yes," Terry said dryly, his eyes drifting to me. "So, where did you girls go after your trip to Margaret Little's house?"

"We can't answer that question without our lawyer present," Thistle replied, grabbing a cookie from the counter. "We demand representation."

"Oh, geez." Terry pinched the bridge of his nose. "Do I even want to know what you were doing?"

"Probably not," I replied. "Besides, it's a surprise." I tilted my head in the boys' direction, the movement deliberate and meant to convey a hidden message. Terry clearly didn't get it.

"What kind of surprise?"

"I've got it." Bay leaned closer and whispered something to Terry – although I had no idea what – and when he turned his eyes to me I considered running. Bay is one of those liars who is gifted one day and challenged the next. Of course, knowing Bay, she might have told him the truth, which meant Terry would arrest me for allowing her to steal a government file.

"I see." Terry's expression was unreadable.

Bay smiled as she walked away from him, stopping close to me so she could pry the lid off the ice cream. "I think he's proud of you."

"And what did you say to him?"

"That we were buying presents and needed to keep it a secret." Bay kept her voice low. "Don't worry. I'm not an idiot. I didn't mention the other stuff."

Oh, well, I'd had faith in her the entire time. I knew she wouldn't screw this up. "Good girl." I patted her shoulder. "That was very smart. It explains why we snuck off and why we're being cagey. You're smarter than you look."

"I look smart," Bay argued. "I'm smarter than you look."

"Hey, don't start talking like your gutter-mouthed cousin." I extended a warning finger. "I happen to like you right now. That could change before you even realize what's happening."

Bay stared at me for a long beat, as if debating whether I was telling the truth or messing with her. Finally she heaved a sigh and nodded. "I'll scoop the ice cream."

"You do that."

I moved away from her, momentarily making eye contact with Terry before grabbing a soda from the refrigerator and pondering how far I should push things before dinner. Ultimately I decided to focus on the fire rather than the boys' unsettled home life.

"Anything new on the fire?"

"Actually, yes." Terry's lips curved into a smile. "It seems that what initial investigators thought was accelerant at the Michaelson house was actually leftover from a lawnmower Ben was trying to fix. He'd been working in the garage and had carried an extra gas can from the back of the house to the front. He used it for the generator in the summer and didn't want to have to run to the gas station in the cold. He's the one who left traces of accelerants around the house."

David lifted his head, his eyes curious. "What does that mean?"

"Well, it means that the fire most likely wasn't intentionally set," Terry explained. "In fact, when the fire inspector went through the house he believed the initial spark happened at the fuse box."

"That would indicate an electrical fire, right?" Winnie asked. She'd apparently forgotten she was attempting to open the drawer, which was good for me.

"We don't have a final report," Terry cautioned, "but it's starting to look that way."

"That's good, right?" Bay carried three bowls of ice cream to the table and slipped them in front of Michael, Andrew and David without prodding. She seemed to inherently know that she should serve them first. "Now people won't believe that the boys in the home caused the fire."

Terry's studied gaze lingered on Bay for a long moment. I could practically see the gears in his mind working. Bay more than any of them picked up on things adults tried to gloss over and hide. This was no exception. "I didn't say that people in town believed the boys set the fire."

"You didn't have to say it," Bay countered. "It was obvious."

"I don't think it was obvious."

"No, she's right," David said. "It was obvious. Thank you for trying to protect our feelings, but it's not as if we didn't know what people were saying."

"This is why I can only work with kids one or two days a week," Terry muttered, rolling his neck. "You guys are all trying to kill me. I can feel it."

"If we were trying to kill you we wouldn't ask questions first," Thistle said, maniacally running her hand over the knife block as she grinned at Terry.

"You'll be on my list, too, if you're not careful," he warned. "As for people in town, I don't think most of them believed the boys were guilty. There might have been a person or two who did, but not the majority of the townsfolk."

"Mrs. Little?" Bay asked sagely.

"Mrs. Little is crazy, so it doesn't matter what she says," Terry said. "We've talked about that."

"Is that what you told her when she called to complain about the yellow snow?"

"I somehow managed to avoid that call." Terry was being evasive. He was so loveable, though, I had to give him a pass. I mean, how many men would spend their entire day working on a model with three young boys who were nothing more than strangers and would be gone in a few days? Terry was definitely a keeper. In fact, there were times I wanted to trade him for every female in my house.

"Well, we were merely running errands," I offered, smiling at David even though the look he cast me was one of extreme doubt. "I also took the girls to lunch while we were out."

"Yeah, that's not suspicious at all," Winnie grumbled.

"What's suspicious about it?" I challenged.

"You never purposely take them out. I know you were up to something."

"That's a terrible thing to say about your nieces and aunt," Clove said, her eyes misting. The kid is a natural when it comes to drumming up fake tears. "I think my feelings are hurt."

"Your butt is going to be hurt if you're not careful," Winnie snapped.

"Oh, my feelings are definitely hurt." Clove's expression was mournful as she knuckled her eyes. "I think I'm going to go upstairs and cry myself to sleep."

"Oh, no one is falling for that." Winnie's expression twisted. "You'll have to do better than that to get anyone to feel sorry for you."

"I feel sorry for her," Andrew said earnestly. "I think she's going to cry."

"She always cries," Winnie said. "It's an act."

"I feel a little sorry for her, too," Terry admitted. "I know it's an act, but she gets me every time all the same."

"That's because you're a sap." Winnie lightly cuffed the back of his head, her expression fond. "She'll be fine. I'm sure whatever covert operation Aunt Tillie took the girls on this afternoon will bolster her spirits while she naps."

I knew Winnie was trying to get me to admit to what we were doing, so I ignored the dig and instead focused on David. He was the oldest and he had a keen ability to read a room. I knew it was dangerous to come right out and ask him the question at the forefront of my brain, but I didn't seem to have much of a choice.

"David, what can you tell me about Carl Lewis?"

"Who is Carl Lewis?" Terry asked, knitting his eyebrows.

"He's our uncle," David replied, rubbing the back of his neck, clearly caught off guard by the question. "What does he have to do with anything?"

"I'm just curious." I was going for a breezy tone, although I had no idea if I achieved it. "He's your father's brother, right?"

David nodded. "We got to see him some when we were younger. He always came by and spent time with us, even after our dad went away."

"Why didn't you go to live with him after your mother died? I mean ... was there a specific reason?"

"He tried to get us."

"I know."

David tilted his head to the side. "How do you know?"

I could hardly own up to possession of the stolen file so I merely shrugged. "I hear things. I'm curious about why he couldn't take you boys. From what I read ... er, I mean heard from random people on the street ... he really wanted to."

"He did want to," David confirmed. "In fact, he told us we were going to live with him. Then it didn't happen. The state didn't want to give us to him because he didn't have a regular job at the time. And there was something else about my father refusing to sign away custody. We had to go to court and everything because Uncle Carl wouldn't give up, but ... the judge said no."

"Does he still see you?"

"When he can, but they keep moving us and don't always tell him," David explained. "He does his best to see us, but he can't always make it. I guess it doesn't matter, because the judge won't let us stay with him."

I had my doubts that would remain true much longer. "Okay. I was just curious. Go back to making your model."

I smiled at Winnie as I grabbed the back of Bay's neck and dragged her to the corner. She ate ice cream as she looked me up and down.

"What?"

"Grab your cohorts in crime. We're going on another trip."

"We'll get in trouble."

"Do you really care?"

"Will you take the blame?"

"You're getting more and more manipulative the older you get," I complained. "I'll take the blame. Just ... grab the others. I have a feeling I might need cute faces where we're going."

"You only want Clove because she makes people uncomfortable when she cries."

"I can admit that."

"Fine. I'll get them." Bay licked her spoon. "We're still going to save Christmas, right?"

"Absolutely."

SEVEN

"I'm confused." Clove held her hands in front of the heating vent as we drove toward Cheboygan. "If the judge won't let the boys live with their uncle, how are you going to change his mind?"

"Because I'm me," I replied. "Bay, you read the file on the way back to Walkerville. What was the judge's name listed on the decision?"

"How is she supposed to remember that?" Thistle complained.

"Judge West," Bay supplied. "I remember because it reminded me of the Wicked Witch of the West … and you say we're the Wicked Witches of the Midwest … and sometimes I remember weird things I have no business remembering."

"Great." I smiled as I passed a slow-moving driver and offered up a one-finger salute for her sloth-like speed choice. "Get off the road, you blind old bat!"

The woman honked back and matched my salute.

"I happen to know Gerald West," I added.

"Did he lock you up?" Thistle asked.

"No."

"Did he want to lock you up?"

"No. Well, maybe."

"Is he going to be happy to see you?" Bay shifted on her seat. "I'm going to guess that he won't and that's where we're going, right?"

I shook my head. "Actually, we're going to see Carl Lewis first. We'll worry about Gerald West later. Trust me. He'll be happy to hear from me."

"I've got twenty bucks that says he won't be happy to hear from you," Thistle muttered.

"Where did you get twenty bucks?"

"I have money."

"Good to know. If I need to borrow some, I'll come to you next time."

"You're my least favorite relative," Thistle grumbled. "That's not just for today. That's every day."

"I'm sure you'll change your mind when I catch you sneaking around outside after dark and don't tell your mother."

Thistle pursed her lips. Much like me, she hates when the person she's arguing with has a point. "I'm not taking back what I said. I don't care how long you sit there waiting for me to do it."

"I don't want you to take it back. You wouldn't be you if you took it back."

"You've got that right."

I bit the inside of my cheek to keep from laughing. The kid has pizzazz. I can't explain it. Bay, on the other hand, was somber as she stared out the window. She clearly had a lot on her mind.

"What are you going to do when you find this uncle?" Bay asked. "Are you just going to ask him to take David, Michael and Andrew, and then send them off to have a happily ever after?"

I shrugged, noncommittal. "I don't know yet. It depends on what he has to say."

"What do you think he's going to say?"

"Why are you asking so many serious questions?"

"Because I'm worried," Bay admitted without hesitation. "I want to make things better, but I'm really worried that we won't be able to."

"I don't think you should worry about that."

"Well, it's too late. I am worried."

I should've thought about that before allowing them to tag along. They're teenagers, which means they're all about themselves most of the time. They're always dramatic. The drama wins out over the selfishness on most occasions.

"Bay, I need you to have faith that I'm going to fix things. I know I don't always do the right thing, but everything will work out this time."

Bay wasn't about to be placated. "How do you know that?"

"It's called faith. You have it, too, even if you don't believe it."

"I do have faith," Bay agreed. "I've also seen you in action when it comes to strangers. People don't like you when they first meet you. This Carl guy isn't going to do what you want just because you act like a friendly little old lady and try to charm him."

Thistle snorted. "She's got you there."

I ignored Thistle's cackle. "Who are you calling old, Bay?"

"I'm sorry. He's not going to see you as a friendly middle-aged woman," Bay corrected. "He's going to think you're crazy."

"That's why I brought you girls," I acknowledged. "He'll melt when he sees you."

"Because Clove's going to cry?"

"Only if he thinks we're crazy," I cautioned. "We're saving that one for when he calls the police."

"I love a good threat of jail right around Christmas," Bay smirked.

"You know ... you're getting quite the smart mouth."

Bay snickered. "Mom says I get that from you."

"Your mother is nuts."

"I'm going to tell her you said that."

"I'm not afraid of her." I meant it. Kind of. Okay, only sometimes. "Don't tell her I said that."

"Your secret is safe with me," Bay said. "Especially if this works."

"It's going to work."

"It has to."

CARL LEWIS LOOKED SURPRISED when he opened the door to

his tidy ranch house and found the four of us standing on his porch. He arched an eyebrow, smiled, and then moved to shut the door.

"No solicitors." He tapped the sign on the door for emphasis.

I shot my foot between the door and jamb so he couldn't close us out, pasting what I hoped was a friendly expression on my face to put him at ease. "I hate solicitors, too. They're a special kind of vermin."

"Okay." Carl opened the door. "If you're not solicitors that means you're probably with a local church. I'm already a member of a church."

"Good for you, sparky." My smile slipped. I couldn't help being a bit insulted. "Do we look like we're recruiting for a church?"

"They do." Carl inclined his head toward the girls. "Although they're not really dressed for recruiting."

"What do you mean by that?" Clove asked.

"I think he means you're dressed like a slut," Thistle replied.

"That's not what I meant." Carl made a tsking sound with his tongue. "I just meant that the church recruiters generally show up in plaid skirts and matching blazers."

"That sounds like a nightmare I once had," Clove noted.

"I'm sure it does." Carl looked amused but eager to get rid of us. "So what is it you want?"

"A few minutes of your time," I answered. "Actually, if things go as planned it would be more like a few years of your time and your heart."

Carl arched a wary eyebrow. "Meaning?"

"Meaning that your nephews are staying with us right now, and I want to talk to you about a few things."

Carl stilled, his expression shifting. "You have Michael, Andrew and David? I've been trying to find out where they are since I heard about the group home fire. I was planning to visit them on Christmas – I have gifts and everything – but no one could tell me where they're staying."

That was odd. "They couldn't tell you or wouldn't tell you?"

"I have no idea."

"Well, they're okay. They're in Walkerville with us and they're fine.

They spent the day building a model with a member of the police force – although not in a weird or creepy way – and my nieces are fattening them up with every baked good under the sun."

Carl looked relieved as he pushed open the door all the way. "Come in. I'd like to hear what you have to say."

"Good. I have a lot to say."

"She's not exaggerating," Thistle offered. "She loves to hear herself talk."

Carl's eyes twinkled as he ushered us inside. "I'll bet you share that trait with her."

Thistle was affronted. "You don't even know me."

"I'm good at reading people."

"Aunt Tillie says the same thing about herself. I'll believe it when I see it."

Carl led us to the living room, offering drinks and snacks – which we politely declined – and then we got straight to business.

"I won't pretend that I understand how everything works, but the boys told us a little about their situation. We want to make sure that they get out of this with a bright future," I started. "I believe you're the key to that bright future."

"If you've been talking to the boys – and kudos for that, because they're not very chatty these days – then you know that I tried to get custody of them," Carl said. "That's what I wanted most. I promised my mother before she died that I would try to get custody. She was too sick to do it herself after my sister died. I've been working on it ever since."

"The boys weren't exactly chatty when they first arrived, but I've been wearing them down," I said. "They've let a few things slip."

"How long have they been at your house?"

"Since last night. We're only keeping them for a few days. That's why I want to figure out the best way to make sure that they go straight from our house to yours."

"Do you really think you're just going to be able to snap your fingers and make that happen?" Carl was understandably dubious. He'd never worked with witches before, so he had no idea exactly how powerful I was. I didn't want to toot my own horn – okay, I always want to do that, but don't tell anyone – but I knew I could make things come out the way they should if I simply had all the information.

"I think I can do anything I put my mind to," I replied. "That includes getting these boys with you. I need information, though."

"Okay. How can I help?"

"Tell me how all of this happened," I prodded. "Why weren't you considered a viable guardian from the start?"

"Their mother, Camille, was a good woman who worked hard and did her very best by those boys," Carl started. "Nobody is perfect, but that woman darned near was. She was a saint, which is why I always wondered why she married my brother."

"What's wrong with your brother?" Bay asked.

"He's selfish. He's always been selfish."

"So is Aunt Tillie, but we still live with her," Clove pointed out, causing Carl to smile.

"I'll bet that your great-aunt is selfish in a different way," Carl said. "Daryl only ever thought of himself. When Camille showed up pregnant with David I thought that he'd change his ways. He was good for a year – right up until she became pregnant with Michael – and then he started spiraling."

"Drugs?" I asked, worried.

Carl shook his head. "He liked to drink. That was his vice. He also liked to gamble. He'd take all the money Camille worked so hard to earn as a nurse and throw it away on football games ... and basketball games ... and even tennis matches when he was hard up for something to bet on."

"She still had Andrew with him," I pointed out.

"I think Camille lived in denial for a very long time," Carl explained. "She wanted Daryl to be a better man than he was. Once she realized that wasn't possible, she wanted to give the kids stability. She thought that was better than them growing up without a father."

I spared a glance for the girls and remembered how Winnie,

Marnie and Twila all clung to marriages that were clearly doomed. "Sometimes it takes a while for reality to set in."

"That's definitely true," Carl agreed. "I did what I could for them. I helped with groceries and played basketball with the boys on the weekends. My brother gave me grief about it, accused me of trying to move in on Camille. I told him I was merely doing the job he refused to do, but he wouldn't listen."

"How old were the boys when he left?"

"I believe David was seven, which would've made Andrew three," Carl replied. "Andrew doesn't even remember him, which is probably for the best. David remembers him as a mean guy who always yelled and made Camille cry."

"Sometimes it's better to live without a father than have one like that," I noted. "David said his mother died from a heart ailment."

"After my brother left I was around more often," Carl said. "I loved the boys and knew my brother did them wrong."

"Do you know where he is?" Bay asked.

"He's in Las Vegas. He works as a dealer at a casino. My understanding is that every dime he makes goes back into the casinos. That's not my problem, though. He didn't even call back when I told him Camille was dead. He didn't even ask about the boys. He just didn't care."

My blood boiled and I had to fight the urge to explode. If Daryl Lewis were in this room right now, I'd teach him a thing or two about curses.

"And Camille?" I asked, forcing myself to remain calm.

"She went quickly," Carl said. "One minute she was fine. The next I got a call that the boys had discovered her on the kitchen floor. She was already dead, but they went through the motions of taking her to the hospital anyway. When I showed up the boys still had hope. But the look on the doctor's face told me all hope was gone the second I saw him."

"That's terrible." I rubbed my hand over my cheek. "Still, the way David talks, you tried to get the boys then."

"I did. I didn't think it would be an issue. Apparently a single man filing for custody of three boys – even if the boys are his nephews and no one else is around to take them – is a huge problem."

"David said something about a job." I hated delving too deep into Carl's private matters, but I needed all the information.

"Yeah, I was between jobs," Carl said. "It wasn't that I was out of work. When I thought the boys were coming to live with me I took a job at the local high school. I quit my old job, but was still a month away from starting my new job. They said that I was technically out of work, so I couldn't have them.

"I thought that it was a stupid rule, but I figured at most they'd be in the system for a few weeks, and that's what I told them," he continued. "Once I started the new job I filed the paperwork again. I hit a different roadblock the second time."

"Roadblock?"

"Daryl."

I wrinkled my nose, confused. "Is he back?"

"No, he's not back, but he has to sign off custody of the boys if I want to adopt them," Carl replied. "He won't answer my calls or sign the documents."

Well that just figured. "And that's the only thing standing in the way of you getting those boys?"

Carl nodded. "I had my brother served with papers, but he never responded. I should've had a default judgment, but the judge doesn't see it that way."

"Judge West?"

"Yeah. Do you know him?"

I let an evil smile out to play. "I definitely know him. I've also got this under control." I hopped to my feet, a plan forming. "Come on, girls. I have a call to make."

"That's it?" The look on Carl's face was priceless. He clearly thought I was crazy. I considered having Clove whip out one of her patented crying displays, but it seemed like overkill.

"Trust me on this," I said. "Tomorrow is Christmas Eve. I'll have the boys with you before the end of the day."

"How can you promise that?"

"Because I believe I can do anything I set my mind to," I replied. "I've set my mind to doing this."

"I'm sure you understand that I have my doubts," Carl said.

"It's fine. Have your doubts. I won't tell the boys my plan in case something goes wrong, but I'd like you to come to the house tomorrow regardless and see them. They'll be excited to spend time with you."

"I'd really appreciate that." Carl looked so grateful I thought he would break down weeping. "I just need your address and a time."

I supplied both and then herded the girls toward the door. "I'll be in touch when I have more information. Just show up in plenty of time for dinner tomorrow. I'm pretty sure I'll have good news for you ... for all of you."

"I want to believe you because you're so forceful," Carl said, "but I've been crushed by the system a few times."

"It's nothing compared to how crushed those boys have been," I pointed out. "Those boys are going to have a happy Christmas if it kills me. I promise you that."

"You should believe her," Thistle offered. "She saves Christmas all the time. She'll do it again this year."

"Technically I'm not saving Christmas this year," I countered. "I'm stealing it. Like Robin Hood. I'm taking from the ... whatever ... and giving to the worthy."

"I'm pretty sure that's not how it goes," Bay interjected.

"How is that even different?" Thistle challenged.

"It's better."

Thistle ran her tongue over her teeth and then shrugged. "Whatever. As long as the boys are happy, I don't care what you do."

"Then let's steal Christmas."

"Yee-haw!" Clove pumped her fist and then shrank back when Thistle glared. "What? It seemed like the right moment."

"I'm totally going to make you eat dirt later," Thistle threatened.

"I'll make you both eat dirt," I warned. "That'll be my Christmas miracle. I'll make you eat dirt and force you to be quiet for one blissful hour."

EIGHT

"That went well."

Bay was happy when I loaded the girls into my truck, her smile serene as she stared out the passenger side window. At times I think she's the hardest to placate. Other times I think she's the easiest.

"It did," I agreed, pointing my truck toward the highway. "I like him."

"He's nice," Clove said. "I really hope the boys get to live with him. It doesn't seem fair that they've been kept away from him for stupid reasons."

"Yeah, I don't get that," Thistle mused. "Their dad is a butthead and doesn't want them, so why would the state people keep them from the uncle who does? That seems to be rewarding the butthead."

I smirked, amused. "Because you're a butthead, I'd think you'd side with the father." I was mostly teasing, but it was true. Thistle had a good heart, but she worked overtime to hide it.

"I'm not a butthead like that," Thistle argued. "And I'm only a butthead to you because you're a butthead to me."

Bay and Clove exchanged dubious looks.

"You're only a butthead to her?" Bay challenged.

"No one's talking to you," Thistle said stiffly. "I'm talking to Aunt Tillie, so zip your lips."

"Hey, don't start fighting," I warned, growling when a woman in a large sport-utility vehicle in front of me opted to drive three miles below the speed limit on a stretch that had no passing lane. "Oh, we're trying to steal Christmas here!" I pressed my hand to the horn and smiled as it blared. "Move it or I'll move you!"

"Why do you keep putting it like that?" Bay asked. "I thought we were saving Christmas."

"We are saving Christmas, but this time we're doing it by stealing," I said. "You started it when you stole the file."

Bay balked. "What else was I supposed to do?"

"I didn't say you did anything wrong," I cautioned. "I merely said you started it. Now I'm going to finish it."

"With the judge?"

"Exactly."

"And how do you know him again?" Thistle challenged.

"Let's just say we've had a few run-ins over the years and leave it at that," I suggested. "I think the hardest part is going to be figuring out a way to get that deadbeat father to sign the document. He's in another state."

"Why not just send a ghost to haunt him until he agrees to sign?" Bay suggested.

I slid her a sidelong look. "Only people like us – you and me – can see ghosts," I reminded her. "He wouldn't be able to see a ghost."

"Yes, but you don't have to send a regular ghost," Bay argued. "I'm not even sure where we could find one on such short notice."

"There's one that hangs around the newspaper office. Edith. She wouldn't help us, though. What are you thinking, Bay?" I was intrigued despite myself.

"I'm thinking that you should just create a fake ghost – maybe one that looks like Camille – and send it to haunt the father," Bay explained. "You have hair from the boys, so you can track down their dad with a spell if you use it."

"Huh." She's smarter than she looks sometimes. It's both a gift and a curse. "That right there is an outstanding idea. I think you're onto something."

"I'm always onto something," Bay said. "You just generally refuse to listen to me."

"I don't refuse to listen," I countered. "It's just that your voice sounds like quacking ducks at times and I have no choice but to tune out if I want to remain sane."

"Since when are you sane?" Thistle challenged.

"Shh." I pressed a finger to my lips as I focused on the road. "I need time to think. Be quiet for a little bit."

The girls lapsed into silence, which Thistle was the first to break.

"You should be quiet," she muttered.

Since she always needed the last word – and I understand what that's like – I let it go. Yes indeed, Bay was onto something, and I was pretty sure things would come together exactly as I wanted this Christmas.

Hallelujah!

"WHAT'S GOING ON?"

The ride back to Walkerville was made mostly in silence, but Bay perked up when we hit Main Street, her eyes shifting to the parking lot next to City Hall. I followed her gaze, confusion washing over me when I recognized half the cars in attendance.

"I don't know," I replied after a beat, "but all of those cars belong to town board members."

"Oh, she's right," Thistle said, craning her neck. "We've egged all of those cars in that front row."

"Hey, what did I tell you about owning up to stuff like that?" I shouted. "It didn't happen unless they catch us in the act, which they didn't. There's no way they can prove that."

"We're the only ones in the car," Thistle reminded me.

"Yes, but if you get complacent with us you might get complacent around others. Practice makes perfect."

Thistle crossed her arms over her chest and rolled her eyes.

"Whatever." I was almost positive I heard her add "you old bat" under her breath. I wanted to address her terrible attitude and the fact that she refused to respect her elders, but the presence of the cars in the parking lot – on the day before Christmas Eve, mind you – made me think someone was up to no good.

And, for once, that someone wasn't me.

"Change of plans," I announced, turning the truck so it bounced over the curb, jolted over the strip of land separating the sidewalk and the parking lot and then smoothly pulled into a spot at the end of the lot. "Let's see what they're doing."

Clove's eyes were wide when I killed the engine. "What did you just do?"

"I parked in the lot."

"But you drove over the sidewalk to do it!"

"So?"

"So … I'm pretty sure that's illegal!"

"No one saw me," I said. "Besides, I would've had to turn around because I missed the entryway before I made my decision. No one has time to turn around."

I pushed open the door and reared back when I found Terry standing at my fender, hands on his hips. "Good afternoon, officer!" I sang out the words as if I was simply happy to see him and not trying to get out of a ticket.

"Officer Terry, I'm glad you're here! We've almost saved Christmas!" Bay hurried to Terry's side and gave him a quick hug. It was almost as if she sensed he was about to lose his temper. "We've had a busy day."

"I see that." Terry forced a smile as he glanced down at Bay. "You girls snuck out of the house again. Winnie is about to have kittens she's so ticked off."

I waved off the statement, unbothered. "Winnie always acts as if she's about to have kittens," I said. "She'll be fine. Plus, me taking the girls means my nieces have more time to dote on the boys. I think they need it more."

"I'd be lying if I said it wasn't good for them," Terry said. "They seem to like the attention. I'd also be lying if I said they weren't a little confused about why you four keep disappearing."

"We're stealing Christmas," Clove replied simply.

"Stealing Christmas?" Terry furrowed his brow. "What does that mean?"

"She's just confused." I forced a smile as I cuffed the back of Clove's head. "The little scamp gets confused far too often."

"Hey!" Clove's face lit with fury. "That hurt."

"It hurt almost as much as when you drove over the curb and our heads almost hit the ceiling of the truck," Thistle added, grinning slyly when Terry's face twisted. She knew exactly what she was doing ... and she was getting off on it.

"Thank you, Thistle," I gritted out. "I don't know what I'd do without you."

"I know."

"Why did you drive over the sidewalk like that?" Terry challenged. "You have three young girls in the truck with you. They could've been hurt."

I made a dismissive motion with my hand. "They're fine. They were in their seatbelts. Thistle is simply exaggerating. That's what she does."

"I don't doubt she's exaggerating," Terry argued, "but that doesn't explain why you did what you did."

"Oh, that. I decided I wanted to see what everyone was doing here, and it was too late to hit the access road."

"You could've turned around."

"Meh. That would've taken more time ... and we're low on time."

"I don't even want to know what that means," Terry muttered, pinching the bridge of his nose. "I saw the cars, too. That's why I stopped."

"Oh, well, let's see what they're doing." Instead of waiting for his response, I grabbed Thistle by the back of the neck and marched her forward. "You're definitely on my list," I hissed into her ear.

"Hey, if you don't have time to turn around and drive on the actual road, you don't have time to make a list," Thistle reasoned.

"I'll make time."

"Not until you get what you want." Thistle was trying to sound rational. "You'll forget what you were even mad about by then."

"I'll never forget."

"We'll see."

I lifted my eyes and found Terry staring as he walked between Bay and Clove. He was clearly suspicious. Thankfully for me, that suspicion turned to outright fury as we entered City Hall and he realized a town meeting was taking place.

"What's going on here?" Terry yelled as he took a step forward.

Margaret, who sat at the head table, made a face when she saw us come through the door. "I believe you'll find that this is an emergency meeting."

"Of what?"

"The town council."

"You can't have a special meeting of the town council without proper notification," Terry argued, striding forward. The look he scorched Walkerville Mayor Harry Buttons with was downright terrifying. "I happen to know the bylaws. You have to make proper notification of a special meeting."

"This was an emergency meeting, not a special meeting," Margaret clarified. "There's a difference."

"No, there's not," Terry argued. "What is this meeting even about?"

"I believe I'll let the mayor fill you in," Margaret replied stiffly, averting her gaze.

Hmm. Her reaction seemed to signify that she expected us to be angry – or at least vocal – regarding whatever was about to happen.

"We're discussing the boys that are being fostered within the township limits." Harry chose his words carefully. "Given last night's fire, we believe that some decisions need to be made if we want to keep the residents safe."

Oh, well, that was so much worse than I initially envisioned.

"Excuse me?" Terry was beside himself. "The fire at the Michaelson house was determined to have come from an electrical box."

"And yet the fire chief says accelerants were used as well," Harry argued.

"No. I talked to Ben myself," Terry said. "I wanted to confirm what he told my officers. Ben said that he accidentally spread the gasoline when he was moving his can from the backyard – where he keeps his generator – to the front. He was working on a lawnmower.

"It doesn't really matter, though," he continued. "The inspector believes the fire originated at the fuse box. That was nowhere near the purported accelerants."

"Yes, and we happen to think that story is a little too convenient," Harry said.

"We?" I challenged, moving forward. "Listen, Hairy Bottom, I know you spend most of your time hiding in a bottle and letting Margaret lead you around by the short and curlies, but if you think I'm going to allow that to happen this time you're crazier than the woman sitting next to you."

"Don't you even think about saying something crass like that!" Margaret barked.

"I hate to agree with her," Terry said, keeping his voice low. "You took me to a scary visual place there."

"Good. That's what I was trying to do." I kept my gaze focused on Harry, the worm. The good news is he's even more afraid of me than he is of Margaret. "By the way, I was talking about his nose hair."

Terry rolled his eyes. "Whatever."

"You can't blame that fire on those boys," I said. "You don't have proof, and I believe this is still the United States of America. That means you can't be punished without proof."

"I think that's a bit of an oversimplification, but I like the overall message," Terry added.

"Besides, they didn't do it," Bay said, her eyes flashing. "They're innocent. You're just trying to be mean ... like you always are!"

"Since when do we allow children to speak at town meetings, Harry?" Margaret asked, glaring at Bay. The expression on her face was enough to infuriate Terry.

"Don't even look at her," Terry warned, stepping in front of Bay.

"She has every right to say what's on her mind. She's a Walkerville resident, too. This is her home. If she doesn't like what you have to say, she's allowed to say why."

"She can't vote, so she can't argue," Margaret shot back. "That's one of the bylaws."

"And this isn't an official meeting," Bay challenged. "You can't make decisions at a special meeting that's been illegally called."

"Bay, what are you doing?" Terry asked under his breath, surprise at her fortitude washing over his features.

Bay ignored the question and strode forward. "You can't call a special meeting – emergency or otherwise – without putting a notice in the newspaper."

Margaret narrowed her eyes. I recognized the expression for what it was: anger. Bay was right, though how she knew that was anyone's guess. Margaret was about to go after her because she knew Bay was telling the truth. Hmm. That was mighty interesting.

"The Whistler is a weekly newspaper," Margaret pointed out. "We can't schedule weekly emergencies, so … ."

"If you don't have time to put a notice in the newspaper then you're supposed to put a notice in the front window of every business in town." Bay's voice was strong and clear as she stood with her hands on her hips. She looked formidable, which caused pride to swell in my chest. It seemed she listened to me a time or two after all. "There are no notices in business windows."

"How do you know that?" Harry asked, dumbfounded.

"I read the township bylaws for my government class," Bay replied. "I remember weird things."

I smiled, amused. "You do indeed. That ability is going to come in handy from time to time." I patted her shoulder. "Good job. I'll take it from here."

"Not if you're going to call him 'Hairy Bottom' again," Terry warned.

I pretended I didn't hear the admonishment. "You have no proof that the fire at the Michaelson house was anything other than an accident. You're using that accident to try to remove children from this town – children you've decided are somehow unworthy – and I won't allow that to happen."

"I don't believe we have to get your permission to do the right thing for this town," Margaret argued.

"Oh, but that's where you're wrong," I said. "If you try to do something that forces those boys out of this town I will make your life a living hell."

"You've already done that."

"It can get worse, Margaret," I hissed. "It can get much, much worse."

"She's not lying," Thistle said. "Instead of yellow snow you could be dealing with red rain ... or purple pimples on your butt."

"Yellow snow?" Margaret narrowed her eyes until they were nothing more than twin slits. "I knew that was you."

"I have no idea what you're talking about," I said airily, shooting Thistle a blistering look before continuing. "It doesn't matter. You called this meeting illegally. That means any decision you make here isn't binding."

"And we can also file a complaint with the state," Bay added. "The town could be fined."

Hmm. That brain of hers comes in handy occasionally. "And we're just petty enough to file a complaint," I added. "Not only that, I will take this story to the local television stations. I will blast your names from one end of the state to the other if I have to."

Margaret made a derisive sound in the back of her throat. "And you think they'll care?"

"A story about children being displaced and treated terribly because of the color of their skin before Christmas? I definitely think people will care."

Margaret was affronted. "This has nothing to do with some of them being black!"

"I don't believe you." I honestly didn't. "I will make sure this story is on every news station before the end of the night if you try something. Walkerville will become synonymous with racism by the time I'm done.

"Think about it, Harry," I prodded. "Do you want to be the poster child for racism?"

Harry swallowed hard, his gaze bouncing between Margaret and me before shaking his head. "Meeting dismissed." His voice was feeble, but Margaret clearly heard what he'd said.

"No!" Margaret was outraged. "You can't do this!"

"I believe he just did, Margaret." I offered her a saucy wink. "Oh, and even though it's the holidays, you should probably watch your back."

"Yeah," Thistle warned. "You're on her list."

"So are you," I snapped.

"We'll see."

NINE

"Get me the ginger root," I instructed Clove once we were back at the house. It was time to put things in order, and that started with "haunting" Daryl Lewis. We needed him to sign some papers, and to do that he had to be willing to put the boys ahead of himself. Because that was never going to happen, I needed to make him believe the only way to save himself was to release custody of the boys to his brother.

"Can we make the ghost look disgusting and stuff?" Thistle asked as she shrugged out of her coat.

"Absolutely." I bobbed my head. "The grosser the better."

"I'm thinking we should make the ghost look like a zombie," Bay suggested. "We should make sure that he thinks the ghost is Camille, but make it look like a zombie Camille."

"Good idea." My girls were growing into their own and becoming forces to be reckoned with. I couldn't be prouder if I'd birthed them myself.

"Or we could just make the ghost look like Aunt Tillie," Thistle suggested. "That would make him crap his pants."

Of course, they're also pains in the behind.

"We'll stick with making the ghost look like Camille Forrester," I said. "That reminds me, we need a photograph of her. How will we get one without making the boys suspicious by asking?"

"Leave that to me." Bay's grin was impish. "I'll take care of it."

"I bet you will." I returned the smile before heading to the kitchen. I pulled up short when I found Winnie, Marnie and Twila toiling over dinner. Thankfully the boys weren't in the room. It was obvious I was about to get an earful. "And how are you this fine afternoon, ladies?"

Winnie rolled her eyes, annoyance evident. "That's not going to work on us," she said. "You're in big trouble."

"You are," Marnie agreed. "This is the second time today you've taken off with the girls without even leaving a note. We know you're up to something. You're starting to give those boys a complex because they think you don't want to spend time with them."

"That's just silly," I said. "We've been out doing stuff for the boys. They're going to have an excellent Christmas. Just you wait."

Winnie, her hands stuffed inside a turkey she was preparing for the following day, quirked an eyebrow. "Do I even want to know what that means?"

"Probably not," I conceded. "I'm going to tell you anyway." I ran through our day, starting from the beginning, and when I got to the end, Winnie was flabbergasted.

"You did all of that today?"

"Don't act so surprised. I'm quite industrious when I set my mind to something."

"But do you think it will work?" All thoughts of giving me a firm dressing down disappeared from Winnie's eyes. She looked hopeful. "Do you really think we can get the boys placed with their uncle?"

"I know I can," I replied. "We're already halfway there. By the way, Carl is coming for dinner tomorrow. We're not mentioning the plan to the boys until everything is set. Just in case I fail … ." I trailed off. I never fail. Still, the boys had been disappointed enough. There was always the outside chance that something wouldn't come together correctly.

"I get it," Winnie said, her lips curving. "You're trying to do a good thing. The gifts are a nice touch, by the way. Terry said something about you buying gifts, but I thought he must have misheard you."

"Why would you think that?"

"Because you're not exactly known for your giving spirit," Marnie replied. "You can't help it. It's just who you are."

"That's not true," Bay argued, appearing at the bottom of the spiral staircase. She had a photograph in her hand, which she handed to me. "That's her."

I looked at the photo, took in the smiling countenance of the woman who given birth to David, Michael and Andrew, and felt myself getting a bit misty. The boys posed in the photograph with the woman. They were all younger, with wide smiles on their faces, but it was clearly a happy family.

"Good job." I shook my head to dislodge the melancholy. "How did you get this?"

"I stole it from David's bag."

"You stole it?" Winnie was horrified. "Bay, what were you thinking?"

"She was thinking we need a photograph to make a convincing ghost," I replied. "She was thinking that if we told the boys why we needed it they'd think we were crazy. They won't even know. Bay can return the photo when no one is looking. It's not as if she wants to keep it."

"I understand that, but ... you know what? It's fine." Winnie held up her shiny hands. "If this works, you'll give the boys the best Christmas gift they've ever had. I refuse to think about anything other than that."

"That's probably wise." I turned my eyes to Clove when she walked into the room. "Did you get what I asked?"

Clove nodded. "We'll haunt the crap out of this guy. I can't wait."

"And then what?" Marnie asked. "Even if you get Daryl to sign the papers, how will you get the judge to do what you want so close to the holidays?"

"The judge handling their case is Gerald West," I replied. "He happens to owe me a favor."

"Judge West?" Twila widened her eyes. "The same judge who gave you custody of us? He must be ancient by now."

"He is," I agreed. "But he's still on the bench. He only does family cases now. Once I call and explain the situation, something tells me that he'll agree to do the right thing."

"Only because he's terrified of you," Marnie muttered. "I still remember when Aunt Willa was trying to petition the courts to take Twila and you stormed in there to tell him exactly what would happen if he didn't throw out the petition."

"I remember, too." Winnie giggled at the memory. "You took us with you. At the time, I didn't understand what you were doing. I understand now that you wanted us to know that you were fighting to keep us together, but back then I thought you just wanted us to see that you could make a grown man cry."

"He was young," Twila said. "Back when he was handling our case, he was young."

"He's not so young now, and I doubt that he'll be as easily swayed," I said. "That doesn't mean he won't come to the right conclusion. To be fair, though, I plan to camp out at his house tonight if he doesn't do what I want."

"You're going to his house?" The look on Winnie's face told me what she thought of the idea. "He'll have you arrested for stalking or trespassing."

"No, he won't." I didn't bother to hide my eye roll "Don't get me wrong, I fully intend to make sure that he wants to sign the papers and get me out of his hair as soon as possible. I have no intention of going alone."

"Who are you taking with you?"

"The girls," I replied without hesitation. "They've turned into wonderfully emotive and manipulative teenagers. If the judge won't do what I want, I'll simply allow Thistle to … well, be Thistle."

"And if that doesn't work?"

"Clove cries like a soap opera diva."

"And if that doesn't work?"

"Bay has turned into quite the little public speaker," I said. "Don't worry. Between the four of us, Judge West won't stand a chance."

Winnie let loose a long-suffering sigh, resigned. "Fine. Do what you have to do. If you get arrested, we're bailing out the girls before you. I'm not sure we have enough money to bail out all four of you."

"I won't be arrested. Trust me. Now, Clove, give me the ginger root. Let's make a zombie ghost, shall we?"

This next part was going to be unbelievably fun. I could feel it.

"THAT WAS NOWHERE near as fun as I thought it would be," I lamented two hours later as I led the girls up Judge West's front walkway. "He didn't even put up a fight."

"That's because he's a coward," Bay said. "You can always tell a coward by the way he reacts to other people's feelings and needs. He didn't care about David, Michael and Andrew at all. He only cared about himself."

"But the zombie ghost was fun." Thistle said. "I especially liked the way you made it smack him like you did. I wish we could've seen more of it in your crystal ball, but the picture was horrible."

"Yeah, that was an inspired touch," I agreed, stopping on the front porch and squaring my shoulders. "Okay, girls, you know what to do, right?"

"Let you do the talking first," Bay replied. "If he doesn't agree with you, Thistle will bully him, I'll make a speech and Clove will cry."

"Exactly." I beamed. "This is the last step for us. We're extremely close to making sure those boys have the best Christmas ever."

To my utter surprise, Bay reached over and squeezed my hand. "They'll always remember you as their hero."

"I don't care about that, Bay. I only want them to be happy."

"I care." Bay released my hand. "Now, let's do this. I'm starving, and Mom was making a chocolate cake when we left. I want to see how much sugar I can eat without throwing up tonight."

"You girls really do take after me. It's fun sometimes." I knocked on the door. "Okay. Here we go."

Judge West was surprised when he opened the door and found us on his porch. It took him a moment to register my identity, and when he did, his face drained of color. "Tillie Winchester."

"It's good to see you again, Judge West." I forced myself to remain calm and pleasant even though I really wanted to launch myself at him and poke my finger into his chest until he agreed to my demands. "I bet you thought you were done dealing with me, huh?"

"I think the word is 'hoped,'" Thistle corrected.

"I did think we were done dealing with one another," Judge West confirmed. "Your nieces are grown women now. Custody issues should be a thing of the past."

"I've moved on to other orphaned children."

Judge West flicked his eyes to the girls. "Are you picking them up on the street now or something?"

"Not them." I waved off his concerns. "These are my great-nieces."

"Really?" Judge West smiled at each of the girls in turn. "I don't remember your mothers' names, but I do remember their faces. You all look like them."

"That's the meanest thing you ever could've said to us," Clove lamented. "I feel like crying it was so mean."

"Not yet," I muttered under my breath.

"Well, that wasn't my intention." Judge West's expression was quizzical. "What are you doing here, Ms. Winchester? It's late and I … really don't want you in my neighborhood. If I'm not careful the neighbors will call the police, and that's the last thing I want so close to Christmas."

"Well, it's your lucky day then." I beamed, hoping I came off as friendly rather than deranged. It was honestly a toss-up. "I don't want to be in your neighborhood. I have to be here for three boys I know. I don't have a choice."

"What boys?"

"David, Michael and Andrew Forrester."

Judge West rubbed his chin, confused. "I recognize the names. They're in the system. Their case has come before me several times."

"And you've made the wrong decision several times," Thistle said.

"I'm sure the nuances of being a family court judge aren't easily acceptable for someone your age." Judge West adopted a pragmatic and yet somehow condescending tone. "Rest assured, though, I have the best interests of the boys at heart whenever their case comes in front of me."

"I don't think you do, and I'm here to explain why," I interjected.

"I don't understand why you're even involved."

"Because the group home where they lived burned down and we opened our house to help a few of the kids," I explained. "We got David, Michael and Andrew. They let a few things slip, and ... well ... here I am."

"Here you are." Judge West didn't look thrilled with the outcome.

"Listen, I don't want to bust your balls ... ."

"She's lying," Thistle interjected. "Just agree to what she wants or she'll never leave."

Instead of being agitated, Judge West cast an amused look in Thistle's direction. "I can see you're built from the same stock as your great-aunt."

"Okay, *that's* the meanest thing anyone has ever said to me," Thistle corrected, causing Judge West to chuckle.

"Technically I'm not allowed to talk about a custody case with you," Judge West supplied. "You're not primary participants."

"No, but we are secondary participants."

"And we want the boys to have a merry Christmas," Clove added plaintively.

"And what makes you think they won't have a merry Christmas?" Judge West asked.

"Because you won't let them live with their uncle and they keep getting separated by the system," Clove answered.

"What do you know about the system?"

"That it's run by 'The Man' and 'The Man' is bad."

I lightly cuffed the back of Clove's head to silence her. "She's exaggerating. That's not exactly what I said."

"I can imagine what you said," Judge West said. "That still doesn't change the fact that until the boys' father signs over his rights ... ."

"But he has," I interrupted, desperate to get the judge to agree to my terms before the hour turned late. What? I didn't want to miss the chocolate cake either. "He came to his senses and is having the document notarized right now. Then it's being overnighted to his brother."

"It is?" Judge West cocked an eyebrow, surprised. "How did you manage that?"

"I'm very persuasive."

He snorted. "I bet you are. Still, there's no way I can push this through before Christmas. You'll have to wait until after the first of the year. It's simply impossible for me to change anything right now."

"Why?" Bay challenged, her eyes flashing. "You've made them wait for years. You've made it purposely hard on their uncle even though he's a good man and the boys wanted to live with him. Why can't you do the right thing now?"

"Yeah?" Thistle pressed. "Why can't you be a real-life Santa Claus and make this the best Christmas ever for the boys? I think they deserve it, and it would take you only a few minutes."

"How do you know it would take me only a few minutes?"

"Because you're a judge," Thistle replied. "You're supposed to be powerful."

"And you're supposed to do the right thing," Clove added, throwing in a sniffle for good measure as tears rimmed her eyes. "You want us to believe in the system. You want us to think you're not 'The Man.' You need to prove to us that you want to do the right thing."

"You need to prove to us that the system works," Bay added.

Judge West pursed his lips as he glanced between faces, finally resting his somber brown eyes on me. "They're good."

"They learned from the best," I confirmed, bobbing my head.

"I have no doubt."

"We're not leaving until you make this happen," I said. "We worked hard to get everything you need to deliver the perfect Christmas to those boys. We've done all the hard work for you. All you need to do is sign some paperwork."

Judge West blew out a heavy sigh as he dragged a hand through his hair, resigned. "Fine. I'll do what you want."

"Yay!" Clove clapped her hands and bounced up and down, her tears miraculously evaporating.

Judge West shook his head. "They're very good."

"They have a certain something," I agreed. "So ... about that paperwork."

"Yes, yes. You might as well come in. I'll need to make a call and fill out some paperwork. It might take a bit of time."

"That's okay. We'll wait."

"But there's cake at home," Bay complained.

"I didn't say we'd wait patiently."

"I'll have that paperwork done in five minutes," Judge West volunteered. "I'd hate to keep you from the cake."

I was really starting to like him. Kind of. As much as I could like 'The Man,' I mean. Okay, he was still kind of a pain, but he was helping with our Christmas miracle. That sort of made him Santa Claus in my book.

TEN

Terry walked through the back door without knocking shortly before noon the next day. The look on his face was murderous.

"What did you do?"

David, Michael and Andrew sat at the table decorating Christmas cookies – they initially declined because they thought it was a "little kid" task, but decided to jump in when they saw how much fun Bay, Clove and Thistle had while tackling the frosting – and their eyes went wide when Terry stalked in my direction.

"You'll have to be more specific," I replied, sipping my coffee. "I've done quite a few things over the past forty-eight hours, but I'm not going to own up to any of them without my lawyer present."

"Then call him."

"I represent myself."

Bay giggled at the look on Terry's face, the reaction just enough to soften his stance. "You look angry."

"I am angry, Bay." Terry wiped the back of his hand over his forehead, almost as if it was eighty degrees and he'd just completed hours of manual labor. "Your Aunt Tillie makes me angry."

"Welcome to the club," Thistle said. "We all go a little mad around these parts thanks to Aunt Tillie."

Terry flicked her ear. "Now is not the time for your sarcasm."

"When will be the time?" Thistle asked, her face stoic. "I need to write it down so I don't forget."

"Just ... decorate your cookie." Terry was frazzled. "What's this?"

Bay handed him a Santa cookie and offered up an angelic smile. "I made this especially for you. It reminds me of when you dressed up like Santa and gave us Sugar."

Terry balked. "I did not dress up like Santa. That was really Santa."

"Aunt Tillie told us the truth," Clove argued. "We don't believe in Santa any longer."

"Then that means you're not going to get any Christmas gifts." Terry accepted the cookie and glowered at Bay. He managed to maintain the expression for only a few minutes before shaking his head. "Fine. You've worn me down. I was Santa. You're getting a bunch of gifts. Thank you for the cookie."

"You're welcome." Bay linked her arm through his. I recognized what she was doing. It was the little minx's idea of flirting, although she wasn't really flirting. She was merely wrapping Terry around her finger to calm him. "You shouldn't be angry with Aunt Tillie. She's been very good today."

"She has," Thistle agreed. "I've only wanted to kill her ten times since I woke up. That has to be a new record."

"I haven't forgotten your place on my list, mouth," I warned. "The day after Christmas, you and I are going to dance."

"You won't be naked, will you?"

"She most certainly will not!" Terry barked.

"Calm down, Terry." Winnie was blasé as she handed him a mug of coffee. "You're off duty, right?"

"Why?"

"Let's just say I added a little something to your coffee to ease whatever anger you've got going on inside of you," Winnie replied. "If you're still on duty I'll need to take it back."

Terry cradled the coffee to his chest and offered up a sour grimace. "I'm off duty. You can't take my coffee."

"Then drink it and chill out." It was the closest Winnie ever got to chiding him, and instead of arguing Terry did as he was told. He took a long drink of the coffee, pressing his eyes shut before focusing on me a second time.

"What did you do?"

So much for him calming down. "I believe I already told you I'll need more information if you expect me to answer that."

"If this is about a tree falling in Mrs. Little's yard so she can't get out of her driveway, we have nothing to do with that," Clove offered.

Terry's eyes narrowed. "How did you know about that? The emergency team that was dispatched there said the root system gave way. It was some sort of fluke."

"That's why we had nothing to do with it." Clove batted her big brown eyes and handed Terry a cookie. "I made that one for you. It's better than the one Bay made. I'm sure you'll pretend otherwise because she'll cry if you don't, but it will be our little secret."

Terry hunkered down so he was at eye level with Clove. "You're going to make some man really miserable one day. You know that, right?"

Clove nodded solemnly. "I'm really looking forward to it."

"I'm sure you are." Terry took a bite of Clove's cookie and smiled. "Very good. You're still in trouble for the tree."

"I don't understand," David interjected. "How can they be responsible for a tree falling?"

"Very good question, David." I beamed. "Tell him how one little old lady and three small girls could take down a tree, Terry." It was a challenge, one I knew Terry wouldn't rise to.

"We're done talking about the tree," Terry said. "Although, I'm going to just bet that you four snuck out of this house, all dressed in black, and disappeared for a bit last night."

"You said you were going hunting for the turkey," Michael said accusingly.

"I knew it!" Terry wagged a finger in my face. "You're on my list. The day after Christmas, you and are I going to dance."

It wasn't much of a threat but it did make me smile. "I'm looking forward to it. I prefer the Macarena."

Bay chuckled as she started making the nearly-forgotten hand gestures that accompanied the song. Clove and Thistle instantly mimicked her motions.

"Oh, this family makes me so tired." Terry pinched the bridge of his nose. "What were we talking about again?"

"How Aunt Tillie made a tree fall even though she was here all night," Clove replied.

"Thanks for reminding him, Clove," I snapped.

"You're welcome."

Terry growled. "Actually, the tree is the least of my worries," he said. "I'm more interested in a little visit you paid to Judge West last night. Apparently you showed up on his front porch with three teenage girls in tow and refused to leave unless he did you a favor."

David's eyes sharpened as he jerked his head in my direction. "Judge West?"

Terry's eyes drifted to David. "Do you know him?"

"He's the judge in charge of our case," David replied. "He's the one who won't let us live with our uncle."

"But ... ." Terry's expression was hard to read as he broke off and pinned me with a hard look. Whatever he'd been keen to accuse me of died on his lips. "Hmm."

The sound of the doorbell caused everyone in the room to jolt. The look the boys shared was almost enough to break my heart. They appeared afraid, terrified even. It was almost as if they expected someone to come and take them away.

That was going to happen, of course. It simply wouldn't be the sad thing they thought it would be.

"You should probably get that, boys."

David slid me a sidelong look. "Are we leaving?"

"No. You have a special guest."

"We do?" David was understandably dubious. "I'm not going to open the door and find a freaky Santa out there, am I?"

I snickered at his worried expression. "In some ways you're going to find the ultimate Santa out there," I replied. "I promise he won't be even remotely freaky."

"Well, I guess I'll have to take your word for it," David muttered, getting to his feet. "Come on, guys. How bad can it be?"

Michael and Andrew fell into step behind their brother, solemn expressions on their faces. They looked as if they were walking to the gallows. Winnie grinned before following, the girls positively giddy as they raced to see who was at the door. They knew, of course. They still wanted to see the boys' faces.

I moved to follow, but Terry snagged me by the back of the elbow.

"I need you to explain what you were doing at the judge's house last night," he whispered. "I got the impression that he wasn't happy to see you and yet did you a favor at the same time. How did you manage that?"

"I'm gifted."

"How really?"

"I refused to leave until he agreed to make a Christmas miracle come true." I saw no reason to lie. As soon as Carl walked through the door, the entire story would spill out. Frankly, I couldn't wait for the boys to find out the truth.

"What Christmas miracle?" Terry was flustered, his cheeks blazing. He turned his head to the door when David pulled it open, widening his eyes when the boys gasped and Andrew enthusiastically clapped his hands.

"Uncle Carl," they all sang out in unison.

"We can't believe you're here," Andrew gushed, throwing his arms around Carl's neck. "We worried you wouldn't be able to find us."

Carl looked so happy I thought he might burst into tears. He held himself together, though, and exchanged a hug with each of his nephews. "I almost didn't make it. A little elf tracked me down and told me where you were. She also invited me to dinner."

David glanced over his shoulder, our eyes meeting. "Are you the elf?"

"I'm pretty sure I should be insulted that you think I'm an elf," I countered. "I'm short, but I'm not that short."

"That's a myth," Bay interjected. "Elves are tall, like Legolas in *Lord of the Rings*. Dwarves are short."

"Thank you, Miss Know-It-All," I grumbled.

"Come here, Bay." Terry motioned toward the pouting girl and skewered me with a dark look. "Do you have to be mean to her?"

I rolled my eyes as Terry offered Bay a soothing hug and then focused on Carl and the boys. "I think some introductions are in order." It took me a few minutes to sort out the Winchester family tree for Carl, but he was interested and couldn't stop smiling.

We'd talked on the phone early this morning. He'd called the minute Judge West's office notified him about the paperwork going through. He'd cried so hard I thought I would drown over the phone. Even though I'm uncomfortable with overt displays like that, I couldn't help being touched ... and happy.

We agreed he'd be the one to tell the boys, and I was almost as excited as him to see their reaction.

"Come in." Winnie couldn't disguise her smile as she ushered Carl into the living room. "Dinner is still a few hours off, but we're happy you came early. I'm sure you have a lot to discuss with the boys."

"I definitely do." Carl was enthusiastic as he sat on the couch, grinning as the boys flanked him. David seemed to be the only one who sensed there was something in the air.

"What's going on?" David asked after a beat.

"What makes you think anything is going on?" I challenged.

"Because you all keep looking at each other as if you know a secret," David replied. "Mr. Terry came by and said you were in trouble, but backed off when he found out you'd been at the judge's house. What's going on?"

"Have you considered that Terry is simply an alarmist?"

David looked to Terry, uncertain. "No. He's been really nice to us."

"That doesn't mean he's not an alarmist."

"I'm not an alarmist," Terry clarified. "I did have cause to worry, but now I'm starting to think that maybe Tillie knows exactly what she's doing."

"I've told you a million times that I always know what I'm doing."

"Yeah, well, I'd rather hear it from Carl than you," Terry said, smoothing Bay's hair. "We'll discuss the tree incident later."

"I have no idea what you're talking about." I crossed my arms over my chest and sent a reassuring look to Carl. "Tell them."

"Tell us what?" Michael asked, shifting. "Are they going to separate us again?"

"No." Carl firmly shook his head. "They're not going to separate you ever again."

"Are they taking us to a new home?" Andrew asked, his eyes downcast.

"Technically yes, but it's not what you guys think," Carl replied. "You're coming to my home."

"We are?" After being jerked around so many times, Andrew was understandably confused. "How long do we get to stay? Is it just for Christmas?"

"It's for good," Carl replied, swallowing as he fought to maintain control of his emotions. He was near tears. "You should know that Tillie worked really hard and managed to get all of the paperwork in order. You boys are officially coming to live with me. For good."

Andrew burst into tears, and Carl gave him a warm hug while David turned incredulous eyes to me.

"Is that why you were at the judge's house?" David asked.

I nodded. "We had a few things to discuss. It turns out that he saw things my way. I barely had to bring out the big guns."

"What are the big guns?"

Bay, Clove and Thistle raised their hands in unison.

"I didn't even have to cry," Clove said. "I was ready and everything."

"And I was barely mean," Thistle added. "I had a lot more stuff stored up in case it was necessary."

"But … is this for real?" David was on the verge of crying. I knew he didn't want to do it in front of everyone, but in some ways I thought it would be cathartic.

"It's for real," Carl confirmed.

"But ... what about Dad?" David wasn't quite ready to let it go. "I thought he had to agree to it."

"Well, I'm still not sure how she did it, but Tillie managed to get him to sign the papers," Carl said, his eyes twinkling. "I got him on the phone just to make sure, and he was ranting and raving about some ... ghost or something ... but he signed the papers. I think your dad might've been dreaming."

"Yeah, I'm sure that was it." Terry's gaze was weighted when it landed on me. "It seems you've been busy. How did you manage all of this?"

"I had a little help." I grinned at Bay.

"So ... we're going to your house right now?" Michael asked, bewildered.

"First we're going to have dinner here," Carl answered. "The Winchesters got some gifts for you, and we thought a big meal with all of us would be nice. Then you're going home with me."

"I can't believe it!" David let loose a huge sigh, his chest deflating and his shoulders visibly relaxing. "You did this for us?"

I nodded. "I think you deserve it."

"You're Santa," Andrew said, jumping up from the couch and taking me by surprise with a vehement hug. "You're the best Santa ever!"

I awkwardly patted his back. "I'm better than Santa."

"You definitely are." Tears swam through Andrew's eyes. "And to think we didn't want to come here."

"We just thought it would be boring," David said hurriedly by way of apology. "We were wrong."

"You were wrong about being bored, too," I said, grinning as I fought my own tears. "So, we have a few hours. What should we do with the time?"

"What do you want to do?" Michael asked, wary.

"Well, remember when I was talking to you guys about yellow snow?"

Michael nodded.

"I thought we'd play a little game with Margaret Little," I explained.

"What kind of game?"

"I believe it's called 'I Win, She Loses' and it's the best game in the world." I clapped my hands to get everyone's attention. "Girls, get your coats. Boys, you do the same. I'm taking you for a quick outing."

I risked a glance at Terry and found him frowning.

"What?" I challenged. "It's Christmas. You have to get in the holiday spirit."

"I didn't hear a thing," Terry said, throwing himself in the chair at the edge of the room. "Someone pass the bourbon, please."

I couldn't stop myself from poking him one more time. "Merry Christmas, Terry."

Terry was blasé. "You do not exist."

"That's good," Thistle said. "You can't arrest her if she's invisible."

"Just go, Thistle." Terry rubbed his forehead. "I'm pretending you don't exist, too."

Instead of pushing him further, Thistle took everyone by surprise when she kissed his cheek.

"Merry Christmas," she whispered.

Terry shook his head. "You're going to make some man really miserable."

Thistle beamed. "That's what I live for."

And, surprisingly, all was right with our little corner of the world. We even had a forecast predicting yellow snow to prove it.

Printed in Great Britain
by Amazon